Praise for *Goliath*

A *New York Times* Editors' Choice

A Best of the Year Pick for *The Washington Post,*
Amazon, *Polygon,* and More

"*Goliath* contains a sprawling collection of characters making their way across a future Earth—already abandoned by the wealthy—that feels vividly, grimly real. This is an arrival."　　　—John Scalzi

"In this ambitious novel, dense with perspectives and social commentary, Onyebuchi dreams up disparate lives in a crumbling future America—with gentrifiers returning to Earth from space colonies and laborers trying to make a precarious living—while leaving room for moments of beauty and humor."

　　　—*The New York Times* (Editors' Choice)

"An ingenious premise: Onyebuchi suburbanizes outer space and makes battered, almost uninhabitable provincial America the frontier. . . . [He] showcases an impressive range."　　　—*The New York Times*

"A haunting take on a future that is caused by events that feel all too real right now."　　　—NPR

"Onyebuchi sets fire to the boundary between fiction and reality, and brings a crumbling city and an all-too-plausible future to vibrant life. Riveting, disturbing, and rendered in masterful detail."

　　　—Leigh Bardugo

"A work of stunningly careful craftsmanship on every level. A vision of a future so plausible it's frightening. Onyebuchi's at his best here."

　　　—R. F. Kuang

"A rich tapestry that is as much science fiction as a meditation on race in modern America."　　　—*The Washington Post*

"*Goliath* is a haunting and incisive look at a world that could very much be our own." —*Los Angeles Review of Books*

"The premise is wry and au courant. In a lesser writer's hands, it could lead to lazy and cynical caricatures, but Onyebuchi uses it only as a jumping-off point into a deeper examination of the idea of home, and what we will do to get there." —*New Scientist* (UK)

"This brainy, brawny sci-fi story uses futuristic concepts to comment on 2022 and eternal issues of class, disenfranchisement, and cold, hard capitalism." —*The Philadelphia Inquirer*

"Impressive in its scale, ambition, and range of voice, *Goliath* is a shattering work that is so much more than the sum of its parts. . . . Simultaneously sprawling and intimate, exploring racism, classism, gentrification, the prison system, and the climate crisis." —*Polygon*

"Onyebuchi weaves together disparate tales about those living both on Earth and above it. And through those stories we question who gets to be the hero of any history. This is an epic of biblical proportions, the kind of sci-fi storytelling that feels ever more vital." —*Nerdist*

"With interweaving time lines and characters, this is a dense read that, like the best dystopias, critiques current political and social problems." —*BuzzFeed*

"Harrowing, visionary . . . It's urgent, gorgeous work." —*Publishers Weekly*

"Onyebuchi's adult novel debut is a full sensory experience of language and imagery. . . . Readers are given a near-future world where race, class, and gentrification still drive the narrative, both on Earth and in the stars." —*Library Journal*

GOLD

TOR
DOT
COM   TOR PUBLISHING GROUP · NEW YORK

TOCHI ONYEBUCHI

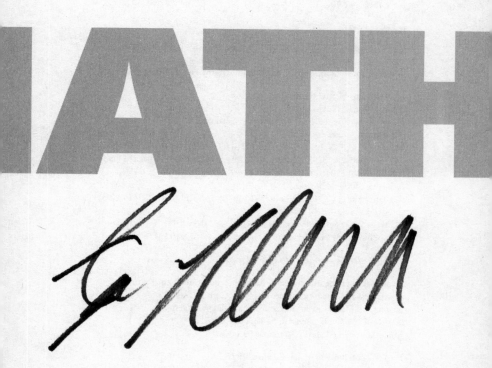

GOLIATH

Copyright © 2021 by Tochi Onyebuchi

A Tordotcom Book
Published by Tom Doherty Associates/Tor Publishing Group
120 Broadway
New York, NY 10271

www.tor.com

Tor® is a registered trademark of Macmillan Publishing Group, LLC.

The Library of Congress has cataloged the hardcover edition as follows:

Names: Onyebuchi, Tochi, author.
Title: Goliath / Tochi Onyebuchi.
Description: First edition. | New York : Tordotcom, 2022. | "A Tom
    Doherty Associates book."
Identifiers: LCCN 2021039437 (print) | LCCN 2021039438 (ebook) |
    ISBN 9781250782953 (hardcover) | ISBN 9781250858399 (signed edition) |
    ISBN 9781250782960 (ebook)
Subjects: LCGFT: Novels.
Classification: LCC PS3615.N93 G65 2022 (print) | LCC PS3615.N93
    (ebook) | DDC 813/.6—dc23
LC record available at https://lccn.loc.gov/2021039437
LC ebook record available at https://lccn.loc.gov/2021039438

ISBN 978-1-250-81448-7 (trade paperback)

Our books may be purchased in bulk for promotional, educational,
or business use. Please contact your local bookseller or the
Macmillan Corporate and Premium Sales Department
at 1-800-221-7945, extension 5442, or by email at
MacmillanSpecialMarkets@macmillan.com.

First Tordotcom Paperback Edition: 2023

Printed in the United States of America

0 9 8 7 6 5 4 3 2

TO AMBER

SUMMER

PART I

Before his flight to Earth, they had warned Jonathan about the "gangs." Even at the Stamford Station where his shuttle had docked, even on the bullet train that spirited him north past brick apartment buildings and houses with gables and turrets, manicured lawns, circular drives, bay windows, even past the shore-front homes of South Norwalk with sailboats parked on the sand or tethered to metal docks fashioned to look as though they were made out of peeling wood, made to look as though they had been there forever, past the kayaks and the fountains and the parks populated by poplars and willow trees, they warned him about the gangs. The admonitions were grave and ominous every time they issued from someone's mouth, but the closer he came to the frontier, the grimmer the admonition. Their crimes, their violence, their predilections grew more and more specific, the anecdotes spawning increasingly specific limbs until Jonathan was made to believe that he could discern the very contours of the lusus naturae waiting for him in New Haven. People who knew people he knew offered their numbers and their contacts, so that once Jonathan arrived, he could pass word of his safe landing. The land was red and burning where he was headed, and if he were not careful, he'd burn too.

He had thanked each and every Cassandra, noted that he would heed their advice, but inwardly, he was grinning. He was shaking his head and grinning. Among the things they didn't know was the sheer strength of Jonathan's thirst for shadow country, the fact that he had wanted to build something ever since the first dreams of returning to Earth had entered his head, that he had spent nearly every waking moment dissecting his plan, putting it back together, testing the foundation and the buttresses and the supports, making sure the electricity worked and that the plumbing was done with a strong enough piping. And gangs. The invariably white folk who cautioned Jonathan against youthful bravado, against infantile nonchalance, knew that gangs existed, which is to say they knew as much as anybody did about gangs, which is to say they knew nothing.

They said gang, and he knew they meant Black. They said thugs, and he knew they meant the n-word.

There were a lot of empty factories in New Haven, which is saying nothing, as Jonathan knew there were a lot of empty factories everywhere in America. When he was a child, those relatives still on Earth, old enough to be dug in at the roots and either too infirm or too set in their ways to make the pilgrimage to the Colonies, would send transmission after transmission to regale their grandson, grandnephew, old friend's child, of places like the Rust Belt. It sounded to Jonathan like a stylish thing wrapped around the waist of a skinny guy with dark and mysterious inclinations, an aura of enticing hurt, the kind of guy Jonathan would want to fix by fucking.

Jonathan's bees sprouted from his hair, buzzed around his head recording the landscape's deterioration. The images beamed, as soon as they were taken, to David's Cloud back on the Colony, a little delayed due to spotty connection.

Stories of the radiation had made their way to the Colonies and even still with the documentation, with the filtered photos on everyone's 'grams and with the news updates and with the video taken by people on their way out, the whole thing had acquired an air of myth. It had always been something that had happened to someone else. The truth was that Jonathan knew no one still on Earth, knew no one who had stayed or had been forced to stay, and he saw it as a deficiency. Life was truly lived here, where it was at stake. The forests were bright green and, as he approached the terminus of the train line, bright red, a vibrancy nowhere to be found in space, where everything was a different shade of gray, where every panel and every pathway was drained of color and only the bricks that came imported from Earth seemed to bear any trace of having had a full and exacting life.

Jonathan collected his bags from the train's undercarriage, then hailed a small personal transport, room for one, that took him past the Protected Zone and into some of the forest outside of Fairfield County. Prior to his departure, they'd made him print out all of his documents and when, now, his comms fritzed with static and his 'gram shots took longer than usual to make their way online, he saw why. The Soviet insistence on printing everything in quintuplet, and the months and months of phone calls and emails prior, had been meant to reassure the authorities on the Colonies that he was no longer their ward. The umbilical cords linking Earth and the Colonies had been snapped. You came here wanting to be forgotten, wearing the odor of an outlaw. The mindset up in the stars was that anyone returning, unless they were seeking to gather family, had nothing left on the Colonies, no reason to enjoy the banal comforts and the safety of the Space Station. If you were leaving, it was because you had been defeated.

There were no more pioneers left in space.

Bridgeport Harbor was now in their rearview. The bees buzzing around Jonathan's hair beamed into his braincase information about the industrial husks that floated by: St. Vincent's Medical Center, which, once upon a time, had been the city's biggest employer; People's United Bank; University of Bridgeport; Housatonic Community College; the Derecktor Shipyards. Wikis on each of the landmarks bookmarked themselves in Jonathan's braincase, and as soon as he scanned them, they vanished into a folder waiting to be trashed. He chuckled and, under a 'gram he snapped of a row of two-story project housing, he murmured a caption in a newscaster's voice: "And here we have Bridgeport, Connecticut, world leader in abandoned buildings, shattered glass, and gas stations without pumps. Come here to see boarded-up windows and wild dogs like no other." Except the dogs here were larger than they were supposed to be and mixed in with all of the industrial decay was a wrongly colored forest, retaking control of the city.

They passed the Ballpark at Harbor Yard where the Bridgeport Bluefish used to play and, before long, they took the off-ramp that put them on Whitney Avenue in New Haven.

Jonathan put his palm to the cabbie's scanner, then pulled it away, frowning, when he saw how much he'd been charged. But before he could complain, the maglev transport was stopped and his luggage was out on the street corner and he'd fumbled for his air mask, barely getting it on before the cab whirled around and sped down a side street, winding its way back onto the Interstate.

Across the street from Jonathan, on a sidewalk torn to pieces by weeds and renegade tree roots, stood what might have once been called a wild boar. This one, however, more resembled a demigod. On four legs, it rose as high as Jonathan's chest, poked at the air before it with a snout longer than it was supposed to be. The spiny bristles ran along its back like hypodermic needles, and its pointed ears wagged to full mast then back down. The sun washed it in shades of ochre and gray. It stared at Jonathan with wild-eyed wonder. It was only after the thing had wandered away, on spindly, overlong legs, that Jonathan realized his own strangeness, the air mask affixed to his face still a foreign object and he very much a stranger in a strange land.

"**NAME** something that follows the word 'pork.'" Michael sounded like he was pushing the demo-truck rather than driving it.

"Loin," Linc said.

The truck groaned. The neighborhood was quiet, exactly how it'd sound if there were no neighbors in it. "Gimme another one."

"Chop."

"Brother, you hungry or something?"

"Belly. Pork belly."

"Okay, after this house we'll hit the bodega." Silence. "You got another one for me?"

Linc thought. "Cupine."

Quietus. "What?"

"Tell me that ain't an answer," Linc shot back.

Michael chuckling. "Pork. Cupine." His seat began to shake. "Cu . . ." The rest was choked in a fit of laughter. "Cupine." Convulsions rocked the cab of the truck. "HWHAT?" Thunderclaps of laughter. "HHWHATT? Is CUPINE?" The truck swerved, Michael laughed so hard.

"Damn, nigga."

"I'm sorry. I'm sorry." He was probably wiping tears from his eyes right now. Sniffing away excess mirth. "But that's the greatest answer I've ever heard."

"It's the right answer."

"I feel you, brother. I feel you."

"On my mama."

"Pow, brother." Another crippling fit of laughter. "Damn, brother, I wish I were recording this. I tell you what, you ask anyone else. *Any*one else, they tell you the same. That you the *only* person who said 'cupine.' I bet you every dollar I got."

The truck straightened its course, resumed its lumbering deliberateness, Michael muttering the "cupine" beneath his breath and trying not to let his howling kill them both.

The sky bled across the clapboard houses that lined the road. Wood domiciles and brick edifices. Single-family homes made after a war that happened before Linc's father's father had been a man. The twelve-wheeled demolition truck hovered over the ground, the maglev strips under the concrete still in working order. Kind of. But the truck rumbled nonetheless. The noise the engine made had the truck huffing like a fat man rounding a corner. The heat and the humidity conspired to stain Michael's third shirt of the day a new color. Linc had stripped down to a tank top and jeans. Even the truck's brow beaded with sweat.

Linc sat in the space between the truck's cab and its bed, that shifting connector where overhead hung the lip of the trashbed. Shade was shade.

He heard the neighbors before he saw them; female voices, generations of motherhood, streamed out of their houses to gripe. Mothers taking care of their mothers, other women taking care of their grandkids, bouncing them on their hips, managing, just by touch, to cool those poor kids down so that they didn't look like black porcelain dolls in the light. They came out one by one, then began to line the streets like trees, following the truck's course.

"When them dead trees coming down?" came a voice from behind the trashbed. They asked like Linc had any say in the matter, like they could even see him and his hammer at all. "When you gonna stop them kids from pushing that dope two houses down from here? I'm pickin' up goddamn needles every goddamn morning!" Someone caught sight of Linc. "You got a job for my son? He's lookin' and he's able to work. Healthy as whatever, no lung rot or nothin'." Another: "My nephew! You can git him some work, he's willin' to do it." Another: "Hell, I can lift just as good as any of 'em. Them checks from Fairfield ain't enough to feed a dog kennel, let alone this family I got here." They announced how well they could tap a water vein and run a hose, how easily they could heft a shovel, how the dying of the earth hadn't yet crushed them, but when Michael's truck stopped, they didn't crowd. This had all happened before.

Linc shifted, ready to hop out from his space. The women started pointing to the abandoned houses on the street. One of them, in a purple blouse, a baby in one arm, the other hand dabbing her forehead with a kerchief, stepped forward. "You finally gonna tear this one down? I been callin' the city for months now. Months!" Another woman beside her stepped up, left behind a little girl who fidgeted with her sundress. "How 'bout that one?" She pointed to another duplex three houses down with a massive tree trunk bursting through to the second floor, branches sprouting out the windows.

Michael leaned out the driver's side window, squinted beneath the brim of his insignia'ed ball cap. "I'm only here for that house over there." He nodded toward a spot two houses in from the corner. A two-bedroom with a gable roof, one half of its second-floor façade charred. The porch was missing its bricks. Some of them saw Linc descend and their target reticles zeroed in on him.

"You tellin' me you're here for just one house? One house?" This one wearing an orange blouse and holding close to her face a tiny solar-powered water-fan. She swept her arms to indicate the row of houses across the street from the one targeted for demolition. "Those are *all* drug houses. Someone got raped in that one on the corner. I called about that one! I been calling all week. I called and called."

Linc's shirt caught on the edge of a groove and the sun lit the puckered course of a scar that ran along the skin just above his hip. An almost-healed souvenir from a house he had cleared a few weeks back. He pulled his shirt down, dragged his hammer off his seat, and hefted it over his shoulder.

"I'm just a wrecker," Michael pleaded. "The mayor don't forward no calls my way." He spoke with a bit of a Puerto Rican lilt; certain vowels and consonants would rise like he was inviting himself over for dinner. The city sent Michael to this part of town pretty often. Linc didn't know how Michael was gonna break it to those ladies that he did have other houses to demolish today but that the rest of those twenty houses stood on the other side of the city.

Linc shuffled toward the house that must have preceded the urban renewal projects that swept through the city during the beginning of the millennium. The houses like these, they were like the Pyramids in Egypt. It made sense that humans had built them, but without the stuff that they had now, such things seemed an impossibility. Digging the hole and filling it with foundation. The ceiling joists and the floor bridging. They probably laid the shingles that had once upon a time been there one by one. Pulleys and men with tool belts. Wood siding put in manually, mortar spread, bricks stacked. Maybe the house had once upon a time been beautiful. The fulfillment of a promise. You work hard, you strive, you take out a loan, and you move along with the business of starting a family. Now, the thing's roof had caved in, trees grew throughout it, and summer heat had made the bulging walls crisp. The women had complained about drug dealers and rapes; some of these places had probably hosted more than a few murders.

The counsel Michael held with the ladies turned to a muffle. Linc entered and could see that the scavengers had been recent here. The floor was soft with mold, shifted beneath his footfalls. Out back, there had probably been a rusted van, maybe without doors, to make it easier for the vultures to load the furnace and the stove, the piping that they had picked out from behind the walls. Maybe they were at this very moment getting paid for their scrap metal. It all probably happened in the time between when the dangerous-buildings inspector had phoned Michael and when Michael had picked Linc up from his apartment. A large, person-shaped lump stopped Linc's boot and he kicked the thing over to find the remains of a face staring up at him. Parts of the body had been gnawed away, some of the fingers down to the bone, the eyes still there, but the cheek jowls torn and hanging. Traces of quicklime lined the corpse. He'd been told to report corpses, maybe they would help out with open investigations. Linc stepped over the thing.

In another room, on top of a molding, rust-pitted mattress slept a wraith. Next to that wraith's head, just underneath its opened hand, was a Tec-9. Red-tops and yellow-tops, wrapped in small plastic bags, peeked out from inside a crinkled paper sack. Linc stooped, gingerly pulled the Tec out from beneath the emaciated hand, doubted the person could have lifted it anyway, pulled out the clip and stuffed it into his pants' pocket. He ejected the bullet in the chamber and tossed the thing into a pile of empty burger wrappers. His hand tightened on the neck of his hammer. The junkie was dissolving into the ruins, turning into the house ready for demolition, and its head would've been easy enough to crash in. The junkie was done living anyway, but Linc moved on.

Descending into the basement, he noted the water damage, but it was far enough along to show that the water had been turned off some time ago. Nothing had lived in there for a long time now. He stayed on the concrete steps for a while, frozen, reminded of the time he'd come down into a similar basement to find a little boy cuffed to a radiator after having passed a man ambling out the back door and buttoning up his pants. He blinked away the vision. Nothing stirred. And if, like the junkie, anything were still breathing, it wouldn't get anything approaching a proper burial. The local cemeteries had long since burst through their capacity.

He came back up for air. The board-up crew had already sealed off most of the space. A roving band of custom-cut sheets of plywood and screw guns. They moved like whirling dervishes, and sometimes their haste left shoddy work in their wake, like bodies that they hadn't accounted for, the ignored junkie or rape victim or dead body or eco-freak trying to make art out of ruin porn.

Coming out of the house felt like emerging from hell. The light blinded. The air, poisoned as it was, cleansed the lungs. The mind-fog and the shell shock dissipated, and all of a sudden, there were new parking lots or bits of road or signage that he hadn't noticed before. Everything seemed draped in clarity. In focus.

Linc gave Michael the thumbs-up. House cleared. His hammer-head dragged behind him.

Michael nodded, then opened his dashboard and out came a small console with a touchboard protruding from its bottom. Empty stim-halers tinked against each other as he stretched and geomapped the house's location, input the coordinates, and armed the drone that would arrive in just under five minutes. There was shade at the bunker, and a radio where he could tune in to the ball game or put on a play-list, and he could operate the drone from there. The console was bigger there, had more equipment and became much more of an immersive experience. Plus, the operating room was air-conditioned. But he had grown to hate it. He needed to be around the people.

On the console would be a high-definition moving image, turning the northwest of New Haven, a span of about a dozen or so blocks, into a midsummer palette of copper and brown and gray, punctuated by occasional, invasive green. The houses, in rows, would be easy enough to pick out, but it was always when he switched to infrared, waiting for heat signals, that the cracks would run through his heart. The ghostly white always stood out against the irradiated landscape, and there was always movement, sometimes the smallest of gestures, until there wasn't. He would linger over well-populated neighborhoods to remind himself that people still lived here, but when he'd have to head over to his target, the blotches would drop off until there was only a blood-red sea below, all twenty-three homes on a once-busy block empty. Sometimes, a sin-gle white snowflake would move among the red, an amoeba lumbering among the charred husks of thirty-five neighboring vacancies.

At the hangar, the only sounds would be the hum of machines and the reggaeton that came from the radio. He'd go through his verbal checklist once he got to the target house, countdown, then mutter his code. And someone near, sometimes a ghost, would whisper back.

Over the course of that incantation, a small gravity bomb would slip from its container in the drone's bottom, fall toward the center of the house's roof, then, as it fell, would pull the house in around itself. The screen would light up with white flame, the smoke would clear, and the crater would stare like an empty eye socket back at the drone's camera. There were times the bomb would malfunction, and the house's remains would sink upon itself, then bounce back up like a rubber band in extremis, pink insulation stretched like cotton candy, paper and plastic and fast-food wrappers and pizza boxes and a basket of unused diapers and tires and phone books and sometimes heroin needles, exploding upward before the bomb resumed its work and sucked the entirety of the place's ghosts into a cube that landed on the cracked foundation right on top of the gravity disc. Before the final moment, there was always an arc made of discarded clothes and, in that arc, every single time, several pairs of children's shoes.

Municipal technicians never figured out how to get the disc to swallow up the more unwieldy parts of the home, so the undigested bricks would be vomited in a pile of architectural effluvium on top of the disc that someone would then have to fish out. And just as his truck would leave or just as they would retrieve the disc, stackers would swarm over the site, harvesting the bricks for building residential units up in the space colonies.

The drone loomed over the targeted house, and by now, residents had set up lawn chairs to watch. Several neighborhoods had gone through test runs where the city government and relevant departments made sure to properly calibrate the tonnage of the bombs. Take down the targeted house and try not to swallow up the ones next to it. The residents didn't seem to care that they sat or stood so near to the blast radius. His truck, even now, was parked dangerously close.

"Feelin' lit, feelin' light," Michael said, cheerier than usual.

"Two a.m., summer nights," chimed Linc, who had, by now, taken his seat next to Michael, surprising the driver.

The bomb dropped and the house did one of those dry-heave things where the bomb tried to swallow everything, then choked up what it couldn't digest. Michael made sure to watch it actually happen, see the browns and whites and greens and blues and reds of the actual house, rather than have the glow of the screen burn his retinas. When he turned, though, he saw Linc's gaze riveted on the monitor, watching as the smoke cleared and small glowing blobs writhed in the wreckage, pieces of the person he was supposed to declare. The junkie was missing a leg, just above the knee, and her blood was hot when it hit the ground, burned bright on the monitor, and she writhed on the ground and reached instinctively for something, for her gun, but couldn't find it, wailed soundlessly and rolled beneath the rubble where she could until she became the same color as the ground.

Michael gave Linc a look, but Linc didn't acknowledge it.

The drone lowered itself, obeying Michael's commands, retrieved the house box, then flew back to the hangar.

He started up his truck, waved goodbye to the ladies who made him promise to come by again—both to take care of them drug houses but also to say hello and get the sweet tea they'd made. The stackers, tracking the drone, had already found the demolition site and just as the neighbors streamed back into their homes, the stackers descended.

One of them pulled a bar of something black out of the pocket of his overalls, undid some of the wrapping, and bit in as he moved to secure his fiefdom.

"Where'd you get that?" asked the second, who sidled up next to him.

The first held it out. "It's Russian chocolate," he said, holding it forward like it was a prize.

"Oh shit, word? What's Russian chocolate?"

"Chocolate from Russia, nigga. Whatchu think?"

Michael's rig rumbled, the engine drowning out the rest, and Linc climbed over to his seat behind the cab.

They pulled out, and as they passed through more desolation, Linc knew, by Michael's silence, that the niggerrican was mad at him for not clearing the junkie. But then they passed into a hood where they were flanked by Craftsman-style homes. Tapered support columns. Stonework porches. Nobody lived on this street but people came out to maintain these houses anyway. Linc occasionally saw the armed patrols that would stalk the block, ready to beat back any advances from drug dealers or whoever was trying to make a new stash house. Their berets and sometimes their bow ties, and sometimes their leather jackets and sometimes their Afros. And whenever there was a new family of Exodusters that had been evicted from somewhere else or another group who had made the Great Migration from cities that had been swallowed up by the blight, they had this neighborhood prepared for them.

Michael turned in his seat. "Gimme a boy's name that starts with H."

"José," Linc replied.

THE kitchen was the only room in the house not bathed in black light. A ratty briefcase lay open on the kitchen counter by the sink with pills of different colors, and acid tabs, and ounces of grass in small ziplock packages lining the interior. Xanax bars, oxy 30s, lean, activis, lunes, shrooms, adderall, and what looked like meth. A skinny white girl—in a tight, torn alabaster half shirt and a Navajo headdress that glowed like the sun, which followed her wherever she went—had brought the case in and mixed an assortment of pills in a blender, pouring the concoction into a red Solo cup and topping it off with a generous pour from a forty-ounce of Olde English. Music thudded against the walls of the kitchen. Jonathan took the cup she had handed him, smiled at her grin, and they sipped together.

She shuffled close to him, so close Jonathan could see the lighting apparatus wired into her warbonnet, and ran her hand up and down his crotch.

When he finished his sip, the cup seemed so big that he needed to grip it with both hands, and her face had turned into that of a cougar's. Her teeth swayed when she grinned, unable to keep form, and she stuck her tongue into his mouth before sashaying to a stool in the corner of the room.

Cup in hand, Jonathan massaged his cheek and walked into the darkness where bodies, electric and glowing with radiation, throbbed and pulsed around his. Hair swishing against his face, someone else's sweat brushed onto his skin. A beige kid leaned against a wall, light flashing over his face, and stuck his tongue out, placed a white tab on it and, staring directly at Jonathan or something past him, held his tongue out for a moment before flicking it back and smirking.

Girls in pink and red halter tops touched themselves, ran fingers down their cleavage. Tattoos ran in single lines up their forearms or along their clavicles or in circles around their thighs where they had raised their skirts. A girl bit her lip as Jonathan swam toward her then away. Someone's mom smiled at him. The wrinkled face was a glimpse in a crowd, then gone. A white guy with ginger scruff carried an armful of unmarked forties somewhere.

Jonathan sipped from his cup, and a blunt, wrapped with brown tobacco leaves, appeared in the fingers of his free hand. Even as he toked, he didn't believe it really existed. Arms wagged in the air around him. Girls in bikinis and neon ski masks stared at him, swaying back and forth, some climbed on tables and were topless as they bounced, forties in hand.

Someone's locs caressed his back through his shirt.

A white dude with short twists, shirtless, torso and arm pocked with tattooed lettering and shadowed animal faces, shifted his weight from one foot to the other and back, head down, before a garish silhouette of a cross.

The ski masks tilted to one side then the next around him. He saw twins, white girls with red hair covering their faces. Then a girl in an armchair with her jean skirt hiked up, playing with herself while two boys watched in drug-eyed wonder.

Jonathan smirked at some mixed kid in a corner who considered him over the bent beer can he had sideways to his mouth and whose end he lit while he toked. The beautiful face vanished behind a cloud of smoke. Glistening curls, someone's head, bobbed by his elbows.

Cameras watched him from all angles. Jonathan, sipping from his drug cocktail and taking the occasional pull from a blunt that wasn't there, made a game out of trying to spot them. Some partiers he walked by had frozen, and Jonathan wondered if they knew about the cameras too and were trying to hide, like if you stood still before a T-Rex and made it so it couldn't find you. The patterned wallpaper moved whenever he wasn't looking at it.

Neon balloons appeared, shrinking as skinny guys with uncut hair inhaled the helium, eyes closed to the music that rocked the sternums you could see through their skin.

In one room Jonathan passed, two boys constructed a blunt on an older woman's bare stomach. Her limbs moved as if she were underwater. She looked at Jonathan, on her back, and he knew, even in his haze, that she didn't see him. Weed stems dotted the skin around her navel. A pearl necklace hung tight around her neck, and one of the boys sat in a chair, dumb, while the other reached out and tongue-kissed the woman. She grabbed the boy's face and pulled him in. The other boy ran out of his seat, Afro bouncing on his head, punched a guy in the nuts, then ran on giggling, swallowed by the sea of bodies in another room.

Oxygen canisters had been mixed with some hallucinogen so that neon gas sprayed out onto a girl's ass. Another had her hands against a wall in an arrest pose while she twerked in a cloud of lambent smoke.

A bearded guy, Solo cup in hand, looked as though he were in the midst of an epileptic fit against a wall by the staircase, but Jonathan heard the music and saw the guy's rhythm and smirked. White guys.

As he moved, the cups got bigger and bigger until they matched his in size.

A girl pulled up her red ski mask and revealed the face of someone who could've been his aunt. Guys standing in the doorway to a second kitchen sucked on Popsicles; their gazes followed Jonathan as he moved past.

Ski-masked girls took a shock-club to a piñata in a bedroom where a girl was giving a guy a blow job, and another girl stumbled to the

doorway and put her coke-nailed finger to her lips, silently shushing
Jonathan with a grin.

In a bathroom, a middle-aged guy sat on the toilet, reading a news-
paper whose letters swirled while a hairless young guy kneeled before
him, his head bobbing in the other guy's lap.

Someone was having a tattoo etched into her skin in another room,
and the whole thing glowed its pattern onto the ceiling. Each mirror
Jonathan passed had his head shaking at all angles like an inhuman
thing, but he felt no movement in his neck. He paused at one and saw
David behind him, resting a chin on his shoulder, and he caressed
the cheek, leaned into the body, then turned around and saw a wild
boar's face staring at him, placed onto the top of a girl's writhing
body.

A godlike girl's face turned to the ceiling while she danced on a
couch, eyes rolling into the back of her head while a group of guys
and girls cheered a kid on as he vomited into his gigantic cup.

People strutted or ambled or shuffled or stumbled by with efful-
gent headbands. Someone's light got stuck in Jonathan's hair.

A makeshift Dome surrounded the house and the adjacent forest,
so that when Jonathan emptied out onto the back porch, he didn't
need the air mask he'd surely misplaced. Already, his augments set
to work, breaking down the pollutants he'd shoveled into his system.
Chill autumn air kissed his face like a sea of someone's hair. As his
head cleared, he scrolled through recent photos and saw a 'gram of the
kid with the bong can; the caption read: #TeamBeige.

On the back porch, #TeamBeige materialized at his side, rolling
up his own cigarette. Crystals glowed in the tobacco. The guy wore a
low-cut V-neck and a massive gray beanie bunched back against the
back of his neck. His forehead glistened.

"There isn't an ounce of cellulite in there," Jonathan murmured.

#TeamBeige took a toke and offered his cigarillo to Jonathan, who
took it and puffed. "You know I left that shit on the Colony. This is
purely a No Cellulite Zone."

"Rules of the Frontier."

#TeamBeige chuckled at that, looked Jonathan over. "Rules of the

Frontier, indeed." He took the cigarillo back. "You're new. When'd you get in?"

"About a week or two ago." A beat. Jonathan glanced over at the young man. "Staking out a claim before I send for my boy." He waited for defeat to register on #TeamBeige's face. Not even a flicker.

"Where're you staying?"

"Got a hammock at a rooming house while I try to figure things out. Looking to buy a house on the West Side."

#TeamBeige took a toke. "Whereabouts?"

"Beaver Hills. Maybe Edgewood."

"You think about West Rock?" He toked again. "Bought a house there last month, in fact." He pushed himself up. "Eamonn." Stuck out his hand.

Jonathan grabbed it, hoisted himself up. Then it turned into a lingering handshake. "Jonathan," he said. "A pleasure."

"Welcome to New Haven."

THE next morning, Linc walked up to the Body Shop to see pieces of the wrecker strewn about the junkyard. Michael had a bit of metal on a stool and was taking his tools to it, but Linc saw the dejection in dude's hunch. Michael hadn't even bothered to wipe the #WhalleyAveWarriors radiation tag from the side of the hangar. That made this the third stash house they'd demolished this month.

He hefted his hammer in search of other work.

inc tugged down the bill of his worn Red Sox cap and closed his eyes against the sweat stinging them. The truck, lifting carpets of ash and dust into the air like someone spreading a bedsheet, provided the morning's only sound. But Linc thought he could maybe hear the excavators that always worked alongside wreckers up ahead, monstrous, steel-tooth jaws spreading open to dump another load of bricks on the growing pile. In the shadows cast by the leaning, crumbling apartment towers stood Black girls and a few jaundiced snow bunnies in leather, neon-colored short skirts, hips kinked to one side while the stone wall supported their lewd poses. The other men in the back of the truck with Linc leaned over the side of the flatbed and whistled.

"Them stretchmarks get me a discount?" one shouted.

"I'm just tryna put one in ya, guh!"

"Love bites, Mami, and so do I."

"I get paid next Friday!"

They laughed and it sounded like thunder, joyous, irresponsible, and even as Linc gripped the handle of his hammer, he couldn't help smiling. He wanted to get at least a little bit of sleep before they got to the worksite, but the heat was a few dozen degrees past sleepy. Why not holler at a few hoes to pass the time?

At least it wasn't raining; at least it wasn't cold enough to aggravate his busted knuckles and the smashed fingers and toes that belonged to any number of kids in various angles of repose in the flatbed. None of them looked up at the red-blue sky threaded with knife-scar clouds and the Colony hovering like a pitted moon overhead.

The sex workers vanished behind a corner, and the young men retreated to their seats. Hunger hung around them like an odor. Linc knew the work would be the best thing to happen to them. Otherwise, they'd be out there just like he was before rehab, letting hunger compel him to destroy the very things he needed.

"We pickin' up Ace?" one of the youths asked. He had his hammer draped across his chest, his head propped against the rickety back of the flatbed, his hat brim low over his eyes.

No one answered.

"We pickin' him up or what?"

Linc stirred, then rapped loudly on the back window. When nothing happened, he rapped again, hard enough to crack the Plexiglas. The driver's side window creaked downward and a leather-skinned Black man with a lazy eye, the ratty remains of a cigar in his false teeth and a straw hat on his head, leaned out on his elbow.

"You gon' break my damn winda poundin' like that."

Linc leaned over to be heard over the rumbling through the abandoned roads by the old Ivy Quarter. "Yo, Bishop, we pickin' up Ace today?"

"Whatchu think?" Bishop spat back. His cigar clung to his teeth. "His place comin' up right now." And with that, Bishop retreated. The window only went halfway up after that.

They drove out of the old Ivy Quarter and the dilapidated houses got smaller, their lean more pronounced. The broken windows with their crumbling frames like Bishop's droopy eye watching them pass. The houses here on the outskirts of that neighborhood looked no different, but out front, piled up on the sidewalk, were mattresses, some with bloodstains like large copper half dollars on them, children's clothes mixed in with dirty linens, ants swarming over half-empty bags of fast food, old radios that looked like they'd only recently stopped working.

Bugs sat up a little in the truck bed and looked around. "There was a riot here when I was a kid."

Linc shot him a look that tried to tell him he still was a kid.

"Cops chased a bunch of us right down this street." He made a sweep with his arm like he was shooting up the block. "Beat the shit outta my homeboy right on that front lawn." He snorted out a laugh, tucking the hurt beneath bravado. "Yeah, the homie Jamal got caught outside the Dome and he died, then a bunch of police came through and tore up the block." He quieted, contenting himself with merely looking around, retracing the ordeal's trajectory through the neighborhood.

It was originally Linc's story. About the boy named Jamal who got caught outside a Dome and who had to lie on his back looking up at augmented cops while he suffocated on irradiated air. And it had happened in Long Beach, not New Haven. And the "homeboy" who'd gotten the shit beat out of him had been his brother Jake. Bugs took the story Linc had told him and left out Linc's mother, who had been trying to tug Linc indoors, and how the cops had been presaged by a band of white Marauders, how they came in on horseback to beat up Black and brown folk, warm 'em up for the police. And how Linc's pops had looked at the whole thing like "damn, not again." Maybe something like this had happened to Bugs wherever he'd come from. Or maybe he just liked sounding like he had more history than he really did. Linc was glad when he stopped talking.

When they got to Ace's spot, a slouching duplex that used to be blue and yellow once upon a time, there was five-oh out front and a couple people that looked maybe like social workers. The County Sheriff was there, a large metal sphere with arms like a spider, one sporting a small-caliber pistol. On its front, a display of a white man's mustachioed face. Remote policing. The cops were partially cyberized, their essential parts replaceable; hence their stomping around irradiated wasteland. But the social workers looked flesh-and-blood enough. One of them looked like she might boot all over her jeans.

Nobody in the truck bed stirred. The chalky dust on their overalls and their jeans and their boots didn't even budge. But they all silently watched the man they'd worked with being dressed down like a bitch in front of his family. Linc wanted to spit but had run out of saliva.

The front door hung open, and inside, Ace could be seen sitting down in his living room couch, his arms around his two kids, boy and a girl, relaxed but protecting them from the officer who, hand leisurely to his weapon, stood over them. Staticky blue and white from the TV flashed on the eviction cop's back.

Linc couldn't hear what was being said, but Ace, from where he sat, raised his voice. The officer never raised his, but eventually Ace shot up from his seat and screamed, "This some *bull*shit!"

Ace stomped out before the cop could make it look like he was being escorted, waited for the cop and made like he was standing his ground. "You ain't got no right. You see this neighborhood? You see it? We the last family on the block. Ain't no one livin' here. So what goddamn difference it make if me and my family make a life here, huh? What difference it make?"

The cop raised his non-gun hand, inches from Ace's chest. "Sir, leave the immediate premises or you will be arrested."

The social workers walked the children and Ace's wife out onto the sidewalk, and already movers had materialized to start offloading the family's furniture. The TV blared. "Do you have a place where you can stay?" the social worker asked Ace's wife.

"No," she said back. She seemed too tired to be annoyed or upset that their life was being brought out into the street like so much trash. "We ain't heard from his family in a couple years."

The social worker's face half crinkled in sorrow. "There are some shelters further out. Fairfield and a few more further down the rail line. Our office can furnish you and your family with rail tickets."

Ace's wife had stopped looking at the social worker as she droned on, looked instead at the growing pile of furniture and appliances, some of them already rusting from exposure to the poisoned air, some of them already growing rusted blood blisters. Her son, six years old in overalls like the ones Ace wore to work, scurried back inside where his bowl of cereal waited on the table for him. The sight of the kid with his cereal, riveted on the TV while the movers emptied his house, reminded Linc of his own dad who, at the same age as that kid, had come home from school to see all their shit on the sidewalk, an eviction notice stapled to their front door. He hadn't told Linc much about it, but Jake told him one afternoon when they were skipping stones off the warped pipes of the California Aqueduct that Dad, as a kid, had spent the following two months living in a truck with his dad, their grandfather.

Bishop turned in his seat. The engine had been idling.

Ace's wife held their infant daughter at her hip.

The officer said "good luck" to Ace and turned away, the silent but ever-watchful sheriff hovering like a pet bird over his shoulder.

"We ain't dead," Ace shouted.

Linc could barely hear him over the engine Bishop had now started revving, getting the car ready to peel off.

"You can't talk about us like we dead. We right here! See this here? This still a family! Ain't gonna break that! Good luck to *you*, Officer!"

The rest of Ace's words were lost in the smoke that billowed from the tailpipe. Bishop shifted into gear and the truck bumped along before shuddering off. No one in the truck bed had moved. Anybody walking by would've thought they were sleeping.

"Guess Ace ain't comin' to work today," Jayceon said, arm propped beneath his neck, head bumping softly against the back of the truck bed. Linc heard implied violence in the kid's voice and wondered what would happen if Bishop spun the car around and caught up with that officer.

Eamonn pulled his Flex out of his shirt pocket, tapped at it a little bit, then handed it over to Jonathan, who found himself staring at screenshots of homes that had been well put together, furnished, lived in, with numbers next to them that represented their bids. The cursor hovered over the main picture, a shot of the house's front façade and its rose garden, its postcard image, and shot out faded shots of the house's other sides, views from above, views of the expansive but well-kept backyard, the small gate that kept the place fenced in. The county treasurer, a wrinkled white man whose neck bulged over his shirt collar and the knot in his blue tie, smiled from the top-left corner of the webpage.

"What am I looking at?" Jonathan asked, facing the stars.

"Online foreclosure auction." Eamonn scratched lazily at his chest. "Houses still being left, folks fell behind on their property taxes, et cetera."

"Wait, I thought this whole place was abandoned. Is the city still going after these people?"

Eamonn shifted on the rooftop, turned to face Jonathan. "You came in through Fairfield Station, right?"

Jonathan nodded.

"Where do you think that money came from?"

Jonathan frowned, turned away from the auction.

"Look, stop by the town halls over in Westville. When the councilor mentions wanting to work with the 'good' residents, think about who he means." He smirked. "You think this is forced relocation, right? Jonathan." He put a reassuring hand on Jonathan's shoulder, moved it down his forearm and wrapped his fingers around the other man's. "There is nothing wrong with what we're doing. This place is, for all intents and purposes, abandoned. We're building it back up. They're talking of expanding the maglev line here." He nodded to the west. "And we got a new air filtration plant going up. Those people'll get jobs. If they wanna stay, they can stay. We're not kicking them out."

Photo after photo of prepared homes flowed across the stream with each of Jonathan's swipes. He pretended Eamonn's hand wasn't warm and pleasantly wrapped around his own. Maybe the someone who lived there wasn't ready to give it up. Maybe her last name was Brown or something and maybe she had hypertension, wasn't quite over-weight, but waddled more than walked. And maybe she had a mole somewhere on the left side of her face and had her hair permed or had some sort of hot comb put to it. Maybe she was retired, or maybe she couldn't retire because she was working in industries where that wasn't done, but she did have disability checks. And maybe she just fell behind on the property taxes, taxes that had been waiting for her when she bought the house a couple years before, thinking she was taking a step up in her play at citizenship. Maybe, when she got the foreclosure notice on her Flex, her brother was asleep, having only re-cently come back from the hospital after his own surgery. And maybe she'd started to tear up and ask her Flex if "they" were really going to take her home from her, her and the Flex knowing exactly who "they" was. And here it was, on the screen before Jonathan's face. A home where maybe all of that happened.

David would have had a field day talking Jonathan's ear off about New Haven's history of racialized housing policies, spouting a detailed and very erudite chronicle replete with riots and interstate highways, and maybe he'd pull up vids or shots of white folks throwing bricks through the windows of Black homes or some mayor's appeal to calm, a thinly veiled command to maintain some asymmetrical status quo.

Jonathan closed the browser window, handed the Flex back to Eamonn. "What they got in Westville isn't what I want. It's not what David wants either."

"You've got buyer's remorse, and you haven't even bought it yet."

"It's not buyer's remorse." It startled Jonathan how quiet his voice had gotten.

"You just don't want to profit off of someone else's misery. Is that it?" Eamonn did not smirk, nor did he chuckle. "Maybe this is gentrification, maybe it's something else. You don't know those people, and they don't know you. Heck, they probably don't even know about you."

"They shut the water off for them and turn it back on for us."

"How do you know your house has running water?" Eamonn asked.

What upset Jonathan more than anything else was how much he had begun to sound like David.

The calls had all blended together: David receiving news that Jo had been hospitalized after falling and hitting her head at home, his manager telling him he didn't need to come into the office next week. Or the week after. Or the week after that. The first call had come while at work, half a dozen holographic screens displayed before him, the chips embedded in his fingertips glowing as he clicked and slid and swiped information from one source to another recipient, the images and news stories and numbers and acronyms somehow translated into stock prices and market share and the stuff that people richer than him used to get even richer. And the second call had come while he sat at his mother's bedside, everything in the room an oppressive, violent white. She was awake and protesting and telling the attendant every way she knew how that she didn't need to be here, then upon discovering the attendant was droid'd, calling her every variation of "toaster" imaginable.

But then—when she'd been asked to name the day of the week and she'd answered wrong and when she'd called him the wrong name before, after blinking several times, correcting herself—he'd had to leave.

Bereft of work, he passed many hours at The Viewer, wearing a groove into one bench in particular for much of the day. As ever, a creature of habit, he noted wryly. Outside the windows that seemed to extend forever in each direction, the stars glowed.

When he let his mind drift, it traced the patterns she'd shown him when they used to stargaze together. The stories—this character's luminous smile, that one's battle axe, that one's flowing hair—like some sort of founding myth. He'd been a child, and she'd talked about some Wild West as though it were Atlantis. He'd tried to imagine an open plain and the thrill of fashioning a new life for oneself, of taking a place and making it home, of carving a slice of self out of the chaos and ambition and shootouts and panning for gold in rivers with your bare hands. Older, now, he knew it was a place she'd never seen, a place David experienced as twice-mythologized, filtered and filtered and filtered, copied and re-encoded and JPEG-compressed until generation loss had made it nothing more than brushstrokes and discoloration and thick pixelated black boundaries. But there'd been comfort in making a frontier out of the stars.

Then, when his cyberization allowed him access to greater information, he could trace deeper, more convoluted, more specific patterns. A burst of apophenia, an overworking of his neural circuitry, and geometric origami would form, patterns with whatever meaning he wanted to give them, designs waiting for a religion to claim them.

Now the stars seemed to randomly dot the dark. Thrown there by careless celestial fingers in puerile fits of reckless abandon. A drowsy, fatuous deity promising order and snatching his hand away at the last instant, laughing.

David began to tremble.

A small sign to his left indicated with an arrow the way to the smokers' lounge.

He rose and followed the subsequent signs until he came to a screen made of glass, the other side obscured by a haze of smoke.

Thoughtless steps brought him past the first set of sliding doors into an anteroom that opened out onto the lounge. People, almost entirely red-bloods like Jo, filled the small space, hovered alone or in small groups, humming conversation in quiet joviality. Some of them stared as he had out the window that opened out onto space. David stood, frozen among them, and constriction returned to his chest. This was a different narrowing, a physical thing like an animal curling in on itself to protect from the wiles of a predator. He coughed.

He coughed again, more vicious than before.

"I think it's supposed to be a cautionary tale."

He spun at the voice, dulcet with a hint of rasp.

The stubbled speaker smirked and moved to his side. He had a slim leather jacket, marked along its front with small pockets, over a small gray hooded sweatshirt, the hood pulled back. He looked at David for a second, appraised him, then turned his gaze toward the expanse. His atomizer's smoke swung between his thumb and index finger before curling up. He smelled of peppermint.

"Want one?" He had snuck his hand into one of the pockets and pulled out a pack, white with a green triangle running down the front. "They're menthols. Hope you don't mind."

"Sure," David said, not knowing why.

They waited.

"Go on, take it."

"Oh." He took the cigarette poking out furthest. The pack retreated into the man's pocket. He held the thing in his fingers, looked around, then stuck it between his lips as he'd seen the others do. A flick sounded from inside the device, flame danced just before his face.

"Now suck in," the stranger said playfully.

David glanced at him, did as he suggested. And the constriction gripped his entire chest. He coughed and gasped, carcinogenic misting in front of eyes welded shut.

"I didn't know any better, I'd say that's your first." The stranger chuckled. David heard phlegm in it. "You're a virgin."

He coughed until his lungs no longer stung. "What did you mean?" he asked when he got his breath back.

The stranger puffed lazily. "What?"

"What did you mean? When you said this was a cautionary tale, what did you mean?"

"Oh." He laughed again. The phlegm had thickened. "Well, you saw the smoke from out there, right?"

David nodded.

"Anybody who thinks about starting up, they just gotta take one look through that window there to know what's waiting for them."

"Oh." It came out as a gasp.

David puffed again. It was easier than before once he followed his rhythm. Slow, easy drags. The nicotine stroked his lobes, put him, oddly enough, at ease. The stars blurred until they began winking out, one by one. Vertigo tipped him.

When he opened his eyes again, he was in the stranger's arms. His heart thrummed at the physical closeness.

"You all right?"

David came to his feet, closed his eyes, shook his head. "Yes. Yes, I'm fine. I'm sorry."

"Don't worry about it. I forget how strong these are."

"No, really. I'm fine." David was straight again, poised.

"You sure?"

He pinched the bridge of his nose. When he opened his eyes, they stung. But no tears came. He exhaled several times, the cigarette's battery light winking out its slow death between his fingers, unheeded. The stranger smiled at David, sympathetically, and turned to leave. "My mother has dementia," David said.

The stranger stopped, turned and looked at him. "Well, shit," he said, and puffed on his atomizer. "Is that so?"

"WANNA butt-fuck?"

David had worn an ashen blister into the polyurethane of his thumb, trying to get his jammed atomizer to work. Occasionally, he'd been told, a concentrated enough external heat source could help stimulate the thing. Like jumper cables. Now, heat rose in his cheeks. He faced away from the man in the leather jacket—his smoking jacket, he'd called it—embarrassed. "What?"

"Your lighter. Seems you've got a bum lighter."

David kept trying. Sparks, but no flame. Aggravating the bituminous swelling until the silvered oval had filled out completely.

"Here, let me." The stranger took the cigarette from David's lips and held its end to his own while he inhaled. The tips of both kissing cigarettes glowed orange. He handed it back to him. "There you go."

David turned the thing over in his fingers, in minor awe.

"Butt-fucking," the stranger said, smiling.

"Oh." He put the thing to his mouth and puffed.

The stranger watched him for several seconds, smirking. "Not all the way gone, are you."

"No," David said between mechanical puffs.

The stranger turned his gaze to the stars. "Yeah, after my dad died, my habit picked up."

They smoked for a while in silence.

"You know, they only put us here to give us an unobstructed view of the Ring."

"The Ring?"

Dying atomizer between his index and middle finger, the stranger pointed at a floating band far in the distance. It flowed horizontally until the walls blocked their view. "It's all junk out there. Trash. Shit we throw out. I mean, it has to go somewhere, right?" He shrugged. "The people in The Viewer, they don't have to see all that stuff. All they see are the nebulae and the zodiac signs. Diana, the silver-footed queen, and all that. Get to stare out there and contemplate their existence." He chuckled, and there was bitterness in it. "Us? We get to look at what we all shit out." He smoked, angrily. Finished his cigarette, replaced the small battery with one out of his pack, and lit up again.

David's lungs no longer burned the way they had before. Even augmented, they weren't built to withstand this genre of intentional damage. Now, they only ached whenever he returned to his apartment. And the vertigo had been harder to chase. But he quietly rejoiced in the man's unassuming company.

"You're in shock now, but it'll pass." He turned to David. "You got people to talk to? You know, friends and all that."

"No, not really."

"'T's all right, I guess. We grieve however we grieve."

She's not dead, David wanted to tell him. Instead, he said, "How'd you grieve?"

He smiled around his cigarette. "I became a smoker."

David saw no reason to return his smile, so didn't.

"I got a group now that I go to. It helps." He shrugged again and his shoulders slumped further. "Just wish to Christ that I'da known him better is all." He scraped the lit end of his cigarette against the anisotropic surface on his pack, deactivating it, smiled at David, and walked back the way they'd come.

FEET. David was staring at feet.

Birds in black ink caught mid-flight amid a canvas of pale skin. Somewhere, faded, muffled, came a voice that said *I love your doves* and another, louder, less familiar, giggled and said *they're not doves, they're crows.* Jo's memories, when David plugged into her now, looked and felt like a video that'd been played so often the tape frayed. Static blitzed in and out, all sound wrapped in gauze. David saw through his mother's eyes the black leather couch this other woman had brought her tattooed feet up on, feet she'd tucked beneath her in feline repose.

One bird had a black wing that ran along the curve of the woman's instep. A couple birds had beaks that threaded the veins of her extensor tendons. Her toes were untouched. But when the woman put both bare feet together, the migration arc turned into a circle. The understanding didn't come to David, but was brought to him by his mother's subconscious. The same subconscious that, when her gaze rose to see a face framed by dark auburn hair that crashed in waves against the smooth, sharp shores of tanned cheeks, told David no one had ever had a greater portion of his mother's love than this woman.

Dee. The same woman who would die in the shuttle crash that had put him in a coma as a child. His mother.

When David left the memory and unplugged from his mother, he saw that she was still fast asleep in her bed, serenity slackening the skin on her face.

"Do you wish I'd died instead of her?" he asked, the question so soft off his lips he wasn't sure he had asked it at all.

DAVID found his fellow smoker on a wooden bench at The Viewer, hands folded placidly in his lap. When he took a seat beside him, the stranger smelled only faintly of mint.

"They're cleaning it out," he said by way of explanation, without looking at him. At David's silence, he continued: "Sometimes it gets so thick that even us hardened veterans start to get that contact high off the secondhand. Gets to be too unhealthy. Violates the Colony Codes and all that. They're okay with us dying, just not too quickly. So they gotta clean it out. Empty out the lungs."

"I do it because it hurts," David said, only vaguely knowing why.

Leather jacket blinked, startled, then turned to him; all mirth and lightheartedness leaked out of his face. "What?"

"The smoking. The damage. I know why I like it." He smiled like a teacher unpacking an understanding to a student. "I like it because it damages me."

"What are you talking about? That's the nicotine. That's why you like cigs. You like it 'cause it releases all those neurotransmitters—histamine, dopamine, serotonin, all of that—and the norepinephrine gets you aroused. Look, I practically failed chemistry; that's why I'm a garbageman. But I'm pretty sure acetylcholine and beta-endorphin *reduce* pain. Mesolimbic pathway, reward system. Any of this making sense to you?"

"But it hurts."

Leather jacket slung an arm over the back of the bench and turned to look at David—really look at him. "This about your mom?"

"Why was she the one who survived?" Then it all came out, a waterfall of words. He found himself stumbling over them, joining them together where they weren't meant to be joined, compound words that hadn't existed before, thoughts clambering over other thoughts until he was out of breath, his mind crowded with images of the shuttle's interior cabin just before the explosion, the debris and people sucked out the hole before the self-repair protocols kicked in, one of his mothers slipping him into his space suit, then him floating in an inky dark that felt as though it would last forever, that seemed as though it were the only thing that had ever existed, that he was a single moment in its life, a solitary grain of sand, that nothing mattered, not even him. He wanted to plug into the stranger's skull and convey the entirety of his vision, realizing this was the first time in years he'd talked out loud about the accident that had killed one mother and ruined another.

He was delirious with joy, vertiginous with rapture. And when he finished, he found the stranger staring at him as though he'd cut off his own arms. Horror and anguish and pity. Sparkling behind that, however, in tears that crowded the corners of his eyes but did not spill forth, recognition.

"You were in the shuttle crash." He blinked, seemed to be coming back into himself. "You . . . your family was in the shuttle crash."

David realized what he'd done and shrank into himself, as though he'd put in the stranger's hands the entirety of him and he couldn't bear to watch someone be less than gentle with it. *He'll drop me and it'll be my fault.*

"That's how my father died too. Shuttle crash killed my pops. Very same one." Then he smiled and sniffed, then wiped a jacket sleeve across his eyes, so that it came back wearing a scar that shone with lamentation.

THE hospital had indicated during the call that something dangerous and urgent was happening, that he was needed right away, that David and only David could solve whatever catastrophe was unfolding. But when he arrived at Jo's hospital room, sedation reigned. Doctors greeted him with a friendly nod. The nurse attendant smiled as he walked past her, through the sliding door that whooshed open. And though Jo didn't have a grin or even an ironic chuckle for him, she was quiet.

David sat down at her bedside and, for a long time, was silent. Just as he was about to speak, to chastise her for making a scene, to curse her out for worrying him, to berate her for being her usual flinty fucking self, she opened her mouth and said, "Didn't remember when I was," in a voice limp with apology.

"You mean where?"

Jo stared at the ceiling. "No." She gulped. "I thought this was just after the shuttle crash." Then that ironic chuckle. "Thought Dee was still alive."

David reached out a hand, put it over his mother's. Though she didn't refuse it, she didn't warm to it either.

"Those damn implants of yours . . ."

David took his hand away and considered his glowing fingertips, the blue that radiated from his thumb. Only a hint at the machinery whirring away inside him, breaking down chemicals, cleaning out toxins, augmenting brain function.

"I'm gonna get the operation."

"What?"

"It's been months now. I know what's happening to me. And I know where I'm going."

"But, Mom, you're too old for full cyberization. It could kill you."

She waved him away, let out half a sneer. "I'm not getting the full package. Who can afford it these days? I just want them to fix my brain a little bit. I'm tired of these half memories." Her voice grew quiet. "I'm tired of always being wrong."

"Jo, it's too dangerous. What if you don't sync up properly? What if they fuck up the partitioning? Mom, this could mess you up—"

"Even more than I am already?" She looked at him when she'd said that. Her features hardened, turning from valley to cliff face. "I'm still cognizant enough to not need your permission for shit. I've already talked to the doctors about it. I'm gonna get the operation. I'm gonna get a cyberbrain. I already have a goddamn outlet." She reached to finger the opening at the base of her neck, then gave up. "Let me forget how to eat and go to the bathroom and whatever else I'm supposed to forget before the end. I just . . . I just don't wanna forget Dee." Her bottom lip trembled.

THE site was so fresh, the chalk and plaster and asbestos so thick in the air, that Linc thought if they'd gotten there a couple minutes earlier, the building might've fallen right on top of them. A couple of the men had once-white hospital masks tucked over their noses and mouths. A few pulled up their bandannas; so did some of the women and other on-siters who came in off the street, all chalky overalls and scratched-up Timberland boots.

The stackers gravitated to their own small kingdoms, the slower ones pushed out to some of the isolated corners while the denizens of Bishop's truck, among the first responders, got their pick of the waste.

"That there's twenty bucks," Jayceon said, indicating with his hammer a mound of rubble.

Kendrick hopped over a ledge, dust rising in clouds upon his landing. "I'm standin' in about two days' pay rightchea."

Linc walked past Jayceon, who shot back at Kendrick, "You standin' in a pile o' bats is what you standin' in."

They went back and forth a few times, Mercedes interjecting with her own putdowns, but before long, everyone was working. Dig, clean, sort, build. Linc flipped his hammer so that the flat claw pointed at the ground. Wide stance, he swung around in sweeping strokes, raking through the rubble, and when he found a brick, he flipped his hammer and, with one swift blow, dashed away the mortar that had clung to it. A quick glance, and it went into his pile. More sweeping, more hammering to clear away the detritus. A couple stackers had shorter handles on their hammers and had to stoop further than was healthy, hands that much closer to the wires, nails, broken piping, panes of glass. With each strike, mortar dust erupted, shards shooting in all directions. Grit settled on their clothes, filled their pores, turned the sweat on their brow into streams of mud that tracked the bandannas over their mouths like tearstains.

Rodney, who moved like a ballet dancer around his war-stiffened leg, had about five hundred bricks. He danced in the middle of his pallet, building his stack around him in the shape of an L. Before long, he had nine layers up, alternating the directions of the bricks on each layer so that the whole thing wouldn't topple.

"How old is you, Bishop?" Mercedes shouted, surrounded by her own stacks.

"Eighty-two next Monday."

"Coulda swore you was at least eighty-five last week."

"Hah!" Bugs shouted from his pile of brick and ash. "Bishop, you been stackin' for least forty-fifty years, that right?"

"Fifty-six years," Bishop said around his cigar, working in smooth, slow, efficient motions. Once his body got stooped to a particular angle, it stayed that way for the entirety of his run. "Lord's help, I just might retire soon."

"That right, Bishop?" Kendrick sang.

"Yep. Get me a nice white horse and set out for Rancho Cooooooooo-camunga." At which everyone, including Bishop, roared with mirth.

"You do that, we might miss you, Bishop." Wyatt this time, athletic build a-sheen with muddy sweat where his muscled limbs showed beneath his work shirt. "Who gon' preach to the congregation here when you gone?"

"The Lord provides," Bishop said. Then again, beneath his breath, to himself, "The Lord provides."

Linc was close enough to hear it under the clink his hammer made when it broke the mortar off a brick.

THE smoker blew rings into the air, swirling, uncertain wedding bands that disintegrated as they floated away from his face. David knew better than to try. He still felt he could only stand in the man's presence, not saying a word. Thoughts were not the things raging inside him, only inarticulate feelings, a storm composed of elements he could not name, thundering and earthquaking inside him. What was Jo thinking? Cyberization would kill her. Was that what she wanted? David had stared at the floor, smoking, almost as soon as he'd entered the lounge.

"How's she doin'?" the smoker asked.

David looked up, startled out of his trance.

"Jo. Your mom. How's she doin'?"

David shrugged, tried for a smile.

For a long time, the smoker looked at him. Kind and scrutinizing. "You okay?"

David faced him at last. His eyes burned, but no tears leaked.

Perhaps his lacrimal ducts had been malformed. But anger blossomed in him at this new physical inability. "Yes. I'm fine. I don't think I should be, but I'm fine." They were alone in a corner, not far from the other smokers, but cloistered nonetheless. He spoke with mechanical quietude. "She wants to cyberize. She thinks it'll preserve her memories of my mom. My . . . my other mom. She won't survive the operation—she's too old—but she doesn't care. And I think this is what she wants. It's like she's wasting it all. Dee died in the accident, not her. And she's just . . . she's just gonna throw her life away." He looked the smoker in the face. "I don't know why I care. It's not like I need her for anything. She's her own person still. She can make decisions for herself. It's not like she's leaving me behind, I just . . . I care and I don't know why I should."

"You're in pain. She's your mom, and you're in pain."

A bitter laugh barged out of David's mouth. "This isn't painful," he hissed. He started, realized what had happened, and demurred. "Physical injury is painful." He itched his forearm beneath his sweater sleeve where he hid the scars he wasn't yet ready to show this new person in his life. The puckering had not yet gone down on the latest. "Smoking is painful. This is empty."

"You should come to my group," the stranger in the leather jacket said gently.

"I don't need a group."

The stranger reached toward him, maybe to touch his shoulder, maybe to embrace him, but David's hand shot out, smacking the hand away and shoving the stranger into the wall. It was only a moment. A single moment where power, fury, roared in his limbs, where he remembered just how much of his body was machine, stronger, more dangerous, than flesh. Instinct had brought the stranger's hands up in defense, but David saw the look in his eyes and how limp the man's defensive posture was, how much he looked like someone this had happened to before.

Before long, the stranger was doubled over, coughing, as though David had broken a gear or loosened the screws on a panel inside him. Phlegmy, greedy coughs.

David winced when he saw how fragile, how little he had made him.

For several long seconds after the coughing fit subsided, the stranger leaned back against the wall, catching his breath and looking aimlessly at the ceiling. Then, with returning strength, he pushed himself off and calmly searched the floor for the pack of disposable atomizers that had fallen out of his pocket.

With a few heavy sighs, he re-fitted the loosened battery of the one he had dropped and was smoking again.

David stared at him, eyes wide with puzzlement.

"I just realized," he said without looking at David, "I never gave you my name."

"Your name?"

"Jon."

"Jon?"

"Yeah, Jon. No 'H.'" He chuckled and let out a cough. "Only family calls me Jonathan. And they're just about all dead. Almost." The coughing grew louder and he doubled over before righting himself. He held the atomizer in his fingers, looked it over, considered it, then put it back in his mouth. "You should come to my group," he said.

David had no more anger left, so he said, "Yes."

THE plastic chairs on Jonathan's balcony were yellow, though, by now, David could tell they had not begun their lives that color. Jonathan was still asleep so David, still glowing from the sweaty, post-argument peacemaking of the night before, stepped into his boxers and out onto the balcony and took a seat in one of the chairs. A pack of Gauloises atomizers sat on a table between the two chairs, along with an empty but soot-stained ashtray and a bowl of plum seeds Jonathan hadn't yet thrown out.

Jonathan's husky found shade beneath the legs of the unoccupied chair and the shelf that ringed the balcony, and David reached down to scratch the back of its neck as the first rays of artificial sunlight reflected off the panels in the Colony ceiling.

He unpacked a cigarette, turned it over in his hand, then flicked it on and smoked. Halfway through the second drag, the head rush hit, a lightness that seemed to spin him into the sky. When the cigarette was about three-quarters down, he simply sat and watched the smoke rise and branch from the tip like a tree blooming before his eyes. The curling wisps, the rhythm of his arm's movement, the vertigo, the impetus to sit outside. This was it. This was the thing waiting for Jonathan every morning when he woke up. This calm. This rightness.

Jonathan's first month back on Earth was by turns moody and decadent. Words and the whistling of the wind sang to him in not-ballads, purring, cantillating, confessing the psychic toll of millennial hedonism. But the fog and falsettos that settled over the empty and silent landscape in the autumn mornings would break his heart every time he was awake to see it. The others moved about him in slow tempos and moaned echoes; time passed as a song. The evening's sybaritic intemperance would turn the block of houses, the makeshift neighborhood, into an existential wasteland with he and Eamonn and the recumbent, intoxicated, zombified women who kept them and their drugs company all waiting for Godot.

Someone had spray-painted "xo" in radiation-tag on each of the houses. An emoticon for a kiss and a hug. Or shorthand for the ecstasy and oxycodone they guzzled every night. And all the while, one question threaded itself around Jonathan's thoughts: Would David enjoy it here?

The two of them, Jonathan and Eamonn, walked the neighborhood as red lit the landscape and the leaves fell from tree branches in shades of rose and orange.

"Find one you like and figure out who owns it," Eamonn told him.

"How much did you pay for yours?" The leaves disintegrated beneath their unlaced boots.

Eamonn stuffed his hands into his pockets, hiked his shoulders up against a breeze that wasn't there. "About three thousand." His lumberjack flannel put him in relief against the autumn. "Place'd been abandoned for a couple years. Belonged to some woman. Bought it from her son. And when I got there, I went upstairs and all her stuff was still there. Furniture, family pictures. A bunch of knickknacks

and old kids' toys in a steamer trunk. There were a couple of 'em actually. Steamer trunks. Didn't feel right opening 'em. And a couple of
'em were rusted shut, so I couldn't even if I'd wanted to. She even had
this picture of some senator. First Black U.S. senator from Connecticut or something. Had it facing this picture of white Jesus so that it
looked like the guy was praying to him. The way the light fell through
the rafters, that's what it looked like."

"How was the place fixed up?"

"Oh, you mean, like, electricity?"

Jonathan nodded.

"Had to light half the place with oil lamps."

They rounded a corner.

"Anybody else live in the area?"

"All the natives moved out a long time ago. Shit, the place is mostly
scrub at his point. The few houses there are, they're there more out
of defiance than anything else. Natural laws say they're supposed
to have crumbled by now, but damn the natural laws, right? Whole
place has turned from city to country." He brought up a holo that
showed the neighborhood from above, then swooped down to focus on a few neighborhood blocks. The only house nearby where the
green silhouette indicated Eamonn's was a cinderblock project house.
"Yale School of Architecture used to do this thing where a bunch of
the architecture students would compete to build an affordable housing unit for the community." He snickered, then the cerulean holo
blinked into nothingness.

They now walked by staggered rows of thick-trunked trees with
dumped boats and hot tubs where their roots rose like tumors or var-
icose veins through the ground. Railroad tiles lay stacked like grave
markers where houses used to be. A young couple necked in one of
the abandoned boats.

When they could no longer hear the lovemaking, Eamonn leaned
in to Jonathan. "Guy was killed in that boat not too far back." He
shrugged again, one of those protection-from-the-cold shrugs. "Fuck
it, right?"

The quieter nights would see them climbing the abandoned air towers, scaling the heights of the air-filtration stations, and, Jonathan having succeeded at not falling through a crumbling roof, they would sit or lie and smoke while they made a makeshift graveyard of their emptied beer cans.

Eamonn, on their first night, pointed out the five tallest buildings. Jonathan felt it was some sort of rite of passage. If you're going to come here, know your place. Everyone who lives in a neighborhood belongs to it. You can't opt out. Not unless you leave.

There was the Connecticut Financial Center, the building at 360 State Street, the Knights of Columbus Building that had been moved closer to Union Station, the Kline Biology Tower, and the Crown Towers, and, pretty soon after, they took to identifying the lesser arti-facts dotting the city: the cathedrals, the schools, the gated courtyards of Yale's residential colleges. The Ivy Quarter's Gothic architecture, choked with massive vines that wound their way through windows and around walls, made the place feel all the more haunted. What-ever noise was made here, it was only quiet licentiousness that wres-tled in the hammocks strung up there or lay in the grass or necked in the hallways or shot up under the arches. That area of town still glowed blue under the protective Dome of a radiation shield. A gauzy, beryl frontier fantasy so close as to be touched.

Linc fished a pack of Newports out of his shirt pocket and lit one up. Bugs, his hands a little less sure, followed suit. Sydney was up ahead, legs hanging through the bars of the oxidized railing. She'd shown up not long ago at a work site, no hammer, no nothing except for her beat-up Converses. And Linc hadn't heard her say a word, but saw the red tint to her hair and its wolfish shape and saw the way the others folded around her, welcomed her, so a part of him called what they were doing now his duty. Showing her around. Helping her get settled.

From East Rock, a ridge grown craggy with poisoned air and sunrays devoid of nutrition, they watched the skyline. Smoke from dumpsters columned into the air, leaned and pitched with the wind. Cracks spread like thick-knuckled fingers through Orange Street, turning the bike lane into a makeshift mountain trail.

The university at the center of the Ivy Quarter jutted like a middle finger amongst the glass-and-steel high-rises, made orange by the sunrise and the venom in the air. The whole place looked contaminated, but Linc appreciated how quiet that made it.

Somewhere in the distance, a shuttle shot off into space.

"Whatchu think it was like for the first nigga in space?" Bugs asked. "Or, like, Mars. First nigga on Mars."

Linc smoked. "Couldn't be me." He didn't want to talk too much in front of her. Maybe if he could maintain the mystery of himself, he could get her to ask about him, to want to know him, but if he gave too much of himself away too quickly, she'd lose interest. And suddenly Linc realized that he liked her. "I wouldn't wanna be the first nigga on Mars," he said and hoped he could leave it at that.

"What you mean?"

He felt churlish, but he couldn't leave Bugs hanging, and this was what it felt like to be an older brother. When he felt himself glaring at Sydney's back, he caught himself. Then sighed and hoped Bugs heard the resignation in it. *Look what I'm givin' up for your sake.* "Well, like, say it's me and a bunch of white people. And I'm the only nigga on the spaceship. And we're on our way to Mars. Soon as you leave Earth, however y'all really feel about each other, all bets are off. So we could get to Mars, and they just be like—" He paused for dramatic effect. "—*'nigger.'*"

Bugs detonated instantly with laughter. The little kid fell onto his side, clutching his belly, and nearly rolled right off the cliff. He laughed so hard Linc found himself chuckling as well.

"Train with these people for five years, you get up there and the nigga just goes . . . 'we doin' slavery again.'"

Bugs squeaked and started sounding like a goose honking in between bouts of breathlessness. "And you're like 'but I met your *kids.*'"

"'Who you gon' tell? The judge? Ain't no judge up here, bitch.'"

"'Are y'all seriously gon' enslave me?'"

"'Ain't no law says we can't. Ain't no Constitution. Go terraform, bitch.'"

Any words Bugs might've had got choked in his throat. Finally, he managed, "'But you can't be racist in space!'"

"'Who said? Who said we can't be racist in space? What're you gonna do about it?'"

"'Nigger.'"

Linc gave in and started laughing as hard as Bugs, not caring who heard or what animals or birds they might've woken up, not caring about how they might have profaned the sunset or maybe ruined the little bit of quiet Sydney had come up here expecting to catch with them. He laughed until his mind went empty and when he was finally upright and had wiped enough tears from his eyes, he saw that her shoulders were shaking too. Fully bent over the railing, laughing so hard she needed the metal to hold her up.

Bugs was still wheezing some residual chuckles when Sydney sidled up next to Linc.

"Whatchu know about space?" she said, lifting the Newport from his fingers and taking a slow drag.

Linc saw her and wondered what this would have been like without this new girl next to him on these rocks. He and Bugs probably would've just smoked and joked about being left behind and would have tried not to sound too mournful about their almost-futures, their never-futures. They probably would've performed that pain-masking they saw on the site, men hurting and lying, hurting and joking about it, hurting and hiding it by hitting someone. And it would've spurred Linc to thinking about Ace being put out on the street like he was and about God making you capable of wanting something you could never have and about precious things falling apart for no reason because that's what they did. But Sydney was next to him and Bugs was still laughing, and right now felt precious.

Bugs, with his chin, indicated something silhouetted against the gray-gold firmament. It looked like a massive crucifix, cross-beam spread over Edgewood. "Looks like we got tomorrow's work if they ain't already pick that place clean."

It was a crane.

This kinda work, you ain't gotta pull a jux," Kendrick told Bugs that first day Bugs had wandered in off the street, lost kid with eyes practically popping out of his head, too young, they thought, to be a dope fiend. But a couple of the stackers wouldn't have been surprised to find track marks on the kid's arms. "First of all," he said between sweeps with his curved-claw hammer, "you get paid for this rightchea. Second of all," a huff, "time you finish stacking your skids, you way too tired to go off and rob someone."

"Beats sellin' roses on York and Broadway!" someone shouted, maybe Timeica, and a few of the stackers chuckled behind their bandannas.

Jayceon told Linc about a guy he knew, used to tell stories about how he preyed on women in abandoned apartment blocks just like this, cornered them where they couldn't run. Linc remembered that time after they'd gotten to a demo site and Mercedes had found an arm sticking up out of her mound. "Goddamn dead body broke my bricks!" she'd screamed. Timeica and Bugs and Linc had helped her cart the thing off, wrap it in a nearby rug on someone's sidewalk, and toss it in a dumpster. The rest of the day, they worked under the stench of burning flesh and smoke filled with human ashes corkscrewing in whorls up into the sky. Jayceon had watched them in silence the whole time.

"This here craftsmanship," Bishop said between breaths.

"Oh, he gettin' ready to preach," Timeica warned from her skid.

"This here what happens when labor meets love."

"Preach, Bishop. Earn that collection-plate money!" Mercedes cheered over her six-high.

"My great-grand-pappy," Bishop said with new wind, "worked

this building site in Virginia. Him and his boys had to drive up from South Carolina every day. The carpenters were all white folk, so 'course them laborers and street sweepers and all them other folk were Black. They'd watch the carpenters work in between their own shifts and they'd bullshit, but my pappy always told me how much he envied them carpenters. Pappy knew the trade some and he used to make that wood sang, woo!"

"Sang!"

"Oof!"

"Preach, Bishop, preach!"

"Made that wood SANG!"

Bishop waited for them to calm some. "So one day, he walks up to the foreman, makes sure no one else can hear 'im, and tells that foreman he sees the job the white carpenters are doin'. He doesn't say how much better he is than them, though he could've and he wouldn'ta been lying. 'Stead, he asks if maybe he could pitch in a little, make hisself useful. Don't even need no extra pay. He still take his laborer's salary. Foreman say sure."

"What else the foreman gon' say?" Kendrick said, clapping his hammer to a brick. "Your great-grand-pappy pro'lly was the best carpenter that side of the Mississippi."

"You ain't wrong, Kenny. You ain't wrong." Bishop had his hammer propped up underneath his two hands and chin. He was like that, could stop working for a bit, finish a sermon, then get right back to it. His back never straightened, though, just changed its angle of hunch. "Anyway, pappy gets to the work site extra early so no one can see him work. He do his work and the foreman's smiling something fierce like he can't believe what he's seeing. Pappy was a blessed magician with wood, and the foreman saw it too. Then they'd hear the white folk truck comin' up over the hill, and pappy would put away his tools, give back the foreman the one's he'd borrowed, and he pick his broom back up so's none of the white folk comin' out their truck got the wrong idea."

Reverent silence settled over the demo-site. A few had stopped stacking altogether.

"I'da let them see me carvin' that wood," Jayceon said, that implied violence thick in his voice. "They'd see I was that much better than 'em. And they wouldn't be able to say shit to me on account of it."

Bishop shook his head, sadly. "And they woulda asked you to come out back, help 'em with somethin' else. And there wouldn't a been nothin' but them six white men, twelve foot of rope, and the peachtree they'd hang you from."

"Peachtrees only grow in Georgia," Jayceon said, smirking.

Bugs watched Linc. Linc felt the boy's swollen eyes on his back and turned on his skid to let the kid see his smirk.

"Whatever tree it is, it got branches. And that's all they'd need." He turned to the rest of the congregation. "So this right here, this all an honest man needs. Kinda work where he can make his own hours. He's his own boss, and his pay is commensurate to his efforts. This is huggin' the earth right here. Getting real, live dirt under our fingernails. This the type of work the Lord meant for us to be doin'. And I don't know about y'all, but I'm a happy and content instrument of His will."

The bedsheets chilled their bodies with sweat-soak, rumpled beneath them. They lay side by side, David and Jonathan, and, behind their blindfolds, they traced the arc their drones made over Earth. Lux levels rose in golden bars just outside their vision as the drones dipped through cloud cover and flew past domed cityscapes. Chicago glowed through a blanket of clouds. The drones swooped upward and dwarf galaxies turned from cosmic smudges into multihued ninja shurikens. The two sleek machines dipped again, satisfied with their glimpses of the constellations, and darted over landscapes swept with porch lanterns and city glare. The flash of an antique smartphone unwittingly documented their passage.

"I miss it sometimes, you know?" David said from behind his blindfold. Below him, below the Colony, was a massive planetary sphere populated with people who had looked to the star-choked sky, depended on it, for guidance. For answers. How did we get here? What are we doing here? Playing out massive, celestial battles of light versus dark, tracking in a star's course a message of gospel. Their futures were inscribed.

Jonathan shifted next to him. "Don't talk like that, David."

"Don't say I don't mean it. Don't patronize me."

Jonathan let out a sigh, returned to his angle of repose.

A line divided the continental United States such that the spheres of gilt were larger on the eastern side than in the south or west. Headlights periodically dotted strips of broken, empty highway. Across the Atlantic, Europe was a collection of shimmering diamonds in the West and a misshapen octagon in the East, whole swathes of the Asian continent draped in black.

"David, it's okay not to have your whole . . . future . . . lined up in front of you."

"What, so most people here are just flying by the seat of their pants? Jon, if I don't figure something out, I'll lose my benefits. They'll garnish whatever wages I eventually end up making. I'll be in waste disposal. A law degree and I'll be taking one of those hoverboards out into space to detonate garbage."

"David, it's not going to be that bad." He didn't say, "But I'm a garbageman."

A supernova flared in the distance. "At least, when I was back out," he murmured, "I had control."

"No, you didn't, David." All playfulness leaked out of Jonathan's voice. "Whenever you pick up, you have no control. That's why you can't."

"But I knew where I was headed," David murmured beneath his breath, more to himself than to Jonathan. "I had a future. Even if it was—"

"David, we're talking about student loan debt. Nobody's died. You're not maimed. You're—"

"Jon, I swear to Christ, if you tell me one more time how I'm going to land exactly where I need to be or how incredibly qualified I am for wherever I end up, I will kick your fucking teeth down your throat." From his altitude, his drone couldn't see the ecosystem of the midnight desert below, the Atacama, but he imagined the beetles and red scorpions he'd seen in holos scuttling across the blued dirt. Gray foxes sniffing the earth, furry viscachas trying to run away. Leaf-eared mice somewhere in the fray. Vallenar toads, legs bent in a crouch on the lomas. Horned owls circling overhead, keeping carnivorous watch over the foxes and rodents. All of it happening in the dark where no one was supposed to see. The drone spiraled upward and cut a course over the northeastern corner of the continental United States, light levels rocketing to 30 lux. "You know, the migratory birds that fly at night, this kind of light is like a siren song. They're feathered moths to the flame. That light that shoots up from the shuttle station and all its lit-up bridges and towers, it draws tens of thousands of birds into orbit around it. The birds think they've found the moon and the stars then, they smack right into the buildings. Dash themselves against windowpanes, then plummet to their deaths."

t was still dark when Dad had Sydney pack her mask and her suit and her Geiger counter and her livestreaming equipment. Dad always carried the heavier of their two packs, but the way the heat sat on the shoulders always got her thinking he got off easy. This time of morning, however, it was only a little warmer outside than inside. As was routine, she went through her usual rounds of jealousy, first envying Dad his lighter meteorological load, then envying Bambi, who always got to stay behind on these runs. "I was so bored I fell asleep," Bambi would always say upon their return, and Syd would almost black out with the effort it took not to slap the taste out of that girl's mouth for not knowing what she had.

"Why's it always so hot?" Sydney had asked Dad when she was still young enough he didn't mind carrying her. He'd told her about what it meant to live in a rain shadow desert, that the Sierra Madre Occidental to the west kept the moisture from the Pacific Ocean from reaching them and the Sierra Madre Oriental to the east blocked the wetness coming from the Gulf of Mexico. But occasionally, if they were lucky, a tropical cyclone would hit them and it might get a little cooler, but they'd be swept away and would probably die horribly if that happened. And maybe he'd been trying to make a toddling Sydney laugh at the image of them being tossed around in a circle, them and their trailer made of corrugated metals, but, looking back at the memory and looking at Dad now, she could taste the bitterness like snake venom in his voice every time he told her this. Maybe a cyclone had done something to him before. Maybe the mountains had too. Sometimes when the Chihuahuans would come by to pick up what Syd and Dad took from the desert, they would bring Sotol with them, and Dad would have Bambi fetch the glasses, and Sydney tried to work up the courage to ask one of the Chihuahuan smugglers what the cyclone and the mountains might've done to her dad, but she never could, so she never did.

By the time it started to get light, Sydney could see the wind turbines in the distance, like copper-penny pinwheels several shades darker than the desert floor they'd been planted in. But they were the ugliest flowers she'd ever seen, and even though the rising sun brought heat-pain with it, the light it threw raised color out of the black grama and the purple three-awn around them. A stomp through floodplain brought them through the sacaton the shape of what popped out the other end of a scrunchie.

Dad put an arm out to block her and did that thing where he bent his head to the side, like he was trying to listen better to the earth or to the sky. Then, after half a minute, he put his finger to his lips and took her hand and, slowly, gingerly, they made their way through the people-hiding grass and out onto the other side.

He only did this when they'd come across something dead or something about to be dead. So Sydney made sure not to make noise with her own pack and not to look back after they'd passed whatever it was that was dying or about to be. Making sure Dad didn't see, she slipped a holo-pen out of her pack, the size of her index finger, and clicked it, timing the button-press with the crunch of gravel under her boot. She'd go over the holo with Bambi later and they'd try to figure out what bit of newness had snuck into Sydney's routine and broken up the sameness of the landscape and the sameness of the heat and the sameness of the trek. "You wanna see a dead body?" And Bambi would inevitably ask her what it had smelled like. Maybe hot leather with an overlay of garbage sugariness.

This part of the desert, the patrols were sparse, but if Sydney listened closely, tilted her head like Dad did, she could hear the sizzle of electric fencing, hear it before she saw the first of the pylons and the sign that said, "PRESIDIO COUNTY, TEXAS MINEFIELD AHEAD ACCESS PROHIBITED." If you got here while it was still dark out and you couldn't see the signs and the insect noise overpowered the fence-sizzle, you could save your life by sighting the Marfa lights, what some called will-o'-the-wisps and what others called the Chinati lights. Them three golden orbs that sometimes changed colors and sometimes popped off then reappeared elsewhere so you couldn't tell if they were ten or a hundred miles away. Right off U.S. 90 between Alpine and Marfa. But sometimes seeing the Marfa lights meant they'd gotten too close to people that weren't her family or the Chihuahuans. People who might sight you down the barrel of a rifle, no warning shot. She'd seen a few coyotes done that way, thankful for the grass that hid her but not for Dad, who insisted on finishing the run anyway before heading back.

No patrollers today and no white-masks, no one shouting Whiteland battle cries at them or the animals they were supposed to be sharing the desert with. Just Syd and Dad and the device Syd was pulling out of her sack, a tripod that unfurled an umbrella skeleton out of its top. With her touchpad, Sydney punched in a sequence of keys. The umbrella skeleton curled, then went sideways, like its tentacles had eyes, turning left then right then left again, before spinning so fast the legs became a blur. Then it beeped and curled in upon itself again.

Sydney was about to retract the device and slip it back into her sack when Dad grabbed her arm and did the head tilt again. Probably listening for that sizzle. The bugs were too loud for Sydney to hear anything else, so she waited. When he was satisfied, they got up and passed the sign. It took them another quarter hour of walking before they hit their bounty.

The cacti spread out in bunches before them. Clustered by type almost as though they'd been organized just for them. Sydney knew there was an air of transgression to what they were doing, but no one told them outright it was wrong. Still, she couldn't help, at irregular intervals, looking to the sky for the glint of light off the wings of a drone.

They made a circuit, cataloging type, and Sydney, work gloves on, pulled up samples, sometimes having to cut them loose with her knife. A lightblade would've been quicker, but it would've damaged the plants beyond selling. The cacti then went into the wagon Dad had unfolded from his backpack and whose sensors allowed it to hover about seven inches off the ground.

Dad reached in Sydney's pack and pulled out a Flex, affixing to it a blocklike device with a wrist-thick antenna angled upward. When it "plinked" a connection, he put on his salesman face.

"All right, y'all. I got your cacti. Whatever you want, I got. Straight from the You-Ess Southwest," he said into the camera. Out of the device would pop holos of buyers in the Marketplace whose messages Dad accepted. And behind those white faces would be telltale signs of the Colonies: a bookcase seen sideways because the Flex-holder was floating in zero gravity or a canopy of stars outside a window that opened out onto inky black expanse or clean, paved streets over which sped maglev cars in perfectly orchestrated flight-lines. "Other sellers only upload photos, and we all know the feeling of getting that package in the post and it ain't even close to what it looked like on the screen. So I'm showing you what we got right as we're picking it." Some of the buyers already had cacti artfully decorating the shelves of their homes or offices, and Syd always wondered if they were cacti she had picked herself or if the buyers had been conned by some faker claiming they had species that didn't exist no more.

"Nipple beehive," Dad continued, and Sydney pulled a nipple beehive cactus out of the wagon she dragged behind her, holding it out to the camera. In the initial broadcasts, she was only a disembodied hand holding a cactus. But one customer had caught a glimpse of her and her smile and had bought almost their entire haul that day. So Dad had tried it again, making sure his little helper got her time onscreen, and, of course, sales skyrocketed. She'd seen how his skin glowed the whole way back on days like that, so she made sure to smile for each buyer, no matter how much her mouth hurt by the end.

"And eagle claws," Dad said, taking the orb-like specimen from Sydney and turning it over so the customer could see. "Straight from the Chihuahua Desert. Check the geotag, brother."

"I believe you," said the turtlenecked customer with a chuckle. "What's that behind you? On the wagon? The one with the red petals?"

"Oh this?" Before Dad could continue, Sydney had the clump of scarlet hedgehog cactus in his hands. "Now this is enchinocereus coccineus, special variant of the Mojave mound cactus you used to be able to find in Nevada and parts of Colorado. Now, blooddirt done wiped them Mojave all out, so this is the only cousin to survive. Last bit of family left here. Got the bright red and orange flowers with the green stigma and the rounded petals. Low to medium spine cover, somewhat flabby stems. Now, get this." His voice got quiet, conspiratorial. "The clumps can have up to one hundred members, each one about ten inches long. You tryna cover some ground, really bring a room together, really brighten the place, this is your baby. Now, filling a room with these is darn near impossible, because, truth be told, there ain't that many left, and these, like it as not, get snatched up soon as a buyer sets sight on 'em. So you gotta act fast, because there's a bit of a queue behind you, and I guaran-damn-tee you, every single one of 'em's gonna want this beauty here."

"And they travel well?"

"Some of the hardier ones, yeah, they can do without light or soil, even water, for as long as about five Colony flights back and forth, but these right here are a little more delicate. You're gonna want it fast, and shipping and handling's where you'll really have to think hard. Hard and fast. So what do you say?"

It went like this for the better part of two hours: Dad moving a customer up to the front of the queue, aiming their holographed face over the wagon full of wares, then pushing hard to get the buyer to pay way too much for what grew plenty here. He'd even say some of them were hundreds of years old when Sydney knew that they were as old as she was. "Radiation makes 'em that way," Dad had told her in confidence one night, counting through their credits. But some of them actually were beautifully rare: the living rock cactus with its rosette arrangement of brown and yellow and gray triangular tubercules, Chihuahuan fishhooks, nylon hedgehogs, Ladyfingers. Whenever one of the prospective customers judged one of these ugly, Sydney's heart leapt, because it meant a part of the haul and, to an extent, a part of her favorite zone of desert would belong to her.

There were a couple customers left in the queue when the gunshot spat a thin column of dirt up at their feet. Mid-sentence, Dad

force-quit the virtual market. Sydney ducked and snapped the tarp
shut over the wagon to keep their wares safe, then they were off, running at a crouch, hurrying as close to the ground as possible. Another
rifleshot lifted the land by her foot, but she kept pace. They were only
scaring her. They didn't mean to kill. Which almost made Sydney slow
down until she saw Dad speeding ahead, the distance between them
widening. The wagon bumped against rocks and rattled and Sydney
spun, still moving, to straighten it, so she had her back turned when
she heard the explosion.

She started when something wet began raining down on her. Plops
of red dotted the tarp like scarlet hedgehog petals.

IT was dark by the time the crunch of gravel beneath Sydney's boots
could be heard from the trailer. She was a silhouette, black against
the blue, and Bambi must have heard the noise, because the screen
door crashed open, and the little girl bounced on her feet on the front
porch. She'd forgotten to turn the porch light on, so she heard Sydney
sniffling before she saw the new red tinge to her hair. But she must
have smelled something. Maybe hot leather and a garbage sugariness.
Because she grew quiet.

Bambi followed Sydney behind the trailer where she unhooked the
tarp and their father's body parts tumbled to the ground.

The dandelion stems came into focus, the seed heads like moons against that part of the sky where red and blue made gray. Gutted apartment buildings and parking complexes hazed and fuzzed in the background, blurred, and the wind pitted the flowers' orbs so that whole chunks would escape, chewed out of the mass then spat out in pieces on a breeze that brought no relief.

"Punk ass nigga." Sydney's face was next to Linc's in the grass, but Linc only had eyes for the dandelions. The grass shifted, signaling movement, and she hovered over him on one elbow. "Come on." She nudged him. "I know you got some." A pause. "Punk ass nigga."

"Nah, you win." It was good to hear her voice, though.

"Busted car muffler-lookin' ass."

He chuckled, then pretended he didn't.

"Baked-potato-for-a-body-ass nigga."

"Nah, you messed it up."

"How'd I mess it up?"

"It's supposed to be baked-potato-for-a-body-lookin' ass. See when you say it like that, it doesn't make any sense?"

She nudged him again, harder this time, and he smirked. In his mind, they were on her mattress. Her face tipped on its side, sheathed in blue night, eyes that shone silver in the moonlight, and hair that was now cerulean, but copper in full daylight like a downy halo around her head, one clump coming at a slight angle across her forehead, her bottom lip just a small bit forward over the top lip beneath a short, rounded nose, those two thin lips a hard line bent upward at its middle into a shy, fighting-against-itself smile. He was surprised because Black girls didn't have that kind of hair. "Picasso painting-lookin' ass."

Vines wrapped around the columns of the parking garage. In a shattered window near the first floor of a high-rise stood the trunk of a tree.

"Y equals mx plus b-lookin' ass."

Ghetto palms growing out of ledges and crevices.

"No-neck-havin'-lookin' ass!"

Linc barked out a laugh and rolled on his side. It was only in the midst of his laughing fit that he realized how quiet it had gotten. "Cue ball from a game of bumper pool-lookin' ass."

"Fit a straw through your gap-lookin' ass."

"Boneless barbecue chicken with mayo on the side-lookin' ass."

"Dick in the butt-lookin' ass."

He laughed so hard he couldn't think of another, and she rolled into him, and instinct wrapped his arms around her, held her so close that her chest pulsated against his with each chuckle, each breath, and he was reminded once again of how she had looked on that mattress in that building on that night.

She was in front of Linc at the market one Monday morning with her EBT card and her arm full of groceries and Linc had told her not to get the bread, because it would spoil easily and the markets only stocked it to look less empty and barren than they really were. She'd said a few words back in that rubbed-raw voice of hers, put her free hand to her chest, cleared her throat, and finished the thought.

More and more seed heads detached from their home bases, so that the dandelions became like the buildings in the distance, pitted and dying, or already dead and decaying. Post-explosion. Well into disintegration.

Sydney's house was one of few on her block. Shabby, well built, maintained enough to still look beautiful, like whoever lived there continued to take pride in that fact. There was another house, and another, each as put-together or a little less put-together than Sydney's, then nothing. An absence so stark there wasn't even a foundation, like no house had ever even been there to begin with. A chunk of American pastoral. You could grow a garden in it if the green weren't so unruly, so intent on the business of empire-building. Some folks were already trying. Then, at the other end of the meadow would stand the charred, soot-covered, alveolated edifice of a home that used to look like Sydney's. But out from the windows shattered to look like dragon teeth, a few dope fiends would peek and survey the landscape, waiting for a dealer or hoping to pull a jux or just lean like barley in the fall weather, their scrawny, lamp-post bodies slumped like twisted wire. After that, a nice house with a porch and a veranda and a rocking chair that had the audacity to stay outside in a neighborhood populated by scavengers and crackheads and neighborhood watch.

Looked like the type of city-half that might have still been alive when Linc was either inside or in the haze of his own world-erasing dragon-chase. Recently deserted. Like Detroit in the 2010s. Linc had never been, but he'd seen holos, heard stories of folks who had left for there or come from there. Linc couldn't imagine the ruined factories there looking any different from the ruined shorefront factories here. Same wood boarded over blown-out storefront windows, same plastic billowing in the wind. Same solitary sentinels, catatonic with something—despair, anger, uselessness—wandering, zombies with an undead grayness in their skin.

In return, Linc had shown her his side of the city, and they'd wandered Union Station in silence where the light came through the ceiling all cheese-grated, the building nothing more than concrete and stone. Vines tortured the tracks the old Amtrak trains used to run commuters on, and heading a little ways north to an overpass whose walls were lush with verdure, Linc parted the weeds to show her some of the murals that had been squeezed into that space.

"You learn how small a city is when you're in love," Bishop told Linc one afternoon on the second floor of a scraped-out skyscraper. Linc's cigarette was flecked with flakes of radiation so that whenever he tapped it, the ash burned purple and red and orange and yellow before vanishing. "She shows you her parts, you show her your parts." They were both looking out over the Green. There was an off-white obelisk in its center, but they had no idea how high it had gone because its top had been cut off some time ago and rain had softened the wound. "You learn her."

Linc figured Bishop was talking about a woman's body without talking about a woman's body so he smiled and let the man talk.

"And I'm not just talking her 'hood. You know, which corner store she hangs out in front of or which salon she gets her hair done at or where her school's at or nothin' like that. I mean her secret places. Those spots she goes to to collect herself, you see what I'm sayin'?" He glanced at Linc, who stared straight ahead. "You get that far with a woman, she starts showin' you her sacred spots. Her church." Bishop rubbed one ashy hand over the other. "Church ain't have to have no stained-glass windas or nothin'. Lord say, 'where two or more are gathered in my name, there am I also.' So when she takes you to that spot, could be a little piece of riverbed or a little hole in a hill, you finna engage in some prayer." He clapped Linc on the back like he was proud of him, and barked a shallow cough with each slap like he was the one being congratulated. "Church is love, youngblood. Church is love."

Linc looked away from the dandelions and back at Sydney. He smirked. "All beautiful as shit for no reason-lookin' ass." The last of the seed heads were lifted away and the gutted apartment buildings and empty parking complexes glowed in the gilt of the sunset.

David was still glowing by the time he stood at the threshold to Jo's hospital room. Her operation was nearing, and a peace had washed through him, as though the nicotine had carried in its wake an industrial dose of tranquility. It dizzied him. Were his mind clearer, he would have noticed how Jo's eyes followed him from the doorway to the chair by her bed. He would have noticed the sneer she put no effort into holding back. He would have noticed the animosity that shone like gunmetal in her eyes. But it wasn't until he was seated and smiling in her face that he saw it. Saw the recoil. The visceral disgust.

"You smoke?" she spat.

L et's go to Earth."

The bedsheets had grown to match their body temperature by now. Their drones had turned off their engines, guided only by the wind, swirling in a holding pattern that spiraled in a small vortex over the eastern coast of the continental United States. Doves as black silhouettes against golden skin. The lux levels made the space before David's eyes aglow. "Why?" David asked, though he knew already that he would go if Jonathan went. He wanted to ask what Jonathan was running from, but Jonathan never ran from. He always ran to.

"We wouldn't be alone. There are still holdouts there. Families. Places where it could be made to work."

At the thought of family, heat burst in David's body.

"People who talk about the radiation are people who've never been. Colony life is the only life they know. And they try to get us to examine our privilege, how lucky we have it here, but do you ever wonder why a seminar on white privilege is just a bunch of white people trying to figure out what's wrong with being lucky?"

The light hurt David's eyes.

"There are people down there who aren't like us. Who aren't like anyone in the Colonies." He shifted next to David, removed his blindfold, and looked at him. "Here, it's all academic jargon. How to Be Conversant in White Privilege Theory. Privilege taught to the privileged children of the mostly privileged."

"You want to throw that away."

Jonathan smiled next to him. "That's what we do with garbage." His drone spiraled into an ever-tighter circle around a swathe of country in the Northeast. "We'll be like the pilgrims. The first batch. The ones who got along well with the Native Americans and had turkey dinners and all that. Just like in the history books." He moved closer to David. "I'll go on ahead, get us set up, and then I'll send for you." What he had left out was the bit about David waiting for his mother to die. To succumb to her illness and to be boxed, then to have her ashes jettisoned out into space to become part of the Refuse Ring.

"And what about the ones who came after, the ones with the small-pox blankets?" David removed his eyemask and turned to see Jonathan still smiling at him, as though he hadn't heard David's fear.

He saw Jonathan about to open his mouth to speak and kissed him. *Shut up, Jon,* he wanted to say. *I'm not ready to fix us yet.*

"Your mother was a smoker," Jo said from her hospital bed. They'd changed her gown in preparation for her operation. The whole room had an aspect of novelty, as though something fundamental had changed. David thought that perhaps it was because they both stood on the threshold of something, the consequence of a choice they'd already made. That moment between resignation and peace. "Sure, she smoked. But she was a *smoker*. She loved it. Talked about it too. Said it made her feel present. No matter where we were or what we were doing, she was always about her smoke." A pause that threatened to wander into something sadder. "You're starting to dress like she used to."

David took a moment to note his unzipped hoodie and the small jacket he wore tightly over it.

"That was her uniform, all right." Jo blinked at the ceiling, and David saw she was fighting tears. "That time you walked in . . . when you came in that time, I . . . I'm sorry. You just . . . you smelled like her."

David wanted to apologize, but he wasn't sure what for.

"We don't die, David. We just change shape."

"What do you mean?"

"Your mother and I, we were the generation that built this Colony. We met in a settlement. All of us coming together, it was so beautiful. She was a bartender but also an engineer, and I was a vagabond but also an engineer. And we wanted a family. We wanted to do it right, better than where we came from. So we made this place, and we made you. And I'm looking at you now, dressed like her, smelling like her, and I swear, if you dyed your hair and curled it, I'd be saying all of this to your mother. I loved her so much." Her face squeezed in on itself in a sob.

David reached out and put his hand on hers and felt that warmth, that welcoming.

"We were young. We thought space would fix us, you know?"

"Jonathan went back."

"Oh?" This seemed to take her out of her sorrow, and David felt grateful he could give her something else to focus on. "And you're still here."

"Just seems wasteful, you know? Everything you did, to build this place, to make this life for me here, why would I—"

"Throw that away?"

"Yeah."

"Ah, you definitely got that from me." She chuckled, and there was no bitterness in it. "Guilt."

And David joined her.

"But that's not why you're still here. You don't want to leave me here all alone."

David squeezed her hand as though to say, *Is that so strange?*

She was a long time staring at him before she spoke again. "When I was a child, there was this candle. There musta been a storm that knocked out the power or something in whatever shithole your grandfather and I had set up shop in. And I remember realizing that I no longer remembered the room around me. The light is just bright enough to make the darkness solid. And I can feel my heart sinking because I might not be able to find my way back to my bedroom, and that is when this thought hits me. This is what it's like to die. Maybe this is what happens to old people. The light grows dimmer and dimmer, then when it's gone, it takes the room, the memory of the room, and everything it ever lit up with it into the dark. When I leave, I'll be taking everything I loved with me. Right to wherever it is I'm going."

"Mom," David said, and squeezed harder. Tears came.

"This memory thing, I hope it helps. Maybe it will, maybe it won't. I think there's two types of memory in our heads. The one that tries to figure out the details. Was she wearing a red dress or a green one that night? Were we picking Red Delicious apples from the orchard or Granny Smiths? But there's the other kind too. The kind that sneaks up on you or that you stumble into. The kind that walks into your hospital room smelling like the love of your life. I have those memories. What the doctors did to my head, it lets me keep those things in me for just a little bit longer. Now, you have to make your own. I'm done sharing mine with you." She scoffed, all of a sudden. "Look at me. Sounding like a mom and shit."

They laughed, and David wiped his jacket sleeve across his eyes.

"I hear it's the Wild West down there."

"Everything's the Wild West with you, Mom. Besides, he's making a place for us in New Haven."

A momentary darkness washed over Jo's face before vanishing. "Your mother and I come from hearty New England stock, you know. Working-class stiffs in Connecticut, back in the day." Her face softened. "You love him, right?"

David nodded.

"Then go to him. I'll be fine."

David thought a point would come when he didn't wake and turn to find empty space where Jonathan should have been and burst open with longing. Jonathan had been on Earth a few months now, and that day had not come. David would pass through stretches of time where he could content himself with aloneness, go about the business of being a young man in the Colonies, in space, by himself. The dutiful son, the struggling post-grad, the sort-of bachelor. Then, suddenly, the tsunami would crest. He could feel it looming behind him, and, a moment later, craving would crush him.

He paced their bedroom now, then went to the closet. Jonathan hadn't taken much with him, so it didn't take long for David to find that leather jacket. Hungrily, David snatched it off the rack and buried his face in it and inhaled. The biggest, greediest cigarette drag of his life.

The house Jonathan chose for David and himself had the better part of a Dodge maglev minivan in its entrails, cut into chunks like undigested meat.

A porch wrapped around the home, which was situated on a tranquil corner next to two empty lots and a few places that were still lived in. They'd watched him from their own porches or from their stoops or as they maintained gardens or set about raking leaves and smiled and shook their heads, all with the air of ritual, as though, just like every other white boy from somewhere, he would be gone in a month or two, stomach full of undigested chunks of ambition.

They called it a house—Jonathan called it a house—but it was a house in name only. Bereft of windows, doors, electricity, plumbing, the absence of which Jonathan could see clearly through the gutted walls. The thing formerly known as a domicile did seem to be pretty adept at holding waste. Piled on a crumbling foundation were mounds of moldy clothing, fast-food wrappers, chewed-through sneakers, empty tin cans, crushed cardboard boxes, diapers used and unused, plaster, rolls of old carpeting, shattered glass, broken furniture, hypodermic needles, and the remains of that Dodge, all of which could be seen from above through the hole in the roof.

"There was a car in my house," Jonathan told Eamonn soon after he had started shoveling to clear space. "Well, parts of a car."

"What do you mean 'parts'?" He took a pull from his beer.

"Like someone put a saw to it."

"Probably an insurance job." At Jonathan's look, he continued. "Someone probably needed the money. Reported the maglev van stolen, then hired a guy to cut it up into pieces and hide them around the city. Half of that thing's probably all over Beaver Hills."

Just behind the oasis in which Eamonn and the others lived was a garden. An orchard, really. Jonathan had to remind himself that Eamonn had been here longer than he had and had seen whole seasons here, had grown peaches and plums and pears on trees, had raised vegetables from the soil that had once been so poisoned with radiation it used to bleed. Had created a place for bees to make honey that they all then collected in autumn. Had projected bootleg holos onto the makeshift skating rink that a backyard pond would turn into in the winter. The idea had come to one of the girls and, that one winter, they set about flooding the backyard with Eamonn taking an iron from his house, plugging it into an extension cord, and trying to smooth the ice over. They had yet to get it right, so, in the meantime, they used it as a screen and stared down from their rooftops to watch the movie.

Autumn saw Jonathan strip the plywood off his place and put in windows that, miracle of miracles, managed to remain unsmashed. The walls that couldn't be salvaged, he demolished, found a hammer lying around and put it to use, swinging in a way that pinned burn between his deltoid and bicep. Fitting hinges to doorframes and installing the doors took several hands, many of the others helping without a request for anything in return. They would haul the planks that had been attached to each other and turn them just so, making sure to trim or cut them where necessary, and when they managed to get the things to click in place, they backed away and huffed, as though they had midwifed the façade of his house into being. Any more wood collection would need to wait until next summer's storms knocked down a few trees that they could chainsaw into logs, drag off the potholed roads, and stack on porches.

In the meantime, one of the neighbors let Jonathan stay in an empty house free of charge, and, as soon as that first night fell, he recalled the stories of burst pipes and frozen toilets, whole rooms charred from the fires set by malfunctioning space heaters.

The first taste of winter, with frost snowflaking on his newly installed windows, had him digging out his wool cap and wrapping himself in so many blankets and furs he had found and taken a torch to that he sometimes worried he'd die of asphyxiation. When his touchboards froze, he put them on oven sheets and heated them over a pot of water boiling on the stove.

He showered in the home of the neighborhood weed lady, next to the room where she kept a fox and its babies, a veritable habitat built around the grass and trees that had become a part of her second floor. Jonathan twisted under the hot water, cleansed, and thought he heard someone singing and strumming a guitar. But whenever he finished, the song did too. And it took whoever had sung those songs with it.

When he told Eamonn about Aurora's fox, Eamonn retorted that it might actually be a small wolf, a casualty of the radiation. The howling at night, he said, buttressed his hypothesis.

The school he and Eamonn and a few neighbors raided for supplies had already been tagged for demolition and boarded up accordingly. When Jonathan broke through one of the plywood-covered windows and snuck in, he felt like a thief, then realized it was how David was supposed to feel, not him. He ripped out the oak cabinets that would go into his own kitchen. In the library, individual books on shelves had melted into walls of brittle stone-colored parchment. A breath of ash covered them. He looked for fingerprints, the evidence of previous visits, and saw none. Another sea of soot had covered them.

On their way out, they stepped over upturned desks, chalkboards covered in the smeared memory of notes, and marble slabs ripped up from the bathroom. Over his shoulder, he could hear David cracking wise, but mournfully, about some statistic related to New Haven's rate of functional illiteracy.

THE original wires in the electrical box had been long since stolen, so Jonathan found his own and replaced the thing in the basement of his new house. It no longer startled him to see a truck from the power company making its rounds. People had lived here and had needed services, and the services hadn't left so much as quieted. Gunshots at night and 911 phone calls still brought police; only, an hour might elapse between the fire and their arrival. Sometimes it was quicker to fix one's own pipes than call in a plumber who could take advantage of the market and overcharge, or an overworked neighbor who happened to be handy with such things. And sometimes streetlights worked, and sometimes they didn't. The wires Jonathan hooked through the top of the box would connect to the electrical pole in the alley between his house and the next. The local electrician had visited when Jonathan, chatting with some neighbors, had chirped about that missing element. It ain't a home till you can turn the lights off. And someone corrected the first person by saying "on," but that first woman stood her ground.

A man the neighbors called Bishop was the guy who finally put the finishing touches on the job, hooking the lines into the electricity pole. His stubble was a field of snowflakes that clung to his face. Faded overalls and something that looked like a small cigar in his mouth but that ended up just being a stick. And a beret throwing shadow over one eye. High on that ladder, he worked in quiet as birds flew by, a massive eagle swooping low under the lines, so close that Jonathan moved to catch the guy, but Bishop never flinched.

When Jonathan prepared to waffle about payment, Bishop held up a hand and said, "Contractor handles it." Then he left, waving to some of the neighbors on his way into the street.

Eamonn laughed when Jonathan came from the kitchen to the basement with rubber gloves on.

"To stop the current," Jonathan said. "You know, in case of any . . ."

Eamonn doubled over.

Jonathan let it all run its course and together they stared at the box. It looked, in ways, like a beat-up braincase, and he made a note in his head to turn that into a running joke when David finally arrived to see it. The box held the house's nervous system, its neural pathways, the foundation on which they would attach the various accoutrements that would sustain their living here: portable air filtration, generators, outlets for them to plug themselves into and recharge their augments, cleaners for the rust Jonathan could already feel building inside of him.

A small oval of light pulled him from the reverie. Eamonn stared at the box, and Jonathan's mood followed.

Jonathan gulped. "Eamonn?"

"Yeah?"

"Get ready to knock me away if anything happens. I might . . . I might get stuck by the current. To . . . you know . . . the box. Or I might be dead. Or we might both blow up."

"Just do it already. I've lived a good life."

A deep breath through Jonathan's lungs, rasping against the rust, then out through pursed lips. "You ready?"

Eamonn nodded.

Jonathan inched his hand forward, finger out, and tapped it against the tip of the switch, yanked it back.

Nothing.

They both let out the breath they had not known they'd been holding.

"Moment of truth," Jonathan said as he reached up and pressed down on the switch. He opened his eyes, and they were both still standing. Breathing. Alive.

Solemnity made their boots heavy against the staircase as they made their way up to the now-cleared living room. They stood before the light switch. Eamonn turned off his flashlight. Moonlight shot wavering cerulean rhomboids over them through the windows. He put his hand to the switch, wondering if he would ever miss the imposed darkness, the mandatory night.

And flipped.

The room burst with light. They could see each other in full view, every feature, every bead of sweat on their foreheads, see it as clearly as if they stood outside by the river in midday. Ambient sizzling from the bulb overhead was the only sound between them.

Then Eamonn let out a whoop and Jonathan doubled over with relief and what felt like tears pooling in his eyes. He gasped his laughter, his disbelief, then looked at Eamonn, then ran around the house. And all night, they went through the house flipping light switches.

On and off. On and off. On and.

Off.

From the window of the public housing unit, Linc watched the maglev bus make its winding commute around the barrier that marked the backyard of the Ribicoff Cottages. Brown, thin-veined leaves littered the ground on the Brookside side of the fence in layers, concealing the envenomed insects that went about their business fucking and dying out of sight.

Before the barrier had shifted, the rolling green hills of West Rock Park would have greeted anyone crossing over from Brookside to Hamden along Woodin Street. You could look at the sky where it passed from crimson red to opalescent blue. Maybe if you were new and didn't quite know how things worked here, you stared for a long time at that fence and you felt safer. You readied yourself to pass into a deeper, thicker layer of God's providence where the heat didn't peel away your skin and where the sweat didn't sting when it hit your eyes and where you didn't have to pass the water through a sifter before drinking and where the ground didn't crack when you put your boot to it.

Linc tried not to feel envy, just as he had learned in the ward and then in the church basements after.

The bus ferried workers the long way around the barrier that kept the clean air in and the poisoned air out. Just as Linc had come out of rehab, residents were making noise about opening up shielded connector roads from the Brookside Estates to Woodin Street and at two other locations between Belden Road and West Side Drive. But Hamden owned the Fence.

Sometimes Linc stared and let alternative histories transpose themselves onto the setting, so that instead of that gray-blue fence that hummed with warning, there was a set of train tracks and a rickety caboose that chugged over them. Sometimes, Sydney is with him in the vision. Sometimes, she's not. Some people have horses, and they all talk in southern accents.

They cut across train tracks and spotted the first batch of workers, moving down the fields in scattered lines. Earlier in the year, the train would pass by and migrant workers from the outlands, some of them onyx beneath their overalls and some of them the color of sun-poisoned topsoil, would leap off the train with their belongings in satchels and bags held together by leather straps and would scatter through the fields, the kids leaping over each other and disappearing in the towering stalks of wheat while the grown-ups set up camp and began to form a long line that led to the plywood mansion at the top of the hill.

Linc would watch the kids run past him, leaping out of a patch of wheat into a moment of visibility before vanishing again in the field, like fish hopping out of a pond, arcing in the sunlight, then evanescing into memory.

He imagined it was easier to believe in God's love in a place like this.

Footsteps announced Sydney. He had been so caught up in reverie that he hadn't even heard her car pull up.

"So," she said when he turned around. After a faux-serious beat, she smiled at him.

He smirked back. "So."

They set off for Hartford, where they wandered Bushnell Park and talked about being kids then about being young adults then about what it might be like to be adults. She told him about some substitute teacher gigs back in Ohio and this one French class she had subbed for without knowing a lick of French. Linc said, "You shoulda called me, I woulda come to your rescue," only realizing later how many different ways he meant it. They ambled through the Capitol Building, squeezing in after a tour of grade-school kids with air masks on and suited-up chaperones flanking them. They felt a bit like fugitive teenagers, or at least Linc did.

It was too warm yet to continue walking outside, so they caught sandwiches from a food cart nearby and, thinking of Wyatt, Linc told her about boxing and about football in high school and about different ways of thinking when your body was involved in something taxing and beautiful.

After lunch, they hopped back into her car and, in about forty-five minutes, the itis hit.

Eventually, they arrived at Elizabeth Park, Sydney's first time there, and found the Rose Gardens and he told her about all the different kinds of flowers they had there without even looking at the signs, and she said that one day in the future he would teach her how to garden, and he demurred and said it was his mother who was the gardener, and she only half believed him. He pointed out the lilacs hanging off vines strapped to poles that connected in a thatched roof overhead. She told him about all the times she'd read of characters in novels smelling lilacs or smelling of lilacs and he urged her forward, and she sniffed at the flower. "So that's what they were talking about," she said with a kind of awe.

He showed her where the herbs were, where the fragrance herbs were planted and which plot was for the medicinal herbs and he showed her the chocolate mint sprouts and said, "Go ahead," and that was when she bent down, pulled off a leaf, rubbed it between her thumb and forefinger, then chewed it. Her fingertips smelled like Peppermint Patties and he giggled at her when she sniffed them.

They got on the ramp to I-91 on their way back to New Haven as curfew descended, and Linc asked her to swing north briefly so that they could ride by the Colt Armory, a big, ancient brown building with a blue dome topped by a little gold horse.

They raised dust on the undone section of interstate that connected the capital to New Haven. Occasional high-speed railtrains chu-chunked by past the pencil-drawn trees lining the concrete.

Linc couldn't tell whether he felt sad or content; the two had braided together to confuse him. When he was younger and still aware of the world around him, still not yet completely blanketed in narcotic oblivion, he had watched wave after wave of entrepreneurs or young city planners come in and try to fix his broken city. He'd read about their attempts in Detroit back in the early 2010s and how, after each metropolis collapsed onto a dwindling tax base, more and more smooth-cheeked, air-masked MBAs would come in with some idea their predecessor supposedly hadn't thought up.

But then corporate sponsorship of space travel. And Colony construction. New and shiny out of nothing replaced new and shiny out of this. And now there was no one left for Linc to laugh at.

Sydney sniffed her fingers when she thought Linc wasn't looking.

They swung through the autumnal desert of Newington. From the Berlin Turnpike, they got onto the Merritt, where there weren't even any nearby trains to rhythm their passage. Eventually, they hit the Heroes Tunnel and when the old West Rock Ridge State Park came into view, Linc wondered if Sydney was gonna leave her car at his place tonight.

When the stars started to poke out, when they could be seen through the cloud cover, they had made their way to the South Overlook where they could see the Dome as well as the Harbor outside it. The Wall was far enough toward the horizon that whole neighborhoods lay in darkness beneath it. As red as the sky would get during the day, it looked just as blue-black at night as it did in old holos.

They sat on the hood of Sydney's car, and she sat behind him, wrapped her legs around him while she got started braiding his hair. She was gentle combing him out, so gentle he almost fell asleep on her, and she worked on him as it got darker and darker, never once asking for a light.

Occasional noise wafted up to them: a bottle broken, scavengers at work. But the block was mostly quiet, having long since been picked clean.

A door opened somewhere and a rickety house exhaled music. Metallic, staticky music that must have come from some radio. Someone was playing indie rock. Stripped-down stuff with a drummer and two guitarists, one of whom was the screamer. No singing, just shrieks, sometimes the guitars, sometimes the singer. Linc grit his teeth against it, squinted, and could hear it more clearly through the fog. Then a light went on and muffled cheering could be heard through opened windows.

Linc forgot about Sydney and the hands at work in his hair and leaned forward to see a door open again and someone wearing what looked to be a plaid button-down with sleeves rolled up to the bicep out on the remains of a back porch. The thing was half firewood. The guy pressed his hands to the small of his back and stretched. Soon after, another white guy joined him. They looked to be about the same height, and their hair was dark in the evening, shielded from the moonlight. One squeezed the other's ass, and they shared a meaningful look before retreating back inside.

Sydney's hands stopped, rested on his shoulders.

"What is it?"

But all he could think of were the air masks the two had been wearing.

Linc didn't turn the lights on at his place, and they fumbled at each other in the dark. Linc trembled and was too rough, too unthinking. He kept remembering Bishop's words, hoping that would bring back the warmth he felt for Sydney, Bishop talking about church and revealing yourself to another person. And it worked for a little, then it didn't.

She slept with her arm over him and, throughout the night, her embrace would tighten. At first, he took solace in her needing him there. But as the sky began to lighten, he realized it was for him.

He saw those aliens and was terrified, and she had known it.

FALL

PART II

SHADOW COUNTRY
Life in a Post-Cataclysm Metropole

The complimentary bottles of water are permanently chilled, and strawberry-mint oxygen fills the lungs. The gas masks, arranged by size, had first appeared when Carlos, a former Latin King (and before that an army engineer), had pressed a button on a remote and a section of their bus's flank had opened, small cumulus clouds of blue chill gasping out, to reveal the rows of masks and their accompanying oxygen tanks. You hang back to pretend that you're cooler than the blond-haired Scandinavians, for whom this is their first "'hood tour," even though it's your first as well. You don't make any bones about whether or not your touchpad and stylus show, because maybe they make you look like a professional journalist. But when you fit that mask to your face and take those first breaths, you feel safer too. No shame. You're way too happy that the thing actually works.

You get sat next to a middle-aged man with two USB outlets behind his right ear and one fannypack, and you have to crane your neck a little because the lady in front of you, the mother of some annoying kid on the bus—take your pick—refuses to tame the beehive that is her honeycombed hair. Fannypack fiddles with his Rosetta, switching languages because he can't tell you're American, so first he starts trying to tell you about his church back home in Finnish, then German, then French, then (mistakenly) Tagalog, before he gives up. You lean out over the aisle, and that's when you get a good look at Carlos, buzz-cut, bumblebee-ink tattoo sleeves (all crucifixes and roses and Día de Muertos calaveras) and a nice neutral white tee over loose black jeans. Before you showed up at the station, a row of buses outside a warehouse-like building with "The Icarus Project" stenciled near the roof, you made sure to do your research. What gang colors you should stay away from; you implanted in your pad a sheet showing every gang's sign, a dizzying series of digital contortions; et cetera.

Next to Carlos, half-turned around in his seat, is Jamal, dread-locked so that he looks like Predator with his half mask on. His shirt is tighter, and you wonder, because it occurs to you with your worldly mindset, if he's filled out his clothes with prison-muscles. He waves at some of the kids while Carlos speaks, plays games with them, throws up a few fake signs and chuckles while they try to imitate. When they get bored, the kids tug on their parents' shirts and beg for snacks. Mostly Pringles.

Part of your research entailed looking into Carlos and Jamal and Devon, the stoic driver. Devon used to be a professional football player, lasted all of a season and a half before a grand jury indictment for a friend's overdose brought him a prison sentence that drained his earnings and paralyzed his employment aspirations. He'd grown up in a gang here in New Haven, and it had followed him into the League, and now this was the only job for which his felony convictions weren't a problem. Through Jamal, he became involved in local community mediation, a group modeled off of the Interrupters in Chicago. Real line-of-fire activists playing Sisyphus with local gang violence. Devon's was a drug charge, the absurdity of the criminal justice system being such that his sentence was initially life. Reduced for good behavior. He was twenty when he went in, and got hired as Carlos's driver pretty soon after he had come out, at the age of thirty-nine.

Behind you, some white kid with a bandanna tied in the style of the early 2000s across his forehead, knot forward, murmurs in a conspiracy-whisper to the astounded kid next to him, "No more boom-bap, this that click-clack get back. Where we don't listen to Bobbi Thicke, but when shit gets thick, they get to robbin' you. Peep. You look new here and before them cats to the left be askin' what you do here, stay close, open those two ears and I'ma hit you with this dic-tionary before you say the wrong things and they pull them tools out

and have you layin' missionary like the concrete is your boo, hear?"
He's local, and has taken it upon himself to scare his poor neighbor
shitless.

Carlos is plugged into the bus's sound system. He flicks a switch by
his jaw and speaks in his stewardess voice, "Red is a very emotionally
intense color." The engine revs, the bus warms with anticipation. "It
enhances human metabolism, increases respiration rates, and raises
blood pressure." The kid behind you: "To burn a Dutch is to float,
to float is getting high. Fetti is grip is deniro, get it you getting by."
Carlos the Stewardess: "It has a very high visibility, which is why stop
signs, stoplights, and fire equipment are all painted that color. Red
represents one-fifth of Connecticut's gang population. Needless to
say, dress properly when visiting the New Haven County area. Also,
tuck your jewelry, and keep your hands inside the vehicle at all times.
Thank youuuuuuu."

A half-nervous, half-bubbly chuckle ripples through the bus.

It was all desolation to begin with, but when you get out to the abandoned neighborhoods, to Newhallville, the places the upper-middle
class fled to get to the Colonies, you see what the post-apocalypse
looks like. The house façades are all gaunt, hollowed faces out from
which occasional black figures leech, ants out of a bleached skull.

"Where are all the streetlamps?" asks one of the blond-haired
Finns, face pressed against the window, stubby fingertips greasing
it up.

"When the Dome went up, certain neighborhoods were sectioned
off, and the city took those lamps to help build materials for the
launch station out in Fairfield." He doesn't sound like he's recounting
an unfairness when he talks, but you know it for what it is. The city
abandoned them.

You're not sure what you were expecting, but it jars you to hear
Carlos and Jamal talk in the past tense. Each corner turned reveals
a new patch of gang territory. Here's where the R2 BWE Black Flags
came up. That right there was one of their stash houses. Jamal is careful not to go too deep into detail as to how the drugs were made and
sold. He has nothing to prove, and it would breach the unspoken rules

of the tour. These are visitors. We are visitors. The black flag, which they wore in their back pockets or had as bandannas or would wave around, was meant to symbolize independence. Red and blue had long since been co-opted. The Latin King branches here had black and yellow. If you were going to Beef With Everybody, then what color was more appropriate than the one symbolizing an absolute void of color, of purpose, of affiliation? It's the color of self-immolation. Of Black kids with death wishes but who don't have a convenient bridge to jump off of or a parent with a well-stocked medicine cabinet. Already, you're romanticizing them.

Newhallville is bordered on the north by the town of Hamden, on the east by Winchester Avenue, on the south by Munson Street, on the southwest by Crescent Street, and on the northwest by Fournier Street. Dixwell Avenue, Shelton Avenue, Winchester Avenue, and Bassett Street are the main drags cutting through the neighborhood. The Farmington Canal rips straight through the middle.

The late nineteenth and twentieth centuries saw industry churn to life in the district. The canal gets converted into a railroad and enterprising George Newhall builds a small factory where the carriages get built. Other factories sprout like weeds around the first, followed by workers' houses and a boardinghouse for the unmarried male workers.

Guns come to Newhallville in 1870 when the Winchester Repeating Arms Company sets up shop, and by the Second World War, the thing covered more than six city blocks and employed over nineteen thousand workers. One-family, two-family, three-family tenement homes surrounded the plant, built by real estate investors either for rental or to be sold on speculation, and when you have enough factory workers, enough breadwinners employed by a single industrial giant, you get butchers and grocers and barbers. Winchester becomes the leading employer in New Haven, so of course, it relocates to Illinois. A machinists' strike in the late 1970s results in the plant being sold to the U.S. Repeating Arms Company, and by the turn of the New Millennium, the place had laid off the rest of its workers. Yale University tried to restore and redevelop the skeleton left by Winchester, turning the factory complex into Science Park. But space travel became too affordable too quickly. Satellite campuses in the Colonies grew into main campuses, and parents had less incentive to send their children to a domed environment where, just on the other side of the shield, the air was so poisonous your chances of lung cancer rose by an average of thirty-five percent. Tax base shrivels, resources dwindle, schools fail, and the kinds of things that keep kids off the streets and out of jail—summer programs, vocational education, church programs— all of that follows suit. Same story across the state. Same story across the country. The tax base left, but the guns didn't.

The bus slows to a stop a few blocks from the cancer'd remains of the old Winchester factory where the one-family and two-family houses now slump. Everyone fits their air mask to their face and de- scends from the bus after Carlos does a quick scan and makes sure the surrounding neighborhood is empty, throws up a baby drone that relays the nearby heat signals, and all is good because the drone, like a hawk, comes back down and folds itself to fit into the holster under his armpit.

A bald, slim-bellied Black guy in a sleeveless hoodie materializes at Devon's side, leaning next to the bus while Devon sits on the steps and several of the people who aren't taking pictures of the poverty porn crowd around. "When did we really know it was real?" Devon's friend/acquaintance/maybe gunman talks like a chunk of concrete has been permanently lodged in the back of his throat. A guttural thing. And you wonder what he must have sounded like as a child. He's got veins casually sprouting like crow's feet from his eyes, and hanging from chains around his neck are obsolete smartphones. An- tique iPhones and Blackberries ornament his chest. "'S pro'lly when we got shot at. For the first time. Yeah. Far as me comin' up? Me and my man's-and-'em. Yeah. It was like 'okay, this is serious.' 'Cause we was hustlin' some shit we pro'lly shouldn'ta been hustlin'. And you know how some guys, the older dudes in the 'hood, they didn't want us doing certain things, and we was doin' it on our own. We wasn't wor- kin' for nobody." He leans against the bus with his legs spread apart, a posture of repose that's almost daring someone to come at him. "You know, we was young. We had egos. We were like 'fuck that; we ain't workin' for nobody.' Then they had to give us some warnings so they actually came by and threw some shots at us." He starts chuckling. "And we were like 'whoa; this is real.' If we gonna be out here gettin' our own bread, we gotta tool up. Gotta be able to, you know, clap back. That's when we knew it was real."

"Have you ever been shot?" asks one mother. She's more curious than concerned. She's not asking someone who could've been her son. She's asking someone who could've been her store attendant. Or her carjacker.

"Yeah, I got shot." He sees a little tow-headed kid peeking out from behind the shelter of his mother's skirt, face completely covered by his air mask. "Got shot right in the head," he says to the kid. "I didn't even know I was shot. Muhfuckas had to tell me." His eyes don't move from the kid's. "I was sittin' in the car, and I noticed an individual I had had an issue with comin' up on me. And I looked at my man in the car like 'yo.' Some things transpired, shots fired. As I got out the car, and it was right there, corner of Munson and Winchester Ave." With his thumb, he points back to the Winchester factory behind him. "Right 'cross the street from the factory. So I jumped in the back, 'cause I was sittin' in the passenger's seat. Got out the car and I ran across the street. You know. Dude ran away, turned a corner, peeled off the block. And my man's when he found me was like 'yo, you got blood on your face.' And I'm thinkin' it's just from the glass. So I'm like 'alright, yeah.' So as I get in the ambulance, dude who came out the back, he took my hat off. And he's got his bot cleanin' up my face, you know? Cop flies over to me, gets a good look, asks me what happened, I'm like 'get outta here, somebody threw a bottle.' Cop's like 'we heard shots,' and I'm like 'I ain't hear no shots over here.'" The little tow-headed boy has completely forgotten his mother. "Somebody was drivin' by in the car and threw a bottle." The boy smiles when the storyteller smiles. "There's glass in my face, I'm in an ambulance, and dude's cleanin' up my face and shit, and dude takes my hat off to let the bot get at, you know, get at the rest of my face, my head or whatever. Anyway, he's cleanin' my shit and he notices there's a hole in my hat. So he looks at the hat, then he looks at me. And he like 'yo . . .'" A dramatic pause. "He like 'yo. Yo. You aight?'" The crowd farts out a few barked laughs, but it's mostly sagging shoulders. "I go 'yeah, I'm aight,'" the guy says into the crowd. "He go, 'yo, you got shot in your head.' It's like 'shot in my head?' You know,"—he's cheesing now too, looking back—"I don't feel nothin' but for a muhfucka to tell you yo you shot in your head, you think you start feelin' something like whoa." He mimes losing his balance, and a few more people laugh. "I'm like 'I ain't shot in the head.' Now, I ain't got a braincase or nothing and even if I did, niggas had Muckrakers woulda tore my whole shit up. But dude showed me that hat, like, the hole, and he showed me a little piece of the shell, and I'm like 'oh, wait,' and he's like 'nah, don't touch it.' And I chill out after a while, 'cause I had to get my shit right, then I tell dude, 'yo, don't. Tell. The cops.' He like 'aight, cool, I gotchu, I gotchu.' 'Cause at first he was like 'yo, ay yo, you could tell me, you was gettin' shot at, right?' I said, 'nah, somebody rolled up by the car' and he didn't even let me finish, he showed me the hat, and he was like 'nigga. That ain't no bottle.' 'Cause it was a Black young dude, you know? So I'm like 'yeah, there was a shootin', but yo don't tell the police, I don't need to be dealin' with all that extra bullshit. And he was like 'nah, I gotchu, I gotchu.' Cops come by on some 'what happened? Who was shootin'?' Look at 'em like 'one o' y'all, motherfucker. Was a beat-walker took shots at me.'" Now he's the only one laughing. "Shit bounced off my arm too. I'm like Terminator or some shit. Nobody couldn't say nothin' to me. No augments. All my shit is natural, red-blood, and I'm invincible. No iron lung, no braincase, none of that cyber shit in my arms, none of that. I was tootin' my own horn after that, 'cause not too many niggas get to toot they own horn like that." You wait for the end because you know it's coming. He's telling this story for us, not for him. "But if nothin' can stop you, eventually, it all stops tryin'. And you the only one left." And you look around at the post-apocalypse and you see what he means. People linger to ask him some more questions, but you're already back on the bus. The door's open, so your mask is still on.

When everyone gets back on board, you can't tell if it all went as Carlos planned or if it hadn't.

Celentano, the K through 8 school, is on Canner and Prospect Street and by the time Jamal gets around to telling about the turf wars that would go down between the Celentano kids and the kids from Lincoln Bassett, over on Bassett Street and Shelton Avenue, you know what it means to clap back.

Devon takes you through Dixwell, and you see a little bit of where it abutted the Ivy Quarter. There are even marks in the concrete to tell how and when the protective domes shrank and when they evaporated entirely, letting in the radiation.

You're reminded of that time in Bosnia and the story of the gravedigger who takes visitors, tourists, interlopers like yourself, up the hill in Sarajevo to where the Olympic Stadium used to be so that you can look down the bowl at the entire city below from where you stand amid the headstones. The gravedigger knows where everyone is buried and walks you to each headstone, then tells the story of that person's life: how they grew up in that neighborhood over there and how their father worked in that bread factory by the mosque and how the deceased fell in love with a girl who went to that school that used to be where the UNHCR offices are now, how they married in that chapel, where their child was born, where they first fell in love and would play when snow blanketed the ground, where they grew old, et cetera. You hear it in Carlos's voice and in Jamal's. That terrestrial longing.

You don't have that in space.

You don't have county jails where men have to sleep and shit with no privacy and where understaffed and half-mechanized guards are as terrorizing as they are terrorized. You don't have the murals tagged with street art, a masterpiece of a rhinoceros charging through a wall painted on that wall, crew names tagged in bubble letters, portraits of the fallen, some famous, some infamous, some simply loved. You don't have the bootleg credit depots for the folks who can't get bank accounts and who need the rations turned into cash so that their kid can make bail. You don't have mothers worrying about that. You don't have mothers trying to figure out how to do it all their first time.

It is all history now, but you wonder what it was like when a place like Yale University ran up against Dixwell. With what marker was the dividing line drawn? Who moved in? Who was pushed out? Who left?

The sociology major in you wants to trace migration patterns. Whites in one direction. Blacks and Puerto Ricans in that same direction. Whites in another direction. And you realize that even then, when the streets were animated with socio-economic caste struggle, this was a place with all history and no future.

In the shade of dilapidated office buildings, the tourists gather. Carlos betrays a hint of worry and you know it's because he knows there are people in those towers, but it's a prime location, maybe the one they've used for every iteration of this tour so far. Many of the kids activate their recorders and the little bees sprout from within their hair to photograph or video record them and their parents throwing up the gang signs they learned before they arrived at the warehouse. Instantly, the pictures are online for all their friends in space who couldn't afford the fare or the parental insouciance or whatever else it is that unchains someone from a Colony.

It's all violence around you, and you're starting to grow nauseous to it. Then you get nauseated by the weakness that brought about your own nausea. Maybe, you realize, it's simply the air pollution, but, no, your tank is still full. And, let's not forget, you're half-mech anyway.

Back on the bus, you guys pull out and ride by a church and before you spreads a rubbled landscape. Mostly open field, some of it untamed jungle or close to it, and in the wreckage of what looks like a recently destroyed building, you witness a small bit of industry.

With bandannas over their faces, many of them in overalls and boots, they sweep and strike at the rubble. And you squint and you see bricks rising like walls around them, as though each of them is building a corner of a house. A couple of them pause, straighten, stare as you ride by, maybe at you individually, maybe the bus as a unit, and they prop themselves on their hammers, the ones you watch, and you wonder why Carlos didn't tell you about them.

Suddenly, those Black and brown bodies squirming in the heat and engaged in the act of creation are all you can think about. And you don't want to ever see Earth from space again.

On the half-built roof, Jonathan found peace. On the half-built roof, work gloves off and his legs splayed out, paint and dirt and plaster dotting his jeans like pockmarks or the boils on a leper, light beige weatherjacket folded in a messy pile by his toolbox, sandwich in hand, sharing an eye level with the tops of the pines and the evergreens lining the road where sat the family pizza spot and the colonial landmark that was the home of somebody famous three hundred years ago and where sat the hairdresser's spot and the ancient Patriots/Red Sox bar, trying to keep the mayo from dripping down between his thumb and forefinger and sliding a stream down his palm, Jonathan found peace.

Aurora had hipped him to the supplies deliveries that only ever went through the remnants of the Little Italy neighborhood by Wooster. And what began as rations and air tanks and breathing apparatuses, through the alchemy of the black market, soon turned into deluxe sandwiches and building supplies and radiation-proof electronics. Plastics somehow reinforced against the poisonous air, Net connection hacks, and if one saved up, one could even trade for DIY dome-building materials. Jonathan could tell which settlers came from Colony wealth by whether or not their building managed already to find itself ensconced in an ultramarine embrace. But now, with this filtration mask around his neck, his shoulder heaved with each breath. The air wasn't nearly as bad here as it was closer to downtown. Enough smaller domes in close proximity seemed to scare the air pollution away. It was all magic to Jonathan anyway.

Amid the detritus of the half-redone roof was a Dunkin' Donuts holder with a couple cups of coffee and a lunch pail filled with burritos. He should know the other two day laborers with whom he shared this roof, he'd seen them work on a couple other projects in the area so far, subcontractors who knew the same guy who knew Aurora and Eamonn. They wore their tool belts and worked like regulars, not quite all the way broken in but definitely more than competent. It struck Jonathan now that maybe this was their side hustle. Either way, it was break time, so he turned away and devoted the rest of his attention to his sandwich and his cigarette.

The first smoke of the day was always the best.

After seven hours of dreamless abstinence, the vertigo was like reuniting with an old lover. He lay back on the shingles and didn't care whether or not his weight caved the whole thing in, nor did he care about whether or not this was a foolish thing to worry about, whether or not the Black day laborers would make fun of him for it.

The workers stirred back into motion and Jonathan rose out of whatever reverie had taken him, leaving even the memory of it behind. After stuffing the remains of his sandwich in his mouth and before turning back to the task at hand, he slipped his Flex out of his pocket, aimed it at the once-downtown with its vines and cracked concrete and evergreen trees, snapped a holo, and sent it to the Cloud he shared with David.

n Mercedes's car, Timeica and Sydney ambled out of New Haven, west-by-southwest, tracing the old Metro-North line. The farther they got from the city, the slower Timeica drove. And maybe Wyatt would've been proud, because other people would have thought she was just moving this way to take in the scenery, like she had never seen backroads so overgrown with vegetation that they'd turned into corridors filled with red admirals and the occasional peacock. They would've thought she was listening to the birdsong and maybe admiring how the departure or death of the people who'd lived here had turned this place into the Garden of Eden again. But, really, what she was looking for, listening for, was threats. The gangs and Marauders filled open road and interstate highway well enough, but the truly fucked up found shelter in forest. Sydney was silent next to Timeica and Timeica hoped that Sydney was thinking this as well. There was no smile on the quiet girl's face, no wonder radiating from her eyes. Maybe she'd seen stuff like this before. Maybe she didn't care.

But their GPS was outdated. Heading into Bridgeport, they were supposed to have passed through at least four radiation checkpoints, even if the surveillance drones overhead told the guards in the QZ that you'd stayed along mandated routes. But every station was the same, abandoned cars stripped for parts, dragonflies and mosquitoes hovering over ponds of stagnant water, a dog lazily baking in the shade of a massive leaf.

Milford and Stratford weren't towns so much as they were two conjoined forests with towns falling apart inside them. And Timeica remembered that time she and Wyatt had stayed in an abandoned house on their way to New Haven that had felt much the same. It wasn't huge, but it told them the apartment they'd grown up in had been too small for their family. And boars rampaging through the forest had given them plenty of meat for their meals. But then a wolf pack had cornered her in the house while Wyatt had been out scouting routes out east, and Timeica had had to use up all their bullets shooting each one of them dead. When she found out later that Wyatt had taken the wolf meat with them, for them to eat along the way, instead of burying the animals, she'd refused to speak to him for a week.

In Bridgeport, the roads didn't really open up, but Sydney sat at attention in her seat, and that was when Timeica noticed that families had started to dot the landscape. An older man in a sleeveless shirt nursing a lemonade under a mulberry tree, kids in a cleared patch of land doing yardwork, so much yardwork that their denim overalls had turned a faded brown, corncobs drying on a line, an outside basin with a cistern filled from a well. And none of them coughing blood into their hands. Sydney turned her neck to watch each of them as they came into view and faded into the distance.

Maybe that was the thing with her, Timeica reasoned. Maybe she's just gone too long without seeing people. She ain't seem feral, and she ain't seem particularly lonely. But she hadn't hesitated when Timeica had offered to take her on a supplies run to Fairfield.

The maglev car eased off a backroad onto the remains of a highway, and the run-down Metro-North tracks were beside them again. The towers of the Fairfield QZ loomed ahead and against the sky was a blue dome, heralding their arrival at a safe haven. The line of cars wasn't nearly as long as Timeica expected.

"Something's wrong," Sydney said, the first words she'd spoken the whole trip.

Before Timeica could so much as agree, Sydney was out of the car. Timeica fumbled through the glove compartment for their masks, rustling through the vouchers she'd picked up from everyone before setting off for here, then was out of the car and hurrying to Sydney's side. "Here," she said, handing Sydney the worn filtration mask and watching her to make sure she put it on properly. She didn't look like the type of person who took care of herself, or who cared to. Before they got too far from the car, Timeica touched the small of her back to make sure she'd remembered to bring her and Wyatt's pistol with her.

Inside each of the cars Timeica walked past was emptiness. They went forward at a slow enough pace that Timeica could stop at each one in the line up to the wall of the quarantine zone and cup her hands around her face as she looked through the dusty window. No skeletons, so at least it looked like people had left in time. No supplies, either.

"This place been gone a while," Timeica said.

She looked around for a response, and that was when a rustling of greenery behind her announced Sydney's departure.

"Hey!" She was more worried than annoyed. Sydney did seem a little off, but now they'd announced their presence, and Timeica only had so many bullets. "Syd!" She whacked aside branches and too-large leaves, ducked under a canopy of tree limbs, then stumbled to a stop at the edge of a broken piece of road. All the while checking for signs of habitation—a campfire, the memory of radio waves shimmering in the air, traces of a small makeshift dome—she noted Sydney's trail.

She slid down the ledge and moved through the tallgrass at a crouch. Sunlight fell in slants through the leaves. She didn't try to avoid it, nor did she try to move too soundlessly. She might have scared Sydney or someone with a hunting rifle. So she walked smoothly, then crawled under a fallen log and vaulted over another. Her body remembered doing shit like this with Wyatt when their travels took them off the road in Appalachia. Squeezing between slabs of dislocated stone wall, climbing through the levels of a deserted parking garage, trying to find their way from one end of a building all the way to its opposite while all the floors in between had rotted through their middles and furniture had fallen to block doors. The puzzle of it all, it was like those crosswords she would sometimes catch him doing on his Flex. While Timeica worried after Sydney, her body thrilled at remembering how to do this thing.

So accomplishment mixed with regret when she came out onto the clearing to see Sydney at its edge, still as a tree, watching three horses amble around and leap into the air and prance around each other while a fourth and a fifth nibbled grass in the midst of it all.

Several moments passed while Timeica took it in, this little glade full of kind, living things, maybe the only things moving for miles. Then she slid down the small cliff's edge and came to Sydney's side.

"How'd you know this was here?" Timeica asked her.

But Sydney didn't answer. When she did turn to Timeica, though, behind her mask there was a smile on her face and a glint of mischief in her eyes like she had the beginnings of a plan forming behind them. And the first part of the puzzle had clicked into place.

ON their way back, the supplies vouchers like an accusation in the glovebox, they drew near the guy with lemonade and the mulberry tree. He looked like he hadn't moved since they last saw him.

Timeica pulled over to the side of the road and handed Sydney her pistol. "You ain't gotta keep it running. I just want to ask him some questions. Find out what happened." She climbed out and shut the door loud enough to make sure the guy heard her, but he didn't seem to be paying any attention. His gaze was fixed on something past her, and it wasn't until Timeica came close enough to see the pulp swimming in his lemonade jar that his eyes shifted to take her in.

"Where'd the QZ go?" she asked, jerking her thumb back in the direction they'd come.

"They cleared that place out a while back. You ain't know?" He moved a little, like he was making space. "Here, take a seat. Bring your friend too."

"Nah, we gotta get back."

"You don't know me, and y'all are two women on the open road, but y'all got a gun on you and mine's is way in the back. You could cap me before I'd ever get close to it. And now that that's out the way, have a seat. I just need someone to help me finish this lemonade."

"I'm good."

The man didn't frown, just sighed. "What's safe anymore?" He shrugged. As Timeica turned to go, he said, "They're gonna reduce that dome too."

Timeica faced him again, almost all the way out of his yard by now. "Yeah?"

"Bunch of Fairfield County went and fucked off to space. That's what killed the QZ. Rations down, so now they just send the drones out with the deliveries. Sometimes trucks too, but it's folks like us driving. Sometimes, when I'm bored, I pick up a few shifts. You from New Haven?"

Timeica didn't answer.

"Sounds pretty poppin' up there. I hear y'all even keep some of the houses standing for the new arrivals. Exodusters really turned that into a place, huh."

"Yeah, they did," Timeica said, thinking back to the place New Haven was when they first got there, how welcoming and set up everything seemed, how good it felt to be around their people again. In a flash of kindness, she said, "You should come sometime. There's probably a place for you there."

"I can't leave my blueberries."

When Timeica said, "Cool," she hoped it didn't sound too harsh. But she was in the middle of the cracked road, broken magnetic rods poking through, when she saw Sydney and then, in her mind's eye, saw the horses, then turned back. "I was serious about the offer. There's people, security, food most days. And domes can get set up for cheap."

"And I'm serious about my blueberries!" He rose slowly. "Matter fact, I gotta start layin' down the straw." At the question in Timeica's eyes, he continued. "You lay down the straw in the fall," he said, exasperated, "so when winter comes, the snow packs it into the ground. I got a straw-spreading rig in the back, so I won't be needing y'all's help, thank-you-very-much. Come springtime, you burn the field, but it's gotta be just right. Day can't be too humid, can't be too windy. And you got this straw-laced field, then you burn it. See, the part of the blueberry plant we see aboveground is just maybe a third of the whole thing. Underground's got this whole world a stuff going on. Burning what's above ground enriches everything underneath. No pesticides, nothin'. Then it's ready for planting and summertime harvest. If y'all woulda come by a month or two ago, I mighta had a bushel or two to sell y'all." He turned and waved her goodbye and, stooped, picked up his glass and his lemonade pitcher. "Come by next year if you want some fresh blueberries. Better yet, come by springtime, help me with the burning, and I'll set you and your friend up with a discount."

Back in the car, Timeica shook her head, smirking. "Burns his field on purpose, can you believe that?"

Sydney had taken one of the vouchers and was folding it into an origami hand-game, adding it, when she finished, to the row of folded vouchers on the dashboard.

"What kinda sense does that make?"

"Bet they taste good, though."

Timeica barked a laugh, then started the car. "Speaking of which, how'd you know about them horses?"

Sydney hunched her shoulders up then down, fishing another voucher out of the dashboard. "Felt something beautiful was nearby. Been a while since we seen a miracle. Felt like we were due." Her words had a rasp to them, from disuse.

"What kinda sense does that make?" Timeica asked, believing her nonetheless.

"'What kinda sense does that make?'" Sydney said, nasally and annoying, in something nowhere near Timeica's voice.

But Timeica laughed, pulling onto the road.

Before Shiawassee and watching Wyatt don a park ranger uniform and bend low, pouring concrete into potholes, and use a machete to clear brush; before him training to hold and shoot a rifle proper and not how they learned to shoot and miss on the road; before Wyatt began bulking up his body and turning it into a suit of armor; before Shiawassee, the two of them, Timeica and Wyatt had arrived at a seawall and Timeica had climbed it, because Timeica had wanted to and Wyatt didn't but she was littler than him, so sometimes, on the basis of that fact alone, she got what she wanted.

They skirted the water foaming against the black rocks that made a natural barrier between the water and the beach, and Timeica skipped ahead on the brown-black sand while Wyatt tried to pull up their digital map. The holograph flickered. With each time Wyatt slapped the Navigator against his thigh, the picture got worse, and that was when he noticed the Geiger counter blinking itself mad. They had to go.

But Timeica was already up the seawall, and Wyatt's shouts were a faint echo of the terns going *kyarr kyarr* over the wave-crashes. She paused at the top and looked out over the first town they'd come across in ages. They'd stayed off the highway, picking at the leavings of each settlement they encountered but only after making sure there'd been no traps left behind. But this . . . this was something else. Something bigger. It wasn't the urban sprawl they'd left behind with its shadowed corners and blinking streetlights and hollowed skyscrapers out of which poked sniper rifles. It wasn't car bombs, and it wasn't stretches of too-quiet punctuated by the too-loud boom and chatter of heavy ordinance and gunfire. This was smaller. But it was still something you could lose yourself in. It wasn't people, but it was something they'd left behind. Not like the scorched earth of those sometimes booby-trapped settlements. This could be made into something.

She shrugged her backpack off her shoulders and pulled out her drone, checking its battery life before turning it on and sending it into the sky. The screen on the back of the camera she held in her hands was small, but if she focused, she could make it her whole world. So she sat cross-legged on the seawall and followed the thing's course over brown-green fields dotted with leafless, coal-black trees. Lining a road were squares and almost-squares somewhere between gray and blue. The drone dipped low to reveal the shapes for foundations of houses demolished long ago. Nearby fields and backyards, the drone told her through annotated holograms, had been used to plant pumpkins and spring onions. There used to be a springtime festival down the road, according to the geotag's annotations. The drone followed the route to what it told Timeica was a nursery school and, swooping down to the front entrance, it zoomed in on a metal rack holding folded, mottled umbrellas. By an empty house, an RV sat camouflaged by weeds. Similar tall grass had grown to colonize other homes whose roofs had collapsed or whose walls had been blown in. Toward the other end of the town stood cadaverous forest. Some of the wood lay chopped in piles. That was the thing about this place. She couldn't tell if whatever happened here had happened last month or ten years ago. But she needed Wyatt to see this. Needed him to see what she was talking about when she laid out the vision she had for them, the park they could rebuild together, the house they could clear out and renovate, the fields they could start tilling, the things they could grow. With no one around to bother them. *See, Wyatt, we don't need anyone to make it work,* the "it" something larger than she had the words to articulate.

"Wyatt!" she shouted, turning away from her camera. "Wyatt! Look!" She turned back to her camera, the drone sliding lazily through windless sky, over and under streetlights, across the empty, soundless place. "WYE-ATT!" Maybe he couldn't hear her over the surf or those annoying terns. She turned around so he could hear her better and saw a shape that looked like her brother sprawled out on his back, looking like something dead. "Wyatt!" She dropped her camera and

scrabbled back down the seawall, sliding for the whole second half
until soft ground jolted her into a crouch and she stumbled forward,
falling onto her brother's body. "Wyatt," she said, smaller, more urgent, hands to his chest, shaking him. A thread of blood ran from a
nostril. His fingers twitched around a Geiger counter and that's when
Timeica saw the frantic beeping and the digital numerals turned to
flickering gibberish.

She shook him, kept shaking him. "Oh no. No, no, no. Wyatt. *Wyatt*. Wyatt, tell me what to do. You have to tell me what to do." Timeica
shook him more and more. "Wyatt, what do I do?" Her fingers dug
into the cloth of his worn-down coat. "Tell me, please. Please."

A foreign sound cut through the shush of the surf. A neigh and
what sounded like someone blowing a raspberry. She looked up and
saw the ghostly white horse that would take them to Shiawassee.
Maybe the mud had hid the sound of its hooves. But maybe it had
come out of the shoreline mist in answer to a prayer she didn't even
realize she'd uttered. She was afraid to touch it lest it disappear. But
she felt Wyatt's fingers spasm again and was reminded of the Geiger counter and the fact of his dying. So she pulled his dead weight
up onto her shoulders, then hefted him belly-down onto the horse.
At the added weight, it pranced, throwing Wyatt into the mud, and
right there Timeica almost burst into tears. The beeping continued.
She hurried to the horse and put her hands to its flank and shushed it
and brought it back and tried again, gentler this time, before climbing on.

Wyatt was heavy on her back and kept slipping, but she stuck his
hands through her belt to keep him fastened to her and by the time
the seawall could no longer be seen on the horizon, she grew accus-
tomed to the weight.

As they rode, thinking it might wake him up or maybe keep him
awake, Timeica thought to tell him about her plans for the place, how
she'd hoped they'd finally made it to a place where they could rest for
a bit, where they could sleep for more than a few nights in a row, a
place where they might some day have neighbors they'd see day after
day, a place that could give them routine, like hanging their laundry

out or talking the shapes of animals out of the clouds, a place that maybe might have a supermarket where she could get honest-to-God pads and not make do with what nature gave them. *I just wanted home,* she thought to tell him, but she couldn't figure out how, so she just said "I'm sorry" over and over for the first three miles, through tears and through their drying, until that had become routine. "I'm sorry" for every time she'd disobeyed him and gotten them in trouble or scared away their food or missed a pistol shot and wasted a bullet or talked too much. She thought she'd be saying "I'm sorry" forever.

They were a dozen miles away before she remembered her drone—which had fallen on its way back to her, on a giant green rhomboid, one in a curling row of thirteen, that held two metric tons of radio-active soil.

Rodney, hammer leaning against his shoulder, skin still coated with plaster, led the white woman up the hill and looked back from time to time to see how she was navigating the weeds.

"What'd you say your name was again? Alison?"

"Yeah, just, Ally is fine." Were her voice an octave or so higher, she'd sound like a sparrow or hummingbird or what Rodney imagined one of those really tiny birds would sound like if they could say human words.

But he liked her where the others grudgingly tolerated her. "Well, Ally, how you doin' back there?"

"All right," she managed to say, words broken up by the effort it took to navigate the brush.

He saw the way she looked at things, turning and staring for long enough to snap a photo with her eyes, and that was how he knew she had a braincase. She probably had a Cloud she uploaded all her stuff to, even though she carried around a tablet fashioned to look like one of those old-school leather notebooks.

They made it to the gravel, and Rodney had her take a seat at the picnic table out front. "You want anything to drink?" She was breathing pretty hard. "A mask? I got one in the house if you need it."

"No," she breathed, "I'm fine. Thanks, though."

"All right." He laid his hammer on the table and stretched his back, then looked out over the place. "That concrete wall you see," he said, pointing at a span of barrier that stretched beyond the vision of unaugmented eyes into the distance. "That wraps around here. We're right in the buffer zone. And this was around when things were real bad at first and they just set about decontaminating things. As you can see, the weeds done got so tall you could climb them to get on the other side. 'Course, there'd be nothing waitin' for you there. Before this spot was decontaminated, the radiation levels in this here yard were about ten microsieverts per hour. Even if you're meched up, that's way over the limit for what's healthy to be around. But the city government and the feds were really dead set on making sure people could still live here. Big PR effort behind it too." He took a seat opposite her.

Her gaze was equal parts earnest and calculating, and a part of Rodney couldn't help but feel bad for her. Whatever it was she thought she was doing, she probably thought it was nobler than it really was.

"There's a spot in the garage. Here, let me show you." And he got up to lead her to the house extension, its door open and baring his tools and dusty, no-tires Benz to the elements. He crouched and pointed to a spot beneath the downspout. "That spot's been decontaminated maybe thirty times since I been here. Rain kept washing the radioactive particles off the roof, turned it into a hotspot. There are plenty of other places in New Haven like that, ten microsieverts at least. And if you don't call the government, then they don't come and excavate. It's only gotten worse since everybody started leaving."

He returned to the table and felt his limp again. His arm sleeve was soaked through, but he wasn't about to show this Ally the metal beneath the peeled-away skin. "You ask me, I think it's good people are coming back. What are they called, 'returnees'?" He chuckled. "I mean, they grandparents, great-grandparents, they the ones that left, and *they* ain't the ones coming back. I know some of the others looked at that first wave of white folk and thought they was all settlers and whatnot come to take over the land and whatnot, but just wait till they water gets turned back on or the roads get fixed. Wait till a dome go up over their place and they ain't gotta pay for it. We'll see if they still complaining."

"You don't worry about house prices increasing?"

"What it cost me to live here? Only a lung and a liver." He laughed. He'd been saving that joke for a while.

Quiet hung between them as he waited for her smile.

"You got anything written so far or you just takin' pictures?"

"I dunno. Still kinda finding my way through it all."

"Only way to finish is to start."

At this, she smiled. Then she unfolded her tablet and tapped it out of sleep mode. It glowed blue. She tapped the air just over the screen a few times, swiped some, then slid it over to Rodney.

"Am I in it?"

"Not yet. I mean, not if you don't want to be."

"I'm just messin' with you. Write what you're gonna write." Rodney took a pack of smokes out of his pocket, tapped one out, then lit up. He made sure he was gentle when he picked up the tablet and started to read.

AFTER he finished reading her article, "I remember that kid," was all Rodney would say to Ally for the rest of the afternoon. She found her own way back down the hill while he smoked.

Good morning, madame."

The voice came from the doorway, and when Mercedes slipped out of her room and into the hallway, she could see that the person on the other side of their threshold was wearing a mask and a yellow protective suit. Her voice sounded filtered, like it was coming through broken speakers. Nobody had come to their door since the start of hurricane season brought red dust up from the mid-Atlantic and the coastal South through their corner of New England and poisoned the water and coated everything not already covered in splashes of copper.

Abuela had on a mask when she opened the door and the other person, a woman, had in her hands a tablet. Instantly, the music in the apartment shut off. Abuela hadn't moved. With a start, Mercedes realized the other woman must have done it.

"I'm from the community residents' association," the woman said in Castilian Spanish. "I'm delivering a notice that someone from Unit 112 in Residence Court returned from outside the city limits yesterday and will be quarantined for fourteen days. The committee is requesting that you and everyone in your household not walk around in the community if you can afford not to. For all essential travel, please take precautions, bring your pass, and register your travel with the association. We'll take your temperature upon your return." When she said that last part, Mercedes saw her smiling kindly behind her face shield.

"Poor thing," Mami said from behind Mercedes. "Her throat sounds so dry." Before Cedes could suggest they get her something to drink, her mother said, "It's probably been a while since she's been oiled." She put her hand to the back of Mercedes's head and turned her away from the door, just as the woman in the protective suit considered her tablet and read through all of the family's data: names and ID numbers of each family member, mobile numbers for each comms device and who they belonged to, even the landlord's details.

"Has anyone in this household been in contact with anyone from Hartford County? Has anyone in this household returned to New Haven from a county other than New Haven County?"

"What if someone lies?" Mercedes asked her mother.

"You can't lie to them." She shook her head with knowledge that Mercedes could only guess at. "You can't hide. Not from them. Come, let's go talk to your uncles."

IT took no time for Mercedes to trick out her Friends app to show her the health status codes of her Close Friends. Everybody in her school who was smart enough did it and with the semester fucked up the way it was, there was nothing to do but mess around with all these apps the government was already using to track your info.

Her back on the rug in her room, Abuela's Bad Bunny blasting through the walls of her sound-dimmed room, she swiped through the holos her friends had uploaded of custom-made masks and shutdown memes. For each username that showed, a notification of their health status slipped across her screen. Green for "nothing abnormal here," orange for "home quarantine," and red for "quarantined at approved facility."

"Yeah, it was so stupid," Mercedes said to the holo of Angelica hovering in front of her face. "Tasha was literally just going on a jog for training, and she was still in the dome. But you know how her family lives right on the border with—yeah, so she was just jogging. Didn't see anyone, didn't touch anyone. And she said the route had been decontaminated literally a day ago. But when she got back to the apartment, the machine at the entrance said"—she changed her voice to sound like a droid—"'Your record shows you left New Haven today; please quarantine for fourteen days.' Like, what kind of bullshit is that? Her health code went yellow just like that. And now she can't even come over to visit anymore."

"You think your mom would let her over?"

"Mami's not the problem. And Grandma wouldn't tell or anything, but there's security everywhere, you know? Ugh, this is what happens when your building's full of white people. All of a sudden, everyone cares about your health."

Angelica's voice lowered. "They started doing door-to-doors in our building too. And there are Augies all over. Like patrols. It's like police *every*where. Fucking Boston Dynamics logos everywhere. I swear to God, if I see another one, I'm gonna scream."

Mercedes thought about what that must be like, all that activity in and around one's building. Even if it was mostly machines, it would've been something. It might've meant hearing new voices or unfamiliar footfalls outside or even just seeing anyone who wasn't trapped indoors with you. Here, it was quiet. So much quiet, except whenever Abuela would play her reggaeton records. She used to be like this even when they were doing in-person schooling before the campus got shut down for the storm. And Mami said that Abuela would leave the player running on purpose even when she was out with her friends, and when Mercedes had asked why, Mami had said Abuela did it to feel like there was someone other than her in the house when she got back. And Mercedes remembered feeling lonely, hearing that.

There was shouting in another room. Mercedes turned her head lazily.

"What is it?" Angelica asked.

Mercedes sighed. "A kid who went to school in Westport came back to New Haven, and Abuela and all of her friend group get into this daily shouting match about that boy bringing la monga into the building."

"He's white?"

"You already know," Mercedes said with her face.

"How are they the ones with all the money *and* all the disease? It's like there's not even a dome over there."

Mercedes let her gaze wander. "Abuela says just shoot all the gringos up into space and leave the rest of us in peace."

They talked well into the night, and all the while, Mercedes watched the health status codes of her friends and the people she followed flit through her screen: green, yellow, green, yellow, yellow, red, green.

"OKAY, so I'm totally not supposed to be here," said the boy in the livestream, "but fuck it, I'm going in." He moved by tiptoe, or at least, that's what it felt like, what he was seeing transmitted via his braincase into the app Mercedes was now staring at while she forked mofongo into her mouth at the kitchen table.

He passed through a threshold into darkness, then arrived at another that had LED lights beaded in an arc over it. A glimpse of his reflection in metal revealed that he held a piece of metal in his jaw, and when he passed through the threshold, a number beeped with a reading in Fahrenheit. Something thrilled in Mercedes watching this boy fake his own body temperature with what must be an implant. Whatever it was also seemed to coat him in permissions from the surveillance orbs embedded as hemispheres in the corridor ceiling.

"We're getting closer. It's wild chill in here. There's, like, no one. It's totally empty, but there's probably a couple Crabs, and I got something for them." He looked down at his waist, where a small EMP hanging from his belt let out a theatrical sizzle.

"The fuck is he doing?" Mercedes murmured around her plantains. If that thing were to go off and not be calibrated properly, it would likely shut down the entire room, which definitely looked like somewhere important.

Then he got to the space, which seemed like it was too big to fit inside whatever building he'd been walking through. It was clear just from his quick panorama that it was some sort of control room. Like he somehow predicted, the room was empty, but the hum of machines operating could be heard even through her phone. Monitors blanketed the walls like wallpaper, each showing a different slice of domestic life: grocery delivery, an argument, watering plants, untangling wires behind an old TV set, head nodding to music, someone with their head in their hands at a kitchen counter worrying over bills, someone drinking in sorrow, someone drinking in celebration.

"Whoa," said the kid.

Then he looked down, and even Mercedes let out a gasp.

The floor he stood on was a floor plan of an apartment complex, and while the monitors on the wall seemed set to whatever the nearest terminal told them to record, his foot placement would call up a scene from the unit he'd stepped on. Whatever the camera or cameras there had recorded, and with each person that shimmered in holographic blue came an array of data in red.

"Oh my god," breathed the kid, peering into the holographic eyes of a mother frozen in the act of balancing an infant against her shoulder while reaching for something out of frame.

The holo showed the woman's age, her degree of cyberization, then, beside that, spilled the household data. The names, ages, jobs of everyone under that roof. Even their Flex details.

The boy took a couple steps forward and saw another projection and another, a malicious smirk on his face as he noted who lived in their apartment and who rented theirs out, which apartments had elderly people in them, whether the women in each unit had organic or fake uteruses, the dating apps the single and married people used, who, living there, was using a housing voucher.

A whooshing sound, and Mercedes slammed her phone on the table, startled. She'd had her pods in. Somebody could've snuck up behind her to see what she was seeing. There was no one around, but the door to their unit had slid open. Mercedes took out her pods, closed the app she'd been using, and walked to the door to find her abuelita, masked up, standing across the threshold from what Mercedes now recognized was the woman from the community residents' association.

Behind the woman, in the building's courtyard, a few people walked the paths around the stone gardens and kids waved their pinwheels and one of them even tried to fly a kite. Everyone wore masks, even though not a single mote of dust caught in the sun's rays was red.

Mercedes heard Abuela joke about the protective suit the woman had worn the last time they'd seen her. Now she had on a flower-patterned romper, her legs hairless the way a mannequin's were. She still wore a mask, though.

The woman peeked over Abuela's shoulder to stare directly at Mercedes, as though she'd known her exact position the whole time. "Señora, could you take our picture?"

Mercedes almost whispered, "What" before she caught the vibe from her abuela that she needed to move, so she went back to the table and fetched her Flex, realizing in the moment that the woman was clocking the fact that Mercedes wasn't taking the picture with her eyes and therefore didn't possess a braincase. The woman had a thermometer aimed at Abuela's wrist and made Mercedes stand close enough that she could get a shot of both of them smiling at the camera in that pose. Her fingers were sweaty on her screen, and it took her a few tries, and with each try, the woman retook Abuela's temperature.

When Mercedes showed her the fourth attempt, the woman exclaimed, "Normal!" beaming at last. "Your abuela can tell you how to send the photo to me." Then she was off, and the sounds of the courtyard rose up to reach their floor.

There was a small courtyard in Mercedes's Chapel Street apartment complex, benches made of steel with wood lacquered over the seats framed the small gardens that had mulch and tiny trees sprouting from them. None of the few dogs that roamed the area, walking through the rays of red sun that shot through the slats overhead, was on a leash. But one of her neighbors walked around, gloved, with a plastic bag in his hand and more on his waist and scooped up their shit. The few residents left might have taken for granted how well maintained the place still was or might've believed it some sort of magic, but Mercedes knew that man cleaning up dog-shit was the fairy godfather behind it. So was the woman who came by to maintain the temperature readers over each doorframe. At first, each unit had a dosimeter hanging outside like a doorbell, but those were too valuable and too easily stolen, so it became the type of thing that was waiting for you if and when you moved in. Like an amenity. To go along with the rec room and the gym and the solar-powered electricity.

One benefit, though, to the emptiness of the place was that Mercedes could play her reggaeton from her Flex at whatever volume she pleased. It was like her grandmother or her grandmother's friends filled the space with her. A way to keep them near. If that were ever taken from her, she knew she'd have to move.

Sydney sat on a milk crate she must've brought with her, and Timeica stood, and like that, they formed a tight circle with Mercedes sitting on her bench. At her side was a little ceramic ashtray, white with a multicolored tile pattern blackened with ash.

"Horses," Mercedes said at last after a puff. "You wanna steal horses?"

"It's not stealing," Timeica said, annoyed, like this was the hundredth time she'd had to explain this. "They wild. No stable, no saddles, nothing. Just roaming around."

"What're we gonna do with horses?"

Timeica shrugged. "I dunno. Feed them? Ride them? We'd be saving them. They looked like they need people to take care of 'em."

Mercedes knew a project when she saw one. Usually, it was women wanting to fix one of these damaged men. The way these pendejos behaved sometimes was close enough to animals. And the woman would smash herself against the wall over and over and over again to save what didn't want saving.

"So what do you say?"

"Cedes, if you just seen them," Sydney said, breathless, in that voice so beautiful it hurt Mercedes to hear.

"Mira, I don't know nothing about no horses. I can't remember the last time I seen a horse, okay? But I know those things aren't cheap. You need chavo. Where will you keep them? How will you feed them? Does anybody in this city even have straw?"

"So you *do* know what horses need to eat," Timeica said, grinning.

"Mija, wait."

"Apples too," said Sydney. "We could get apples easy."

"How many horses are we talking?"

"Three or four," Sydney said.

"Is it three or is it four?"

"Five," Timeica said firmly. And with that, it felt as though Mercedes had been drafted.

There was no resisting. They were gonna do this with or without her, so she might as well make sure they were safe. "The plan is easy. A bunch of us drive in—"

"With my car, of course." Mercedes lit another cigarette.

"And we ride the horses back out."

"You been on a horse before?"

Timeica smiled a "no but what could go wrong" smile.

Mercedes shook her head, cursed under her breath. "And we get the horses here. Where do we put 'em?"

Timeica lifted her chin resolutely. "I'll talk to Bishop about that."

"What's Bishop got to do with . . . You know what? I'll let that one go."

"Good. Sydney's gonna go on another Fairfield run, and she's gonna get a good look at the horses again, make sure they're still there and nobody's gotten to them yet. Also gonna look for surveillance. It was pretty light on the way there, but you never know."

Mercedes arched an eyebrow at Sydney. "You're not going alone, are you?"

A grin split Sydney's face. "I'm going with Linc."

A snort escaped Mercedes before she could stop it. "Another fucking project," she said out loud.

Linc and Sydney had left Bishop's truck around some brush on the side of the Merritt Parkway and hidden it beneath vines and large leaves. Then Sydney had removed any part of it a scavenger might've deemed valuable—took off the rims, eviscerated what was under the hood, even twisted off the side mirrors—and scattered those pieces in nearby woods. She didn't say why, but had a just-in-case look in her eyes. She'd done it all with practiced movements, looking like she knew what she was up to, like she knew how to put back together what was broken. Because she looked so confident doing it, Linc trusted her.

Bishop was always loath to part with his truck, but when Linc told him that Sydney wanted to take him on the next Fairfield run, Bishop had smiled at him and readily lent him the keys. Linc and Bishop both suspected that there was no more food to be collected there, that their vouchers were all useless, because there weren't even droids to process their claims, that now the trucks came to them—whenever they did come—but he'd handed over his truck nonetheless. So that Linc could spend some time with his girl.

She had eyes for the greenery that consumed the roadway, the stuff that stuck up through the cracks in the concrete and twisted the underground magnetic lines into breaking. She seemed to spend most of her time with her eyes skyward, tracking the tree canopy. Linc couldn't help but follow her gaze and catch the leaves at the beginning of their turning. Wind was cutting through the tunnel the landscape turned the roadway into, and Linc drew closer to her and slipped his arm over her shoulder. She didn't resist, but she didn't slip her arm around his waist like he'd hoped. Maybe it was because his knapsack was in the way. That's what he told himself as they passed exit after blocked-off exit.

Barricades blocked most of the off-ramps, and it was clear from the imprints in the ground and the occasional buzzing in the air that, once upon a time, mechs had guarded the border of a dome here.

Thunder boomed distantly.

They both spent a few moments looking up at the sky and the suddenness of the gray before heading into the forest shelter. The rain would thicken the radiation, marrying the airborne dust of it together to make mud. Sydney pulled Linc deeper into the forest, away from the side of the road, again like she knew what she was doing, and Linc imagined they were both thinking about Bishop's truck and whether they'd buried it deep enough to save it from the worst of the acid.

Before long, the soil squished, wet and noisy, under their boots. Running would've splashed the stuff all over them, so they walked as fast as they could until Linc heard the soft pattering of rain on something that wasn't foliage. Cloth. He followed the sound, holding Sydney's hand and only belatedly realizing. Then, in the middle distance, they saw it. A tent.

Their steps slowed, so that they could better listen through the rain for other sounds: a grunt, footsteps that weren't their own, a gun cocking. But there was nothing. As Linc edged closer, box cutter in hand, he skirted the perimeter of the camp. The only other evidence that a human had been here was the graveyard of spent dragons behind the tent. He was a long time staring at them before Sydney appeared at his side. He couldn't remember the last time he'd seen that many before, and it brought him back to a moment, a random moment, when he'd found himself waking up in an abandoned, bombed-out apartment building.

His eyes were open when the sun rose again and revealed what someone had done in the interim. Around the hand propping him up, emptied dragons. His whole body, bent as it was against the wall, felt stiff and brittle from the final edges of the high. Intermittently dotting the alley were piles: discarded wood, welded scrap metal, broken tools, cigarette packets, soda cans, trash, all politely organized.

The rising sun threw their shadows against the abandoned building opposite Linc where several of the other stackers slept or didn't. A wooden stepladder and shards of unwanted wood made a young girl with tousled hair and the silhouette of her dress flare out in a breeze that wasn't there with her head angled toward the sky. A metal stand curved to hold balls of copper wire gilded by the sun made two faces silhouetted against the wall of the second floor, a man and a woman, bodiless, facing each other, on the verge of words. Two wooden step-ladders and twined poles became two girls sitting on stools, slumped forward, one with her chin resting on the palm of her hand. Bags filled with shit formed dunghills on which rested black plastic trash bags and wood to make the shadow on the wall that of a young woman reclined against a rest with another woman's head in her lap, the first looking forward while the second faced insouciantly skyward. Shadows play-acting at living.

Sydney squeezed his hand, bringing him back to the forest. "Let's go inside," she said so quietly it was as though she hadn't opened her mouth at all.

The cloth musta been lined with something, because the floor was completely dry. Who would abandon a thing like this? Which got Linc thinking that whoever it was probably got themselves killed but had maybe, Linc hoped, killed the other person in the process. So that no one would come looking for this bit of haven.

This probably wasn't what Bishop meant by "spend some time with your girl" but it made him warm to know that he wasn't alone, being trapped in a forest and having to listen to the angry patter of poisoned rain all around him.

He tried to look at her while pretending not to look at her, tried to casually brush the skin of his hand against hers and see if she was down to fuck right now as much as he was.

She turned to him with heat in her eyes and did that thing where breath seemed to catch in her chest, so that her mouth was partly open and welcoming and just when Linc was about to press his lips against hers, she smirked against him and said, "Wanna hear a poop joke?"

"What?"

"A poop joke." She said it with that husky voice of hers.

"Sure," Linc said, hoping Sydney clocked how annoyed he was.

She settled on the dry ground. "Aight. So, there was this time after the war and where I lived there was this hill. We were in a spot by the water at the time, and the hill was kinda steep, and you kinda had to do that hill if you wanted to get anywhere downtown. So one night it had been rainin' hard. Like, fat-ass raindrops. And just comin' down like washin' through everything. And you had to be careful, because electricity was still on in parts of the city, right? So"—she pressed her hand to her chest and cleared her throat—"so, you had to watch out because the poles that got knocked down during the war woulda lit you up if you stepped in any puddles. But the next day, I was walking up the hill. I forgot what I needed to get from town, but there was this line of cars"—she traced the line in the air—"long-ass line and everyone's honking and shouting and it's just wild, right? And they're all stopped behind this one car. It's broken down and half the drivers are like 'yo, fam, keep goin' what the fuck' and the other half are like 'nah, go back, go back!' and that's when the smell hits me."

She'd never said this many words in one go to him, or at all, really. And Linc wondered if maybe she was nervous or scared or preparing for something, working up the courage to do something. He wanted to tell her to chill, to not worry, that he'd be gentle with her like all the other times, but he didn't know how to say all that without sounding mad thirsty, so he said nothing and just listened to her work her throat raw with talking.

"So the driver's got his foot on the gas and the car is just VRRRRRRM, but it's not goin' anywhere, right? Just stuck, and shit's just flying everywhere and people are screaming and you wanna know what happened?"

"What happened?"

"The storm was so bad the night before that the sewer system just bust wide open and this manhole got popped up into the sky and people's shit literally came down like rain on the hill."

"The hill you were walking on?"

"Well, yeah, but I turned around and picked a different hill after that."

Linc started chuckling, then got mad at himself because the story Sydney told was too involved, too real, too close to where they lived to be a good joke, but then she was giggling, and it didn't sound like her throat hurt, so Linc let go of his anger and laughed with her.

The sound of rain lessened. In sync, they peered out through the tent opening to see the rainfall replaced by mist.

"We good?" Sydney asked with her eyes, back to being quiet again, and Linc said, "Yeah, I think so."

He stuck a hand out and held it in the open air for a little bit, then pulled it back and got ready to step out. Sydney squeezed ahead of him. An idea hit just as she passed through the opening. He flipped the knife in his hand, searched with his free hand where the tent cloth had been bolted down, and started hacking away at it. As he'd hoped, the cloth—no matter what was reinforcing it—came away smoothly. Then he rose, holding it over him and wrapped an arm around Sydney's waist, bringing her into the shelter.

She leaned into him and closed her eyes, letting him lead.

He had no idea where they were but, rather than remain hyperaware of their surroundings, he let his mind wander. He liked to linger on the small bits of herself Sydney gave him and extrapolate, storytell. If she was in a city during the war—maybe it was called The City, where she was from—then maybe she spent most of her days underground. Maybe there was artificial lighting or maybe shit was just tunnels with lightbulbs strung up and maybe it was a maze but you learned it all pretty quickly, learned everything that distinguished tunnels anyone else would say looked exactly the same. Maybe to cross from one part of the city to another and avoid bullets from white militia or the Black folk trying to protect you or anyone in between, you had to scurry through this underground city like a rat. And maybe it did something to her skin and maybe the dust got into your lungs and there was no way to breathe anything like real unfiltered, unvarnished air. Maybe the only time you got to spend above ground was in buildings with roofs or ceilings over your head, anything that could collapse on you and kill you but make you bleed out first. So maybe when she was finally able to come out from underground, she would wander the city aimlessly, just trying to take part in every public space, to imprint herself in the air there. Maybe she would jump onto park benches and run through the craters in parks and maybe it got so that the hill she would walk up and down wasn't just a piece of earth but a reminder. Like someone high and important was telling her she didn't have to live underground anymore. Maybe the hill was evidence that the war was over, or, at least, as "over" as a thing like that can get.

And maybe she and her friends who survived the war went to the beach and sat on the rocks and took that water spray to the face and they didn't care about all the garbage that had collected there because they weren't underground anymore. And maybe Sydney jumped into the water and waded out but then felt something touch her leg and jumped out. And maybe she shrieked and held herself close while another friend, braver or more reckless, swam out to see what animal it was, then maybe stared at the water for a while before laughing and telling her that it was a piece of shit. A piece of shit had touched her leg because no one had fixed the sewage system during the war and it was all going out to the sea or the lake or whatever body of water this was. And maybe that got everyone laughing except Sydney at first, then maybe Sydney started laughing.

She moved her hand in a circle on his chest. "Whatchu laughin' at?" she asked sleepily.

He hugged her closer. His way of saying, "Nothing."

A house came into view. Linc had no idea how long they'd been walking, but the place glowed with the prospect of safety from the ir-radiated wetness outside, so he hurried the two of them across the ex-pansive front yard with toppled, worn-down stone statues and down the weed-choked gravel pathway to the front porch with its awning overhead. Out of the rain now, he gave Sydney the tent covering, then went to the nearest window. After too brief a glance to surveil the situation inside, he smashed the window with his elbow, cleared away the glass, and hopped through.

A cabinet blocked the front door from opening, so he stuck his head out the window and said, "through here," and Sydney climbed in.

Once inside, Linc offered to take the cloth cover from Sydney, but she just smiled and wrapped it around her shoulders like a cape, then spun around and let it flare. It looked good on her.

They wandered around, from room to gigantic room. He thought he'd be used to walking through houses like this, places so big on the inside you could cry for help and a person at the other end wouldn't hear you. You could hide in a place like this. The bathroom with the broken tiled floor had a tub big enough to sleep in, to drown in. There seemed to be three separate living rooms on the floor, though one of them could have been a dining room with all the furniture stolen. Eye scanners and thumb pads sat smashed next to every door. He stepped up the spiral staircase and, knife out, gently nudged doors open. After a while, he lost count of the bedrooms, then he made his way up yet another flight of stairs to what looked like a series of studies and art rooms. Even though dust and soot coated the walls, he could see the squares where pieces of art might have once been. Framed paintings or posters, a spot on a desk where a small statue's base might have stood. But beyond that, he couldn't imagine what else would fill a once-carpeted space this size.

The place had grown too quiet, so he went back the way he'd come, on the way passing by a second-floor bathroom. There were still a few floors above him that he'd neglected. But this house looked like it had been here long enough that everything of value was either gone or spoiled.

He sheathed his knife and walked into the bathroom. There was no tub here, but the space where it looked like people showered, you could have a whole picnic inside. Over the sink hung a single mirror shard, a small, sellable thing that hadn't yet been taken. And he stepped closer to it, close enough that he could recognize his face. He wiped the smudging away with the palm of his hand and could see, for the first time in too long, what he looked like. The pitted, lined skin; the hollow jaw; the grayness of his flesh. The silver sunlight that came through the open window space, he blamed for the ghostliness of his reflection. But he bared his teeth and could see the discoloration. The spaces where some were missing struck him like chastisement. Like he was being berated. But it was the grime that got him. So much of this place, picked apart as it was, seemed so much cleaner than him. This house that no one had taken care of for so long looked like it was in better shape than he was. People had gutted this thing, stripped it of worth and almost entirely of function, and it was still a thing that could inspire awe. It was still a thing that could have a kid like him wandering around, slack-jawed. He sniffed and backed away.

"Dinner is ready, please proceed to the first floor dining room."

The droid's voice startled him. He whirled around. His hands found the edge of an exposed pipe, and it came loose with a vicious ripping-and-scattering sound. His mind went empty. He stalked to the droid, who repeated, "Dinner is ready, please proceed to the first floor dining room." And he raised the pipe and swung. The thing slammed to the ground sideways, its wheels whirring against air. "Dinner is ready, please proceed—" SMASH. "Dinner is ready—" SMASH. "Dinner is—" SMASH SMASH SMASH SMASH.

Its once-rounded head was a mess of circuitry by now, but he couldn't stop. He covered its torso with dents, caved its legs in, swung and swung and swung, and oil splashed up against his cheeks and coated his clothes. He kept swinging, down, down, down, even as his shoulders shook. He wanted this thing gone, wiped from the face of the earth. SMASH SMASH SMASH SMASH SMASH. He couldn't stop, so he didn't. And a part of him knew that this was the best place for his anger, something cold that wouldn't resist him and wouldn't look at him afterward with fear, wouldn't nurse any loathing for him in its heart.

He realized he was kneeling over the thing, his knife to several of the wires in its neck when he paused.

Sydney stood a few doors down in the hallway. The sound. She musta been drawn by the sound.

After a beat, he stood, wiped the oil from the knife onto his pants, then sheathed it.

"The rain," Sydney said, and Linc knew she was back to keeping her words from him.

He listened for movement outside and heard none. It had stopped. "Yeah, we should get back. Curfew." As he shouldered past her, he wanted to ask if she'd found anything, just to hear her speak, just to hear her say "nothing," but he didn't want to hurt her too.

There was no work the next afternoon. When everyone got to the worksite, there was nothing but bats in the rubble. The drone had eaten everything else. A few of the stackers wandered off back home. Some hitched rides, but the rest stayed. Wyatt made a table out of a bunch of the stones and people fashioned their own seats and someone brought out a deck of shimmering holocards. A holo-deck of cards that scintillated blue and projected pixelated suits and numbers. Sometimes, they malfunctioned and switched or showed the wrong suit or hue and the dealer had to reshuffle.

Jayceon took the deck and made a show of flipping the cards more deftly than his predecessor, his hands a blur. The deck turned into a single blue cube in his hands. Rodney, sitting across from him, stretched his stiff leg out and sighed.

Linc sat on a porch step a couple feet away, the rest of the house gone behind him. Sydney, sitting a step above his, had her legs around his while she braided his hair. He had his head leaned back in her lap, eyes closed, and could hear Snowflake holding counsel with Mercedes and Timeica not far away. Snowflake—only Rodney ever called her Alison—had her touchpad in front of her, tapping furiously, then holding it up to take pictures of the stackers getting ready to play.

One of them, before the game, said, "You really wanna chance it with that deck? I don't wanna lose no friends on account of a bootleg deck o' cards."

Jayceon chuckled while he shuffled. "Nigga, you done lost family for less. This is Spades; you ready to get read for filth or not, nigga?"

Sydney was gentle with his head and would occasionally massage his scalp beneath his 'fro where the sun itched him, always a step ahead of him asking. The sky was purple over them, but the heat told him it was still around midday. The type of heat that would follow you into shelter, the type that no shadows could beat back. So they took it. Like a whip-scar over your entire body.

"Hell, you can play Spades anywhere. 'Course you can play on a shuttle," Timeica was telling Snowflake. "If you're somewhere and someone says you can't play Spades, they're not trying hard enough. You might only be missing a table to flip when some bum-ass nigga reneges."

Mercedes, chuckling, lit up a Newport.

Linc didn't hear Snowflake's question, but Timeica responded, "You sit down at a Spades table at your own risk. You finna get called everything *but* a child of God."

"I didn't talk to my husband for a month after a Spades game," Mercedes said around her cigarette.

Kendrick shook his head, walked away from the table, and sidled up next to Linc on the porch. "I don't play Spades with Black folk," he breathed. "I got too much to live for. Niggas act like they playing for freedom papers."

Timeica turned to Snowflake, her new coconspirator. "You play Spades like your whole reputation, your 401(k), and your credit score are on the line. A person will form their entire opinion of you based on that Spades game. How valuable you are to them."

"Shit is irrevocable," Mercedes opined.

The journalist shook her head in wonderment.

Mercedes shrugged. "You don't have to be a genius or anything like that. You just can't renege."

"Don't you ever renege," Kendrick said loud enough for Mercedes and Timeica and Snowflake to hear.

Mercedes gestured with her cigarette. "See that table over there? All stones and shit? Probably weighs over a hundred thirty-five pounds. You see how it's mostly old bambalans at that table? Veterans and shit. Jayceon's probably the youngest by at least a decade, maybe two. If he reneges, any one of them old heads would probably flip that table all the way the fuck over." She laughed like she was watching someone do it. "Eighth deadly sin, reneging."

Timeica took a stone to the claw of her hammer, banged against its edge to bend it while she talked. "You renege? That reneging will follow you for the rest of your damn life. Don't matter if you was two years old when you did it."

"How do you not renege?"

Mercedes mimed holding cards in her hands, cigarette smoke winding around shiny, curled fingers. "When you get your cards, arrange them by suit. Alternate the colors." She winked at Snowflake. "You're welcome." She leaned back on the column behind her, elbows out. "Spades, you either choose to learn or you stay in the absolute fucking dark. There is no middle ground. None whatsoever."

A clang from Timeica. "Reneging ain't the only way to suck. You can overbid, underbid, cut your partner. But understand this: Not taking the pill is an accident. Burning your house down because you left the hot plate on is an accident. Cutting your partner? That's grounds for an ass-whooping."

Snowflake paused. "What's the worst thing your partner ever did in a Spades game? How did you react?" She spoke with a professional reporter's mechanical detachment. She was curious and earnest, Linc knew that much. But he couldn't tell if she really cared. If he had told her Spades wasn't a game, it was a way of life, she probably would have made that a pull quote and thought nothing more of it.

Timeica barked out a laugh, stopped forging her hammer. "Ay, Jayceon! What's the worst thing your partner ever did in a Spades game? He still breathing?"

Jayceon dealt the cards, stared intently at his. "She cut my lil' Joker with a big Joker. Started breathing maybe five minutes later after I throat-chopped the fuck outta her."

Linc spat out a choked laugh, his scalp twinged. Kendrick hiccupped his mirth. Mercedes murmured, "Word."

Timeica turned to Mercedes, "You, Cedes?"

Her cigarette burned down to the butt. She tossed it down, stamped it out with her boot heel. "Let's just say there's some cabrona in Paterson, New Jersey, with a bald spot that a weave can't cover."

"Oh, Lord," Timeica said, her hand over her mouth in mock horror.

Kendrick craned his neck. "I seen a girl get smacked with a Sprite bottle because she missed one book to have a bubble."

Mercedes laughed herself into a blood-thick cough. Linc felt Sydney grin behind him.

One of the old heads, his face shadowed by his fedora, itched his salt-and-pepper stubble. "I'll never forget it." His voice was a flattened tire rolling over gravel. "Last Christmas. My sister-in-law cut over me with a big Joker. There was liquor involved. Also, I already couldn't stand that bitch. So you know all hell broke loose. I was half-blind with the whiskey and stumbled my ass outside into the snow. Took a box a sugar with me outta the kitchen. Poured it all up in that bitch gas tank. She wanna underbid and shit. I'm like 'bitch all we need is a seven, we made four!' And I asked her specifically, are these Whitneys and Bobbys strong? That's what I called my books: Whitneys and Bobbys. So I went out with a box of Dominos sugar and filled that bitch gas tank." His shoulders shook with chuckles. "To this day, she still don't know who did it."

Linc watched the expression change on the white girl's face. Watched her shit fall all the way into her shoes. She looked at Jayceon like he was on the verge of losing his life.

Rodney patted his leg, moved his cards around with his free hand. "My mom went into labor with me during a Spades game. I was born during a seven and a possible . . ."

The others howled. Sprinkled it with "get the fuck outta here" and "you are a cotdamn fool, Rodney" and "you know that nigga's serious."

Kendrick smirked. "Grandmama is legally blind in one eye, but I bet three books in, she know what everybody got in they hands."

Snowflake gave Timeica her whole face. "So, would you say Spades is the precursor to a lot of violent crime?"

Only Sydney could tell she was joking.

Linc nudged Kendrick and reached into his pocket. Out came a small canister with "G4S" in red and black labeling along the side. "Check it." He handed it to Kendrick. "Sydney and I found it over by West Rock."

Kendrick held it up to his eyes. Turned it over. "Air canister."

"Yeah."

"Who the fuck's walking around with air masks?" He flipped it through his fingers. "Ain't that old, either."

"No, it ain't."

"Shit." Kendrick eyed Linc, turned to look at Sydney, who worked diligently on Linc's hair. Then he stuffed the canister in the pocket of his overalls. "There more?"

Linc nodded. Then he nodded at the reporter who sat with Timeica and Cedes in their bubble of hilarity. "Lil' Miss Pop Star over there, I don't like her. Why's she interested in us? In this place? She's writing whatever she's writing, and who's it for?"

Kendrick tapped his breast pocket where the canister bulged slightly. "You think we in trouble? I mean, shit, look at all this."

Sydney coughed, mean and wet. A little bit of it splashed onto the back of Linc's neck. She wiped her hand on her lap. Linc's own hand went to the back of his neck, and when he looked at his fingertips, they were red. Quickly, he scrubbed it into pink, then wiped what remained on his jeans. He felt weary; his shoulders slumped with it, because he knew he couldn't run and settle in another place. New Haven was the only city he'd been sober in since he'd watched his brother hang from a streetlamp in Nevada. "I can't do this anywhere else," he whispered.

Sydney's fingers skipped a beat, and he knew she had heard him. She sniffed and it sounded like she was fighting a sob.

The white lady held up her touchpad, looked like she was taking a picture, then turned back to Timeica and Mercedes, who crouched over to see what she'd documented. Kendrick cut his eyes at the group.

Linc caught a glimpse of the image, which flashed briefly as a hologram before Timeica told Snowflake to cut that light. It was a hand, someone's hand. Maybe Jayceon's. Everyone's fingers looked wrinkled and thick and ashy. Three diamonds: a six, a three, an Ace. Two hearts: An Ace and a ten. A King of clubs. Five spades: eight, Queen, Jack, two, Ace. And two Jokers.

"How many books can this hand win?" asked the white lady.

Mercedes glanced sideways at her. A little you're-quick mixed with some watch-yourself.

Timeica squinted at the image. "Eight books and a possible."

Snowflake had that eager student look on her face.

"The gods done blessed you with a hand like that." She spoke in a hushed whisper. If it ever got into anyone's heads that she had some-how fucked up the game, she'd have to go stack somewhere two states away. "You got the four highest cards. Two Jokers, Ace of spades, and a two. If. You're playing deuces high. If not, you still got the highest spade, the King. Whether or not your partner has it, you can still snatch five books. Easy. Those red Aces'll get you another book. Smart thing would be to play them early before the suit runs out and people start cutting you. That's seven. You can use the two of spades and even the eight to cut once you're out of clubs and hearts. That'll net you two more."

Testing the waters, Snowflake whispered, "What happens if I played the five or the six?"

"Then you're an underbidding trick-ass mark and you deserved to be cussed all the way out."

Mercedes shifted, moved her ass back and forth against the ground. "If you ain't ready to throw down, nena, picheale a ese tema. You got no place at a Spades table."

Linc tilted his head, Sydney leaned down to his ear while she worked his scalp. "Could run a Boston with that hand." She nodded toward the trio.

"She's eatin' that shit up," Kendrick muttered beneath his breath. "Exotic fuckin' tigers 'n' shit is what we are."

"I'm a proud monkey," Linc smirked.

Kendrick got up. "I almost want her to try playin' a game. Just to watch one of those folks over there fuck her up." He patted the dust out of his overalls. "That's how you deal with invadin' motherfuckers. You invite them to a Spades game."

Bishop had Bugs in his truck while he worked on the wooden electricity pole. His chewing stick rotated between his teeth, his gloves slumped in his pocket. He knew it was dangerous to do this work without them, and that it hurt, but it attacked the numbness and made him present. And it distracted him from the white boy staring up at him with worry wet in his eyes.

There were more of them now, which meant more work that wasn't stacking. Sure, he could fall from this rickety-ass ladder and break every bone God gave him, but stacking was a slow death. Even wearing a mask, you got the dust in you; not only that, you could barely breathe beneath the thing. And stooping like you had to do, especially if you had a short hammer, meant that your body figured that was its natural state, that hunched over was how you was supposed to be, so when you stood upright again, trying to look somewhat dignified and whatnot, the body rebelled. "Pick one," your back kept saying to you.

Birds flew low over him, and he almost stopped completely to admire the eagle that soared over his head. The animals that did show up here in autumn were bigger than they were when he was growing up, but they seemed natural. As many people as lived here, the animals didn't seem to mind.

After he finished, he was slow getting back down the ladder. The others watching him—the white boy and the mixed one who had his arm wrapped around the white boy's waist—probably saw him as some old nigga trying to convince himself of his own usefulness by taking on unnecessary danger, on the warpath to make the whole rest of the world understand he wasn't obsolete. Not yet. But the neighbors who knew him knew why he took his time coming down that ladder. He liked to linger here. The air was cooler here, the small domes more robust. Not the patchwork, rickety contraptions near the city center. Folks really had it better here. Even with the stash houses and the empty lots and the houses that had long since been foreclosed on, they had it better here. The roads might not've been anything to write home about, but they really did have it better here. The animals weren't too shook to show their faces, to commune with the rest of God's creatures.

He couldn't fault the white folk for picking this place for a landing pad.

On his way to the front porch, he watched the white man—Jonathan! That was his name—fumble in his pocket for change like Bishop didn't have a credit exchanger in the truck. And something about it made him feel sad. His chewing stick twitched between his teeth. "Contractor handles it," he said, raising a hand to stop the boy.

The relief on Jonathan's face deepened his sadness, so he nodded at him, tugged his cap slightly, then picked up his toolbox and walked off.

Around the corner, his truck came into view. Bugs was in the passenger's seat tinkering with the boxy credit exchanger, turning it over in his ashy fingers. Bishop made as much noise as he could, tossing his tools onto the backseat, then climbing in.

It was good to see Bugs be curious and kid-like again. When he was around the others—around Jayceon and Linc and the rest of them—he always talked like he was older than he was, and Bishop knew—he'd seen it too many times before—that if he left Bugs to himself, then Bugs would fall in with those other boys and absorb their violence or their tendency toward it. Left to himself, he'd spend more time in his own head and find more and more ways to get out of it. The track marks on his arms were healed, but if you knew what track marks looked like, you'd know that's what they were. And what did it say about a kid who still did those drugs and couldn't even afford dragons?

"Where we goin' next, Bishop?"

"Just gotta run a few more errands. You got somewhere important to be?"

"Nah, just bored. Shit is boring here."

Bishop laughed as he started the car. "You get older, you'll realize how good bored is. How lucky you is to even be bored."

"I ain't got no kinda plans to be that bored. You crazy, man."

"Maybe I am." And with that, he peeled off.

BISHOP'S truck was parked on Orange Street, flanked by shuttered coffee shops and workspaces. Behind him, a few East African restaurants had their "Closed" signs up. But every so often, Bishop peeked over his steering wheel and around the corner toward the library, next to which sat City Hall.

Bugs was still messing with the credit exchanger.

"Hey, can you put that down?" he asked with too much bite in his voice. "I'm tryna look for somethin'."

The noise stopped.

Bishop clocked the sun's height in the sky to tell what time it was. He started drumming his fingers.

"That help you think?" Bugs asked, sharp.

Bishop stopped.

The sun sank a little further, and Bishop was about to turn the truck back on when he saw a figure start to jog down Elm Street. At first, they were a white speck coated in blue, then as they got closer, they became a white man in a translucent blue bodysuit with a headband holding back sweaty, flowing tree-bark-colored hair. The city comptroller had augmented lungs, Bishop was sure of it, so running like this was pure vanity. Just to be seen. But Bishop had been counting on that.

He got out of the car and crept around the corner, clinging to shadows, even though it woulda taken nothing for the white man to see him. And he made his way up the block. Then, just as the comptroller was about to round the corner, Bishop swung out, slipped his pistol from his pocket and smacked the man in the head, toppling him sideways.

Before the man hit the ground, Bishop wrapped him up in his

arms and frog-marched him to the truck. With one hand, he pulled open the back door and tossed the man in, then jumped in behind him and sat on his legs.

"Where's our food rations?" Bishop hissed at the comptroller.

"Wha . . ." A voice that had been calibrated to automatically add bass came out scratchy and like static.

Bishop pulled a device that looked like ancient headphones out of his back pocket and forced them onto the man's ears, even as he writhed and struggled under Bishop. "Don't bother calling for help. The drones can't see you. And you shoulda fuckin' shelled out for security, but you ain't skim enough off us fucking people, ain't you?"

Bugs had turned in his seat but there was only a moment of surprise on his face, a brief raising of the eyebrows, before he turned back around and even seemed to relax against the seat.

"Credit station at the Fairfield border been closed, so when were you gonna tell us?"

"I . . . I don't know what you're talking about."

Bishop smashed the gun butt against the man's temple. No blood came out of the wound, but a dent did mar the manufactured curvature of the comptroller's temple. "You was just gonna let us starve."

"We . . . we are in the process of preparing a transfer of—"

Bishop hit him two more times, this time trying to actually break the wound open.

Something changed in the comptroller's posture. "I've seen your face."

"No, you ain't. Because I scrambled your shit too. If you think you can threaten your way out of this, you fuckin' with the wrong nigga. I will blind you forever, homeboy, now where's our *fucking* rations?"

Now the comptroller started to tremble.

"If you don't answer me, your daughters in Westport *been* in trouble. Fuck with me."

"Okay, okay, wait, wait, wait."

"Next city council budget meeting, if we don't see the right numbers allocated for our fuckin' community, this'll be a love tap compared to what's next. Now, tell me how you're going to fix our food problem."

"I don't know . . . what . . ."

Bishop pressed the barrel to the back of the man's knee. "You wanna run again, my nigga? Answer the goddamn question."

"Okay, okay. I'll take it out of my own salary. Ration distribution will begin next week. The distributors will be reprogrammed tonight and the new routes will be put in and it'll all be set, please, just, not my legs."

A small part of Bishop felt vindicated that the man was more visibly distressed over the ability to flaunt his partially mechanized body than the prospect of harm coming to his daughters in their domed community. But that was what men his type were like. Mid-level bureaucrats who didn't know the right people to make cushy careers for themselves in the Space Colony. Grifters who were stuck here, none of them by choice, forced into their fiefdoms and molded by their greed and small-mindedness into ant-sized tyrants. Bishop felt more respect for the robots they programmed. At least those were governed by a code.

"Now, you're gonna make good on your promise right now. Stick your hand out." When the comptroller hesitated, Bishop hit him again. Again and again until the man stuck his hand out between the driver's seat and the passenger's. "Aye," Bishop said to Bugs, "take his index finger and put it to the scanner."

"Wh—what are you doing?"

"Shut the *fuck* up!"

Bugs took the man's finger, as commanded, and pressed it to the credit exchanger's scanner. Immediately, digital green numbers appeared on its screen, the total rising higher and higher until Bishop said, "That's good."

The credit exchanger disappeared.

"What I said about the next budget meeting stands." Bishop kicked his back door open, then shoved the comptroller out of his vehicle.

When Bishop came out after him, he made sure to step over the man and linger, gun barrel pointed at the man's face the whole time, before getting back into the driver's seat and spouting red dust over the fallen man's face as he turned the corner and sped off.

BUGS'S legs dangled over the bridge in Canal Lock 12 of the Farmington Canal. Bishop's truck was parked a little ways down by the gate and the old lock keeper's house. The leaves around them had started to turn so that the two of them on that crumbling stone bridge over that dried aqueduct sat beneath an umbrella that was just beginning to gild and redden.

Bugs munched on his taco while Bishop spooned bits of already-brown salad into his mouth. His stomach couldn't take whatever that beef shit they put in tacos and burritos now did to it.

"It was the niggas with money that was doin' the thuggin'," Bugs said around a mouthful of taco. "Mama was around when all them rappers were runnin' around talmbout gang-bangin, and she ain't see none of them niggas around."

"You listened to rap?" Bishop almost added "as a kid" like the kid still wasn't just that.

"Nah, my mama loved me!"

Bishop's chest heaved with laughter.

"On the real, though. A gun's expensive as shit. You broke, you can't be broke with a gun. It was always the middle-class niggas was the turn-up niggas."

"That so?"

Munch. "Yeah. Some of those rap groups was gettin' niggas' whole 'hoods crashed. Mama used to gang-bang and she could tell who was really out there and who was just tellin' they homie's stories. But that shit ages you, bro."

"Bro?"

"I'm sorry. *Unc.*"

Bishop chuckled.

"Nah, when you out gettin' into situations and all that, it just speeds up your shit too much. It's exhausting. You gotta think about what street you can walk down to and from school. After a while, you just stop goin' to school because it's too dangerous. You know you're gonna get banged on. Ain't nobody got a job, ain't nobody breathin' clean air, and it's just drones everywhere, droids up and down the block and niggas ain't gettin' enough credits for food or school or whatever and when that's all you know, it's what you get sucked into, then you grow up a little and you ain't tryna have time for all that."

"How old is y—"

"You could see the homie get shot dead in front of you and die on the street literally at your feet and two weeks later niggas is moved on. Rest in peace to the homies, but when you see that—when you see the homie die in front of you who all these people say they care about, then they go about they business—you know ain't no afterlife or nothin'. The light just go out and that's it. And I'm not tryna get into all that."

Bishop watched him eat in silence for a while before asking, "So what you lookin' to get into?"

"Here? I dunno." Munch. "I seen the way them birds be bothering you when you was up that pole. Shit was hilarious." He grew pensive. "I know I'm supposed to say some shit like school or whatever or try to make it up to space, but I got more sense than that. I know what this is. I dunno. I guess I seen you up there, old-ass man tryin' not to get your ass beat by an eagle, and I was like 'I could see that for myself,' you know?"

"Thought you wasn't tryna be old and bored no more."

"That was before I seen you rob a government nigga." Smirking, he popped the last of the taco into his mouth, halfheartedly wiped the grease on the paper wrapping, tossed it into the trash-strewn aqueduct, and climbed up onto his feet. "I'ma be in the truck."

"Aight, Bugs," Bishop said quietly, hoping to linger a little bit longer on the bridge.

THERE hadn't been air sirens for a long time, but the sound was rarely absent from Bishop's dreams. Repurposed tornado sirens in one city, fire alarms in another, voices over loudspeakers muffled into unintelligibility. It was always at least one of these waiting for him every time he went to bed. Earlier on, in the loft on State Street, he would sleep with the pump-action shotgun cradled against his chest, but one morning, he woke to find a massive hole in his headboard and his lieutenants at the door with their hands on their pistols and he'd had to watch them look at him with worry and pity when he shooed them away with a gruff, "Bad dream." So he kept it just out of reach. He would have to get out of bed and with deliberation to get it. Night terrors wouldn't take his life. Not after all he'd gone through.

But tonight it was a different sound that woke him.

Thoughtlessly, he slipped his legs over the side of the bed, grabbed a bathrobe from the walk-in closet, then came back for the shotgun. Half-sleep still fogged his mind as he mumbled assurance to the guards outside his door, then took the elevator down to the ground floor.

He came up short when he almost stepped on the winged dog that flitted by his feet. The thing had orange fur and matching feathered wings, all the color of napalm, and moved in hops. Thing was the same color as the chickens that ran riot on his great-grandfather's farm. So many generations of God-man occupied that land that it was assumed Bishop would follow in their footsteps. It was in his name too. And they'd watch approvingly as he preached the Word to those chickens, trying to keep them enthralled, trying to corral their attentions. Praying over chicken births, conducting chicken funerals when one or two of them had been picked for slaughter, baptizing them in the face of their furious flapping. There wasn't a name for what had skitted across Bishop's feet just now. He doubted it woulda listened to him. He had only a little more power over it as a gangster than he mighta had as a preacher.

The sound—now a cacophony of different sounds—drew him in the direction of the Long Wharf waterfront district. He felt, behind him, the presence of the maglev Range Rovers. Protection even though he doubted he needed it.

Hammering, wedging, sawing, splitting. It sounded like the simultaneous tearing down and building up of things.

The vision slowly clarified, blurs growing edges, until he saw a single man tearing down his own house. Instinct had Bishop cock the shotgun and hold it like he was about to cap this nigga who was making the only bit of noise to be heard for miles, but he stopped.

In a city filled with craters and an administration falling over itself trying to follow a fleeing tax base, in a city pockmarked by desolation and disrepair, this man was destroying his own house. And Bishop watched, transfixed, remembering vaguely that there'd been some warning from county officials about fire lanes. Whether to protect from militia strikes or from whatever blazes the red dirt and the poisoned air could start, the lanes would hopefully localize any fires that broke out. He'd seen kids just out of school in days past clearing roads and pathways to make space for the wide fire lanes, backpacks bouncing on their shoulders while they worked. And now here was this man, tools moonlit in the night dark, taking apart his own home.

It's all gonna be gone.

After the worst of the storms had passed through and the tsunamis and the red dust, he'd twisted his power to force the big out-of-town construction companies to hire locals as subcontractors, and he'd believed he was doing the right thing, a durable thing. And he'd do it again after the next disaster and the next. As long as he had money and as long as people listened to him when he talked and got out the way where he walked, he'd do it. And it'd be a good thing to rebuild a city. A city that wasn't his, wasn't his birthright, but a place he could participate in anyway. No one was from anywhere, right? Being an Exoduster proved that.

He'd told himself that to be a good man was to build something that would last. And he watched that lie get taken apart right in front of him.

The winged dog did something that was half-bark, half-caw. It kept trying to achieve liftoff, and Bishop was consumed with bitterness. If he stayed any longer, he'd shoot that animal and that man, so he turned and went back to his apartment.

The main entranceway spritzed cleanser all over his body and the agent sank into his pores, fighting whatever radiation he might have picked up while suitless outside and when he got to his unit, he took the hose from what was once a sink and sucked in the filtered water, trying to rinse his mouth. But the grit never left his teeth.

BISHOP wasn't really angry they'd dragged him out down the highway for their little adventure. He was set, as far as money and rations went. And, sure, he did find solace in the work, but the weather was chilling and the world's cooling was unkind to his joints. He didn't miss the stiffness. Plus, they weren't using up the voltage on his truck. Still, he made sure to grumble every now and then to make sure Timeica and Mercedes and this little Sydney girl heard it. He did have a reputation to maintain.

The world outside looked freshly rained-on, and it had that mulchy smell to it. Didn't smell like desiccation and dehydration and lung rot. Smelled, instead, like that joke people used to tell when things started going bad, that humans were the virus and the earth was healing. Best thing that coulda happened to the planet was all the white folks left it.

"Ay, put on some music."

Mercedes, in the driver's seat, turned her head slightly. Though it wasn't raining anymore, her windshield wipers were at work, sliding the glowing motes of radiation to the corners of the Plexiglas. "Whatchu wanna hear? I got some reggaeton."

"Nah, put on that Freddie Gibbs."

"Who?" This from Timeica in the passenger's seat.

"Y'all don't know about that Freddie Gibbs."

"Bishop, is that one of your rappers again?" Mercedes said it with such playful disdain. "You listen to a lot of drug music for a preacherman."

"It's poetry. Y'all got no idea the poets we used to listen to back in the day. Freddie Gibbs, Pusha T. Oh, man, that Pusha. King Push. He was the Poet Laureate of Cocaine Rap."

"Thou shalt have no other gods before me, right, Bishop?" Timeica said, then guffawed.

Bishop sulked. "We contain multitudes, girl. Sometimes, you just gotta put something ignorant in your ears. Sometimes, I'm ready for gospel, and sometimes, I wanna hear about robbin' the plug. Ain't nothin' wrong with that."

"You are so *old*, Bishop!" Timeica shrieked, and that got Mercedes nearly collapsed over the steering wheel until they hit a bump that sent them through the air and quieted them a little bit.

"And there's education there," Bishop continued, undeterred. "Y'all ever heard that Young Jeezy? You ain't e'em gotta go to college. Just listen to the *Thug Motivation* intros, that's all the education you need."

Mercedes: "So, I sell a kilo of cocaine and no more student loans?"

"Sí, señora!"

Sydney laughed softly with them. She'd been quiet the whole time. While Bishop knew she generally wasn't much of a talker, she had an energy the whole ride that Bishop recognized. He knew they all wanted to show him something, even though they were vague about what. Sydney had the look of someone who'd come up with the plan. Real G's moved in silence. A rapper had said that.

"Y'all ever seen a moose before?" He aimed the question up front, but really just wanted to hear Sydney say something.

"What, in person?" Mercedes asked. "Where I'ma find a moose, Bishop?"

"I'm just sayin'. Among God's creatures, you might not find one more dramatic. You'll find them in spaces where there's a lot of trees, and sometimes their antlers will have velvet on them."

"Wait, their antlers have fur?" Mercedes asked.

"Not all the time, but when them antlers first grow, they got a layer of skin on them. That's called velvet. And that nourishes the bone while it forms. When it's done its work, the velvet comes off, so if you ever see a moose scratching its antlers against a tree, that's what it's doin'. Gettin' rid of the velvet." Thinking about moose made him think about when he was once trapped in Maine, lost somewhere in its northern half, wandering trail after twilit trail. And someone sometime long ago had told him something about moose and dusk, so that to distract himself from the constant fear of being killed by someone who didn't like the look of him, he kept his eyes peeled for antlers. For branches that swayed not from wind but like they'd just been stripped of their leaves by moose-mouth. He lingered by clearings, peered into forests, tried not to kick the dirt too hard in frustration whenever he thought he'd seen moose hide but it turned out just to be shading that leaves cast over the bushes beneath them. A part of him thought if maybe he gave up or were on the cusp of giving up, a moose would reveal itself to save his spirits, and it would point him in the direction of an exit.

But there was no moose, not that time, and no pre-night deliverance from that maze of forest. There was no single sign or North Star to lead him out, but somehow he had escaped and he had established himself farther south, made a community, secured a plot, and made it back up, almost like he had a score to settle. And he'd prepared to spend a week, two weeks, looking for a damn moose, as long as it took, because he knew the poison air and the poison dust and the poison rain couldn't have killed all of them. If it hadn't killed him, then it couldn't possibly kill those beasts.

And almost instantly, at the mouth of a side street maybe ten minutes' walk into the forest, was a moose, antler-less, with its neck elegantly dipped so that it could sip water from a puddle. With languid movement, it raised its head and stared at Bishop, and he thought he could even see it arch an eyebrow, then it went back to its puddle, and Bishop left, wondering about the nature of grudges and if there were ever a way of holding them that didn't leave a man exhausted and wanting by the end. But he'd chuckled to himself all the way back home.

And he found himself chuckling now, even as Mercedes pulled to the side of the road.

"This it?" he asked, nudging his door open and stepping out into the mud.

"Nah, a little further," Sydney said beside him.

He looked down at her with surprise, but she just smiled that impish grin he'd glimpsed on her earlier, then hurried ahead with the rest of the women.

They led him into the forest, and it worried Bishop a little that there were maybe two guns between the four of them and no one had drawn a knife. Especially since the path they walked looked like it had been tread a good bit. Other people had been this way. As they got deeper into the green, he realized that *other people* was them.

Mercedes slowed down until she was beside Bishop, helping him down ledges and through gaps in stone. A part of him wanted to shrug her off, but that was just pride talking, and he knew it. He wouldn't refuse the help.

"What's this surprise, y'all? Is it a new truck?"

Mercedes smirked, and this time, there was some of Sydney's mischief in it. "Nope."

"Y'all finally got me a pulpit, but you need me to move it, big strong man that I am."

"Nope, not it either, Tío."

They climbed over a log and slid down a little bit of hill. Timeica and Sydney were gone by now.

"Stop guessing."

"Y'all got me a dolphin. Please don't tell me I gotta swim to this dolphin."

Mercedes cackled. "A dolphin? What the fuck? No, it's not a dolphin."

"It's a record collection, that it? Y'all act like y'all don't care for my music. Y'all think I'm some old head who talks too much, but you found me some Jeezy, and y'all thought 'aww, Bish would love these.' You shouldn't have." He batted branches away and was grateful for the talk. Felt good to laugh and not worry where harm was gonna come from. It wasn't like this in cities. Cities, he knew how to move, where to go and how to get there. Needed only a day and a night, maybe half a week at most, and could find everything he needed and quite a bit of what he wanted. Cities called to him. All the places that weren't cities contrived to hurt him, to confuse him. He didn't need that mess in his life, not at this age. Not after all he done went through.

"It something we can fit in your car?"

"Um."

And that was when they got to an opening in the trees. Mercedes stood at his side while, ahead of him, Timeica and Sydney stood or, rather, Timeica stood. Because Sydney was sitting on a horse.

"It ain't a moose," said Mercedes.

"No, it ain't," Bishop breathed. He didn't care how loudly the wonder hummed in his voice. Nor did he notice that he'd already cleared the space between him and the horses, that he already had his hand to the side of one's face. And without realizing, he had both hands against its flank, sensing that it was about to experience distress and heading that off at the pass. "No, it ain't."

He remained like that for some time, long enough for every other living thing to move so that it orbited him: Mercedes, Timeica, Sydney, the other horses, even the dragonflies and hornets and cicadas. All these things turned into planets, moons, celestial bodies revolving around him and his horse. Already, it was his horse.

He took his forehead from the horse's flank and faced Timeica and Mercedes, while Sydney continued to sit imperially on her horse.

"We was thinkin'," Timeica said, "to bring them back to the city." She shrugged, looking shy. "Don't look like they belong to anybody. They just been out here, probably since before Sydney seen 'em maybe a month ago. Winter's coming, and they'll need somewhere to stay. And it'd be good for the others, you know, to have something like this. For themselves."

Mercedes jumped in. "We figured you'd be able to help. Maybe you knew about horses."

Bishop snorted. "And why would you think that?"

"'Cause you old, nigga!" Timeica shouted, and they all laughed. Even the dragonflies and hornets and cicadas seemed to be laughing too.

ON his mattress, alone, Jonathan plumbed his memory for downloaded evidence of Eamonn's ancestors, an intimacy deeper than coitus, that data. Eamonn had given Jonathan an access key to his Cloud and, with Eamonn's superior Net connection, Jonathan had downloaded several folders of data and now waded through the flotsam of proof documented by Eamonn's ancestors that they had lived here or somewhere like here as long as a century ago. Still photographs, published essays, journal entries, blog posts, social media status updates, so much else.

Across from Jonathan is the yet-to-be-assembled bedframe and in the sunset's dying light, it blurs, its edges dissolving, until Jonathan slips completely into the simulation, blurring, his edges dissolving.

You're a student again, and you're returning to the home the family moved to after Dad died. You spent much of the bus ride working on your cover letter for a summer gig overseas.

But about the time the bus passed the exit for Sandy Hook/Newtown you put away your work and stared past the pretty girl next to you out the window. All bare branches and winding hillside road until you hit Waterbury and you started to see the spires of church towers and the smoke billowing from a nearby factory and the commercial district neatly arrayed before you as you descended the highway. From above, everything looked sharper than you remember. Cleaner. Even when you got into Hartford and there were cleared spaces that you don't remember, new parking lots, new building façades, all of it seemed sharper. More focused.

You spent most of the trip on I-84, heading steadily east in what proved to be a much speedier route than originally planned. Serendipity had you on that bus after prudence had urged you to get to Port Authority several hours early.

But when you did look out at your home state as it welcomed you back, you felt you were in some kind of shell shock. It all looked crisper. Kinder than you ever remembered it being.

You came home and after Mom picked you up from Union Station and went to bed, you played video games to keep from weeping with joy, all the time filled with images of your state as viewed from that mountain-road stretch of highway, a place that looked exactly and completely like a kingdom.

You were afraid to return to this place, terrified of experiencing the place without your father present. He was a deacon in a church there, Bethel Alliance Church on Stanley Street, but served no truly essential function in the town municipality. He was a gear, necessary the way every gear is necessary. Replaceable, but someone's machine stops if he is gone, someone's machine is in need of repair, needs to be fed.

You imagined going back someday for the long term. To live and grow there. Maybe do the family thing. Maybe you're a father by this time. And maybe, before this return, you take your son or your daughter on that ride, familiar to you, novel to him or her, on Metro-North between New Haven and Grand Central, the twice-daily voyage you made throughout early sobriety, when you were in the course, along with others, of rebuilding yourself. And maybe your kid will point out the window and you'll follow their finger, seeing the smoke billowing from the smokestacks in Bridgeport, the blackened, dilapidated cars in the junkyard, the small cathedral and the emptying factories that surround it. And you hope your kid will marvel at this, and you imagine you will smile, as if to say, "This is a beautiful kingdom and one day, it will be yours."

You won't have replaced your father. But maybe the machinery, the family that was disrupted by his removal, can hum again with unfettered, unabated life, sated, properly fed.

This nigga didn't spend no kinda money," Bugs said to no one and everyone as he lifted another batch of planks from the bed of Bishop's truck and staggered down the path to the clearing where the rest of the planks lay. "He had to move one time because shit had got hot for him, and he had just come into some money, and he was like 'aight, bet, I'ma buy a new car' 'cause he wasn't tryna be seen around the set. And his manager, who was the homie, was like 'yo, don't let 'em talk you into spendin' no kinda money on no car. You need to? Paint your mama car, but don't let 'em trick you into spendin' that money.'" He dropped the planks with a crash and didn't bother arranging them. "I was with him when we went on tour and it was like his first big festival and he had just got some of that advance check." The others moved around him, clearing more paths for the shuttling of supplies, laying down the foundations for what was supposed to be some log cabin, spreading out blueprints in another place for what looked like stables. "And we went to the ATM 'cause he had wanted to get some money, and he put his thumb on the screen and got rejected. It had said he had no money. And we're buggin' out, 'cause he don't spend like that. No car, just his bills, his mama bills, that's it. But he looked at me and he was like 'some niggas done stole my money' and we was like 'wow, we really gonna have to kill somebody.'"

Hammering filled the clearing. Jayceon and Kendrick were digging a small moat at the clearing's edge to catch rainwater and whatever would drain from the forest. Even though Rodney and Linc weren't close to the same size, they carried a big log over to this part of the forest where they could stand between two tall trees that were about eight feet apart. Then they started fastening the log perpendicular to the trees with paracord.

"But ain't nobody stole from him. It was just cost of livin', feel me? That's the thing, yo. Bein' alive is so expensive. But yeah, we ain't kill nobody over no ATM shit."

Clackin' and thumpin' filled the clearing the next day.

"That's why I can't fuck with video games, man. The rapper friend, a homie of his kept blowin' up his line, straight up harassin' him. Talkin' all kinds of shit, like gang shit too. And you know what he wanted to do? Nigga wanted to play video games. On the dead homie. Real life, he one of the nicest dudes ever. He got a wife, a kid, I think he mighta actually retired a long time ago, but you put a controller in his hands? Shit is not a game, bro. I done seen puppy-dog eyes-lookin' niggas turn into savages playin' Super Smash Brothers. Nigga could be at your cousin's baptism, then the next day, you see him on the console, he look like he ready to shoot up a school, on the dead homie. Me and the homie had went over his house one time and it wasn't even on some make-music shit. Like, we didn't really have rapper-friends like that. Like, we had niggas' numbers and we knew niggas, but we pick up the phone, it ain't to talk about no rap shit, niggas got kids and shit. Anyway, we at the other nigga's spot and he just call up a screen, 'cause he had one of them holos, and he had on the gloves, and he just starts goin'. But the whole time he lookin' at us like cuz what is you doin'?! He not even lookin' at the screen. And I'm sittin' there not tryna disturb him or fuck up his flow, but it's like he ain't even payin' attention like that. He talkin' to us about his grandmama Jamaica recipes and shit, askin' if we wanna know, because he know we be wanting to drink something fresh at the crib but only really be fuckin' with workin'-class joints. He's Mexican. But, yeah, man, you put the gloves on that nigga hands, he will *wash* you. And, like, me and the homie, we nice, but we not *him*, know what I'm sayin'?"

Bishop had told the group that the best thing was to have the structure open on one side so that it was facing the sun in the winter and so that in the summer, the prevailing winds would cool the horses. And the next day, Jayceon and Bishop got out of Bishop's truck with a ton of sheet metal and Bishop had said it would have to do because fiberglass was too hard to come by. Linc made runs with Mercedes and Rodney for more materials to store under the lean-to. And Rodney was digging holes two feet deep and one foot wide for the wooden posts to go in. Then Timeica showed up with premixed concrete to pour in, then the rest of them set the 4 x 4 posts in place, shouting back and forth about whether or not they were plumb.

"Yeah," Kendrick was saying, "the Red Store. It's like . . . I dunno, a convenience store or corner store or something, I dunno."

"So, like a bodega, then?" asked Mercedes.

"Nah, you can't get alcohol there, I don't think. But I would go there for loosies and—"

Jayceon shook his head. "Kendrick does *not* sound like an Atlanta name and you a Atlanta-ass nigga, I'm just sayin'."

Rodney tamping down as he backfilled to make sure the post was square while Bishop used a string line on the front and back to keep it in line.

"Anyway," said Kendrick. "I would always go to the Red Store with this nigga who was riding bikes. Like, *bicycle* bikes. And I would go with him because he was a licensed gun carrier. He was always wearing baggy clothes and tank tops and shorts and he would have the hammer in plain sight. Nigga would take over whole lanes of traffic and what were you gonna do? What're you gonna say to a nigga with dreads on a bike with a red bandanna and a Springfield 45 on his waist. And he sold me my first fixed-gear bike when I was a kid, because we had lived in Edgewood, we moved there when I was like ten or so."

Mercedes and Sydney running a skirt board along the back and sides of the pole barn and Linc and Bishop working to set the stringer six feet from the ground. Jayceon rushing in to help Sydney, set it on an upended box, raise the front end up to the eight-foot mark.

"Mama was a Exoduster, and Atlanta's where we wound up because we heard there was Black people there, but also the place just had this huge musical history, and she was really into that. But we

was down bad. Like, I would get bike rides to go back and forth to
the Red Store for loosies. We was by the housing projects and there
was always sirens and always toasters rollin' up, and sometimes it was
like even if bad shit was happening, you didn't want them to show up,
because then it would turn from somethin' local into some extra shit
and our place mighta been a little fucked up, but it was ours. And,
like, even then, there was this, like, young energy to it. It was kinda
crazy."

"What's the story, nigga?" Jayceon called out.

"Fuck you, nigga." Kendrick turned back around. "Anyway, we get
to maybe I been there eight, ten years, right. And you can tell things
are startin' to change. Maybe gettin' some returnees. Domes start
poppin' up in places, air starts changing, and you can tell that the shit
you're lookin' at is not how it's gonna be in like ten years, maybe five.
Maybe even two. So cherish it. But it's this one night. A summer. And
it's supposed to be dry, but the rivers make it humid and sweaty and
I was sleepin' on niggas' couches and floors by then 'cause Mama had
died and I was just broke and angry all the time but wantin' to make
music. And there was this house on Hutchinson Street that I would
stay at and it was kinda snug right in between these two other houses,
so if one person was like 'hey I'm throwin' a party tonight,' the other
two were probably okay with it. Seven days out of the week. And it
would turn into like hundreds of people showin' up. And you'd have
girls twerkin' but also weird shit like this one dude who would always
show up and he smelled like pennies and he would be in this tank top
and he'd organize these dung beetle battles. And the dung beetles,
'cause of the way the radiation hits down there, they almost the size
of dogs. Nigga, I'm not lyin'!"

Half the crowd groaned, half the crowd laughed. Then they
switched off.

"Anyway, we're at this party, right? One of these epic summer parties. And, like, the homie Hurley had just bought a 357. We called him
Hurley because he was always wanting to buy one of them motorcycles
and look like one of them rednecks out west, but could never say the
name right. He was white, but he was just as broke and left-behind as

the rest of us. Anyway, he got this gun he just got, right? And people show up to these things with hammers all the time. People are showin' off their shit out back and in the hallways, people are fuckin' in random rooms. That kind of energy. But yeah at one point, Hurley comes out of his room and he's like 'someone just snatched my Flex.' And he had *just* bought this thing. It was one of the big joints that you had to attach to a separate touchboard but it could call up multiple holo screens at the same time. And he had bought it the same time as the gun. So he runs outside and he's like 'someone grabbed my shit, what the fuck' startin' to go crazy, and we're askin' people. And that's when you hear this car peel off. FRREWWW. Just like that, and you *know* that's the niggas that took his shit. And Hurley, poor guy, is runnin' after this thing in his fuckin' big-ass boots he's always wearing even though it's hotter than fuckin' donkey balls in Atlanta at that time. But the night kinda ends with that sad, despair-type energy. Because Hurley, man, he had so little, and to see a guy like that lose, it just kinda fucks everything up. The party's still goin' on, so we're startin' to tell people 'yo, you gotta leave,' you know, kickin' them out. Until I see Hurley go out front. Literally right in the front yard of these houses, and he raises his gun in the air and starts bustin' shots. POW POW POW. And that gets everybody out."

Add another 2 x 4-inch (5.08 x 10.16 cm) grit on the side, level with the one you placed against the bottom of the stringer at the back.

Mercedes: "That'll clear out a party."

"So we're all just kinda sitting in this dude's living room, feelin' sorry for him. But there's still that energy in the air, so it's gotta go somewhere. And you know that weird friend you have, who's like, into prog metal and like holo-hentai and shit, real weird but watches anime and could kinda fuck you up? We nicknamed him Tetsuo after this old anime we would watch on his dusty-ass Blu-ray player. Anyway, he gets everybody goin' over the night. Like, who was there, who was where, when this person came in, when that person left, whose car they were in, all this shit. Like actually sittin' there cracking the case of who stole my man's Flex."

Nail the 2 x 4-inch (5.08 x 10.16 cm) wood flat on one end. Use

2 x 6-inch (5.08 x 15.24 cm) wood for the roof rafters that sit on 4-foot (1.22-meter) centers.

"Fast-forward to the next day. We're in Hurley's room. Everybody's makin' calls, trying to figure out who was at this party. And Tetsuo's on the socials and he finds a picture of this girl and he's like 'that's it; that's the girl. I know this the shorty that took your shit.' And I'm asking why he thinks that, and what's also in that girl's account is a photo of the dude who he thinks took Hurley's shit. And then underneath is a caption: 'these dumb niggas.'"

"Holy shit," from Timeica.

"And then he's like, 'look, dude has on a purse.' And it was one of those purses you kinda wear across your front and, like, over your shoulder. Oh, I forgot. Dude also took Hurley's bullets. So all he's got to his name is the gun and the bullets in it."

"Six, right?" Wyatt asked. "357 holds six."

"Yeah, but he bust half them shits into the air the night of the party."

"Oh, shit." Wyatt reared back a little. The reporter's eyes went wide.

"But anyway, so that's the caption, and I'm like 'this is it? This the evidence?' And he's like 'one *thousand* percent.' So we head out, but just as we head out, we get a call from *another* nigga who was at the party who was like 'I know where the nigga be,' all cryptic and shit. And he's like 'you ain't hear it from me. Can't let nobody know I know, but this where the nigga be.' Then click."

Fasten metal hurricane hold-down straps to the posts and to the rafters to prevent high wind gusts from pulling the roof off of the support posts.

"And now there's like four, five of us, and we're not all, like, goons and shit. We're weird kids who watch hentai-holos and listen to trap metal. But it's go-time. We all know what we gotta do. We need to get over there and get Hurley's shit back. But we squeeze into the car and there's like five of us squeezed into there and at least three of us are carrying firearms. And not all of 'em got permits. So we go on a drive, and we head up toward the Lennox area of Atlanta. Now, get this. Tetsuo had even geotagged it to the specific apartment they were in."

Overlap 29-gauge galvanized corrugated roofing panel by 2 inches (5.08 cm) to the skirtboard, stringers, and grits. Cut to fit using a circular saw fitted with a metal cutoff blade on the sloped sides.

"So we get to the apartment building and this nigga Tetsuo even disabled the scanners by the entrance so they wouldn't tag us for being exposed to too much radiation. Or something, because somehow we got in there and we go up in the hallway, and I'm like 'okay, so we knock on this door, what are we about to do?' Like, we could really all be finna die in this hallway, you know what I'm sayin'? And over what? A Flex? I don't know how it wound up this way, but I wind up bein' the nigga that gotta stand in front of the camera. So I knock on the door and this girl opens the door and is like 'who the fuck is you?' And I'm thinkin' I'm gonna just cut straight to the chase, so I tell her 'you were at my house last night. Something went missing. I'm just here to get it back.' Now, remember, there's a gang a niggas right next to me at the door, but she can't see 'em. So she's like 'look, you need to get the fuck outta my house. I don't know what you're talking about.'

"Soon as the homies hear that, they all come in behind me, so she sees it's like five niggas on the other side of her open door and she. Breaks. Down! I'm talkin' snot-crying. 'Oh my God, I'm so sorry, I didn't know!' Just crumples. Two of her friends come out, see what's happenin', they go down too. Flump! We thought we was gonna have to bust in this door and be like 'aye I'ma beat this nigga brains in till he confess' or 'I'ma sew his asshole shut and keep feedin' him till he tell me where my shit' or whatever. Like, we really thought we was gonna get in a shootout with some niggas over a piece of technology the size of my fuckin' palm. But, no, it's just five niggas in a room all of a sudden tryna console these girls who have just completely lost it by now. And I'm rubbin' the first one's back like 'I'm so sorry, I ain't mean to come across like a threat, we're sorry for scarin' you' like, when I tell you how funny it got, just like that?" Kendrick snapped his fingers, and the reporter started. "Then she starts tellin'. Snitched on everybody. Said the caption wasn't talking about us but about the niggas she was with. Told us this is where he is, this is where he hangs out, all that. And right there on the counter is the box of bullets."

Add doors to the front by building a 2 x 4-foot (.61 x 1.22-meter) frame. Use the same sheet metal as the roof and walls, and hang it from the post.

"Then one of the homies grabs my arm, and he's like 'we gotta go' and I'm still thinkin' I still gotta convince this girl I'm not about to kill her, but he's like jerkin' me out the room. And I'm like 'what's up' and he tells us that there's a guy back at Hurley's crib who says he beat up the dude who stole Hurley's shit. Right at the old West End MARTA station. That's our train system. It was still runnin' in certain places around that time, but they shut down a bunch of stops. West End was still goin' tho. So we're in the car, and the dude's on the phone like 'yeah, I saw the nigga and I knew he was the one who took Hurley's shit so I just started bustin' his ass.' And on our way, we pass by the West End station, and Tetsuo's like 'STOP! STOP! STOP THE CAR!'"

The reporter's mouth hung open. "What was it?" she breathed.

"Hurley's Flex, sittin' right on top of a bag. Apparently, during the fight, dude getting whooped just dropped the bag and booked it onto a train while the doors was closing. And the whole time—because that fight was happenin' same time as we ran up on them girls—the whole time between that ending and us gettin' there, no one took the shit.

"So that's how we found Hurley's Flex."

Finish with preformed foam sealer strips that fit between the roofing and joist.

"That is an Atlanta-ass story," Jayceon said, hands on his hips while all of them—Bishop, Rodney, Mercedes, Timeica, Sydney, Bugs, Kendrick, Linc, and the reporter—looked up at the horse barn they'd built. "You a Atlanta-ass nigga."

"Thank you, kind sir," Kendrick replied, eyebrow arched, shoulders aching, smirking at their barn.

Bishop made the rounds, picking everybody up from where they lived downtown. It was almost like he was getting them ready for work. But none of them had their hammers with them, just themselves and a sparkling sense of mission. It was early in the day, the blue-dawn hour, dew-fresh and cool. There was no plan, no time set to go pick up the horses from Fairfield and bring them to their new home in West Rock.

There'd been some residual touches put on the stables, the clearing away of brush and the installation of a bootleg filtration machine for Lake Wintergreen, just east of the mountain ridge. Linc and a few of the others had gone back to add extensions to the barn, and they'd worked in relative silence. No storytelling, no real out-loud joking. All conversation happened in their bodies, put this here and slide that over there, fasten it here, lift, hold, nail. And like that, more stables had been built. It looked like the populating of a small town on that field in the shadow of the south prominence of West Rock. By now, some of the housing development residents had come down, either to gawk or complain or help or marvel or joke. And every time one of the children asked what was going on and Linc said, "Horses," the kid's eyes would light up like they were made of diamonds. Stoic and near soundless, the men even let the kids sometimes play with the old power washer they'd borrowed from Bishop, feigning injury and death when the little warrior turned it on them.

One morning, a few of the young men had come back to see saddles hung on nails in the tack room. No note left behind, no evidence of past ownership. No idea where they'd come from, but the boys looked at them and knew what they said. They said, "This place is ours." So they silently thanked the residents and took the saddles with them, and now the saddles sat on their laps as they rode in the back of Bishop's truck to that small clearing in Fairfield where the miracle horses lounged, munching on the grass.

None of them said a word as Bishop pulled over on the side of the broken road and the crew piled out and moved in hushed, whispered steps down the path through the forest. Even the stackers who were making this trip for the first time stepped with sureness.

Sydney and Timeica led the way, followed by Bugs. Then came Kendrick and Jayceon and finally Linc. Rodney, citing his leg, begged off.

When they finally came to the clearing, they stood for several minutes in awe, watching the horses be. Bugs had his jaw open the whole time, the rest of the world gone to him. Jayceon drew a sharp breath, brought up short. Kendrick crouched on his haunches and smiled. Linc began to tremble.

Sydney and Timeica grinned at the group, satisfied with their work. Then, one by one, the boys passed their saddles to Timeica and Sydney, who saddled the horses and tugged and made sure everything fit like it was supposed to.

Jayceon was the first on his horse. There was a moment after Timeica helped him up where he looked unstable, like he was ready to fight the thing underneath him. And the clearing held its breath, and Sydney shot him a warning, as though to say, "Don't you dare hurt this horse," but a relaxing flooded through the space, and Jayceon grew taller and gentler at the same time.

Kendrick was up next, looking as though he'd been born on a horse. Linc let Sydney help him up, but before she boosted him into his saddle, they looked at each other and put their foreheads close and seemed to kiss. Then he was up on his horse. Bugs rushed to his own horse, electric with energy, and the horse, not knowing him yet, reared and skipped backward. Timeica got the horse by the reins and called Bugs out in the softest voice possible, then led the horse back and let the two of them speak silently before it seemed Bugs and the horse had come to an agreement and Timeica boosted him up.

Sydney and Timeica were the last up on their horse, Timeica with her arms wrapped around Sydney's waist.

Sydney said, "Like this," and led them in a slow circle around the clearing. They formed a line and followed her, squinting at how she moved her legs, squeezed her thighs against the horse's flanks and loosened, how she held the reins, and each boy became an item of homage to her. They made circuit after circuit after circuit until she could tell that their bodies had learned it all, that they didn't need to think about it anymore, and just like that she led them up out of the clearing, sticking to flat ground and winding around the base of the cliff to another, smoother incline. The forest chirped and sang around them. Then they emerged onto the street, closer to the QZ and farther from Bishop's truck than when they'd first entered the green.

It was Rodney who first saw the group coming from behind him and Bishop.

Bishop was working his chewing stick and had his elbow hanging outside his window. His gaze lost itself somewhere in the middle distance, and it was Rodney who brought him back.

"Look at 'em," Rodney said, and it was the awe in his voice that got Bishop out of his truck and into the middle of the road to watch them coming. Five of them in two rows with Sydney and Timeica up front. Clopping regularly and deliberately, not like an army, but like the people who command one.

Rodney clambered out after Bishop, and they both had their hands on their hips while the royal family drew near.

Bishop looked up at Sydney and Timeica, who sat imperially on their horses, the sun silhouetting them from behind.

"Y'all need an escort?"

Sydney looked to Timeica, who smirked and nodded, then she turned back to Bishop. "I reckon we'll take one," she said in a Kentucky accent.

Bishop snorted. "Will it scare the horses if I honk the horn a few times? Announce our arrival into town?"

"We got it, Bishop," Timeica replied with a wink.

"All right, then. Let's get a move on, then. Mercedes been at the farm all day." He shook his head on the way back to his car. "Can you believe that, Rodney?" he said once they were both in.

Rodney adjusted in his seat and chuckled. "Changes a person. Bein' on a horse." His accent had changed.

"Not you too," Bishop said, starting the car, smiling.

Others had helped Jonathan load the furniture, some of it wooden, some of it metal and misshapen, into the husk of a living room, but when Jonathan, soaked through his layers, turned to thank them, they were gone. The Black neighbors and other nearby residents who saw this lost, misbegotten white boy trying to do an impossible thing with almost no help. Maybe they were laughing at him. Maybe they were too occupied with the business of their own lives to laugh at him. Sometimes, though, he would hear laughter.

Like now.

Around him, wet paint in open buckets; over his mouth, his filtration mask, waging war on two fronts, against both residual radiation and paint fumes. In one hand, a thick paintbrush, and in the other, his Flex.

There was still no blue dome on his street yet, nor could he afford a single-dwelling shield. Perhaps it was the David in him that was secretly content not to have one, not to have those helping him find in his home the safety of fully breathable air only to return to their irradiated reality when he's gotten what he needed from them.

Impatient, he scrolled through the instructions on his Flex: How to Properly Paint Your Furniture in 5 Steps.

Step 1: Sand it. A paragraph followed, first telling of all those erroneous tutorials that dispense with sanding. Then, after that disclaimer came instructions to use 150-grit sandpaper. A link brought him to a separate page about orbital sanders and where to buy them from. Jonathan recognized none of the store names, had seen nothing he recognized in all his time in New Haven and its environs. Getting ahold of a car or truck to go searching would take too much time and money he didn't have, and he couldn't bear begging the neighbors for any more than they'd already given him. Be careful not to gouge the surface, you just want to give the primer something to adhere to and—

He had no primer. He couldn't get past Step 1 because he had no primer. And what the fuck even was primer?

The paintbrush trembled in his grip. He saw in his mind's eye the aftermath of the tantrum: the paint cans kicked over, the walls gouged out even further by some hammer that must have been lying around, the metal table with the bent legs bent even further, the window glass shattered from whatever broken piece of wood he'd thrown through it. And he had risen to bring about the vision when the laughter arrived.

He realized only now that he'd been standing. He dropped the paintbrush onto the floor he knew he would have to tear up again at some point in the disordered list of tasks he'd put together over the past several months.

Then he was on the ground, staring at the ceiling.

The windows. He forgot to open the windows. Why didn't he open the windows?

The ceiling melted toward him in the shape of Eamonn, and it was like wood and plaster dripping from the ceiling where it melted and landing on his cheeks and sliding into his ears and landing on every other part of his body but with the force of a stone thrown so that every joint ached, every piston rusted and every gear made the sound of bone against bone, the sound of protest. Plaster dripped onto the rest of the apartment's upturned interior: it rained holes in the cushion of his futon, it splintered the wood of his desks.

Then, the ceiling throbbed with the shape of David. Jonathan willed his eyes to remain open, fearing that if he should close them, if he should blink, the vision would change back, and David would leave him, and Eamonn would be what was left. Eamonn and the black closing in on him from the edges of his vision, swallowing the world around him without chewing until—

The laughter drew him out of the swamp. His body moved before his mind could follow, and he found himself at his front door. Wind whistled through an open window.

For several long seconds, he stared at that window. Not open, but opened. He blinked himself awake and passed through the threshold.

The air had cooled some. It no longer sizzled with late summer. And the kids were wearing jackets, jackets with holes in them and patches taped up, jackets as worn down as the laceless sneakers on their feet, and they all seemed to be running in one direction, a whole gaggle of them, then another bunch would round the corner. And watching them winded Jonathan. He coughed into his hand, and oil-colored blood spilled through its nozzles. He knew he should go around the house and open the rest of the windows, it occurred to him that it was an act of stupidity to try painting with them closed to begin with, but all he seemed to be able to do was stagger all the way through the front door, the screen door clattering shut behind him.

Nobody noticed him as the kids vanished in the tree-smothered distance. The spoiled filtration device that had been affixed to his face came loose, and he let it fall to the landing.

Drunken steps took Jonathan down his porch. *Follow them,* his body told him. As he came to the street, he turned to look at this half house of his, this thing he'd been so excited to prepare for David, this thing he'd hoped to have finished by the time David came, this work he thought he could wring out of the earth with his own hands, and he wiped his palm over his eyes and forehead, trying to dash away tears but only coloring them red. This was what he had to give David. This was the best he could do. This monument to his inadequacy.

So he turned back around and followed the children.

He followed them down the cracked concrete and the twisted fencing, past the chipped painting on the awnings of their homes, past the duplexes, down past the backyards with the tarp covering the pools and past the sheds where the grills and tongs and other picnic tools gathering cobwebs. He followed them down wood trails and through scrub brush until he crested a hill. By now, the laughter, a siren song, had grown louder, fuller. A chorus. And out in the field beneath him were stables and, amid the children and teenagers and their parents, horses.

It was a dream. It had to be. Even as he made his way down the hillside path to the fence enclosing the field, he felt it was a dream. Some of the neighborhood children had their faces pressed up against the gritty metal fencing, giggling as some of the parents went about distributing masks. There was no dome here, but perhaps this place didn't need one, existing as it did somewhere outside the confines of this coastal city, somewhere beyond the bounds of despair and thwarted ambition.

People Jonathan didn't recognize rode tall atop the horses, some of them with long-handled hammers in their saddlebags, and children crowded around one of the riders as he emerged from the stable on his horse and then broke away and did a circuit of the field at a fast canter. Beyond was more field, and maybe this was where the galloping happened.

And Jonathan didn't know how long he'd been standing by that fence, mouth agape, in stupid wonder, before a Black woman nudged him and held out a single-use mask. Reflex almost had him telling her that he had mechanized insides that would last longer than her natural organs, that his lungs were built more durable than hers, that he was repairable, but he couldn't figure out how to tell her these things without telling her she was not, so he took the mask and fitted it to his face and watched the horses and thought of David, how beautiful he would find this sight.

The kitchen cupboards blew dust at Jonathan whenever he opened them, stinging his eyes to the point of tears.

"Mosta the heavy lifting's been done," said Eamonn from another room in the abandoned house. "But there are a few things in the basement we were saving for later."

Jonathan couldn't let go of the cupboard doors. "Yeah," he murmured because he knew Eamonn had said something, but he couldn't remember what, couldn't hear it, wouldn't have heard it if Eamonn had said it right into his ear. They were too full of the memory of horse hooves thump-thumping against the grass.

In the living room, there was no carpet, no photos, no calendars hanging from the pins in the wall. Jonathan wasn't even sure the lamps worked. There were only two folding chairs, carrying basement dust and rusted into an eternal seated position.

In the basement, no longer cramped with boxes full of old toys or whatever other old school stuff families always left here in between their children's school semesters, stuff which, as they would all get older, would remain with greater and greater permanence where they stood or sat or leaned, the duffle bags with broken zippers and the rolling shelves and inadequate laundry bags and small detergent containers and sports gear sticking out of their shadowed corners. Every time Eamonn brought Jonathan here for another raid, there was less and less stuff.

In the gutted and almost noiseless basement, they loaded a large freezer onto a wheeled cart. The only sound, birds and rustled grass and a game of cornhole played in a neighbor's front lawn, came through the opened shed door.

The plan was to get it upright, leaned at an ideal angle, and up the stone steps through the door and out onto the backyard by the drive-way where Eamonn's truck waited.

Eamonn secured the thing on the wheeled cart, moved with ease around the weight of it, practiced effortlessness, as though this were the type of thing he took from houses all the time. Jonathan got one foot on the first step, the other propped beneath him, ready to step back and pull the thing while Eamonn lifted.

"You get the top, I'll get the bottom," Eamonn said.

Jonathan had the open air to his back.

"You got it?"

Jonathan nodded, exasperated, eager to get the thing up and out. "Yeah. Yeah, I got it." Jonathan waited for it, then it came, the tight-ening in his back as the thing moved, step by jolting step, up the stairs. Jonathan wondered if he was doing it wrong, if it hurt too much the way he was doing it and there wasn't some easier way to go about this.

They hauled the thing up and got it straight and upright on a cor-ner of driveway close to Eamonn's truck.

Jonathan straightened, the small of his back aflame. "Look," he said, back arched, frowning, narrow-slit gaze pitched toward the ce-rulean sky with clouds floating like stuffing from a slit pillow, prepar-ing himself.

"Yeah?" Eamonn asked, and it sounded like he was lighting another cigarette.

"I can't see you anymore."

The atomizer flicked. Flicked. Flicked.

Jonathan saw him light up and straighten, crack his shoulders, ro-tate them a little bit.

"Now, we just gotta get it on the truck," Eamonn said without finishing his smoke.

But Jonathan found he couldn't move, and suddenly, tightness took his chest and squeezed and squeezed and squeezed until his breath came out in a single sob, and he didn't know if the tears in his eyes came from the constriction around his heart, air-poison at work, or from some deeper, more profound well. But here he was, bent over his knees, hidden by furniture from the man who had helped him find this home, and whatever he felt that made his hands tremble as he put them together, shaking, to his lips was a misery large enough to dwarf the cramp itching the small of his back, large enough to snatch at the air from his lungs, to squeeze it out until, even closing his eyes, the tears rolled down his cheeks and he forgot where he was and when he straightened, trembling, a hand resting against the freezer for support, he looked around to try and see if anyone else was watching. If David, somehow, from his perch in the Colony, could see him. He sniffed, wiped his eyes with the heels of his palms. Sniffed again. He could breathe. Several large breaths later, he turned to face the work of lifting the fridge and was startled when he saw Eamonn staring at him.

"I'm sorry," Jonathan said, not knowing why. "Fuck, yeah, it was just, it was something in my eye."

The expression on Eamonn's face didn't change. "What did you say?"

Jonathan sniffed. "I'm not fucking you anymore." Something powered his arms and his legs, told him to work through the hurt in his back, that the labor would clear the emotional congestion from his chest. He'd already gotten his hands on the fridge and the wheeled cart. "C'mon," he said, gesturing with his head toward the truck, "let's get this loaded before it gets too dark. The streetlights don't come on here."

Eamonn still stared, not with judgment, not with pity, not with anything Jonathan recognized. Then, face still made of stone, he joined Jonathan, and together, they unstrapped the freezer and loaded it onto the flatbed, and Jonathan dusted his hands on his jeans and looked at the thing where it lay and was happy he could still breathe and that the only pain he felt, the only immediate pain, was the cramp at the small of his back.

They climbed into Eamonn's truck, and Eamonn pressed his index finger to the ignition pad, Eamonn's finger glowing as the thing rumbled to life.

"He won't know about us unless you want him to," Eamonn told

Jonathan as they backed out of the driveway and onto the darkening road.

"Thank you," Jonathan said back, though the words were lost under the growl of the engine.

This wasn't the first thing Timeica ever remembers, because even her earliest memories have Wyatt in them, him having preceded her by almost six years. But her first memory of being alone, not lonely, just alone, was in a backyard, on the edge of a forest. Night, just fallen, had turned the whole world sapphire, and there must've been little to no light pollution, because the stars could easily be counted and the moon cast its own guiding light over the patch of grass on which she sat.

She had the soles of her feet pressed against each other. She couldn't remember if she was wearing shoes or not, but the wetness beneath her ass chilled itself into indelibility. The place wasn't recognizably Chicago. But she always attached the place to what Chicago meant, made it the second entry in the dictionary's definition of Chicago. It always seemed to be nighttime in the memory, even as she knew she had wandered that forest during the day. Maybe it was the furtiveness of it, the transgression that wandering entailed, that unheeding of Mama's "get back here" and "Heaven help me if I find you" and "where's Wyatt" that cast night over every remembrance of the forest and her promenades therein.

It could have been forest anywhere. Not just Chicago, but all throughout that line in the Midwest that she and Wyatt had followed when lung rot had gotten Mama and they'd lost their last reason to stay. At first, Wyatt would hound Timeica for her wandering like she didn't already know about the white Marauders that would kidnap you in your sleep and kill you or sell you to some place you could never come back from and the cannibals and the mechs and the sheriffs and the low-grade war between and among them on those gray swathes of former neighborhood. But everywhere they stopped, outside of every domed city, was some vestige of forest.

The farther east they migrated, the less alone Timeica felt on her journeys. That prized lonesomeness, that privilege of solitude she had gathered about her in the quiet of the verdant tranquility, the red of the sky and the gray of the earth began to leech. Paper burger wrappers strewn around tree trunks, hypodermic needles crushed beneath a stampede of heedless bootheels or plain bare feet. Used and unused condoms. Sometimes hotplates or a makeshift rice cooker, or a pot of hot water and cut-open Coke cans for cups. Evidence of people leaving in a hurry. She could no longer be alone in these places because the shame of what people had done to each other hung thick from the branches like rotted, blood-dotted laundry, choked the pride and dignity out of the whole enterprise and left her walking back to Wyatt with shoulders hunched, feet dragging, in a posture of shamefulness, as though a guilty conscience were pulling her back to confess her sin.

Along a side of highway, they couldn't tell which one as the signs had long since rotted, Wyatt leaned against their car, chewing bits of a taco he'd bought a while back. He had wanted to get far enough out of town that Marauders or less organized bandits wouldn't see them enjoying their meal. Timeica wanted to needle him about how ridiculous his caution was, but then she remembered sneaking past Wyatt's room one time when Mama was alive and hearing her reprimand him for wearing his red Blackhawks hoodie out at night, chiding him with great desperation about how dangerous it was, and Timeica had thought she was talking about gangs but would later learn she was talking about cops. Mama lit into Wyatt fierce about it, in his ear about how we had to be twice as good for half as much and how they didn't need an excuse to make you a corpse and Timeica had stood frozen by that crack in the door, staring at Wyatt with his head down looking at his lap, utterly still because he hated hearing this stuff again and hated even more that it was all true.

From the back seat, Timeica looked out over the unending sprawl of former farmland. It was desert on both sides, rendering this slice of southern Illinois indistinguishable from the Texas she saw on the Net or in the pictures Madeline would send her via Flex of her own family's odyssey through the South.

Telephone lines sagged toward the earth, the poles to which they were connected curled like a gang sign. The occasional abandoned house or dwelling that Timeica would think was abandoned but Wyatt would warn her was not had melted windows and sometimes a roof was missing and sometimes dogs chewed carrion out front and sometimes a banner would be hung or a name spray-painted in radiation tag marking the spot as territory belonging to one set or another. Whenever they drove by, Timeica would follow the outposts with her gaze, trying to figure out how street gangs adjusted to a place where there were no more streets. How could their ambitions expand to fit such vastness?

Timeica asked Wyatt this around a small fire by the side of a highway, in a little ditch that managed to hide much of their flame, according to Wyatt. And in Wyatt's face was a moment of contemplation, of empathetic projection. "Maybe it's like when you realize you could do something physically that you couldn't before. Like you short your forty-time or you do a few more push-ups than you could yesterday. You can stretch yourself out a little bit. Imagine you claim a set and instead of a street corner, you get all this." He waved his arm up and down the strip of highway, indicating its entirety.

She had an idea of what he was talking about, but couldn't square it with why someone would want all this. "What do you do with this, though?"

Wyatt shrugged. "Own it." He was thinking of the purple, patterned banner hanging down the front of that last house. A cemetery, someone else's cemetery, lay in a plot right next to it.

She squinted into the darkness. "Is this what happens?" A memory of their old kitchen and Mama and one of their uncles sitting across a table and that uncle wearing glasses and drinking something dark and sweet.

"When you push someone out, yeah. This was before your time, before the red dust, but it's like what they did to Brooklyn decades back. New York, really, before it got evacuated."

"Like when the rent goes up?"

"Yeah. Like when the rent goes up."

There was nothing she could see in the darkness, but she looked anyway, the wall just as impenetrable as it had been a moment ago. "Who're we pushing out, then?"

"We ain't pushin' anyone out. You think if white people wanted any of this, they'd let anyone from Grove Street have it?" He chuckled, and Timeica didn't quite understand why.

They'd get to cities—Gary, Indiana; Cleveland, Ohio—and Wyatt would tense for the first week until, she realized, he knew where the patrols were and where they weren't, whether the police here skirted the perimeters of the Bounded City with red-blood cops or mechs and would seem almost goddamned relieved when he saw a purple dragon in profile tagged on a wall or the Grove Street marijuana leaf.

She grew to grudgingly accept the cities, so that by the time they'd arrived in the East, she could wander the collapsed opera halls and hollowed-out factory buildings and voided school gymnasiums and find in them the same reverent quiet she'd once looked for in forests. Her footsteps, in those moments, echoing in the cavernous maws of the opera hall, the factory floor, or the gymnasium, would be the only thing wrong with those perfect places.

Wyatt never let Timeica see his hurt, tried, at least. And Timeica remembered much of their trip thinking he hurt for having lost Mama. But in those soft, warm moments stopped on the side of the road or seeking shelter beneath an overpass, from flying mechs or Marauders or the wild-eyed, double-jawed monsters that only seemed to move across that land at night, Timeica saw him smile a smile that wasn't yet wistful.

Chicago had still been teeming with life by the time they'd left. Too many people for the jobs that paid. And within the Dome, folks were still tearing each other to pieces. When Mama died, their blood-tie to the place broken, they knew they had no choice but to leave. It was what Mama would have wanted.

Here, farther east, Wyatt's smile turned into the kind that recalls a memory or a place where something was better, kinder, freer, and it never occurred to Timeica until then to think of her older brother as a frontiersman. They'd been privileged, she realized, to have lived on the edge of undiscovered country, and it hurt Wyatt that they'd had to give that up.

In West Virginia, there was still forest. Varying green shades that rose up small mountains into misty diadems.

One fogged morning, Timeica rose before Wyatt and bounded into the forest by the side of the Interstate, her pistol slapping against her thigh, her knife sheath bobbing beneath her armpit. Giggling, giddy, she soon remembered her proper posture and let her shuffles become the only noise announcing her passage.

The forest ended.

Like a blanket had been lifted from her eyes, a pitted, ravaged moonscape lay before her, bits of honeycombed earth held up on stilts where the things hadn't yet collapsed.

Shock kept her from crying until she returned to their tent, and when she did finally start bawling, Wyatt held her like he knew why she was weeping. And she let him hold her because she knew he did.

Jonathan had a wool blanket draped over a coat draped over his shoulders as he sat on the front porch of his yet-unfinished home. The new freezer deep in the bowels of the house had brought with it a new serenity, what one of the other settlers called an insh'allah attitude, something she'd learned traveling somewhere in Mesopotamia. A sort of "it'll get done when it gets done" mindset. A leaving-behind of control, so that everything that happened was its own miracle. Even the mug of hot chocolate in his gloved fingers.

David hadn't said what time he'd be arriving at, as neither of them could guess at the time difference between New Haven and the Colonies. As soon as news came that David's paperwork had gone through and the next wave of arrivals was scheduled to fly out, Jonathan had insisted on being at the shuttle station to meet David, and when David had rebuffed him, Jonathan had insisted on meeting him at the Fairfield Station. But David had said no to that as well, perhaps understanding without even having to be told that Jonathan was in the process of assimilating this new mindset into his thinking. Learning that he didn't need to be the dictator of all things. How had David changed in the meantime?

He arrested that line of inquiry before it could spiral into paranoia and instead schooled himself into being present for this quiet, for the sound of winter around him and the feel of it in the seat of his torn jeans. For the moonlit clouds and the lights winking out in window after window on his street, some of them staying on for Jonathan to wonder at what sort of life was lived in those rooms. When David finally came, Jonathan would begin introducing him to their neighbors and showing him the stable, closed for the season, where kids rode horses.

A truck rounded a corner and emerged from the darkness, sounding of Eamonn. But when it pulled up in front of Jonathan's house, Aurora was at the wheel. "Look who I found," she crowed, just as the passenger's side door swung open then shut and David revealed himself, standing still in the street, gilded by the truck's headlamps.

For five of the longest seconds of Jonathan's life, they held each other's gaze, not knowing where to begin but wanting to tell it all and wanting, at the same time, to hold some of it back, to tell it in its own time. *How much life have you lived without me?*

"Come to the bonfire!" Aurora hollered. Her fox had migrated to her lap, its tail feather-dusting her face.

Jonathan stood, too suddenly, and hot chocolate splashed onto his gloves and his blanket fell off his shoulders. He heard chuckling behind him as he turned around and was secretly grateful he could give David this to laugh at. "One second, I . . ."

"No, come on! They're already getting started. David said he's already down. Bring whatever it is you're drinking!" Her commands overrode whatever objections might have grown inside Jonathan, so he gathered his blanket into his arm and tried to negotiate his self-insulating mug, pressing the button that slid a lid over it, and he made his way down the steps.

David said nothing as he opened the back door for Jonathan and Jonathan climbed in, only smiled. He was still smiling as he came in after Jonathan, sitting beside him, close, lovers-close, and Aurora set off.

Jonathan still struggled to muster something meaningful to say, but David pulled out his Flex.

"Look," he said, in a quiet voice as he pulled a video from his Cloud. "We passed the sun on the way in." He started the video. "These are the magnetic fields coming out of the sun's active regions, and this is the hot plasma tracing them." Ribbons of gold undulating in arcs and fans, as though sustained by movement. "When the loop breaks, you get a solar flare, and the charged particles go speeding out into space, and that's how you get aurora at the Earth's poles."

Jonathan stared, transfixed.

"Did you catch it here?"

"No," said Jonathan quietly. "I think we're a little too far south to see these, but it's beautiful. You saw this on your way in?"

"We did." David ended the video, then leaned his head on Jonathan's shoulder and was soon asleep, even as the truck jangled over the poorly laid magnetic lines under the cracked concrete.

Later, around the fire, David remained quiet while the others danced in their flannel jackets and passed around spiked cider someone had made.

"I was reading," David said at last, "about these people at the South Pole." His voice was softer, his words slower, and Jonathan wondered if that was still the travel lag dragging at him or just another deep and meaningful change Jonathan hadn't been a part of. "They set up camps in the emptiness and look for meteor fragments. They camp near the base of the Graves Nunataks—it's an Iñupiaq word, a rock exposed over an ice sheet. The temperature gets below negative-twelve Fahrenheit, but there's almost no wind, and when it's there, it kind of walks slowly over the snow. The light has this flat quality to it. And it's one of the few remaining places where the atmosphere is transparent enough that the mountains in the distance—those crisp edges—can seem so close, even though they're so far away. And you'll be kneeling over this patch of bluish ice, surrounded as far as you can see by snow, and you'll be looking at this tiny thing just below the surface. People go there looking for meteorites." At this, he looked up at Jonathan and smiled.

"That sounds so . . . isolated."

"Doesn't it?" David replied dreamily.

Jonathan considered the boy huddled next to him. *What if it never snows here?* "Come on. I want to show you something." He hoped David couldn't hear the desperation in his words or see the furtiveness in his movements—see him looking for any trace of Eamonn—as they moved through the woods. If David wanted a place cut off from the rest of the world, a place where no notification could ping on your Flex and nothing could be added to or removed from your Cloud, a place devoid of announcements and news and questions, a place encased in magic, Jonathan would show him.

So he hurried this boy he loved through the woods and brought him to the hill's edge and pointed at the darkness that encased the field.

"What am I looking at?" David still had his mug of cider in his hands.

"There's a field there. Adjust your eyes."

And David did, calibrating his eyesight, tuning and adjusting frequencies.

"Do you see it?"

"Is that a . . . is that a stable?"

"For horses," Jonathan said, grinning.

David shook his head. "How do horses happen here?"

Jonathan laughed. "Magic, I dunno."

"Do they have implants? Are they mechanized?" The questions were breathed, as though they weren't even meant for Jonathan, who suddenly felt so stupid standing next to this man. Why did he think David might ever want a place teeming with life, with birds flying across the sky and plants growing, with animal tracks remaining in the soil until rain came or humans with their own bootprints? Why did he think David might have ever wanted to hear the gurgle of flowing water?

"I'm sure they're beautiful," David said, indicating in the way he turned that it was time to head back to the group.

Moonlight cut through the forest almost at random, but sometimes David would pass through a beam, and that was when Jonathan saw it.

The patches, the tears, the worn-ness of it. His old leather jacket.

It fit David perfectly.

You get rough hands," Linc said to Jayceon, feet dangling over the flaking steel waterfront pier. He felt the patches where duct tape had been put over his holes. Took off the gloves to stare at the skin of his palms, pale beneath the moonlight. Kendrick picked up bits of stone and shrapnel behind them and tossed them into the ocean. The whole place smelled like seaweed and skunk, but the moon shone bright overhead and he could pinpoint just where in relation to the celestial body the Colony hovered. It was a speck no bigger than the farthest star, but he imagined he could see it rotating. "Rough feet too, walking around in them boots all day, kicking piles of trash. Feel like I'm turning into a brick." He turned his hands over, let them sit in his lap. "You think anyone up there got hands like us?"

Bugs was on Linc's other side, hands limp in his lap, just staring out into the water. The look on his face telling of the moment you're watching something drift away and it finally settles in your brain stem that you'll never see it again. Maybe being reminded of his old neighborhood when they'd gone to pick up Ace and seen him get thrown out his house had done something to him. Realizing how little must have been rebuilt after the storm, how Bugs could no longer pretend it was a place he could go back to, maybe that was what had his face like that. Linc wanted to pat him on the leg or punch his arm, but instead just looked away, pretending his own thousand-yard stare, hoping his posture said "it won't feel like this forever" loud enough for Bugs to hear, and certain enough to hide the lie.

Kendrick tossed more junk into the sea. "White folk ain't got our constitution. Can't none of 'em swing a hammer like I can."

"Goddamn right," Jayceon said quietly around a new cigarette.

Linc turned and could see, seated on a bench, Mercedes, with Timeica leaning against the back of the thing, testing its strength by propping herself on it by her arms. Mercedes was rolling a Turkish cigarette that glowed with flecks of radioactive dust.

"You ain't a stacker till you smash your thumb," Timeica said. "First busted finger I had, the nail turned all the way black and just fell off. Took about a year to grow back."

Mercedes didn't seem to be listening.

Timeica laughed, then let up off the bench, came around, and sat on it.

Linc didn't hear the rest of the conversation, but saw Mercedes wearing the look of someone whose head keeps falling off their hammer, someone frustrated, realizing any light at the end of the tunnel's just more tunnel. She looked ready to die.

"You seen Ace around some?" Kendrick asked no one in particular. He'd stopped throwing shit into the water.

Jayceon lit up another Newport. "He somewhere he can't stack." The flame danced at the end of his cig. "Might be there for a couple years."

Winter was on its way, and Linc could already see in his mind's eye the warehouse they'd huddle in, the rusted garbage can whose burning refuse would provide their warmth. He could already feel the cold biting through his duct-taped fingertips, could see the stackers dropping off who caught pneumonia and couldn't get it treated. He could feel hammers accidentally breaking hands, leaving them monstrously swollen and constricted.

"We ain't dead," Linc whispered to himself.

He looked up at where he thought the Colony sat. "Good luck to you, Officer," he said before walking back the way he had come.

It had been less than a second, but, in the way that daydreams stretch time like a rubber band, it had felt long enough to hear a whole sentence. Long enough to see Kendrick turned into Jake, tossing debris into the California Aqueduct and Linc turned into a little boy, legs dangling under the bridge railing, and Mama standing behind them. Long enough for this smaller Linc to feel her smile on his back and to hear Pop walk up behind her, Pop before Nevada and the drink and Jake hanging from a tree and the family splitting up and Mama lost in her grief and Pop taking his last remaining boy to join the Exodusters, Pop before his dying, and wrap his arms around Mama's waist and lean in and lose his face in Mama's hair and murmur in a voice dripping thickly with love, "Hey, Miss Pepper," and smile because Pop was the only one who could still make a joke over Mama's name and not get hit for it.

Less than a second but long enough for Linc to have felt it, to have held it in his beat-to-shit hands, and collected it, the memory so heavy in his pockets that it slowed his walk.

He didn't mind.

WINTER

PART III

PART III.

Leaves moved across Rodney's target reticle, crisp and flaking with veins like gnarled spines. A mountain wind carried them through Sniper's Alley. Reflected in the shards of glass beneath his one straightened leg: food wrappers, the remains of cheese-and-flatbread sandwiches with half moons chewed into them, cigarette butts crushed and leaning with some of them curled in on themselves, sticking like stubbed tree branches out of mountains of ash and soot and silvered dust.

It was dusk.

Weeds split the concrete floor by his other boot, pressed as it was against a stump of once-marble, what had maybe a long time ago been the base of a column. Fiber-optic snakes coiled through the cinders and flakes. Angled toward him was the screen of a small, foldable tablet. It flashed with scrambled images. Interrupted by dead-channel television grain: a school building in the aftermath of an artillery attack with its steel supports bent like half-flexed fingers and the bars over the windows crimped like fangs in an animal with no face above its mouth, hospitals where even the blood had been incinerated and where building and pulverized bone corkscrewed into the sky, wafted by waves of burn. Somewhere above him, clutched in a corner of the roof, was a wasp's nest. And every morning, a metal swing would creak with activity, hung from a crossbeam coated in blooddust, the floor beneath it scuffed soft as flour.

A fallen column propped his back up. Stopped being discomfort a long time ago and was now numbness. Small, rotted bits of ceiling fell down to splash on his outstretched thigh. His shooting arm lay at his side. Palm facing the ceiling. Eyes closed. The fingers of his left hand twitched. Electricity hummed in the veins of an arm that bled cables. His right, he crossed over his stomach.

Cords from his left arm ended at the monitor in which rippled harried shots from the cameras held by scouts and a remote Land Rover. Flashes of faraway machine-gun fire, explosions that growled like a Tamaskan Dog held back by a muzzle. The occasional glint of light off an errant piece of glass that burned back, in its reflection, length after length of shadow to unearth another sniper similarly angled.

RAKIM had talked at Rodney. Not to him.

Rodney would listen, and Rakim would speak about how dangerous militia forces had made it, sounding all of eighteen years old. He was always moving, Rakim. Always moving, so that his camera always powered on with coordinates far away from its previous check-in. But in the few instances Rodney caught an errant glimpse of his body in the static gray of a monitor, Rakim wore a different set of clothes. Rebel forces, one night, had come to his house to look for him and when they couldn't find him, they'd arrested his brother. He had vanished for a time, and Rodney thought he was dead and didn't bother mourning him, then found his timestamp and IP address again on a new montage of chemical attack sufferers later that week. The kid had found bribe money, and the bribe money had found the hands of the right border guards.

They looked the same, the journalists and the rebel fighters. Early twenties with close cut or carefully tousled hair with a beret maybe, many of them in olive green or urban gray. Camera-ready at every angle. And their forever-posture was Morosely Charismatic.

In the beginning, when Rodney had arrived at the city and looked over its eastern border from his bluff, he saw that mountain ridge that surrounded the city and made it a bowl, and, with his rifle slung over his shoulder, he had watched the deluge of refugees pushing and swarming in both directions. Families, fighters, filmmakers.

Rodney had seen fear before, had noted through his riflescope the dilation of pupils, the raising of eyelids, the recognition of the moment

that films the eye with the beginnings of tears. The huffing and the
shouting and the weeping at the border, the grunting and the shoving
and the slipping of sandals and sneakers against pulverized ground,
Rodney had noted all of it. What brought him here was a mystery until that moment at the border, watching that wild swirl of humanity
ordered through and across checkpoints, in caravans or in pockets or
as individuals.

It was to cure an itch. It was the curing of the same itch Rodney had seen in some of those entering the city, those with cameras
disassembled and hidden about their persons, pieces of documentary
tools strapped to them, a pencil here, sheets of a notebook there, eyes
glinting with the same longing, craving, mania he felt when paying
witness to wartime grotesqueries.

When Rakim's first images graced Rodney's screens, it did not escape Rodney's notice how intentional Rakim had made the appear-
ance of bits and pieces of his own body. An arm, a thigh, a few fingers
caught in the frame of a massacre's aftermath's documentation. More
than the shake that charted the handheld course of a gun battle, this
seemed more than instinct, more than the human impulse toward
survival, more than fear. Rakim was playing. On the other side of the
camera, never filmed, never photographed, was Rakim smiling.

Rodney had wondered if Rakim knew this sniper was pirating his
data stream, stealing his eyes. And when Rakim began his running
monologue, Rodney had wondered to whom the boy spoke. How
many followers did he have? How many people was he talking to
when he told them about the mold that crawled along the walls of
his "cave" and the maggots and the carcinogenic that hung like a
blanket in the room where he slept and edited. How many people was
he showing where he kept his packs of Gauloises Reds and his BIC
lighter, where, through the blink and scratch of the security camera
Rodney had hacked, Rodney saw the array of digital cameras that
hung from the water pipes running along the wall? Where a rebel
fighter, emblem'd uniform folded to make a pillow, lay wrapped in a
blanket some shade of blue by the chair that Rakim occupied when
he worked?

Longing brought Rodney back to his body and the stiffness that burned in his angled knee. The tiny pebbles filling the space between the wall and the small of his back. The sweat-sour that told him it was time for another fix.

When the air shimmered like this and the walls bled into the air that touched them, the kill brass littering the floor by his thighs, once golden and now rust, became indistinguishable from his dragons. Evacuated inhalers, pushers deflated, openings where he would fit them to the crimson, corroded sockets in his arms and along his neck.

Pain curled the fingers of his organic arm into a half fist. The low-level ache that sat just beneath his skin grew pins and needles that pricked the thigh of his outstretched leg. The sight of the small, black blur that had scurried into the scope of his rifle awakened him. Something in him stirred.

His organic hand fumbled in one of the pockets in his vest, but he knew. He'd long since outlasted his supply of dragons. Evidence of the craving was cluttered around him. Occasionally, when he still had some left and the leviathan would stir inside him, the bars of its cage rattling, its growl escaping his lips as a sharp intake of breath, a gasp, he would fight it. Keep his hands clenched in a trembling fist. And some days he would last half a minute. Some days he would last a full minute. And in those joyous moments of righteous agony, he could feel the light getting closer. The longer he held out, the brighter it became until it was enough to sear his eyeballs. The pain rendered him ecstatic. The harder it got to breathe, the closer he got to climax. And after the pain became the high, he would reach into his pouch, touch dragon to outlet and let the narcotic wash him beneath wave after wave of orgasm. He would shudder. And a small, limping smile would curl his lips as the sun faded away and night carried him into sleep.

But, now. Now, there was only the graveyard of used dragons, his kill brass, and the figure that had wandered into his field of vision. The first bit of human motion all day, and his focus tightened.

Rodney knew what the kill would mean, what itch it would cure. And he redoubled his efforts to keep from firing the shot, even as the figure swam behind the shelter of a mortared bus. A small curve of scalp could be seen through one of its empty windows. Air thickened in Rodney's chest. He bit his teeth against the urge. Sweat beaded his forehead and ran down his ash-covered cheeks in muddy rivulets.

A second shadow darted into view to join the first. Rodney's heart quickened and he closed his eyes, but the men still glowed as heat signals in his brain, images burned behind his eyelids by the rifle to which his arm was connected. They glared against the cooling soil.

The walls of his home shrunk and expanded in the same instant. Time swam in a cloud around him. The world fell away, columns collapsing outward, roofs crumbling, the floor disintegrating with bits of it falling into empty white void, apocalypse, and he welcomed the alabaster ego-death. It burned. How it burned. Resist, and you will inherit the earth. The message rumbled his bones inside him. It gripped him and held him still while the space around him tore itself apart and lightning struck in his brain and thunder crackled, and suddenly, a bolt louder than any he had heard in weeks struck him into oblivion, and his eyelids slackened and behind them was the white flame and, in its aftermath, the pieces of the two men rolling about in the crater. They struggled to hold their bodies together, to gather their separated pieces, and their blood, when it left them, glowed hot, steaming itself cool when it touched the ground.

Slowly, their colors dimmed. And dimmed, and dimmed, until they were the same color as the ground on which they lay.

A sigh left Rodney deflated. Silence had returned. He knew that were he to touch the end of his sniper rifle, his hand would come back burning. A new shell casing joined the others on the floor around him. The rifle reloaded automatically as the kill brass welcomed its brethren.

Dusk deepened into night.

As the clouds shifted, Rodney watched through a narcotic haze a few civilians who still dared the snipers and drones by inviting friends over for tea they warmed by the barrels around which some of the homeless huddled to heat their limbs. A couple climbed onto their rooftop to make love, writhing in near-silence beneath their blankets.

Children who didn't know better found a back alley in which they could play a game of football. One of them would call an audible before every play. Sounds of men and women wrapped in cloaks to shield their heat signatures gathering the remains of the murdered scratched and itched into Rodney's earpiece. Somewhere nearby, others dumped weapons and the remains of a camera in a nearby river.

Inherit the Earth

On April 17, 20—, in Long Beach, California, a man selling mobile water filtration systems leaves a customer's house and stands on a sidewalk invaded by weeds. Briefcase in hand, he watches a sea of Black and brown and white people surging through the street. Among them are men and women in their early thirties, a few youths in their twenties, and a cabal of Black teenaged boys. They are running from the police.

Along the street, windows slam shut, and the salesman sees now that some of the officers and the police-bots zooming like raindrops caught in the midst of a rare rainfall are raising their pistols at the windows. Low-grade mechs stomp from far away, gobbling up yards of concrete with each stride. No firecracker pistol shots punctuate the spring afternoon, but the salesman watches two police descend on a Black boy in a baggy white T-shirt. Tackled and pinned to the ground with an officer's knee on his neck, he lets out a choked yelp with each blow of the shock-stick. The salesman hurries down and asks: "What'd he do? You're gonna kill him." When the police tell the salesman to "get over here," he asks, "Why?"

For that question, he joins the youth on the pavement beneath the hail of electrified blows and four others, much younger than the salesman, in the back of the police van that transports them to the local precinct, where their beating resumes. Among the names shouted at them by their assailants are: "dog," "shitbird," and "nigger." In the corner of their cell lies an older man, Hispanic, absolutely still, undisturbed by all the racket. Recovering, later, the salesman asks one of his cellmates if the older man is still alive, and the young man who responds, a bleeding lump having erupted on his forehead, says that the old man is a neighbor of his and "when they saw the cops out there beating us up, he asked them what was going on, and they just turned around and clocked him; like, he didn't even have a chance to put his hands up or protect his face or nothing." His question was of the same genre as the salesman's and so too was their punishment twinned. The salesman, upon a brief, fraught stay in St. Mary Medical Center after his release, lost an eye out of the encounter and gained a limp. It is easier now, he says, for the cops to notice him on the street. And to act accordingly.

No charges have been filed as a result of the encounter, and calling it an "encounter" lends it the very quotidian designation that seems to hover over these incidents, the frequency of which has skyrocketed in the wake of increased space flight, incidents which many believe smoothed the way for the race riots that spilled through the city that summer and which were a shock to *The New York Times, The American Standard,* every other nationally syndicated publication, and much of the rest of the world. Indeed, the only people who did not seem to be shocked by the riots were the residents of color in the city that burned around them.

Since construction of the latest outer space departure station began in South Bay, urban centers north and northeast of there have been increasingly defined by their constriction, an effort all the more accentuated by the directing of air pollutants into those metropoles. The result is that the very sky above largely depopulated, resource-deficient cities like Inglewood and Lawndale and Gardena is policed while a corridor is prepared for Orange County residents to travel at leisure to the Colony. The invisible sphere bounding those cities has turned them into one broad swathe of Occupied Territory and law enforcement has treated it as such.

Ostensibly, the discussion has centered on the decisions made regarding what to do with the lingering effects of irradiated waste. Municipal governments must finally contend with the results of scrambling to meet increasing energy demand with swiftly dwindling supply, and the results are being felt in urban areas across the nation.

Discussion of diagnoses and solutions has fallen along predictably political lines with conservationalists applauding the forward thinking of state government leaders and civil rights activists arguing for the free-air rights that should be the same for everyone. The retort of the conservationalist has typically been: "So everyone should walk around with lung rot?" Even though distinctions of Northerner and Southerner have long since become irrelevant, the same fault line haunts this dilemma as has haunted the country since its founding, and it is everything from willful blindness to malicious intent that keeps discussion away from the demographics, away from the fact that rates of lung rot have increased exponentially among communities of color concentrated in cities, but have remained steady elsewhere. And commentators, notably civil rights activists, have come to use the term "white flight" not to designate an exodus to the suburbs but rather an exodus to the newly constructed space colonies. TV pundits argue about the economics of space flight, and when the term "affordability" is used, it is code for the emptying suburb and the pregnant ghetto. What is not said but is widely known is that where the sky is red and where the sky is blue is very much a matter of Black and white.

Jonathan Crawford, 32, among the rising leaders in this latest wave of rights-based activism, spoke at length about the federal government's facetious efforts to deal with the inequality between protections for urban residents and protections for the rest of the country. Invitations to shuttle from Chicago to Washington would proliferate, arriving like clockwork, and Crawford, he admits, would succumb to the routine, "like I was on a Broadway show with a 10-year-run," and sit with one highly placed official after another. Before long, once the curtain had been raised on the drama, Crawford realized, he says, that when they asked what would happen that summer—any summer since the first wave of red dust washed from Charleston over Detroit—they were really asking what would "they" be taking to the streets for this time and about how many of them would there be. Who would cause trouble, and "what could I do about it?"

Crawford does not deny the increasing potential for violence in cities like Detroit and Chicago and Long Beach: "the sky turning red is when people began realizing that their quality of life was plummeting. It's been going on for two decades now, and kids are now coming of age that have not known a world where lung cancer rates weren't at least 65 percent in their neighborhoods. These kids grew up very early on seeing that where they lived was not like where other people lived and any time they wandered too far out by accident, they got the shock-club. Or they got jail. Some of us remember what it was like before, and we have pictures and video and holo-recordings and VR, but to those kids, that's not reality. Their sky's burning, and pretty soon, the ground at their feet will start burning too." When asked if the Washington meetings held any potential, Crawford replied: "Five summers now, they've been making the same call. And the summer's always violent. Nothing's getting done. Next spring, I know my phone's gonna start ringing again."

Across the country, legislatures have enacted laws adapted to these Bounded Cities, essentially calcifying their demographics. And in the aftermath of each convulsive push on behalf of the trapped to escape into the suburbs or the sparsely populated land outside their bubble, in the aftermath of every burghal paroxysm, entreaties are made to respect the law. Which, for many, is simply to submit to the edict that they are forbidden from space travel. They are forbidden the right to breathe clean air or to look at the stars from any other vantage point than the gutter.

Jamal Rice-Dominguez, 12, was left to asphyxiate when police officers, upon finding the boy outside the bounds of the Citysphere, encased his head in a breathing mask and reversed its settings. Immediately, it was said that the police had killed the boy because he had wandered into illegal space. Because he'd been trying to escape.

Jamal Rice-Dominguez was pronounced dead in a hospital bed in St. Mary Medical Center on April 16, 20—.

The next day, a man selling mobile water filtration systems witnessed an entire neighborhood flee the police chasing them for trying to escape the bounds of their city. That day, he lost his eye and was given his limp in the same hospital where Jamal Rice-Dominguez died.

This story can be and is being written in Philadelphia. It is being written in Detroit. It is being written in Chicago. It is being written in Los Angeles and Boston and Cleveland. It is being written in Washington, D.C. The byline changes, but the title is always the same: The Meek Shall Inherit the Earth.

[May 17th, 20—, 5:25 p.m.]

Fires and floods, baby. Story of my life. Fires and floods. [Laughter.]

I don't remember much of Little Rock, we moved to New Orleans before I could make memories, really. That's where a lot of the extended family was. You could say my parents being in Little Rock was their little experiment or rebellion, before they came back. But some of my kid years were spent there, in Arkansas. I can barely remember it, but yeah. But, even as a kid, I was always thinking about past iterations of myself. Not in any reincarnation type of way, but . . . so, like, my grandparents had the *Times-Picayune,* right? That was the only real news where they were, and I used to wonder if an earlier me woulda been able to afford something like *The New York Times.* Could I ever get around or behind its paywall. I don't know why I was so concentrated on that, this idea that the news, or access to the news, could separate a group into two: those who could afford it and those who couldn't. It's even weirder when you remember how we grew up. The Internet was everywhere. People walkin' around with whole galaxies in their pockets. No blind spots, no black areas. No information silos, really. Not like it is now with shit closed off. It can feel like you got access to everything, but it just means you're seeing more of what the world's like, you know? I mean, I'm a little nigga, so I can't quite articulate it that way, but it's what I was feelin' at the time, know what I mean? They always said I was gifted as a kid, that I saw things I wasn't supposed to see. And it wasn't like I was peeking under the stairs or walking out past the city limits. It was more like I was lifting the curtain on the world a little bit. NOLA was the most European and the most African city in America at the time, and I had an idea of what that meant even if I didn't know it completely, know what I mean? Slave pens, bacchanal, the music. I saw a girl dance on her grandma's coffin once. Can you believe that shit? [Laughing.] Now, to look at that from the outside, you'd think that was the highest dis- respect, right? You talk about dancin' on someone's grave, you must have some real spite in your heart for that person. But this girl was cuttin' up, bright green dress with a white ribbon in her hand, twirling on the wood soon as they set her grandmama's casket on the ground. She was a sight. I mean, look at her move. I can't find the video now but it was on Twitter for a bit waaay back in the day and there was this whole back-and-forth about whether or not that was an actual tradition, whether she hated her grandmama or whether this was all outta love, some celebration of the older woman's life. The tweet's long gone, but here's a little clip of my dad and grandma gettin' into it about that girl and the coffin. You gotta toggle a little bit to about the two-minute mark. Storage space on this thing is small, so I don't got too many of Grandma's memories on here. But, yeah, I can't say either way whether that girl was dancin' out of respect or disrespect, but it looked like she was moving out of love. You know how sometimes you do things that look damn near inscrutable from the outside as a way to deal with your grief? Maybe you're even a mystery to yourself. But your mind gets out of the way and you just let your body move. Most times, people just collapse, like all their bones disintegrated at the same time, but sometimes you do the opposite. Grief sets you on fire. Sometimes, you see bursts of that where I'm from or where I been in my life. Enough people dying and someone's bound to dance on a casket. One cat I knew had an interesting spin on it. He mighta been an Exoduster, so, when I knew him, he was always on some spiritual tip. But one day I told him about that girl and that coffin, and we're grown by now and a lot of life's happened to us in the meantime, but for some reason, that day, I'm remembering the girl and the coffin and he tells me that maybe they're tappin' into something going far back, you know? Past the slave ships to the shores of West Africa. Tells me, you look at the soil in, say, Uniontown in 'Bama and you see black and red earth, tough as shit. The type that old, old, old ladies used to chew to make their blood stronger. And you head back to the shores of West

Africa, you see the same stuff. And you start to wonder if the old, old, old ladies there chewed it too, to strengthen weak blood. Maybe they just didn't need to. You ever listen to Sun Ra? My folks were heavy into his stuff, and he named an album after Birmingham. Magic City. I think he was tryna say something about the future. You know, how the South has the past, is the past, but is also the future, you know? Like, if you wanted to know which way the country was headed, look no further than the Black Belt. All of this was coming. The devastation, the ruin. All you had to do was look at the way our graves got put up against the landfill. Look at where they put the chemical plants. You were gonna see where they put the nuclear reactors. Then you were gonna see where they put the water walls and then you were gonna see where they put the domes that filtered the poisoned air. I dunno, I'm starting to ramble, aren't I. You ain't ask me about Alabama.

We moved to Reserve when I was a little bit older, but it was still in what was called Cancer Alley, which runs up along the Mississippi River. Louisiana had some of the most toxic air in the whole United States. I mean, you look at the levels around the country now and you probably start asking what were we even complainin' about back then, especially since now nowhere's safe to breathe unless you're in a Domed City. But, you look at a map of Cancer Alley, and Reserve is nestled right there in the middle. Highest rates of cancer in the whole country at the time. Fifty times the national average. People wanted to try to call it Resurrection City much later on when they were trying to make things better, but when we moved there, it was a ghost town. Everybody knew somebody who'd died of cancer. Maybe you lost a whole family to it. It's a riverside town, and I remember there was one woman and you stand on her porch and look left, there's her brother's house, he died of cancer. You look right, another brother's home. Empty. Him and his wife got it. 'Cross the street, neighbor fighting cancer. You know how, with jail and prison and shit, you walk down some blocks and everybody knows somebody who's been locked up? It was like that with us and cancer. And no matter who it take, it's the same sort of thing. You gotta watch them lay in that bed, whether they was guidance counselor or gangbanger. Coulda been healthy as an ox a year or two earlier or maybe they was born to the poisoned air and the poisoned earth, but no matter how they was before, this was how they were now and you couldn't do nothin' about it. It could change you just like that. Shit would straight-up gentrify your insides. [Laughing.] No, but tell me that's not what it looks like, though! Some juice shop shows up like a tumor in your 'hood, then you got a Whole Foods and a yoga spot, and you turn around, the whole cancer's metasta- sized. Lungs, liver, pancreas. Whole neighborhood gone while your back was turned. I seen a whole neighborhood gone in eight months. Tell me I'm lyin'. Anyway! What was I sayin'? [Laughing.]

   Right. Reserve.

I SLEPT through all of it. Corpse at my side, I slept through the entire slaughter.

   My understanding was that when the Specials had fired on our carriages and sliced open the remaining fabric of our coach, they'd seen me wrapped in the same blanket as the corpse of my war buddy and taken us both as deceased. Which explains how I managed to keep my ears.

   But when I woke, I was by myself on a stretch of dirt with a twist- ing trail of blood behind me. Crowder wasn't far, tangled as he was in his blanket. And when I waited long enough and had gathered enough strength and courage to hazard a glance at my surroundings, which smelled thickly of charnel and tasted of smoke and copper, I saw that Crowder and I had fallen down the side of a ridge, and we had both lain together in darkness. How many nights had we spent fighting the Spooks in precisely that posture?

   I don't remember any of the attack or why what was torched was torched and what was spared was left for the buzzards. I don't remem- ber anyone screaming for help or begging for their lives or anyone shooting back or anyone pawing the air by their head where their ears once were. I don't remember the warnings.

   But I know it all happened.

   I remember climbing that ridge and seeing what remained of the caravan on the plain and wishing I could unsee it, unremember it forever, whispering to myself the whole time, "God in heaven, God in heaven, God in heaven." Some of the bodies had white kerchiefs around their faces, ensanguined, some with hoods over their heads and holes for their eyes, looking less like men and more like crippled ghosts.

I'm sure they came how they always did, the Specials. Black bodies practically descending out of thin air, landing in your midst, and you've got a moment's worth of life left before a single shot from the cannons fitted to their bodies craters your insides or bursts your head open or guts you or brings the building you stand in down on top of your head. Then they're gone. Just like now.

The desert is littered with dead things.

Beetles on their backs no longer struggling for purchase and having given up the ghost, leathered coyote skins, sun-polished bones of whatever the coyotes had eaten before they'd died, dog cactus and prickly pear flanking my path. Spanish dagger and catclaw and lechuguilla punishing me where patches in my clothes leave exposed flesh.

With the creosote bush and the mesquite and the blackbrush, I wonder how often it's rained since I was last here. Whether this flora saw any hint of relief in the clouds. Whether they will provide me shade when I collapse from thirst and hunger and debility.

I hear the thundering of many hooves.

I turn and see clouds rushing toward me. Massive, ominous walls of dirt and dust and detritus. Through the brown, I spy white cloth. Were I to squint harder, I'd probably see white skin under all that dirt and mud. Skin-folk. My rescue. I bet someone's even got a horse for their fallen comrade.

I look around and all the Specials are gone. There coulda been twenty involved in this skirmish. There coulda been two. You can never tell anymore. Deaths in this part of the country don't get more mindless than this. Still, I should count myself blessed even now, for having ears to hear my deliverance rumbling toward me on the desert winds. Pregnant with promise.

The War is over, and this is what we're reduced to. White men on horses forever looking over our shoulders for the spook about to whisper our end in our ear.

[May 17th, 20—, 5:48 p.m.]
At night's when you really see the Pontchartrain Works chemical plant. You hear it during the day. Sometimes it's a hum and sometimes it's a roar. And you always smelled it, day or night, that's how close we all lived to it. It was practically our backyards. But night was when you really saw it. When I was younger, a bunch of us would climb up onto our roofs, even though our parents wanted us all inside with the windows closed—on account of the smoke coming out of the plant and all—but we would get up on the roofs and in the summers when the days were as long as possible, we'd sit up there on those roofs and watch the chemicals fuck up the sunset. There was purple and there was gold and there was green and you know how little boys get with their jokes. All fart noises and vomiting and jokes about poop and sex and all that. And we'd say some of those things about the sky. How sometimes the clouds looked like spoilt milk, all chunky and discolored. Or sometimes the smoke would make the clouds look like they boo-boo'd on theyselves. You didn't think nothing of it at the time, just figured it was like those summer thunderstorms where you get the dirty lightning forking sideways through the sky. This was just what happened. But then you spend enough nights sleeping with your window open next to a chemical plant, and one day you wake up and you fall out of bed holding your chest, tryin' to tell your mama that you can't breathe you can't breathe, but all that comes out is gasping like you some kinda fish washed up on shore.

They took me to the hospital and the doctor told me and my parents that I had asthma and even as a kid you can tell that this isn't like when you get a cold, you know, something that comes to you then goes away. No, this is a permanent thing. This is a thing you're gonna have to live with for the rest of your life. This thing on your back don't ever go away. You just hunch your shoulders to fit it, then you forget that there was ever a time when you didn't have trouble breathing. So you got your asthma and, of course, you got the lead poisoning from the lead paint they used in the homes. And then I'm in high school when the fuckin' respiratory pandemic hit? [Laughing.] When I tell you that Reserve was built on the site of an old plantation, would you believe me? Feels a bit on the nose, but I ain't even a little bit lyin'.

DuPont didn't get there till like the 1960s, I think. So we're talkin' almost a century ago. Way before I was born, but it always felt recent to the generation before, like one day the grass was green and the air was clean then the very next day kids are dropping like flies from asthma and you've had to bury half your block from cancer. I'm sure it was more gradual than that. What's the word? [snapping his fingers] Hyperobject? Yeah, nonlocal hyperobject. It's a living thing, but you can't touch it. It's so massively spread out over time and space that you can barely perceive it. That's what global warming was. You look around now, and you're like *duh,* but back then, growin' up, nobody who could do nothin' about it seemed to care much. Anyway, so DuPont arrives and Pontchartrain goes up, and it's a rubber factory. They made neoprene. You know, the stuff that they use to make tires, wetsuits, all that stuff. You got slavery, then Jim Crow and a whole lot of white folk pushing the place down economically, then suddenly this factory comes to town and it's got jobs and it ain't goin' nowhere—because nobody else wants it—so of course you're gonna work for the place and make it work for you. What choice you got?

Mom and Dad weren't tryna have no kids die early, so they got me up out of there pretty quick when they saw how bad it was in Reserve. I knew they was tryna protect me, but all I felt at the time was loss, you see what I'm saying? Lost my friends, lost the little nooks we would play in, lost the grass we would run around on. Lost them damn beautiful chemical sunsets. And when I got up north to live with my auntie and uncle, all there was was trees. Blocked out the whole entire sky. Just green everywhere. But the air was cleaner. You could feel your lungs expanding with it, like the cage around them done rusted and fell apart.

They actually lived in Connecticut. Go figure! But it was weird. It's strange thinking about the place now before there were domes and before all the white folk went off to space. It really does feel like a whole other planet. But there was all type of person there. Where we lived, you had working-class people, like cops, teachers, people who did, like, roofing work, that sort of thing. You had that, you had Black folk and Puerto Ricans in some of the big cities. And you had some refugee communities too. And you had fuckin' farmland up north in the state. Cows and tobacco and all of that. And then in the southwest, the part that was closest to New York City, that was all the waterfront property and all the rich Republicans and all that shit. But to be honest, the place was kinda emptyin' out by the time I went to live there. We lived in one of those working-class neighborhoods. Mostly white folk, and super defensive about it, but at that age—what, twelve? thirteen?—I'm online most hours of the day anyway. Okay, post your little conspiracy theories or whatever on Facebook, I got a video dance challenge I'm doin' with my followers. But you also gotta remember too that there was a big movement at the time and a lotta people were being made hip to racism and all that that might not've cared before. Don't get me wrong. White people are still white people. No offense. But at least some more of them were marching or even organizing protests and stuff. And that was the thing about the Internet back then. Like, a cop pulls a Black dude over and then shoots him while his baby's mama and their child are in the car with him and that video is everywhere. And when you got the video like that, and the cops haven't touched or edited it or anything like that, it's . . . I dunno. Evidence? Shit. But I'm a kid seein' this shit. Whole generation. The shit that happened in Minneapolis that kicked off that whole round of shit, that was when Mom and Dad were maybe teenagers or had like just met. So it's 'look on your phone,' racism. Look outside your window, racism. [Laughing.]

But, growing up, it wasn't a whole, like, staring at my phone type of deal the whole time. That's what we had too. They could be the same size as a Flex, but they couldn't hold *nearly* as much data. Like, you couldn't hold actual neural data in them. It was all videos and pictures and music and stuff. It was all copies of stuff or experiences or whatever, not like you got now. And certainly not no holos. But yeah I did actually spend some time outdoors as a kid.

I have this one memory of a possum corpse rustling inside a plastic grocery bag.

Uncle's driving this turquoise Ford sedan, and we're on the way to school, and he's pulled over to the side of the road where these huuuuuge columns of grass are just bent under this breeze by the abandoned Stanley Works factory. And I'm a kid so the building just reaches so high over me its top vanishes in the clouds. It's morning, and, in my head, Uncle, he's more of a moving shadow, bending light around him, than a real flesh-and-blood man. However old I am in the memory, I know he's gonna die in less than five years. Like a premonition. Anyway, I'm watching Uncle Jim exit the car and he's got this possum in this plastic bag in his hands. And I hear the shuffle of movement. I don't see him get out and throw the thing over the fence, and I don't see him get back in. I just hear the car door creak open and then thud shut. Uncle's back in. He smiles at me, and then he drives me to school.

That was a weird summer with the possums. They always came for the trash. But our backyard was huge, though. Had a green chain-link fence all the way around, and we had a swing set we never used, but there was this big tree in the back. Musta been like a oak or something, I don't know. But I'd take some of the rocks at the base of the tree and crack them open and you could see these rings on the inside. The iridescence ringing their cores.

I remember the night Uncle killed the possum, actually. They'd been at us and our trash for a while now. So, one night, Uncle grabs this massive tree branch and walks outside, and [inaudible]. Then, later, he comes back with his shoulders slumped, and he's tired, and I knew he'd just beaten the thing to death. Never saw the process, only this massive, powerful . . . I dunno, demigod who'd gone out, murdered a thing, and came back pretty much unscathed. But yeah, Uncle died probably a year or two later. Cancer.

THIS musta been what it felt like to be a Confederate soldier after the Civil War. Almost two hundred years later, history don't repeat itself, but it sure as hell rhymes.

Negroes, shackled at the ankles, bang out another stretch of rail-
way. I think of when I'd seen those self-same silhouettes pockmarking
the green vistas of corn and soybean that stretched for miles further
south. I'd shredded my Whiteland militia coat and used it for fire at
nights during my ride home and what patches I couldn't bear to burn,
I sewed into a blanket I never ended up using. They would see me, the
recently victorious, the new ruling class. Moon-white eyes staring out
from night-black faces, little kids hiding in the forest, taking shelter
under heavy-leafed branches, maybe running about them just like
Sam and I had done in our Kentucky youth, pausing when they heard
the hoofbeats of my passage and staring, faces absent of judgment, of
fury, of anything. The impenetrability of expression cultivated after
hundreds of years of a white man's boot on their neck, an opaqueness
that frustrated police and school principals and scholars and camp
guards who could not divine the Nigger's hopes and wishes and fears
beyond those endemic to all humans, who could therefore not ma-
nipulate them. Those children that followed me with their eyes would
probably never unlearn that skill.

Later, I see their fathers working the fields and I wonder what's
changed. What the hell did I shoot at all those gene-fucks after the
Cataclysm for?

My horse takes me on the main road cutting by the tracks of tim-
ber the family used to work and a part of me expects desolation while
another part expects to see more Blacks working the plot, but I squint
and, burrowed into the mountainside, calling up a chain of commands and shout-backs, is a familiar band of whites, some of whom
turn around and wave at me as I ride by. I can't tell whether it's because they remember me or because they can tell what I've been up to
these past few years.

This swath of the country belongs to white folk once again. Those
Blacks with devil-bequeathed ambition came, then there was war,
then Occupation, then more war, then this simulacrum of peace. But
whatever's happening in Charleston and Washington, it's quiet here,
and there are more white faces than not. Which is solace enough.

I'm home, but I feel like it was my life's work getting away from this place. Like it's repelling me and pulling me further in all at the same time. Nothing has changed.

Before I know it, I'm in front of the bar and I'm hitching my horse and in my head is that time when Virginia came in and caught my eye and was smelling of gin and juniper and that time when two Hetlund boys stumbled in already drunk and wound up facedown in the river and that other time when Uncle Al was behind the bar and couldn't get me to stop drinking because Virginia was gone and Sam had gotten himself hurt by a falling tree he hadn't paid attention to while logging.

And I try to think of how I could've stayed away so long from the comfortable burn of whiskey passing down the throat, how I could've gone through that many years of warring against those negroid abominations without tasting a drop, what horrible discipline must have powered me. And even as I think it—that the drink never helped nothing and that believing that, even when it wasn't true, had kept me alive—I find myself walking in, catching lazy sunlit dust motes against my face, and taking a seat across from a bartender I don't recognize.

I wonder, fleetingly, if Pa is still alive.

The bartender pours me a double shot, turns to go.

"Leave the bottle."

He pauses, scans me, and knows, then, that I've come from the War, that I've seen terrible things done to white folk. He puts the bottle next to my shot glass and vanishes without another word. Doesn't even tell me about the price.

In the morning mistiness, the dust motes hang in shafts of light that have burst through the windows overhead to illumine an auroral walkway, leading straight to the bar. The place is quiet. A drunk snores in a corner. Robins dance on the windowsill. The world outside this shadowed place is all light and coruscating tree branches. There's the clink of bottle against bottle and the bartender emerges from the backroom with a case of bourbon, the glass unmarked, unlabeled. Because anyone from around here knows exactly what make it is. I watch the bartender place the bottles, wipe down the counter with a dishrag, and snap the tops off the whiskey he intends on using today. No one ever wrote a set of musical notes so pretty.

I'm the only animate customer in the establishment, and in these few
quiet hours before the place becomes rowdy and raucous and overflow-
ing with too much noise, I can enjoy a drink in peace. Maybe watch
an out-of-towner salesman amble in, hat off, and ask for a Kentucky
bourbon, and I would smirk and joke with the bartender like we knew
each other: "Pour him a bourbon and tell him it's from Kentucky."

I laugh at the daydream.

THE Negress takes a seat one away from mine.

"You know horses?"

I bite back a snarl in response to the woman's query. "Enough to
ride 'em," I say into my drink. My thoughts are a swirl of mint juleps
and summers with people richer than me, afternoons spent in the
shadow of barns, watching from far away as sable beasts, mounted
by nigger jockeys and tiny whites, sped around a track and people
screamed at the things, at those beautiful animals, who in the course
of a race could erase an entire family's riches or turn a lucky man
from a pauper into a prophet. I'm a child before the end of the world.
Run fast, turn left, run faster. "You ever go to the races?" I don't realize
until I finish the question that I've asked it.

"'Nawl. We didn't race 'em where I was from," says the Negress
before tossing back her drink and, with titanic impertinence, pouring
herself another from my bottle. She's covered almost entirely. A rag-
ged coat, cloth wrapped around her gloved hands, the fingertips poking out through sand-colored fabric. Outside of her face and those
fingertips, there ain't a lick of black skin to be seen.

She ain't there but to be ignored, I guess.

She smirks, shyly, shifts the battered hat on her head, comes across
a little sideways, maybe turned mad by having been born that color.
Maybe she's paramilitary. If she was, she'd'a killed me by now. "You
do any railwork? I knew some folks did some railwork, Blacks mostly.
Following the length of rail westward or wherever it spun 'em.
How old were you when they came 'round? When they told you
you could get paid to work horses and round up Blacks that didn't

have paramilitary Specials to protect 'em? Bring back slavery." She's talkin' to me and herself at the same time. "One of 'em sees you had killin' in you. Takes a likin' to that. 'N' it's not long 'fore you're called on to do your duty."

The air sizzles. Pops. This has to be a dream, so I keep my mouth shut.

"But you were smart enough then to know that when they said roundin' up unprotected Blacks would be your job, that they really meant the other thing, and that's what that one fella wanted to see you do." The Negress pulls rolling paper out from the folds of her jacket. Fiddles with it. Starts rolling. "You ask him now, he'd tell me you didn't mind killin' 'em and missin' the payday. That you'd figured them for animals anyway, not deservin' of life, and were simply restorin' things to their natural balance." She stops, collecting herself. Trying to remind herself of something. "I dunno. Maybe I ain't givin' you enough credit." And she dares to look me dead in my face.

Before I can leap out of my chair and show this nigger what's what, she slaps something cold and metal and glowing around my wrist and a memory seizes me entirely. The air is aswarm with Virginny accents and everybody is louder, just trying to be noticed looking well and well dressed.

An electric shock rips through me. My mind goes white. Then—

A horse race. Last night's rain has softened the ground into mud and several drunks, some in expensive jackets, already lounge in the effluvium, scrambling aimlessly to right themselves like upturned stag beetles. I remembered Billy and Hollis's warnings the night before over brandy, their chuckled admonitions that I exercise caution, their claims that it could not possibly get as bad as last year, their secret hope that it might. The clubhouse perpetually on the verge of being burned to the ground by errantly struck matches, raving drunks stumbling about in clouds of vitriol and delusional fury, aiming to settle ancestral scores, everyone with a mint julep in each hand, vomiting across aisles on each other so that the runways were slick with bad decisions and people slipping and grabbing on to you to keep from slipping further and being stomped on in the mad rush. More drunks pissing themselves in the betting line, stooping over to snatch their soiled money from the sticky floors, fighting each other to get back upright again.

"Come now, we mustn't miss the actual race." Uncle Al grabs my arm affectionately and half hauls me down the sidewalk, already crammed with people moving in all directions, down toward Churchill Downs.

I'm about to find my groove when I see, across the street amid the pulsing throng that's less walking in any direction so much as vibrating with life, Virginia. Flower-patterned sundress, freckled alabaster skin smelling of juniper trees, head haloed by reddish-blond hair. She glows and seems to move blissfully unaware of the fact. She's got new wrinkles, a curving fold just by the side of her mouth, a small tree of lines by her eyes, and her hips have filled out slightly. Cushioned by her hair is a wide-brimmed summer hat half a season too early, and I know she only wears it for her husband in whose arm she threads her own, and it's exactly that consideration that draws me to her again, expels all other conscious thought, and I follow the course of her movement as it parts a stream through the crowd before her and takes her off into the distance.

Uncle Al pulls me toward him, whispers in my ear, beneath the sound of wooden gate-doors swinging open and shut and people shouting at each other, decency diminishing with each second, under the slap of bootheels sticking and sucking out of mud and the distant neighing of horses prepped for their big turn this afternoon, "Five million dollars will be bet today." And I'm led to believe that a piece of that will fall squarely into my own pockets, simply because I belong to this family.

This place is still standing, this land, because when Black folk with the power to blow you wide open without a second thought came by, these members of my race put up no fight. Just let 'em rush through, hoping they were on their way to somewhere else, bankin' on being left alone if they stayed docile enough, content to be left making the money they've been making off other white backs. I know this is a memory, because I haven't yet taken up arms against the Specials. I haven't yet joined the Normal forces in ridding the country of the scourge of Spooks. Right now, I'm just young and dumb and in love with someone else's woman.

I see, in the infield, among the milling swarm of stained dinner jackets and sticky beards and rumpled sun hats, Virginia's beatific face again and resolve to get near her. On my way out, someone shoves a drink in my hand and I down it, then shove up to the bar and order two more drinks, none of which survive the trip back out past the outdoor betting windows, past the regular Blacks drunk with the power of handling their own bets and the resentful white men shoving past them, and the younger whiskey gentry, running about like the children they are, with their girlfriends hoisted on their backs, hats waved above their heads like they were cowboys riding their steeds bareback.

No one selling drinks out here, but the air reeks of stale whiskey and beer splashed on shoes and staining dress shirts. I've eyes only for Virginia, passing through the gates, one by one descending into a more atavistic tract of bowel until I'm shat out, through a tunnel, stepping over bodies, elbowing my way through a throng of people, striking out at loud voices, uncaring of faces that regard me with shock and disgust and could care less about the race none of them can see from here.

She is an island of gilded effortlessness in the midst of the chaos. I grab her hand, and instantly our fingers are entwined, no argument, no resistance, and we float through the masses and past the entrance of the adjacent Bingham Gentleman's Club and the pristine white tablecloth and the politicians and well-to-do legislators and landowners and their ladies, past the smell of their untainted-ness, past the immaculately groomed lowhill whites serving them, past the corruption tightened in their faces, and into the spacious, cushioned ladies' room, where, in the confines of a stall, I hike up her dress, one leg thrown over my shoulder, press her against the wall, and kiss her, the fingers of one hand wrapped around my neck while the fingers of another fumble at my belt buckle.

The gates all open at once and Morning Glory speeds out, fast and sable as a cloud of dun-colored geldings thunder close behind, and their hooves strike the ground near enough to crack it with rhythmic pounding and the onlookers are screaming and shouting, each for their own bets, the sound like tumultuous waves breaking against a sheer cliff face, and as a man absently, nervously chews the edge of his program and grips it in a white-knuckled embrace, the horses pant, nostrils flaring, sweat-sheen drawing out the contours of each starkly defined muscle, flexed in the movement, when, rounding the bend, Water Lily, before on the outside, kicks harder against the ground and gallops hard on the turn, pushing ahead, women in the stands, gloved hands slapping the railing slapping the stall door men with necks stretched forward like the horses, inching them ahead as if through mimicry they could push the horse with a bit more energy, whispering beneath their breath Go, go, go, keep going, keep going, yes, come on Angel, the women on their feet, without regard for their husbands, both screaming madly, faces contorted in rage and ecstasy, the hooves thudding enough to drown out every sound until just before the end, which they feel mounting with every left turn, there is silence, two horses having broken away from the pack and Morning Glory's jockey with the switch in his hand raised high poised on the brink of violence, the horse pulsing beneath him with each stride, and all is silent in that brief instant before the horse crosses and the air is thick with release and relief and yes, oh God, yes, thank you, yes, a trickle of foaming blood issuing from each of Morning Glory's distended nostrils.

"What'd you do?" I'm shaking and darkness settles over the bar's interior. The sun is gone. Clouds have extinguished it. "Who are you?"

"Jason Lingerfelt?" She already knows the answer to that question.

I'm paralyzed. My fingers refuse to wipe the whiskey from my overgrown mustache.

She's got her hand on a chain linked to the bands around my wrist. She'd moved so quickly and quietly that no one, not even the bartender, notices my predicament. No one here will save me. Steel shines in her newly argentate pupils. She's a Special. "Jason Lingerfelt, you're under arrest for the kidnapping of Margaret Morgan and her two children from the Specials-Occupied State of Ohio to the Whiteland State of Texas. And for the murder of Absalom Morgan, her son."

[May 17th, 20—, 7:52 p.m.]

I got into a private high school on scholarship. [Laughing.] Yeah, one of those New England prep schools. Let me tell you, best four years of my life. You could feel like you were standing on a precipice though with everything that was going on in the world. We were doing virtual classes. And it was tough for a lot of people, because not everybody's got the same tech or not everybody can, like, find a quiet room to do their classes in when they gotta share an apartment with a whole-ass family, know what I mean? It's one thing, you know, if it's school in your own community and like how it used to be way back in the day and people got the temperature readers in their homes and the schools got the hand sanitizers and everybody kinda knows where everybody's been, right? But, like, the private schools, that was a whole other game. You got people from all over the country, all over the world. And they tried to do the in-person thing for a few years kind of on-and-off, but the pandemic was like nah, fuck that. This was a couple years before me, but the big thing was when, like, international kids started coming here and getting sick then bringing that virus back to their home countries, and you really saw like, wow America's the ghetto. [Laughter.] But, yeah, it was like that. Like, you hear older generations talking about how, like, immigrants used to come here or *their* parents came here looking for a better job or a better life or whatever, and you look around, and you're like "for this?" Meanwhile, most people I knew were like, oh you're American? Stay the fuck away from me, man. I remember talking to kids—and it was a certain brand of kid too, who, like, knew shit but wasn't, like, too tied to this place—and they were always like "get me the fuck *outta* here, bro." Sometimes, if you're from a place, and you love it, you wanna claim it, and part of that is also wanting to improve it, right? Meanwhile, for a lot of us, the only America we known is basically a country on fire, right? Like, America's somehow the only country that could not only fuck up response to a global viral pandemic, but *keep* fucking it up, and you also got all the race laundry out in the open like that, and, granted, it's stuff anybody with a brain and half a conscience *knows* about, but now it's all happening out loud, you know? And that's just what you're born into. So then it started happening to us, you know? Some of us started thinking like the generations before us. Like our grandparents' or great-grandparents' generation. Like maybe life in America ain't it. Maybe we could build a better life for ourselves and our families somewhere that wasn't here. Growing up for them, you couldn't actually *go* to another country. That's how bad it was here. Other countries *banned us* from traveling to them.

I think white folks got so fed up with being told where they could or couldn't go that they finally got serious about putting that first Colony together. Buncha companies or corporations, I forget who was the first to announce. Probably the Tesla guy, but then the government got involved and was throwing all this money at it. And before you know it, people are actually going up into space. I'm in school with these rich white kids and by the time we're getting ready for college, their parents are getting set up in space. That's how fast it was. Them shits even had the Amazon logo on the building sites. All over their uniforms, all of that. But yeah, all of that's happening while I'm in high school.

The whole place was like a mini-college. Classes were tough in the beginning. I wasn't used to that kind of rigor, you know? But I remember it as a good time, generally. People were kind. Went out of their way to take care of me. By now, Auntie was my legal guardian. I didn't know that all types of stuff was going on behind the scenes. Mom and Dad caught the virus and that fucked me up for a while. Then there was Uncle Jim dying, and I was too young to process all of it. My whole mind was escape, you know? Just, like, bury yourself in your schoolwork. Bury yourself in getting out of this country. Just finding a way out. But one thing I did learn? How to go to school with rich white kids. [Laughter] It's an honest-to-God skill! Made college a lot easier. But, you could definitely see the change in them too. The bad ones get worse and a lot of the good ones turn bad, because that's the world they're in and that's how their parents are. Some of the good ones stay good. But I had some Black teachers and I didn't find out till much later how lucky I was.

In prep school, white boys start to grow into their superpowers, figure out all the things their whiteness and their manhood gets them access to. By the time they get to college, they're full-fledged villains. [Laughter] But I was an orphan, know what I mean? I came from slave land in the South, up north to a dying factory town, the type that people point to and say "deindustrialization" or "post-industrial" or something like that, practically a Rust Belt type of city, then I get here. And I say to myself, "You know what? You're working-class." And it wasn't really embarrassment for me. When we were kids, me and my cousins used to help Auntie out cleaning and disinfecting office buildings all around Connecticut, but we were just kids and we figured this was just how the world was ordered. And I was good enough in school that I could flex on the other kids in my class. Nobody made me feel like they were better than me. You know how white folks do, no offense. But I got to college and saw how rich white people get and it started to stink. It smelled really, really bad. If my soul had a nose, it spent most of that time all the way wrinkled up.

THEY chain me like a nigger.

Manacles around both wrists, a chain looped through to link with the shackles around my ankles so my hands have no choice but to sit in my lap. I ponder asking the marshal across from me for a cigarette, just to hear her break up the silence between us when she tells me why she has to say no, but I think better of it. Out the window is honeyed pasture our train's cutting an iron-straight line through.

Will they hang me right away? I almost ask her.

I hope they don't. I hope they give me time to get used to Ohio air for a bit, maybe write a letter to Ma and let her know I'm not sad about how things turned out, hope they'll give me a chance to explain that I wasn't a deserter, I just had some lucrative business to attend to, running down lonely Spooks and sellin' 'em into them labor camps before my home was overrun with Spook-sympathizers. And I hope they'll let me shave so I can die smooth-faced and dressed as well as I can afford and greet God in better condition than I'm typically known for maintaining.

I smirk because I can trace the woman's thoughts. "You think my family gon' kill you once they find out you done took me under the auspices of the law of a country ain't none of 'em reco'nize?"

By God, she don't even blink.

"We ain't that backwards we don't recognize a government's capacity to restore order and civility and whatnot, make men outta us barbarians. I ain't sour 'bout how it turned out, but I am quite perplexed at havin' woke up to a world where a Negress can look a white man dead in the eye, who's wearin' chains like a nigger and be all right with that situation."

The train rumbles in silence.

"You ain't chained like a nigger." She shifts, makes herself more comfortable. "You chained like a man broke into a family's home, kidnapped a mother's kids, sold one into a camp, and kilt the other." Sun's shining straight through the window, but it's no match for the shadows covering the marshal's face.

"You sayin' I deserve this, then?"

"I'm sayin' deserve's got nothin' to do with it."

"You gonna watch me hang?"

"I don't think so." She says it like she's deciding which boot to put on first or whether she'll roll herself a smoke or just spit 'bacca instead. It unnerves me. "What's it to you? Me showin' up or not to see you hang."

"It'd be the completion o' yer duty, for one."

She squints at me, has trouble figuring me, it seems.

"For another, I'd need someone to bring my message back to Ma." I shrug, but it seems a heavier, more mournful gesture than I'd intended. "I don't know too many people in Texas I'd trust with that."

"I ain't a courier, if that's what you're getting at."

"It ain't."

Out the window, the pasture is charred and brittle.

It looks how I remember it from the thunderstorms that attacked the homesteaders on the prairie when I was younger and stupider and runnin' with men just as violent and hungry and desperate as me. Blackened patches where lightning struck and where tiny homes had turned into conflagrations, swallowing up the year's harvest before the locusts had a chance. But this burn has a different smell to it; I can tell that much through the winda. It smells like salt poured into open wounds, like kicking a downed man, like rampaging after the war'd already been won. Or lost. It smells like the planet took revenge on us. It smells like Specials.

I don't catch a reaction either way from the marshal as we near the devastation, passing indications of carnage and whispers of sabotage, military maneuvers practiced on civilians, a few garrisons sparsely populated, the occasional horseman paused, lone and silhouetted, on the hilltop, scanning our passage, maybe wondering at our mission.

Through the window, the air smells of cedar and burning, though there ain't a forest for miles.

[May 17th, 20—, 8:58 p.m.]
After college and droppin' out of grad school and a few years sort of wandering, I came back to Connecticut. Moved in with a Boricua friend from when I was younger and we got a two-bedroom in Hartford. Downtown. You wanna hear the story of America, just look at Hartford. Used to be the Insurance Capital of America. So much money was made there, they called it America's Filing Cabinet. But none of the money stayed. You could walk through downtown Hartford, even in the middle of the day, and feel completely, utterly alone. Not like in New York, where the city's whole business is being anonymous, knowing it's heads or tails whether someone would help you if they saw you in trouble on the street. This was different. Even full of people, the place was a ghost town. People talked about making it a sort of tech city, a New England Silicon Valley or whatnot, but that never took. There's no downtown scene. People drive in to see the theater at the Bushnell [Performing Arts Center], then drive back out to the suburbs. The little café where we lived opened at 10 a.m. and closed at 3 p.m. Even the Dunkin' closed early on Fridays. At some point, they built a Dunkin' Donuts baseball stadium, but whenever we drove by it, we were always asking, "Who did they build that for?" We chuckled when we said that to each other, me and Freddie. But you

could hear the sorrow in it if you really listened. Living there affected
Freddie more than it did me. Park Street was where the Puerto Ricans
lived and all the Blacks lived in the North End. Main Street was kind
of the dividing line.

It's a shame, because there's so much damn history in that place.
Take the Wadsworth Atheneum. When I was in grade school, we went
on field trips there around Christmastime and the whole place would
just light you up. The art, the Christmas trees. Oldest public art mu-
seum in America. And by the time Freddie and I moved there, they re-
did the library, freshened up Bushnell Park, even though you could still
catch the crackheads there if you went at the right time. Or the wrong
one. But, yeah, man. Those office buildings. When the people working
in those places left, it's like they evacuated. That's what it was. They
don't leave, they escape. I was old enough by that time to know about
tax bases and property taxes and the way schools are funded, so you
could see the injustice in it, you see what I'm sayin'? You look at the
statistics and read about "economic activity," but it's all just white
folks moving money from one pile to another, and none of it stays in
Hartford. No art scene, no nothing. If you wanted to be a writer or an
artist or whatever, you could go and starve in Boston or New York. You
didn't have to do it in Hartford, even though we paid $525 a month for
our apartment at the time.

That mighta been why I came. I mean, I was close to Auntie, who
was getting older. But I guess I thought that maybe I could do something for the place. Improve it. Fix it. Make it alive again. But you just
can't get money to stay there. Try walking around that place and buy-
ing a cup of coffee. Mayor after mayor, governor after governor, all
trying to get business to come to that city by giving them tax breaks,
and look at what it did.

I don't want to say it was a difficult time. Maybe it was. It's all sort
of foggy now. But I was in my twenties and drifting between postgrad
study and unemployment and temp jobs. If you were my age, left college in those years, you could kinda blame the recession. The country
never really recovered from that outbreak. But sometimes you feel
like it's a personal thing, know what I mean? Like there's something

wrong with you. Everywhere I landed, I didn't really feel like I belonged. Doing postgrad stuff, I felt like I didn't have any skills. Just felt unaccomplished. I was just there to ride out the downturn, and I felt like everybody knew it. Then there's the shame of unemployment, because I wasn't really unemployed. There were plenty of people who were actually looking for jobs. Auntie had lost her job as a tax analyst, turned around and became a nurse. Felt like I was ducking and dodging responsibility. I was just overeducated and useless, taking a job from someone who needed it and deserved it more than me. Got put in a psych ward after a suicide attempt, and when I was in that place, I didn't even feel like I was really depressed or really going through it. Felt like I was faking it to get out of something. Like I was avoiding work. Felt like there was no place for me, because I wasn't capable of working. All my friends who studied econ got jobs overseas, and I was just walking around taking up space. Led to my first try quitting the drink. Really quitting it.

I did it in the middle of a winter. Hartford was getting as cold as it would get all year, and I moved to New Haven. [Inaudible.] It was too cold for a jacket. Too cold for a hoodie. So I put them together and I really dug how it looked, you know? How it made me feel. Throw on some snow boots and I looked exactly like the kid they didn't let into the Ivory Tower. Outside churches, donning my uniform, huddled in little circles on the sidewalk around the light of a half-dozen Newports, I felt like that kid too.

We'd do meetings on our phones or whatever, but sometimes we would meet up anyway and of course we'd have to get our temperatures checked or whatever, but sometimes we would just hang outside and shoot the shit. Inside the Rooms, I met people who looked and felt like I did. I mean, they were mostly white folk, but they had the same insides as me. They hated themselves and they probably felt like some potato-bug shell of a human being. But they said "hey" and your name every time you announced you were there and introduced yourself. They said it collectively. And when they did, they sounded like the church choirs back home. And over the next couple of months, it felt like they were sacrificing to help me. May not have looked like it. But, the shape we were in, you give a stranger your number, you're opening yourself up to a person who, once upon a time, was used to lying and stealing and doing whatever to feed their fix. And they did it without asking. Didn't expect no repayment. Sometimes, they did things like that without me even noticing. We were in the foxhole together. With our hoodies and the jackets we wore over them and the jeans and the snow boots and the Newports. That was our uniform. We were doing the work. The necessary, dirty work. Rebuilding our capacity for love. And we knew, somewhere deep in our hearts, that we'd never see the completed building. We're building this church, this cathedral, but we'll die before it's finished. We could imagine it. Most days, it was that image in our heads, this idea of our repaired lives and rebuilt existences—the way we could take up space in the world—that was what got us through. You know what they say: scar tissue's stronger than skin.

Thinking that way made me feel hopeful about people and places, you know? Like when cancer happens to a neighborhood and mutates it, maybe people can come and change it back, you know? Maybe the cancer goes into remission. Places like Hartford or other parts of Connecticut, you saw it all over the country. Sure, rich people were leaving, mostly white people, but they were sometimes takin' their juice shops and their yoga studios with them, know what I mean? We were getting our cities back.

I love New England. It's where I'd spent so much of my life. But I think some of it is made up. Told myself lies about myself, made it seem I was made out of different stuff than I was really made out of, you understand what I'm saying? I have these memories of being a kid and raking leaves on the lawn in autumn and standing on the front porch beneath this tree that had a branch over our front yard and the leaves were just on fire they were so red. Velvet. That's what color they were. And I have these memories of Auntie eventually calling someone to cut that branch down, even though the tree was rooted in our neighbor's yard, because she didn't want that branch falling on the car or on any of us. And it's so vivid, that memory, but I don't know if it's mine really. You tell stories to people in your life and they

tell you their stories, you exchange things. And after a lifetime of doing that, you sometimes forget which are yours and which are theirs.
[Inaudible]

I'm sorry. I don't know why I'm crying all of a sudden. Shit just
kinda happens like that when you get older. Sneaks up on you. I don't
know if it has to do with loss, plenty of people die. Happens in waves,
you know? You're young and it's birthdays, then you get older and
it's weddings, then you get older again and it's funerals. Not even
funerals, even. Sometimes, you hear about a person, what happens to
them. Whether it's violent or not. Natural causes and all that. Sometimes, people just drop out. And you don't think at the time that you're
talking with that person that it's the last conversation you're gonna
have with them. Last time you're gonna hear them speak right in front
of you, close enough to touch. I dunno. Been a long time since I got
to speak this long all at one time. Just remembering a bunch of last
conversations. Whole lotta last conversations.

It was like that in the Rooms, you know. I don't know how much
you know about AA, but it was like that for me in my twenties. People
drifting in and out. You get sober with your cohort, and as broken as
you might be in the beginning, it always does your heart good to see
the same people showing up over and over. Means they're doing at
least that thing right, you know? They might relapse but they come
back. They might find some other way to backslide, give in to their
character defects, but if they're in that room next week or their face
is in that little box on your screen, you know they're doing at least
that thing right. But then a face goes missing. Maybe one week they
don't come because they got themselves a new job and they gotta
go to new meetings. Maybe they move away. Maybe there's a family
thing. Or maybe they're dead. You lose people like that. They just turn
into absences. There's no marker. Just one week they're there and
the next they aren't, and they don't come back. Gave the whole thing
high stakes for me in the beginning. I was desperate. I wanted to help
Auntie out after she lost her job and I couldn't do it while I was in my
cups. That was part of it, but another part of me also just wanted to
live. And wanted to do it different than how I was doing it. I just wanted

to not be in pain anymore. Maybe, at least, know where the pain was coming from. Some of it's just the knowledge you come into, growing up Black in this place, seeing all the ways you can be hated, all the places you're kept out of. I'm sure there was other stuff too. Losing my uncle when I did didn't help. And I never really dealt with Mom and Dad dying either. Never really gave myself time to. I know diagnosis ain't cure, but it's close, right? I dunno. I think I just preferred knowing to not knowing, you know?

Fellowship at the time was mostly white. Poor and white but still white. Never felt like they were hostile against me, but whenever we got together, it was like, "hold up, you gotta leave your Blackness at the door." So, in the beginning, it was like being a Black dude and my political consciousness and all that had to be separate from being sober. Online was different, though. Big fellowship of people of color. I remember, the first POC meeting I logged onto, the speaker was this Bangladeshi cat, and he started out talking about being the son or grandson of immigrants and how the rap he listened to as a kid helped him get politically conscious and got him more involved in being Muslim, and he's talking about how he had to basically be this chameleon to fit in with all the white kids at school or at parties or whatever, and it's like five minutes into his share and I'm bawling. Thank God my video was turned off. [Laughing] Never got to meet any of them in person, but that fellowship saved me. Didn't have to conveniently forget I was a Black dude in those meetings. Saved my life.

Still, you're lonely, know what I mean?

It's just hard being with people sometimes. I mean romantically. Found out somewhere in the mix after college that I had bipolar, and I remember what it felt like to hear that. I'd been so hyper and productive as a kid, even in college. I could get all the work done and then some. Could party as hard as anyone. And then some. But I just figured I was makin' up for the time I lost not bein' able to get out of bed. Kinda explained why I loved the drink, but it wasn't the kinda explanation that's one-and-done, you understand what I'm saying? The bipolar and the drinking, they danced together. I could drink while I was hypomanic and be the life of the party. Or I could drink to pick me up from the depression, but sometimes it would just bring me lower. You know how sometimes you'll be in a depressive episode and it feels like you're locked in a room with no ventilation? No windows, no doors. And there's no conceivable way of getting out. And someone on the outside, someone bigger than the whole room, keeps raising the temperature. Up and up and up and up and up. Till you're suffocating, and you'll do anything to get out. Even something stupid.

IF survival instinct was such a goddamned primitive function in beasts, then why are flies so intent on getting themselves killed? In my prison cell, the mindless things seem to have been created for no other purpose than to remind me of just how far my chains allow me to stretch. I'd reach to swat at some buzzing beside my head only to have my shackles yank my delinquent wrist back to its proper place. Maybe they aren't earthly creatures but rather totems of torment. Creatures governed by powers and principalities beyond my seeing, powered by the same wills that shook autumn leaves from trees and cracked the sky open with thunder and set families at war with each other when the red dust came.

The fly I thought I'd killed—I'd felt its plump body crash against my fingers—alights on my thigh and, in the dying sunlight that comes through my window, is showered with motes of dust like snowflakes in miniature, a small devil of everyday life basking in celestial luminescence.

Sometimes in the cell, I will hear a voice, not speaking anything intelligible or anything I recognize as speech, but a voice nonetheless, humming, familiar and alien all at once, and I'll sit up from where I've been napping and I'll look vainly for who had spoken, only to realize that the humming has turned into the buzz of a nearby fly and the air isn't so much populated with spirits as it is with insects.

They sound like Samuel sometimes, and in those moments when I'd get up from my nap and think he was near, my frustration links with a new sorrow in my chest and I feel like I've been falling forever, even though I'm sitting down on a cold hard slab of rock. I'll hear his voice, unmistakable, despite him humming a tune he had no way of knowing and the fly that will settle on my shoulder or the top of my ear or somewhere in my hair would be spared another swat, for I'll, in that moment, become convinced that it holds the reconstituted essence of my brother who, before I head off to go lose a war, gets himself cut in half by a Special he'd thought was his friend. He was simple like that.

The same feelings catch me when the dying light would bleed on the wall in front of me a silhouette I recognize of a more shapely Virginia or sometimes Dora's face in profile, the stone and light mixing to make something that rests somewhere between the physical and immaterial, a thing I'm convinced I can touch but that will fill me with fear and wonder upon that touching. An angel, even in the shape of a fly, is an artifact of glory and who am I, a degenerate horse thief and Marauder, to kill such a thing?

Stars are on their way. I can tell from the lessening of light through the window. And the flies' buzzing grows even louder now that there are fewer animals about, my prison guard retiring for the evening. Maybe this is Dora's last attempt at reforming me or maybe it's Sam finally saying that, as they were cutting the ears off of every white they could find, maybe those Blacks tearing hell through our country weren't so bad.

Maybe I'm just desperate.

Hoping, in my desperation, that I'm a bigger man than this. That if one squints and takes my life in its brief entirety, one might see a pun, a thing vaguely resembling the universe, my own dereliction mapped to cosmic movements.

The fly hops up off my thigh and disappears into the night that has invaded my jail cell.

A dog barks outside and I twist on my seat to watch the figure of one of my jailers duck-walk under the nighttree with a metal saucer in hand. He kneels to where the dog, back arched, tongue lolling, stands and barks, and he takes the bits of meat from the saucer and holds them out to the dog, who licks and chews and is quieted. There's flatness for miles. In the near-silence, absent the buzzing of flies, I can hear the man whispering nonsense to the beast he has just fed. Loving, considerate nonsense.

I sit back down, waiting for the flies to return. Or at least the one that sounds like Sam.

I hate Ohio.

THE lock turns.

I lie on my side for a bit longer, eyes adjusted to the darkness, and see in the entranceway the Negress's silhouette.

"Where's the body?" she says and I can tell in her voice that there ain't no more of that mutual "respect" we'd cultivated during that train ride from Kentucky to Ohio. "Where's the body?" she asks again.

I sit upright, my chains slinking about me, and make a show of wiping the sleep from my eyes. How many nights had she ridden, state to state, crossing from Specials-Occupied territory to Whiteland and back, searching for what I told her might or might not be there?

"You said the body would be over in the valley. That desert trail you took to get back from here."

I wait.

"It ain't."

In the near-darkness, I can hear the change in the marshal's voice, the new steel in it, the hardened will of a woman who suspected she might not get to do what she had set out to do. I smile. "You cain't find twelve white men in all of Lorain County who'd convict me under color of law for kidnapping." I'm more than a little astonished at my fortune. Anybody saw my record of bets at the racetrack could tell I've never been that lucky. Lucky me that it's against their law to strap me to a chair and plumb the depths of my beshitted mind for proof of the crime. "Bet they all died in the War, didn't they. And you cain't find that little boy I allegedly ran down with his momma. And that nigger woman I ran down—allegedly—is off in the wind. Which means, all that's left is the one I shot. Allegedly." My smirk enlarges. "Without that nigger's body, it looks like I don't get to hang, don't it."

"Don't it."

Looks like we're goin' to Texas.

Before I can raise my hands to hit back, the marshal is on me, keys wrangling the locks on each chain and in a few moments, my shackles fall away. My instinct is to rub my wrists, then as the marshal kneels before me and finishes undoing my restraints, I hold back the urge to wrap my fingers around her neck and engineer a new path to freedom. But she stands up and says in a voice that seems to grip the collar of my shirt, "Let's go find that body."

I let her pull me with that voice because maybe if I walked the way I walked, I could carry the illusion that I was the one holding the trump cards, that I could go the other way whenever I wanted and that I chose out of some mysterious motive to stay. Maybe it's myself I'm trying to convince. That I'm really going along because I don't want to feel that glowing collar around my neck yank me somewhere I don't want to go. So I step with the Negro marshal. Follow her to the stagecoach that, when it gets going, moves with others before and behind it as a caravan. Sit beside her as she fiddles with the loose wrapping around her hands, more relaxed than she'd been at that bar, the both of us listening to the two nigger gravediggers who sit up front under the night-sheet pocked with stars, shovels erect between their knees, telling a story I can't understand, that sounds, when I drift off into sleep, like something that could have only existed in a dream.

[May 17th, 20—, 10:48 p.m.]
I heard there might be jobs down south, that the South was sort of rebuilding itself. A lot of young professionals at the time—highly educated, city folk—were headed to the South. Atlanta was the mecca, but there were other spots. And it really felt like there was a fight to take it back. I mean, you had the police shootings and whatnot, and it really turned Ferguson into a heavy place. Reminded you that there was Black folk suffering there. You got little spasms like that in the news. Mom and Dad were in college when Hurricane Katrina hit in, when was it, 2005? Yeah, '05. Dad was a freshman in college at the time and had a roommate from New Orleans, he hold me how he was lookin' at him, and really couldn't believe he was talking about the same place Grandma and Grandpa were living. Same city. And when

the hurricane touched down, all that white kid ever talked about was his family's properties. That's right. Plural. Properties. But he assured Dad that his family's houses were in the "safe" part. Mom was always gettin' on Dad for showing me news clips from that time, but you see all that aerial footage and if you look closely, there's bodies floating in the water. And you look around now and it's like what's changed, you know? What the fuck has changed? They lived through the Ferguson uprising too. That whole era of police killings caught on cell phones and uploaded to YouTube. Some of them had been doing it since Oscar Grant. Michael Brown was the flashpoint for a lot of them. And this cinematographer friend of Dad's from Kentucky sometimes came to visit when I was little and he and Dad would always talk about that time and about working in these white offices. Practically everybody's white. Your bosses, the other reporters, the copy editors, the fact-checkers. I mean everybody. Covered in snow. And Dad and his friend would rattle off these names. John Crawford. Kajieme Powell. Eric Garner. Ezell Ford. George Floyd. Ahmaud Arbery. Breonna Taylor, Tamron Parker, Miriam Ortiz, just goes on and on. Had a work buddy who was one of those guys going back and forth between St. Louis County after that kid Michael Brown's death, waiting to hear if the police that shot him would face charges. And everyone was nervous because you know how it goes, but you're still stupid enough to hope. And the decision came down and everything exploded, but what got to this guy, what ate at him, wasn't the decision itself but the hopelessness—I'm talkin' sheer hopelessness—in the faces of those young men he saw gathered around those fires on West Florissant. Told this cinematographer friend who told me that he cried for about three weeks after that. Freddie Gray and Walter Scott, those were just names to me, you know? Boogiemen that Mom and Dad brought out to tell their little boy how to be when police were around. But these are people who look like these fellas' cousins and uncles. I saw pictures of them and they look like my cousins and uncles. The way Dad talked about it, was like war reporting. You come up for air after diving into the deep end on segregation in McKinney, Texas, after a little Black girl gets body-slammed by a cop at a pool party, and two breaths later, you gotta write about what your generation thinks of that white boy that shot up that church in Charleston. Mom didn't talk much about that stuff, and I think she just wanted to raise me to grow up in a better place, you know? More peaceful? She didn't wanna kill the hope in her little boy. I mean, she knew what was what. She knew what the world was, knew what this country was. But I'd hear her chew Dad out after one of his friends came to visit or called and they got to reminiscing.

But the South was what was happenin'. We were different from our parents and grandparents. Supposedly. Not to say that they weren't as strong as us or that they just took it on the chin while we were ready to fight for what we wanted. Not anything like that at all. We got what we got because of what they took and how they faced the worst of white people.

One time, Dad's cinematographer friend, he told me that whenever he ran into some difficulty or some challenge making a movie, he would think back to growing up in Louisville and what the lighting was in those moments. He was all about using what lighting was available. If it was dark in a room he was filming in, like nighttime, then he would use Christmas lights, that sort of thing. Or he envisions the light in his aunt Mary's kitchen. Told me whenever he had an issue or couldn't figure something out, he would tap into those memories. [Inaudible]

I don't know why I thought of that just now. Maybe it's just all this talk about what the South meant to me at that time. Maybe what it meant to a lot of us. I grew up in the North too; they had their prejudice. Whenever some white politician would roll back women's rights—and you'd have a white woman governor signing an abortion ban into law, stuff like that or when a cyber police budget would get approved and those fucking robot dogs would show up on our block or a school had to shut down because the state government got lax about virus stuff— people would be like "oh we should burn down Alabama" or "Mississippi is just a buncha hicks" or "Georgia should go ahead and secede if they wanna go back to the Dark Ages," as though there weren't all kinds of Black people fighting for their lives against all the white folk trying to kill them down there.

So after I left that tech job, I headed down South and that's where the stupid thing happened. Actually happened on the way there, but there's no need to get into all that. But yeah, I was in my early thirties the first time I saw the inside of a prison.

THE carriage stops.

One of the Negroes in the wagon up ahead, monstrous, steel-formed giant of a man, staggers off the wagon bench into the brush by the side of the path, coughing blood into his palm until he stops and vomits over some cacti. That tax you get for walkin' around this radiation-ridden plateau gotta get paid somehow. Even if you got augments.

He heaves again, chunks in a stream of red and pink. Like he's trying to expel the demons that God had stuffed into his body upon conception. May cancer kill him dead.

The nigger walks back to the wagon, still a giant, but one whom cancer has hollowed out, whose steps clang against the desert floor with an empty, excavated ring. A shell whose important parts have rotted away.

Two deputies flank the marshal on her bench, one of them holding the reins. And they chuckle to each other.

"I know that field," the one on the marshal's left remarks, pointing off past a rounded mound of sloping hill. He shifts his rifle between his legs as he talks. "Would come out with Joe in the mornin's before chores and shoot off a couple rounds to get good."

"What'd you do that for? Nothin' to hunt here in these parts 'cept coyote. And I'll be goddamned if you went and picked up a taste for coyote."

The first deputy shrugs. "Wasn't about eatin' what we shot, really. More 'bout shootin' it and nothin' else."

"Shootin' just 'cause?"

"Shootin' just 'cause."

"You think that big fella's gonna make it all the way till sunup?"

"I wouldn't bet against it."

"It or him?"

"Whatchu mean?"

"When you said you wouldn't bet against it? That mean his livin' or his dyin'?"

"His livin'."

"That so?"

"You seen the size of 'im. Could probably beat a steam drill just like that John Hardy fella."

"You mean John Henry."

"Do I?"

"John Henry's the fella beat the steam drill. Hardy was a gambler."

"Naw, I heard it in a song—"

"Well, you heard it wrong. And I got about a dozen friends and family members back in Talcott, West Virginia, willin' to tell you so to your face."

Time was, they coulda just looked it up on a computer.

The first deputy shrugs again. "All right." He spits. The jet of sputum shoots out like a train from a tunnel, disappears, and lands with a splat against a rock. "Still wouldn't bet against it."

The rolling of the wheels over the desert's debris becomes its own lullaby music until it stops and the marshal is standing at the carriage's side, waiting for me to step out. She has rope in her hands and when she binds my wrists, I don't protest. I imagine she is pretty sore about the last stop.

She walks me out the carriage and one of the deputies walks with us as we cut a path through the sharp-bladed desert grass and sagebrush that tower like sentinels over their arid fiefdom. We walk until the caravan is out of sight and the way the deputy cradles his rifle makes me wonder if I might have to dig my own grave out here soon. Cheatgrass and Mexican horsetail scratch at my ankles and I am glad when we stop, but that gladness flees me when I see the well not ten meters away. The others wait for me to say something, to verify that their suspicions are correct and that somewhere in this vicinity a body is buried, to plead for mercy having been spiritually aggravated by proximity to my crime, I dunno. But whatever it is, I don't do it, and the marshal sees that I won't, so she sniffs, her deputy spits, and she says, "It ain't here, either, is it."

And I look around because I feel I owe them that much, then shake my head.

The marshal turns to lead me back, but the deputy stops me.

"We could be standin' on that boy's grave right now, not knowin' it, and this guy's laughin' at us. How you know he ain't full of shit right now?"

The marshal turns to me. "Are you?"

I shrug. "I was drunk when it happened. And it was dark out." I look around at the mounds that seem to be, in the light from the deputy's lantern, constantly changing shape. I'm sober as a stone, but it all looks like a massive dreamscape. None of the lines stay still.

"You sure 'bout a well bein' there?" the marshal asks, not seeming the least bit exasperated with me.

"I, I don't know. There mighta been."

"And there mighta not been," the marshal says to herself, and that ends the conversation.

Silence burdens the air between us before the marshal brings me back to my carriage and leaves me to go talk with her deputy, who hasn't moved and who wears a look of indignant obstinacy on his mug. Even from where I stand, I can hear the sheriff snoring a few wagons ahead, face engulfed by hat, fingers laced across his chest, boots up on the bench in front of him in the wagon bed. The niggers speak in hushed tones above me, either not caring that I can hear or not knowing I can.

"You think the sheriff's gonna realize how far gone we are?" the first asks.

"Fool's fast asleep. I were in the same car as him, I'd kick 'im just to show you. Fool'd sleep through three thunderstorms in a row, wake up wonderin' why the grass was so wet and who knocked them trees over. Fool can't barely put his gun in his holster 'thout shootin' hisself. How he gonna know we as far gone as we is?"

"I only bring it up 'cause that white man they say killed that lil' boy, he might could go free if'n that body's far 'nough out west. Ain't no law there in the Territories." He means Whiteland.

"Homesteaders, though."

"White folks just as stupid as that sheriff, you ask me. Ain't nothin' out here but could get a man killed. And here they are just chasin' it like a babe after candy. Don't know nothin' but violence."

The second groans. "You start philosophizin' again, I'm f'in to walk back."

"We get out into other counties, we'll be walkin' back anyhow."

"Maybe we won't have to dig none. Shit, it's hotter than all get-out."

"Nigger, we ain't that lucky." The first harrumphs. "Ain't got that white man's luck." His voice dips, as though he's hiding it even from his companion now. "White man can go and get drunk as he want, shoot a free no-Special-type nigger ain't do him no kinda harm, and have us niggers sweatin' till the Third Comin' chasin' our own tails, diggin' holes in the goddamned dirt while he snickers at them that caught 'im. I tell you, two bits says we don't find no kinda body out here."

"You willin' to bet your pay on that?"

What did it matter? The sheriff is oblivious to the fact that we sit at the ambit of his dominion, that if we keep on for much longer, whatever body gets found would mean nothing in the case for me hanging. The part of me that loves hearing myself talk wants to nudge the man awake and warn him, wants to skirt a little closer to the quicksand's epicenter, but learned prudence keeps my mouth shut.

[May 17th, 20—, 11:56 p.m.]

They had me at Gladden Correctional in South Carolina. Bishopville. In Lee County. Largest max in the state, and it had eight other prisons to compete with. Here's a thing about South Carolina, at least at the time: one in ten prisoners was servin' a life sentence. If you were doing a long bid, you had to do at least 85 percent of your time. That's automatic. No getting around that. You could be an angel on the inside, no getting around that 85 percent. If you got twenty years or more on a felony charge, you ain't gettin' out till maybe seventeen years later. If all goes well. And here's something about Gladden specifically: year or two before I got there, seven inmates died in a riot. Apparently the deadliest in the twenty-five years prior. Quarter of a century. That's where I was headed. No prior incarceration, no jail experience, no prior charges. Decade earlier, I was studying abroad in Paris. Hell, I went to Yale! Just . . . wrong place, wrong time, and there I go. You know what's really wild about the whole thing? I'm still thinking about what this means for my student loans! [Laughter]

The riot mighta been after I got there, I'm not sure. This is where things start to get fuzzier. I was always stressed, practically to the point of breaking. Because, at that age, you have a pretty good idea of all the different ways you can be hurt. Physically, psychologically. You know your pain threshold, or you think you do. So you spend quite a bit of time wondering what it's going to be like when you're finally raped or whether or not you should do like in TV or the movies and walk up to the biggest guy in the yard and try to hit him just to prove you're not the one they should mess with. Doesn't occur to you that a big part of prison is the boredom, you know? The tedium of it. You don't learn that till later, sometimes till too late. There's all kinds of ways you can hurt. Another thing you realize is that a lot of the racism you mighta seen or experienced out there is milk and cookies compared to what's waiting for you in here. It's like the curtain's raised on America in there and you see the country for what it really is. You see what people are like when you tell them to let go of their inhibitions. I ain't never seen anybody hate another person the way a white South Carolina CO did beating a Black inmate with his nightstick on the causeway.

But there are things you pick up. Some of the guys who had phones would make these short little videos to put up on the socials and show people on the outside what it was like and how you could do certain things. Like how to make your own electrical unit. They used to be called "droppers" back in the day. Like, way back. Like, Attica-back. And what you'd do is you'd take two razor blades like this, see? And you'd put matchsticks between them and wrap them together with string or thread, whichever you had near. Take a paper clip to hook a piece of lamp cord to the thing, then place the whole thing in water and boom. You got yourself a heater. What's the process? Electrolysis? Yeah, that. The heaters were contraband only when the COs felt like giving you a hard time. But being caught with one could get you put in AdSeg. Or sometimes, instead of AdSeg, they'd just lock you in your cell. They did that sometimes when solitary was too full. Figured it was about the same. But things were just inconsistent a lot of the time. You thought you knew how a CO was, whether this was one of the hard-asses or this was a guy who respected you if you paid him respect, then they'd turn around and dock you for something they let slide a week or two ago. Even the guys who'd been there a while, it got to them too. Because you figure a man can endure just about any routine. But it's the back-and-forth of it that gets to him. The fickleness. If the only constant is chaos, then you're always primed for static. If nobody's gonna give you peace, ever, then you gotta be ready for blood all the time. And if you took anybody's blood pressure at Gladden, you woulda broke your machine or whatever.

I heard how it used to be. Like at Attica in the 1970s. Nobody who was alive then was alive now, but these things get passed down.

The state only gave you this thin gray coat, two work shirts, three pairs of pants, one pair of shoes, three pairs of underwear, six pairs of socks, and one comb. Everything that could be gray was gray. Then, once a month, you'd get a bar of soap and a roll of toilet paper. One roll. That's all you got for free. You can't even say they fed you. You just get used to going to bed hungry. That's why you angle for jobs in the kitchen or mess hall. Sure, it's seven days a week rather than five or two or whatever, but at least you can get some leftovers. To get anything more than that, toothpaste, deodorant, extra toilet paper, you needed money. You wanted to call your loved ones or have them call you? You needed money. Hell, sometimes you even needed to grease a palm to get visitation rights back. So you worked or you hustled or both.

Going to prison at that time was like going back in time. On the outside, smartphones and cyberization and Colonies, and on the inside, concrete and transistor radios. [Laughter] You could ask for magazines or books and there were some organizations that made it their mission to send stuff to you. But especially after the latest wave of protests and riots and stuff on the outside, they got real old school about all that. In theory, everybody's mail could get censored.

Or opened. Letters got thrown away. Stuff blacked out. Every time a magazine was sent in, it had to go through the administrative committee who would review it. But if you were Black and put in a request, more likely than not, it wound up on the prohibited list. It was like that for a lot of the Arabs there too. Almost nothin' we wanted made it past the mail room. My heart went out to the Puerto Ricans and the Guatemalans there. Anything written in Spanish got thrown out immediately. Couldn't have no common-law wives or husbands come in or any kids you had with them.

One cat in there, Puerto Rican cat, had me help smuggle this letter out for him. And you're probably wondering if I read it already and whatnot to make some sort of judgment about the type of person I am who would read someone's letter like that . . . but, yeah, I read it. [Laughter] He said for the person he was writing to not to write their name when they wrote back, so the letters won't get confiscated. Because he was being retaliated against by some COs on some nonsense or something or other. He told this person he listened to WVOC or WDXY, one of the AM radio stations they got in Bishopville. Told this person he listens between 6:30 p.m. and 7:30 p.m., because that was after dinner. Call in and the DJ will take requests. Even though it was a news talk station, they had this part of the night when they could let listeners call in with a message for somebody in one of the prisons. Ask them to play a song or just say hi. Just to hear the other person's voice. They started it when the pandemic first hit, as a sort of goodwill thing because prisoners were dying left and right and the jails and whatnot wanted to put on a good face and stay open. So, if they could make sure everything was copacetic, they let the calls happen. Lot of people let up on the prisons after that. Anyway, the reason this is important—this story—is because he writes the other person's name in the letter. Tries to be coy about it, but I can see, even with the Spanish sprinkled through, who this is headed for. It's goin' to Freddie. What do you think about that? Wild world, right? Freddie! The Puerto Rican cat I lived in Hartford with all those years back! Gave me even more questions about what Freddie'd been up to all this time. Anyway, I couldn't turn around and tell this guy that I knew the dude he was writing to, otherwise, he'd know I read his letter. So it just stayed with me. Didn't tell no one. And Freddie had no idea where I was or that I was in here and that he could write to me too. Just a little bit of cosmic choreography I had to keep to myself. Fella's name was Joaquin, and it turns out, he'd been just a year or two before me. The story seemed to be that, for the most part, the prisoners did what they were told, all about trying to do their time and get out, right? And prison's got routine for the most part, even if that routine happens to include regular opportunities for you to get the dogshit beat outta you by a CO or someone in another gang. But lately, there'd been a different crowd coming in. Some of them were new kids who got picked up off the street, some of them were transfers from out of state, and they were young. They were young, they knew what was going on in the world, and they knew what they were talking about. Could quote Mao and Malcolm but they'd read Audre Lorde too. bell hooks, Angela Davis, all of that. Their parents were protesters and activists and you could tell stuff was getting bad on the outside with the space stuff because of how these kids were coming in. And you'd see these cats standing up for themselves even when they didn't have a gang of fellas with them and it was just them and the CO. Was like watching a white guy poke his finger in a cop's face and tell him his taxes pay that man's salary. It's thrilling in that car-crash kinda way, know what I'm saying? Part of me, though, sees a brother and feels sick. Like, I know what's in that kid's future. And it was like that for a lot of 'em. But they didn't bow. Some of them would get beaten damn near to paralysis. But they had this air about them. And it's not like it was all them either. Them bein' at Gladden unlocked something in the rest of us. You spend all that time cut off from the world, and you forget that almost right before you came in, it was normal for someone's name to be a hashtag on the Twitter app and it come out that they'd been shot eleven times runnin' away from a cop and that there was video evidence and that you had to watch that and that the cop would get off scot-free, first with paid vacation, then they're back on their beat. So these kids were a reminder of that. And it'd get into this cycle. You had the CO decide to be a jerk. Then the kid would take it standing on his feet, and so would a bunch of the others. Then that'd make the CO get his posse and they'd come down even harder on the kids, who'd find their own way to respond. And you could tell it was making everyone antsy, because every CO there knows that their life and their safety depends on us prisoners feeling a sense of respect and that if we have a legitimate complaint, it'd fall into a willing ear. You lose that, then you're one dude walking 120 inmates who don't like you all the way to breakfast. But a lotta people are COs that got no business being COs. Not only that, your population of guards is pullin' from the rural South Carolina job market? Lotta poor white people bein' left behind while the planet's gettin' warmer and the rich folk are fuckin' off to space. A lot of the bad stuff white folks did to Black folk, they did to these kids. Some of these kids came into here beyond hope. They watched their parents get spied on by police and picked up in unmarked vans. Had their first taste of first-gen toasters. They just knew how the whole system was. They knew, and they didn't give a fuck. I think it just made them more likely to blow the whole place up. Ain't no cage for their kind of angry.

CAYENNE startles. Shakes away the residue of Jacob's shadow, which had darkened the corners of her vision.

The desert is empty before her.

That ringing in her chest sounds again, and even though she knows she is the only one to hear it, the sound ripples over the plateau, winds down the path that cuts through the hills and, like quicksilver, swallows the landscape until it is gone, and that invisible tugging that has so far led her to the horizon lessens and Jacob is no longer so loud a voice in her head that she can hear nothing else.

Behind her, the sheriff and one of Cayenne's deputy marshals argue in hushed tones about how far they've traveled, the sheriff insisting they could not have already covered fifty miles, the deputy declaring that the sheriff had no way of knowing that they'd traveled fifty miles because he'd slept through most of them. They buzz back and forth at each other for several minutes as Cayenne leads the caravan. Then Cayenne hears the sheriff's horse approach, prepares herself.

"How do we know this jackal's not leadin' us into an ambush, Marshal?"

"He ain't had no chance to round up a posse."

"He's got brothers know he's been arrested."

"Ain't had no chance to reach 'em, tell 'em where he's goin'."

The sheriff looks for something to hit, tightens his grip on the reins. And because Cayenne is a Special and a marshal and somehow still alive for breathing in planet-poisoned air after all this time, Cayenne cannot be hit. "We're sure he's takin' us to the body? You talked to him during your ride down here. That what he said?"

Cayenne sniffs and spits. "He didn't say much worth repeatin'."

The sheriff follows suit, squints at the rolling lumps of hillside in the distance, at the desert past that, doesn't trust any of it. "Haulin' us out into the goddamn Whiteland wilderness is what he's doin'." He halts his horse. Cayenne clips ahead, then stops, turns around, sees the sheriff cast that calamitous, not-born-yesterday-on-the-lookout gaze over the desert. "I've had about enough of this."

He wheels his horse around, and Cayenne sits quietly atop hers as the mustachioed, ample-bellied, thick-armed sheriff rides to the prisoner's coach, dismounts, and drags the prisoner out, yanking him by his rope. Cayenne quiets her horse beneath her as the sheriff drags the prisoner across the ground, raising small puffs of dirt, drags him to a small copse of sagebrush and kicks him, twice in the legs, then angles toward the stomach, then the head, each kick building in wordless fury. Cayenne's deputy trots to her side and the two watch the prisoner's resistance diminish until each kick becomes an already-accepted fact of existence and it is only the prisoner's duty to bear it.

It's the own man's folly that's got him here, Cayenne tells herself, on the ground taking a beating from a lesser man than he. And the marshal wonders why the prisoner doesn't just open his mouth, acquiesce to the strangling, and vomit the location of the body that's surely buried somewhere in this country. Then she chides herself for wondering. If the train ride proved nothing else, it proved that there was no knowing some white men. That there were those who bled red like her but were governed by impulses alien to her, driven by foreign engines, and that the hurt and the pain that some fled from, others ran toward. White folks were, to one degree or another, predisposed to madness even before the War.

The sheriff's boot comes off the prisoner's cheek, then thuds in the man's stomach again and the sheriff stands over the prisoner, huffing, spittle dripping down his chin. Realizing himself, he wipes it from his mouth then stalks back to his horse, leaving the man's rope in the dirt.

Breeze from nowhere stirs the prisoner's clothes.

Cayenne dismounts, walks to the man, gathering rope as she approaches, and turns the man over to see his blood spilling from gashes on his face. The prisoner spits out a tooth, coughs phlegmy red strings into the brush, then comes up to one knee. He topples over, and Cayenne slips the man's arm over her shoulder, the rope coiled in her free hand, and notices there's no smile on the prisoner's face.

"You got a cigarette?" the prisoner asks in a whisper before they get close to the caravan.

Cayenne pretends not to hear, helps the man slowly mount the steps against broken ribs and a new blood-rich cough. She waits while the prisoner takes his seat, then pulls a rolled cigarette out of her shirt pocket.

"The hell you doin'?" the sheriff bellows.

Cayenne looks at him, the gesture explanation enough.

"Put that away. Don't give 'im that." The sheriff stomps to where Cayenne stands, snatches the cigarette from her fingers, then looks to the prisoner. "He ain't gettin' shit till he's earned it." And stomps toward his horse, forgetting that Cayenne is the federal authority of this party of lawmen for the duration of this search, remembering that Cayenne is Black.

Cayenne mounts alongside her deputy, who had remained atop his horse the whole time, and the caravan resumes its course until they come across a stream, whereupon Cayenne dismounts, helps the prisoner down from his coach, and washes the man's face with water.

The river is already dark, but Cayenne thinks she can see where the man's blood renders the river violet. She can't tell. She pauses in the act of drying the prisoner's face and, on the man's cheeks, the glistening water melds with the streaks of half-dried blood, like tears.

Almost as though he had been crying.

HER horse moves beneath her.

Her lids drift closed in half sleep.

She removes her hat, wipes sweat from her forehead with her forearm, squints through the stinging moisture.

The sheriff's horse clops at the same steady pace behind her, the carriages rolling softly over rocks and snakeskin. Cayenne tries to shake herself into wakefulness, fits her hat to her head.

The caravan moves onward.

Something pointed and invisible knifes Cayenne in her chest. She sees a young man's face in the waking dream that haunts her, and it is Jacob's face. The air is thick with him, his smell, the heaviness of his voice, the swelter of his rage. Then Lincoln's dark, star-dappled face fills her vision. Placid, settled but all the more terrifying for carrying Jake's rage too. *I left you,* she wants to hiss and weep at once. *Leave me alone.*

A homestead looms in the twilit distance.

[May 18th, 20—, 12:41 a.m.]
Word got in through the prison admin grapevine about these new inmates, and as soon as they got to Gladden, they were held in keeplock. Twenty-three hours a day in their cells. Half an hour for rec, sometimes meals brought to their cells, sometimes not. I don't know what the thinking was but it just made everyone harder, and that's why we did that first hunger strike. For a lot of the guys, they didn't even need that much pushing. The food had started to taste worse, and the water was coming in a different color. Kinda had a reddish tint to it, like the dishes and cups they came in were rustier than usual. Was only twenty-four hours, but a few of the guys got sick. Would turn out, they had cancer, and I figured they came from places like I came from,

brought a piece of home into prison with them. So you got the sick bay overcrowding and our medical care already left a lot to be desired. But it was getting bad for some of the guys. Vomiting and some had sores coming up on their skin, nasty stuff. Real nasty stuff. Either the prison staff didn't know or they didn't care what was going on. Besides, only quarantine option was to throw the sick guys in AdSeg. Some of the guys caught fever, others got really bad headaches. After the hunger strike, the commish sent word to Gen Pop that he was willing to hear our grievances. By now, some of the guards were starting to worry too. We noticed that there was a lot more bottled water on their side of the bars. There were some staff reductions and that didn't make things any less tense. You had a lot more guards calling in sick. Some mighta actually been sick. Some probably just figured the overtime wasn't worth walking through what the place was turning into.

Now, if you look at Gladden from above, get some drone footage, you see there's a spine in the middle, connected at the long ends by an overground tunnel to two main admin buildings. Then on each side of the spine, you got these smaller, what we called "dorms" or housing units. They look like butterfly wings. You had about 250 inmates to a dorm, but apparently, the day of what happened, there were about forty staff on hand to handle about fifteen hundred, sixteen hundred inmates.

Anyway, everybody's already tense, and we go out into the yard for our rec time, and two of the guys from my dorm start getting into it. Turns into a little scuffle, nothing big. Couple of the other guys watch, some of the younger dudes wanna jump in, because they ain't get the violence they came in here with drugged outta them yet. But one of the COs comes over to break it up. I think the guy's name was Roof or Ruuf or something. I remember us thinking it was funny, what his name was. He comes over, and usually when that happens, there's a little bit of shouting and everyone calms down. But, for whatever reason, maybe it was the wrong kinda summer-hot—you know, the type that gets angry kids out on the stoop, the type that gets kids shooting each other, that type—but Officer Roof comes over and tries to calm people down, and before you know it, Joaquin—he was Freddie's friend—he hits the CO. Right in the chest. He didn't get him across the face or nothing, nothing to leave a bruise or anything like that. But he hit dude so hard he took a couple steps back. Maybe Roof was just stunned more than anything else. Like he couldn't believe something like that could happen to him. As scared as the COs are all the time, they still fancy themselves some kind of invincible, you get what I'm saying? Anyway, Roof goes back to the other guards, and gets one or two of 'em—I think it was two—to come back. And by now, everyone's pretty shook, as tense and jumpy as we all been. Because we know something evil's about to happen to Joaquin. But the guards that come, they just say that there ain't gonna be no reprisals, no payback. They get that everybody's tense, conditions have been rough. And the guy's actually talking about what we been going through. Like he gets it.

Anyway, next day when our block's off to breakfast, Joaquin's cell won't open. He's been put in keep-lock. And we figure we know what's gonna happen if we leave him alone. They already don't need a reason to beat you, but because of what he did, they just might kill him. So we stop. Right there in the hall. None of us move. Somebody says we ain't eatin' if Joaquin ain't eatin' with us. Then another guy chimes in with the same. Pretty soon, we're all sayin' that out loud, and, sure enough, they pop the lock on Joaquin's cell, and he makes it to mess with us. Turns out, it was the CO who popped the lock, and he called an audible. None of that went through the higher-ups. We didn't know that at the time.

Now, it's standard procedure to have all the gates open at times of the day when there's a lot of foot traffic. By the time we're heading back from breakfast, word comes down that our dorm ain't gettin' rec time. None of us. Apparently, letting Joaquin out was some sort of security violation, even though none of us was really responsible for that. Wanna know how we find out we ain't gettin' rec time? We get to our gate to get out into the yard, and it's locked. Nobody told the CO, either. That's right. Singular. One CO.

There's another group coming back from mess and they're in our dorm too. They see that we've been locked in our tunnel, and they figure out pretty quickly that it happened on purpose. The COs start ordering us to stay in line, but soon as you hear that quiver in their voice, you know it's over. I can't remember who snapped. Mighta been somebody who wanted to protect Joaquin or maybe somebody who wanted revenge for their cellmates—couple guys had got it bad from COs last week for another yard incident—or maybe it was one of the metal shop boys. [Note: the previous April, a work stoppage organized by Muslim inmates at Wateree River Correctional Institution turned into a six-month protest against the conditions of confinement, which included a lack of religious reading material and violation of dietary restrictions during Ramadan. Violent reprisals occurred just after that year's Eid al-Fitr celebration and dozens of the victims were subsequently transferred to Gladden. The event is known as the Eid Uprising.] But all of a sudden everyone's lashing out. It's like don't nobody care about these guys carrying guns or pepper spray or nothin'. Doesn't take long to overwhelm them. One of the guards, pretty quick actually, has blood streaming down his face. I mean, comin' down in waterfalls. And I ain't got no grudge against them personally. Whole time I've been in, I've managed to dodge the worst of what happens here. But you could see on some of the guys, they had the sores, and I seen some of the guys in there that had been coughing up blood. Seemed like after mess, even more guys had gotten sick. We wouldn't find out till much later that there was stuff wrong with our food and water. There's theories that we were being poisoned. Some sick way of reducing the prison population. Call it "reform." But I known it was the reactor.

There was a nuclear station. V.C. Summer Nuclear Station. In Jenkinsville. Fairfield County. See, there's Fairfield County, then east of that, Kershaw. Then, next is us.

THE place is a mystery to me.

I can't figure out how that cow in their yard manages not to look sickly or how storms haven't already pulverized their house into nothingness or how the beginnings of a community (seen in the distance, but of which this homestead is very much a part) can contemplate itself in so barren a wasteland. It is a different post-apocalypse than what had swept other parts of Texas that Spooks had charioted through and claimed with their flags. If that was the barrenness of after, this is the barrenness of before. Makes me think of what the Earth mighta looked like before the Lord spoke its flourishing into being. Before He conjured up plants and healthy animals and people to eat them. When the place wasn't yet meant for living.

And it shows on the homesteaders' faces. The man with a hat that's falling apart and a gun in his hands in about the same condition and that defiant snarl-frown melted on his face by the desert's night-heat. The wife in a threadbare gown, standing in the doorway, backlit by an oil lamp as her cow-faced daughters stir to wakefulness. The homesteader stares us down. Every muscle hardened by difficulty, every wrinkle in his face and elbows chiseled there by bad luck and climate, by calamity and cataclysm and misfortune.

They look feral more than anything else.

I wonder, then, stepping down from the carriage—minding my ribs—to stare at them alongside the gravediggers, when was the last time they saw this many humans at once.

The sheriff detaches from our group and, with the marshal at his side, ambles over to the homesteader, who hasn't let his gun drop an inch, and the three speak in whispers, mostly the sheriff speaking with the odd, brief declamation from the marshal, and the homesteader listening in coiled silence. The homesteader sees that the marshal is Black. Maybe he wonders if she's come into Whiteland to kill him. Maybe he wonders what she's doing with all these whites that are somehow, by the grace of God, still breathing.

The marshal breaks away from them to contemplate the landscape alone, and after a few more moments the sheriff returns and the deputies leave their wagons and follow him back into the homesteader's building. One of them holds the other end of my rope and pulls me forward, lest I think I've been forgotten.

WE are fed tough strips of meat that taste like what I imagine coyote would taste like and given milk in small glass jars. The sheriff and a few deputies hold congress in the adjacent kitchen and in their talk is all the gruff politesse of men at work, men who are always at work, men for whom work is sustenance, breathing. Though to imagine that sheriff doing anything more strenuous than eating a pastry nudges a few chuckles out of me. The place looks bigger on the inside than its outside promised, but I still have to curl my legs at the knees to provide space for the lawmen that sit with me and the marshal, who, by now, has joined us inside.

"Tough livin' out here, I imagine," says the sheriff in the other room, stating the obvious. "Noble of y'all to make a go of it like this."

"We do well enough," the invocation to God parenthetical in the homesteader's graveled voice.

"Coyotes a problem for y'all?"

The homesteader shifts in his seat, announced by the rustling of his overalls. "Not more than's expected."

"Mmm." The sheriff munches on something. "Good milk here."

"Thank you."

And so it goes, back and forth, without substance until talk migrates to the future and what westward expansion might portend for these folks on the outskirts of Eden County. One of the niggers outside starts coughing up a lung again and everyone quiets until he's finished, or dies, by the sound of it, then picks back up again. The marshal reclines against a wall, standing, rifle cradled in her arms. Some of the deputies recline where they sit, pistol-belts loosened or wrapped and lying next to them on the wooden floor, while they finish eating and some of them slouch in slumber. I feel the marshal drilling a hole in my back with her stare, and that's when I notice I'd been eyeing a deputy's loose guns. The pistols fit snugly in their holsters. I look away and bring the glass jar I'm holding to my lips and realize it is already empty. Guess I'm determined to look like a fool.

"And you can bet your ass on my word that I've got no more love for them Charleston suit-and-tie guttersnakes than I do for them scorpions I'm always pickin' outta my boots every morning," bellows the sheriff. "Parasites, always tryin' to stick their hands in the next man's pockets, 'stead of building what they need they own damned selves.

And not stoppin' of course until every parcel of land is subject to their whims and wishes as scribbled out on them parchments they dare to call laws in this part of the world. Last I heard, they're regulatin' where you can and can't set up a dome, protect yourself from the radiation. Think they can put a price tag on good air."

"Yeah, that don't carry too much truck down here."

"Give it time." Takes a drink. "Give it time." He stifles a belch, sighs. "Don't understand that hard work's a God-ordained virtue."

Not knowing, I want to tell the homesteader before sleep takes me, that God originally intended it as punishment.

[May 18th, 20—, 1:22 a.m.]
Anyway, the guys beat the shit outta most of the COs, but this older guy throws his body on top of one of the guards to keep him from getting hurt too bad, and a couple of the other guys do the same. He looked like the type of guy if you asked why he did it, he'd say he done seen enough violence in his life, that sort of thing. By now, we've got a hold of everybody's keys, so we're jamming them in, trying to unlock the gate into the yard. At that point, people just start streaming out. Like it's a flood. Me and the older guy, we lock some of the guards in an office room on the upper floor, mostly for their own safety. They could still radio their buddies in the other dorms, let them know what was up. But for some reason, I don't know why, they didn't. I mean, this had happened a few years prior, prison riot that killed about seven of us. None of the guards were hurt, but it was just some typical gang stuff. Thing is, it broke out in multiple dorms at the same time. Maybe like three of them. So it's not like this type of thing could never happen. That whole thing ended with a bunch of bodies piled on top of each other by the barbed wire ringing the whole prison. That's how that sorta thing squares out in Gladden.

Anyway, guys are streaming into the yard and they catch people right after the mess hour, so a bunch of people still haven't made it back to their dorms. Somebody shouts that we're taking over this place, and that's all it takes. Wasn't nothin' coordinated. But I'm still in my tunnel. And I see one of the guards has been hurt real bad. Probably a head wound. Bleedin' from his nose, mouth, all over his face. And kinda shaking on the ground. Me and the older fella pick him up and carry him all the way to the admin building, which we can walk to freely at this point. We try to get his name, but he ain't in any condition to talk. So when we get to the main admin building, we can only bang on the door and say we got a guard here that needs help. There's enough glass in the building for the admin people to see that there're a lot of inmates that aren't where they should be right now, and they know something's goin' down. Found out later that the alarm wouldn't go off for ten minutes. Which means all the chaos that happened happened in less than ten minutes. We're banging on the door trying to get this guy help, but they're just staring at us. Warden's in there, I think. Prison superintendent. Bunch of the head guys.

Musta taken us a whole 'nother ten minutes for them to open the door and take him in. I'm pretty sure if they'd done it sooner, the poor guy woulda lived. Then again, he mighta died during what happened after. Or he mighta died from the food or water we were given. Ain't no tellin'. All I know is that when the guys would find out, that would be it. We'd have the death of a CO on our sheet. That's murder. And they'd get all of us on it, no matter if we'd hit the guy or not. Me and this older fella too.

We get back and there's almost fifteen hundred inmates in the main yard. They've taken over the Spine, and it looks like a bunch of the dorms are wide open. Still, there's this weird calm over the place. Not, like, calm. But order. Time gets real weird around this point. Real elastic, because all of a sudden, it's the afternoon. And stuff's been set up. I don't know where the guys got these supplies, probably from the metal shop and the various offices and whatnot they had access to during the rumble. Because someone's set up a table and there's a bunch of medical supplies stashed under it and around it. And another table's been set up, and somehow [laughter] somebody set up a speaker system and a microphone! Like it was a block party!

At the time, it didn't feel like the calm before the storm. It felt more like some sort of validation. I came out worried that some race war was gonna break out. You could see how the whites were sorta separating themselves from the rest of us. But you get a little closer and try to see if maybe you gotta get more almost-dead COs to the admin building, and you get there and you see that there's this circle of Black and Arab fellas, and they're facing out. They'd made this sort of protective circle around the hostages. Yeah. That's what the COs and prison staff out in the yard were now. Hostages.

I get there and, suddenly, the old fella's not at my side anymore. He's standing up on this table with a microphone and he's speaking. And you could tell he was from around here. Super South Carolina dude. Said it was time to come together, put aside our racial differences. That we were in a special situation. We had power. And we could use it for petty stuff, getting revenge on people who wronged us here, gettin' high tryin' to forget our worries or forget the fact that this was where we were. Or we could band together and help make things better for all of us. "They have to listen to us now," he said. "They got no choice." I don't know how he did it, but he managed to get through to all of us who weren't already in the bathrooms shooting up or who hadn't already started raping smaller inmates we mighta had our eye on for a while. And then a couple other guys got on the table and started talking and introducing themselves. Couple of them were transfers. Two were Black Panthers, a couple started out as community organizers in places like Ferguson and Milwaukee, fella from Oakland, type of folks to have had tear gas shot at them by police. Coulda come from the same middle-class households as me, just got caught in the dragnet and thrown here. There was a guy from the Young Lords, who repped the Spanish set. And there was some white Marxist cat. Sam something. Started with an M. We called him Red. Anyway, the old guy gives his speech in the beginning, then at the end, he announces that they're setting up a counsel and negotiation team. People can volunteer and people can nominate others. I don't know why, but I volunteer. Maybe goin' to Yale had convinced me I was some kinda smart dude. But I know I wasn't like the transfers who had actual negotiating experience, you know, dealing with the folks at their old facility. I think a reason nobody had a problem with me joining was because I didn't have beef with nobody. Wasn't a part of any crew. Managed to keep my nose clean and all that. Matter of fact, I was pretty well liked. I'm just assuming that last part. Sometimes it doesn't mean people are doing nice things for you. Sometimes, it just means that people aren't doing you harm.

One of the Black Muslims, Rasool, he ends up being the chief medical guy and he organizes trips to the sick bay to get medical supplies. Far as I knew, he wasn't any kind of doctor. But he knew there were guys that needed treatment for things like diabetes and Rona stuff and other long-term-type illnesses. Then there was the issue of the sores and the vomiting that had hit a bunch of us. Pretty soon, though, he's got it all pretty under control. I guess, you give a guy a chance, he can rise to the occasion.

Before the day was done, though, we'd started seeing a response. One of the dorms had been retaken by police or prison guards or the army or whatever. Think it mighta been the Goon Squad. During the initial chaos, we'd been fuckin' afraid of them. Terrified. No-mercy type cats. They wouldn't beat you, they'd cripple you. They don't see no kinda response except just short of lethal. And I guarantee you: quite a few of our guys who died before and after this died specifically because of the Goon Squad. If they could, they'd chop our heads off and put them on spikes outside the prison. They had sharpshooters on the roof, and I didn't even want to think about what was happening to the prisoners still locked in there. For sure, their dorm was on lockdown. Pretty sure the whole prison was, but I wouldn't have been surprised to find out that, say, they'd even cut off the water or whatever. Electricity, water, all of it. That mighta actually saved a bunch of them from what was coming.

We figured them retaking the prison was inevitable. Just a matter of when and not if. You could already hear police sirens wailing on the other side of the barbed wire. Didn't seem to faze the security team, who had taken to wearing red armbands. Saladin was the head of the security team. He was the guy made sure everyone was safe. Everyone. Hostages and the rest of us. Woulda been too easy to let everything go sideways. Lord knows some of us wanted it, but maybe that's why the Lord saw fit to put others in charge.

They set up tents in the yard and made sure everyone got fed from basically what was a community bucket filled with things that people went and swiped from commissary. Candy bars, sandwiches, juice boxes. Imagine what it feels like to eat for free what you used to pay an arm and a leg to get. I bet you think we turned into gluttons, just wasting food and whatnot. But some of us couldn't get it into our heads that we deserved more than we took. Some of us barely took anything, just a little more than our usual portion or what we could normally afford. Sure, there's some rebellion in that fact. But we just wanted to taste free, you know? In the back of your head, you know the bill's gonna come due, and in the worst way possible, but you can't let yourself get bogged down by that. Not in the moment. In that moment, you're free. You can't be thinking of the spiked cage they're building for you.

CAYENNE feels, in the homestead's embrace, an echo of home. Its heartbeat, recognized. As though, at any moment, Jacob might step in from another room, slouch against a doorjamb, hands in his pockets, and smirk.

The others are on the verge of sleep, some having already slipped beneath the lapping waves. The talk between the sheriff and the homesteader has softened and the gravediggers outside have ceased their shuffling and Cayenne imagines them maybe having a smoke and plotting their own mythology in the constellations above their nappy heads. When the lawmen recline, some of them with their hats over their faces, they carry the physical ease of children in their unconscious, a young boy's understanding of his own limbs and the length to which they stretch, the perfect angle at which to pitch one's back for comfort, the easing back of shoulders a man's obligations have pushed up and forward. They are relaxed, and it is the first time she has seen them so.

Cayenne shakes away sleep. Her blood itches at the memories trapped here, someone else's memories, someone else's Pa putting that bench together and someone else's Mama working in the garden, her dress pooled in white around her kneeling form. It was another life.

But Cayenne needs to watch the prisoner, who needs only a moment's inattention to escape and never be found again.

Jacob was here. With his people to come and complete what the storms and flooding and fire and red dust had started. To cleanse the land. Maybe this had once been a town with a town hall and a grocery store and maybe a strip mall and a Main Street and homes populated with white folk a world away from the tornadoes and hurricanes up north and the flooding and the earthquakes and the fires everywhere else. And maybe Jacob remembered what Marauders had done to people who looked like him, and maybe he'd felt like these white folk had needed reminding.

Voices quiet into silence, the lawmen descend further into slumber. But out of the kitchen, a glow hovers, moving slowly through the air until it has entered the main sitting room. Cayenne blinks at it and only after a few moments of confusion sees the figure of the girl silhouetted by the oil lamp's flush. She does not recognize her from the faces that stirred in the window upon their arrival. This one is different and floats more than walks. Glides.

Jacob slouches inside her, hungry.

The girl drifts to the farthest of the sleeping deputies and as she nears, the young man stirs awake and, upon opening his eyes, gapes at the girl for several seconds. He appears caught in a trance, unbelieving of this thing standing in front of him, this evidence of celestial design. She leans forward, her lamp balanced on a tray that also holds up small glasses of warm milk. And the deputy, seeing her offering, takes a glass, all the while wondering at her face and the expressionless luminescence that gilds it.

She is this way with all of them.

Their nap, when they loosened the stole of steely masculinity from their shoulders, was the only precursor to this vision, preparation. They see her and, one by one, they are children again, faces drained of skepticism and flint and filled instead with bewilderment and awe. Did Lincoln ever look at anything like that? she wonders, before biting her lip against the wondering.

Jacob unfurls his claws, Cayenne feels the movement scrape her insides. The girl draws near. Leans forward with neither smile nor frown on her face and offers the tray, which holds only a few remaining glasses. Cayenne hazards a glimpse into her eyes, amber flecked with minims of green and shards of morning. Each of the lawmen, upon holding silent communion with her, had been startled into a posture of recognition, of remembrance, and Cayenne feels herself drawn to the same angle.

The girl then serves the slaver a glass of warm milk and Cayenne watches her fold the tray against her chest and, lamp held at her side, vanish into another room. The prisoner smiles at the girl, and Cayenne takes consolation in that exchange. She decides she won't watch that white man hang in Ohio.

[May 18th, 20—, 1:52 a.m.]
The negotiation team has pretty much all its members, but they wanted to have a better process for putting together their council. Wanted a person from every dorm that was present to be represented, and you could volunteer, but you had to be elected. Once that was settled, they kinda let anybody take the microphone for a bit. That thing hardly went untouched. People made all kinds of speeches. Some were really out there, but some of those fellas, well, they coulda been preachers in another life. This goes on for a while, and you can tell some of the guys are starting to tune it out and figure out what it is they want specifically. But then it comes together pretty quickly that the next step is to write up demands.

I get picked. That's when I got the nickname "Yale." Plenty of the other guys in there had gone to college, some had finished enough course credits there or in other facilities to be able to graduate or whatever, but I think I mighta been the only Yalie in Gladden Correctional Institution. So they go, "Let's have Yale do it!" So me and a white guy, Heath, we put our heads together and basically take all the cacophony and chaos of the past, maybe five hours, and turn it into a list of twelve demands. We were typing, sure, but we also had to be decision makers and translators. Somebody's talking about how the food they get served is against their religion, we gotta translate that into "non-pork diet for select inmates" or if someone's complaining that when we get out, it's impossible to get back into school, we write "better communication with academic institutions to allow for transfer of credits." Also, these issues had to be voted on. In this new "spirit of togetherness" [laughter], you can't let it seem like one person or one group is getting privileged over another. We know what that looks like because the COs do it all the time. And we also know how fragile this whole thing is. It's funny. Sometimes you have an idea of what you're taking part in, that it's history. Mom and Dad talked about that, growing up during a pandemic when the whole country was basically falling apart. Sometimes, you know you're living through a chapter in a history book. But sometimes you're just thinking about the next day or how you're going to get through the next minute. Prison collapses time like that. Somebody stupid once said you only do two days, the day you get in and the day you get out. Now if that ain't the dumbest shit I ever heard in my life! [Laughter] You do every single goddamn day of your sentence! Anyway, I say all that because this Heath cat keeps saying "Attica, Attica, it's just like Attica" over and over and over! Just "Attica, Attica, it's just like Attica!" I'm just like "my man, calm down, we gotta get this list out or this whole thing goes sideways."

Apparently, at some point while we were doing this, the superintendent got on a bullhorn and demanded to know what the hell was going on. So a delegation got sent, and apparently it was four or five guys tricked out in face shields like the Goon Squad had and, like, makeshift bats, kinda for protection but also kinda to protect their identities. And apparently when they got to the pathway, they all start talking at once and the super tells them to shut up, real fuckin' mean. And there's just silence, and they just stare at him. Then one of 'em, mighta been Red—he was a wild boy like that—he says, "We talk to the commissioner, or we talk to no one." Just like that! [Laughter] The superintendent just storms off, and that's that. And that ends up being why this list me and Heath are putting together is so important. We're going to the commissioner. Straight to the commish.

The sirens outside the prison are far enough away that you can still hear people talking in the yard, but there's another sound, softer, and you realize it's cameras clicking. Reporters are here. Heath then comes up with this idea. Usually, if we needed to get info to our lawyer or a reporter or just online in general, like, up on the Socials, like a pic of our face after a CO beat us up or maybe blocked-up toilets or other evidence that what we was going through was damn near unconstitutional, you had to smuggle in a cell phone, snap the flicks, and somehow get the pics out to them. If they unblocked the wifi or data usage, then you could upload shit directly, but you needed, like, burner accounts on the Socials for that. Direct communication was always safer. You could text, or sometimes even find a way to upload them onto a computer at a workstation and send a bunch of files. But they been cracking down on illegal cell phones and blocking the wifi, so that got too tough after a while. Here, though, we had the chance to bring the news to us. And now it was them talking about "Attica, Attica" and that's when it starts to set in that maybe this is one of those history moments too. So we were able to get word out that reporters were welcome and their safety was guaranteed. You could probably guess how skeptical they mighta been. Their whole idea of Gladden was that a year or two back, we'd had a gang riot where seven dudes died. We're the most violent max in the whole state. Everyone's afraid of us. All together, we're the boogieman. So they weren't the first people to see us. First person to see us was actually the commish.

We couldn't really believe it when he came through. I know there musta been some negotiations and stuff that happened between the team and the admin staff, stuff above my pay grade. [Inaudible] But sure enough, out the admin building and into the yard, flanked by this huge, 'roided security team, actually surrounded on all sides by those dudes, is the commish. Bald head, kinda skinny dude with a little bit of a belly. Doesn't look too much like a supervillain in a movie. Has a kinder face than you'd expect on someone in his position. Turns out, he was new to the post, which might explain why he didn't yet have that hardness you get in the face. Maybe one of those people who thought he could turn the place around, so to speak. Make some real reforms or whatever. And, well, if that don't get beat outta you quick . . . [Laughter]

Anyway, he's surrounded by the security team, who bring him to the negotiation table, and I'm sitting right across from him. Everybody's real cordial with him. Black even gets him a juicebox from the food pile. I notice that they made sure he had a clear view of our tents, our sick bay, and all the medicine we had to treat people. Made sure he saw how organized we were handing out food and water. We were organized! That's how they wanted him to see we were. How *we* wanted, actually. You hear about this guy and the power he has over our lives and here's a chance to make a real impression. He ain't just a voice on the shortwave radio, he's here sitting down right across from me, ready to negotiate. Oh, and they made sure he saw the hostages, all surrounded by their own security detail, those dudes I mentioned earlier who were facing outward, they had those stone faces on, not like they're daring somebody to try them, but that they don't have time to play around and that you test them at your own peril.

When we finally laid eyes on the commish, couple of the guys called him Stretch, and the name took. I wasn't gonna call him that, but, for some reason, I can't recall his name. So he's gonna be Stretch in this story. Maybe Mr. Stretch if I'm feeling charitable. [Laughter]

First order of business was finding out why he hadn't responded to our little manifesto earlier. A lotta work had gone into that document, and to be brushed off like that ticked a lot of us off. Made it seem like he was just entertaining us, not takin' us seriously. He told us that he had [finger quotes] taken our demands under consideration. That's what he called them: demands. But that the doc seemed just like a copy of some other stuff that'd been circulating in some California prisons around the same time or a little earlier. So, ultimately, he thought we were just making a ploy or whatever. Maybe he didn't truly believe things were as bad as they were and how close we were to exploding at that time. He coulda prevented a lotta pain and broken bones by just listening to us, but you know how these things go. Whenever we try to talk about our demands, I'm talkin' about the ones we sent out earlier during the uprising, he kept trying to move the discussion to the hostages. We made sure to let him know they were being taken care of. Fed, clothed, hydrated, protected. We made sure he had a good line of sight on them too. But that was all he wanted to talk about. We knew, though. We knew they were the only thing keeping us from getting pretty much killed. Without them, they woulda had no problems straight up storming the prison and leaving our blood on the walls.

That was a thing we asked him about. If he could take care of. Could you get some of the snipers off the roofs? Maybe scale back the police response? We figured we'd showed him that we weren't a pack of animals. And, just under an hour after we started discussions, after he was getting ready to leave, I told him, in a low voice too, "You see, Stretch, we got you in and we're getting you out unharmed. Ain't nobody lay a finger on you the whole time you was here. Remember that." Then he went back to his people, who I imagine weren't too happy that he didn't have the hostages with him. Easy to underestimate a bunch of convicts. Not just prison admin staff but even activists, reporters, all of them. They think they know what we need and want more than we do. Wanna tell our stories for us, because they think we can't read or some shit like that. Like we're primitive thinkers, like we got no sophistication or nothin' like that. Anyway, our sophistication kept us alive that day. And not only did Stretch get the police to pull back a little bit, but he even got the water running again. Some of the pipes got damaged in the initial riot. We also had him check in on some of our friends who were being held in solitary and who we hadn't heard from. Next time he came to us, he had a couple reporters with him. I think they saw him come back unscathed and figured their chances were pretty good. The *Columbia Record, The Sun, Greenville News, New York Times,* even someone from *USA Today.* Prison still wasn't allowing any drones in the airspace over the facility, so it could only be on-the-ground footage. There mighta been some other smaller pubs in there, some online joints, but we didn't care. We were ready to answer whatever questions anybody had for us. Some of the reporters were cyberized, but because they didn't have to go through any metal detectors, they got in and could snap flicks of everything that was going on. Beamed some of that shit straight up to the Colonies, I heard.

Didn't matter who we talked to, just as long as we got the word out about the big thing that was happening here. The extraordinary thing. Samson was in this prison. We were Samson. You know the story of Samson? In the Bible? Mighta seemed like we had small ambitions at first, and I don't know about the others, but I started to feel like maybe, just maybe, we could bring this place down. Not actually bring it down but make it livable. Turn it from the hellhole it was into something you could walk into and still maintain a sense of dignity. Me feeling this had nothin' to do with the reading or the education I had before I got in here. Had nothin' to do with the type of life I lived beforehand. Because I think everybody comes to prison, deep down, wanting that. Or at least some version of that. Who comes to prison wantin' to be turned into an animal?

OUTSIDE, she visits the gravediggers who hold counsel with the stars, their kinfolk.

[May 18th, 20—, 2:51 a.m.]
The old man, one who'd helped me carry that injured CO to the admin building, he said as much. Right when the newscasters and everyone got to the center of the yard, he—the old man—got up on the table with the microphone. Said he was speaking to the people of the United States of America. I don't remember his exact wording, but I remember how the speech he gave made me feel. Everybody was quiet. You could hear a pin drop. Was like nobody was even breathing. And he goes into how we'd asked the prison administration for many things, but they'd only given us murder and brutalization. That's what he said: "brutalization." He told them, "We are men. We are not beasts. All of us, every single man in this facility, is worthy of dignity and humane treatment. This isn't the beginning, this is merely the continuation. We have set out to change the conditions of our confinement and resist the way in which our bodies are brutalized and discarded. We are not disposable. We are not beasts. Listen when we tell you this. We

will be seen. And we will be heard." There was more, some of it was about our specific demands, some of it went into his own background, growin' up local, in South Carolina, and seein' how climate change was fuckin' up his home and how Black people were bearing the brunt of it. But that's the part that stuck out to me. Made sense that he was a preacher's son. He had that bearing about him. A little bit showy but really feelin' like he was being guided by a higher purpose. Kinda like what they talk about in AA. You may not feel it while it's moving you, but you look back and see that you were being guided by this current winding through your life. It's carrying you. And you feel it best when you submit to it. That's what I think the old man felt he was doing, submitting to this higher purpose. You could tell it in the way he spoke. His voice didn't crack, wasn't dry from the poisoned water we'd been drinking, he didn't sound weak from the infected food we'd been getting all summer and going into that September. *That* was our Samson right there. Short hair too. [Laughter] You could feel him pressed up against the pillars of the temple, everybody crowded around him, police watching, even from their drones in the sky. And you could see him pushin' and gettin' ready to bring the whole place down.

After that round of negotiations broke down, some of us were kinda scared that the concessions we'd won—like getting the water running again and establishing food lines—might get taken away. But then talk reached us that they were gonna send a doctor in to check in on the hostages. Not only that, but some local politicians were gonna be coming through. It really felt like a weight was being lifted from us. Every time we looked at the roofs or even outside the barbed wire around the prison, seemed like there were fewer police and army folk. The reporters had thinned out a little bit too, but we didn't think it was 'cause they weren't interested in us. Maybe they just went somewhere we couldn't see. Or they were able to let drones in to record everything.

Outside, you could feel the wind. Like, really feel it. I realize now that was 'cause it was starting to pick up. It was howling a bit and some of us wondered if that was why it felt harder for us to hear each other. They sent a doctor in, not one of the doctors that had already worked in the prison. Those bitch-ass niggas couldn't give a fuck about us when we saw them, whether we needed psych meds or a tooth had rotted in our mouths. There were even stories that they experimented on some of the inmates, sterilized them without their knowing, infected them with all sorts of shit. Anyway, this doc was a new doc. I think he was from a nearby hospital. Anyway, he came in and saw that we'd already put sutures on those who needed it and splinted fractures and all types of stuff. Rasool was in on a murder rap, he was never gonna see the outside of this place. But Doc trusted him enough to send him back and forth for supplies and to help take care of the hostages and the people who needed it. Watching them work together was some kind of magical. You shoulda seen it. Like two peas in a pod. Just straight business. You watch that and it's like you've opened a portal to some parallel universe right next to ours, and you're lookin' at what coulda been. Pretty soon, the doc leaves, and it's just us.

It'd gotten dark and the wind picked up and it was drizzling a little bit. But everybody pretty much decided to sleep in the yard. If we was gonna get attacked, let us at least see it coming. Remember that weight I was talkin' about? The one being lifted? You *really* felt it come up off you now. There was guys in there hugging, somebody started up a drum circle. At one point, you could hear singing, real barbershop-quartet type stuff. I saw Heath wiping his eyes at one point, just kinda standing by himself. He was sniffling and he'd either just finished cryin' or was about to start. Maybe both. I asked him what happened, figured maybe he just got some bad news about family or somethin', and he just kinda stood there for a moment, glowing a little bit, and he looked up at me and just said it'd been so long since he'd been able to get close to someone . . . I'm sorry. I'm just . . . remembering that night. Before so many of us died turning back to look at what had happened to us. Just . . . that night.

Anyway . . . later that night, the old man found me and just kinda stood with me. All my time there, people had been fascinated with me on account of my background. Some people thought I made up the whole Yale thing, but other people would latch on just to hear my story like I was some exotic animal, but the old man, he wasn't like that. He was sure of himself, you know?

You know what he tells me? I'll never forget. The rain was starting to come down pretty hard, and the wind was gettin' really loud, and it wasn't like he was raising his voice or projecting or nothing like that. Matter of fact, he's speakin' real low. And he goes, "It's been so long since I'd seen stars. It feels good. Like a blessing." He gets quiet, then he says, "Story says that there weren't even ten good men in Sodom and Gomorrah. I think there were. And I think before the fire came down, they got a good look at those stars. They felt loved. I believe that."

THE marshal has my ropes wrapped around one fist. Hat tight on her brim, she leads me forward toward the glowing purlieu. The sun is coming, and the sky blues along the horizon toward which we move. Horses clip-clop behind and alongside us. My steps have no more energy in them. The marshal seems in about the same condition as me, driven more by inertia than any other propulsive force. As much as this landscape resembles anything we have walked through before, it is different, sparks a deeper recognition. The marshal doesn't resemble that Spook child at all, but I'd had the kid that many paces ahead of me when we'd last taken this trail.

Air sizzles around us the farther into the desert we amble. No one speaks, but I take it everyone assumes I'm leading us the right way. It feels right. And if they feel I am deceiving them, it wouldn't be a thing for them to kill me and bury me right here where no one would ever know I'd once been alive. A beetle tips itself over, slipping from a rock and landing on its shelled back, sharp, segmented legs clawing the air for purchase. A vulture cries. When I look up to see where the call had come from, there isn't a bird to be found.

We all look ahead to see three black dogs gnawing at a small off-white cloth protruding from the earth. The sheriff fires a round into the air, startling the dogs, and when they see we aren't going to alter our course, they skulk away. I notice now that we have entered a small valley through which runs a barely breathing river.

The sheriff calls out to the gravediggers and they answer by running with their shovels, the big former steel driver trailing behind them,

toward where the chewed thing stands erect. When we see that it's
the toe of a boot, we all quicken our pace and pretty soon we form a
loose circle around it.

Rain has churned the soil since the last time I'd been here, raised
some parts and buried others, and maybe that's how the body came up
like that amid patches of moss and errant greenery. I recognize the pattern along the sides of the upturned boot-toe. We all stop at the thing
and look at it for some time, then the marshal snaps to attention and
cannons out an order and the gravediggers begin disinterring the body.

"Careful, watch the head. Don't damage the head, you stupid. Dig
around the body." The sheriff skirts the edge of the makeshift tomb
like a housecat searching for the right angle of attack. The gravediggers mumble to each other as they work in a language discernible
only to themselves, one of them setting about where the head's buried
and the others angling around the erupted earth by the foot, caving
the ground away to reveal the rest of the leg and the other foot as well.

"Now, go on and get the sack," the sheriff says to one of the marshal's deputies, who looks to another among the deputies, who in turn
looks to another, silent accusations in each gaze. The sheriff, upon seeing that no one has moved, gazes in befuddlement at the young men,
all of whom shrug when his eye falls upon them and who, in the face
of his mounting anger, struggle to hold back renegade chuckles.

"Can't believe this horseshit. You mean to tell me none of yous
had the wherewithal to bring the sack with you when we mounted up
outta Oberlin?"

Nope, their expressions say.

"Christ a'mighty." He paces. Stops. "Well, get the rug, then. We'll
wrap him up in the rug. Lord knows, he ain't ridin' in my carriage."
The deputies sour, and the sheriff turns to the body that has now
been, for the most part, excavated.

I expected the nigger boy's eyes to be gone, plucked out and eaten
by one animal or another, but there they are, agape in wonder at the
sky they're finally getting to see. The gravediggers carve out the sides
of the makeshift grave and stop when they hit metal, look at each
other, then at the sheriff, and resume digging until they've unearthed

a rusted shovel. Everyone stops moving and the sheriff looks at me
with something akin to horror on his face. The deputies stop their
banter. Even the marshal looks at me as if I were something new and
alien to her, like we hadn't spent all that time on the train together.
And the question hovers in the air over us.

You made that boy dig his own grave?

I show no remorse because I am past that, merely sniff and spit at
the ground. Rope burns my wrists.

The gravediggers toss all the shovels out over the edge and one of
them climbs out and positions himself to catch the body when they
roll it up. The deputies arrive with the rug that had served as a place-
mat for some of them during the ride. It unfurls by the nigger standing
over the grave and the two other gravediggers, one of them the cancer-
ridden giant, lift the corpse, twice nearly dropping it, and roll it onto
the rug. It's smaller than I remember. They climb out and start rolling
up the body, when the sheriff shouts, "Wait a minute. Just wait a minute." Pointing to one of his underlings, "Go get me some parchment
and some stove polish. And a bench too, or somethin' to write on."

I still remember a time when we typed things on tablet screens
with our fingers. Christ, I've gotten old.

The kid dashes away, returning in a few moments with a makeshift
writing station. He kneels on the desert ground, back erect, with the
small cardboard box holding the paper down. After a moment, he
undoes his gun belt and lays it neatly at his side, then relaxes into his
posture.

"You ready?"

The kid nods. Everyone but the kid stands in an aspect of rev-
erence, like scattered penitents of a church congregation finally
gathered in the presence of a process bigger than themselves.

"Date: the eighteenth of July in the year of our Lord twenty fifty—"
Dogs bark and I don't catch the rest. We wait. The dogs stop. "Location: Eden County, Texas." He looks to one of the suited men, probably
a magistrate or a magistrate's errand-boy, for confirmation. And when
one of the marshal's deputies nods, the errand-boy nods too.

I shuffle my feet, suddenly bored.

"The deceased, Absalom Clark Morgan, aged"—a pause, then aside to one of his factotums—"how old are we sayin' here?"

"Does the prisoner not know?"

The sheriff regards me. "How ol' was he? General range-like."

I shrug. Gene-fuck property ain't got that kinda age. "Adolescent. Kid-like." I think. "Maybe sixteen. But just barely."

The sheriff frowns at me like I'm playing a joke on him, but I guess that's to be expected. He returns to his former attitude. "The deceased, Absalom Clark Morgan, aged fifteen, was found under a patch of earth within the boundaries of Eden County. Approximately seventy-five yards from the valley ridge a corpse was buried in the ground and upon recognition of said corpse, officers of the law proceeded to dig up and exhume the body. Among them Sheriff John Bell of Eden, Deputy Sheriff Bill Oates, Deputy Magistrate George Hawkes, U.S. Marshal Cayenne Jackson, hailing from Lorain County, Ohio, and several of the marshal's deputies from neighboring counties. Upon their arrival in Texas, they traveled over the course of many miles in a single evening to reach the spot at which lay the final proof of a crime committed in the Specials-Occupied State of Ohio."

The scribe scribbles as the sheriff dictates.

One of the marshal's deputies steps toward the sheriff. "We're not doin' all that autopsy business here, are we?"

The sheriff looks around, shrugs as if to say "why not."

"Ain't a doctor-type among us, Sheriff. We should take him back into town. Least so's his people can identify him." The young man's face softens. "Be a nice bit of closure for the family," he finishes, softly.

Doesn't occur to any of 'em that the boy ain't got no more family, none that can be found, anyway.

I realize then how young all the deputies are, especially the local ones. They have hair on their faces, sure, and they have a man's bearing about them, and they wear their guns the way men should, but many of them don't have the spiritual wrinkles that come with manhood, those devotional foldings that show up as crow's feet or gray hair or arthritis. Those that have it, I notice, seem like the war-hardened back home. The rest, it turns out, had managed to avoid that hardship and haven't yet had the kindness beaten or shot or cut out of 'em. They have a bit more aching to do.

"Yeah, we'll do that," the sheriff says back. He faces his congregation. "The corpse of the deceased, after it was decided that present conditions did not allow for a full and thorough autopsy, was transported back to Galveston, where it was to be transported back to Ohio, reunited with the deceased's family, and prepared for burial." A pause. "You get all that?"

A moment's scribbling, then a vigorous head-nod from the scribe, who fans the paper, then folds it and slips it into his jacket pocket.

Everyone is standing now, silent, unsure of what to do or how next to proceed.

"Y'all can roll him up now," says the sheriff, saving us. And the gravediggers do just that while the big fella fills the hole back in with the shovel I'd made that Morgan boy use before I'd murdered him. The marshal jerks my length of rope, pulling me away, and we all walk back to the caravan while the nigger toils in silence.

I walk close to the marshal, but she doesn't seem inclined toward speaking. Maybe she's got no more cigarettes. Maybe seeing that extra shovel in the grave, that indication of a particular cruelty, has changed her mind about me.

Sunlight bleeds down the valley wall in strips.

I think maybe I'll ask the woman for a cigarette anyway.

The nigger giant batters the rest of the delinquent earth into the ground with a thud-dull smack, and joins us.

A sideways glance at the marshal confirms my suspicion that she ain't from no Lorain County.

[May 18th, 20—, 3:30 a.m.]
Anyway, that was the last thing I ever heard him say to me.

You see, Gladden sits between Black River and Lynch River. And the reason it looked like there were fewer and fewer people outside was that they were being evacuated. We were so busy dancin' in the rain that we didn't notice. The reactor I told you about, it got flooded and was leaking its shit into the soil and the water. And the river waters were starting to rise. We had no sandbags, they hadn't even given us enough bottled water. It was either September 13 or 14. One of those days.

Because, the next day, Hurricane Faustine hit us.

That night, we felt the shock wave from the explosion. The power plant had flooded. Was supposed to have been decommissioned, but the state wanted to try out nuclear energy again, I guess. Core exploded. Just gone. Afterward, people were talking about graphite falling straight out of the sky. You pick it up, your hand melts. Anyway, stormwater came. Hurricane took the ash. Wind and flood brought it straight to us.

Washed us all away. It was hell. They left us in hell. No one came to save us. It was . . .

It was . . .

[Inaudible.]

Lot of us were too sick to get out and avoid the worst of it. We'd been fed poisoned food and water for months now. Eventually, clean-up arrived. People said, afterward, that they looked like ghosts. With their masks and their gowns. Some of them were dripping in whatever they got sprayed with to protect from the radiation. Those of us who didn't get out in time, they got shot. Those bodies are under the concrete now. Whole place was paved over. Never saw Freddie's boyfriend again. I don't think he got out. Don't know why I was so sure the old man did, but I was. Even though they got rid of all of it, I was sure. Anyway, they razed the whole state of South Carolina. And buried that prison underneath layer after layer after layer of concrete.

And that's how it started. That's how . . . all of this got started. The red dust storms, the radiation, the fallout, the war, the Exodusters. All of it.

THE dead body grows pustules in the heat and even a few wagons away, can be smelt by Cayenne and one of her deputies, with whom she rides back to Galveston. She wonders why she doesn't yet feel completed.

She tries to speed her thoughts already to the next job, but instead parallel presents and imaginary pasts capture her. Clipped with scissors and stitched together with thread, a variety of recollections that fracture her sight like a broken mirror. In this one, Jacob checks the buttons of his shirt, then the cuff links of his collar, then brushes some of his hair while he stares at his reflection in a fingerprint-smudged bathroom mirror. A job interview. In this one, Jacob sits on his bed in darkness, with the stillness of a mountain, while she kneels before him in their Vegas apartment and dabs at the cut above his eye with cotton and cleaning fluid. Already, a cemetery of copper cotton balls soaks in the bucket at her bare heels, toes peeking out from beneath the patterned wool of her nightgown. In this one, Cayenne shovels dirt onto her son's grave after having cut him down from a streetlamp while his father watched. She is preparing it for anonymity. And in this one, she is unearthing the corpse untouched by maggots, carrion unsullied by pillagers and pestilential tenants. In this one, she sweeps the bedroom floor and her two children, unknowing of the apocalypse they've been born into, read quietly on their beds. In this one, Cayenne lies on the desert floor, foot still twisted in her stirrup, life leaking out of the gunshot wound in her chest. And in this one, mirroring the choreography of the previous, she is not frowning in confusion, nor is she weeping with regret, but rather smiling. Faintly. With the corners of her mouth. Hoping no one else sees it. Cain finally harmed beyond fixing, the mark of the beast no longer an infernal protection from the After. In this one, she is running with her second son, now half-grown, through a field of waist-high grass that bends in a breeze shepherded by fortune from the surrounding mountains. In this one, it is that boy leading her. In this one, this second son, her Lincoln, is a pace or two ahead, his hand rough and scabrous and firm against Cayenne's: the origin of the heat sweating her palm.

THE desert is littered with dead things.

This is what it's gotta be like. Slate-cleaning for those of us comin' after me. Settling here, making this place anew. I don't look at us, doin' what we did, as janitors. No, it's more cosmic than that. We was a flood. Space ain't a home. The Colony ain't a home. It's a waystation. A place to catch your breath. We know that truth to be self-evident. Powers the heart of every Marauder. Somebody's gotta keep this place warm for when the returnees get back.

Truth is, this place never stopped being ours.

I content myself with dreams as we ride back. Thinking perhaps that in some other future, we make it back to Galveston and a bunch of the Morgan family is waiting for us and they see me and the sheriff and the marshal and the deputies rush to my aid to beat back the rioters and preserve my life for just a few more days. Thinking that as the company holds back the vengeful relatives and the Specials sympathizers who've taken up the Morgan family's cause, I catch sight one last time of that woman, Margaret, and see everything in those eyes I'd been wanting to see for the past half decade. Thinking that she might have at her side a little boy, who looks a bit like the marshal but smaller. And as they take the body into the hospital and the doctor waits with the gravediggers who are just there to fill space because no one knows where else to put them, one of the niggers spots the little boy in the doorway, a cousin maybe, peeking surreptitiously through the crack in the door at the boy only a little older than him on a slab of wood. The large nigger is sitting down, fatigued in his entire body, but the smaller one has a coin in his hand, probably a week's wages in Whiteland, and closes it in his fist, then opens it again for the child to see his empty, lined palm. Then he pulls the shining thing from behind the kid's ear with an expression of mock-wonderment, and maybe it nudges a smile onto the boy's smudged face.

With the creosote bush and the mesquite and the blackbrush, I wonder how often it's rained since I was last here. Whether this flora ever saw any hint of relief in the clouds.

THE train stops and for an instant, neither the marshal nor Lingerfelt moves, captured as they are in the inertia of the journey. They regard each other. Between them passes some unseen communion, some silent remarking of the day's passing, and it is then that the door to their compartment opens and one of the marshal's deputies enters to let them know they've arrived at Oberlin. The rest of the troop enters and, together, they escort the prisoner out and into a rusted town car that spirits him into the night.

Tim sidles up beside Cayenne at the hilltop as they watch the transport head toward the prison; the music of chains clanking grows softer with each passing second, until it's nothing. And Tim rolls a cigarette. Cayenne wonders why she is waiting, what she is waiting for, knowing, as she waits, that she'll find no ram caught in the bushes and that the prisoner will hang and the future will unfold as it will. She wants to hate him the way Jacob would've hated him.

Guilt wraps its arms around her chest like her husband used to do. She can't help but feel she had something to do with that little boy's murder. She fights back visions of her two boys, the one dead, the other abandoned. But each time she sees a Black boy's lifeless body she also sees her own Jacob hanging from a tree, strung up by whites maddened by the end of their world, and she sees her second boy, a baby, cradled in her arms and she sees herself walking away, from the memory of the one and the reality of the other. She's grown so comfortable in the body of this heart-hardened woman, and she hopes, as she does with every mission, that some sense of completion awaits her. She's waiting for the day she can say to herself, "Both my sons are dead, and here are their bodies." Someday. Not today.

"You're lookin' a little sideways, marshal. Prisoner give you a hard time?"

Cayenne wishes she could find a way to quiet the ache thrumming in her chest. "Nah, Tim. Just tired." She straightens. It doesn't feel like revenge. Maybe it still is. It doesn't feel like reparation, but maybe it still is. She says nothing more to Tim and watches them take that white man away in chains.

A man shuffles past with a long-handled hammer leaning against his shoulder. He shoulders into her, and the head falls off, thuds into the ground. She stoops to pick it up, and that's when she sees the man has stopped.

"You dropped—"

The Preacher

How two deaths in New Haven, Connecticut, illuminate the intergenerational plight of the Exodusters

On the 29th of April, in 20—, Bishop died. The precise hour of his passing is not known, but by the time the riot had ended, he was gone, hunched over in Saint Michael Church with a young man asleep on the floor next to him. On the morning of May 2nd, a small, makeshift caravan ferried Bishop to a nearby graveyard, traversing roads made winter by smashed plate glass.

Beneath a sky whose red and whose blue swathes wrapped around each other like rival gang bandannas, the caravan moved through tranquil post-apocalypse. The brutality, enacted with drone strikes and augmented police officers and makeshift radiation rockets, was Old Testament in its indiscriminateness. Looking around, one expects to see the corpses of frogs littering the sidewalks, flanking a stream of blood. One looks at doorposts for any markings shielding that household from the Angel of Death. It is, more than anything else, the realization of a vision. Whose vision, it is perhaps impossible to tell, but the tragedy of this is its inevitability. All throughout the New Testament, the Book of Revelation sits and waits. The Dome above shimmers, the colors of the sky fighting against themselves, and if this isn't apocalypse, it'll do until the real one gets here.

I had only spoken to Bishop directly on two occasions, each instance in the basement of the duplex he squatted. On the dresser and the mantel were bricks, mementos from worksites, propping up flower vases or acting as paperweights. One brick, he collected the day he met a stacker named Ace and Ace's family; he had written the date on that one. Another, he had picked up to find $100 beneath, all of which had made its way into the collection plate at the Town Green Methodist Church in which he served as deacon. Some of them bear a name and a date, and in our first interview, Bishop had confessed that it was to mark new arrivals. He had been a part of the first generation of Exodusters, making their way from points west and south to the East Coast, where rumor had it things weren't so bad, the air was halfway breathable and there were no toasters to be seen. "Anywhere without Marauders and police was Eden," he had said that afternoon. He points to the brick that marks Jayceon's arrival, the one bearing Wyatt's visa stamp and Timeica's, gestures indiscriminately as there is no organizing recent arrivals and old-timers. Mercedes has no brick because she had staked a claim for herself here while Bishop was winding his way through the middle of the country. She'd had a husband he would like to have met. Despite their lack of arrangement, there is an order to them. Spend enough time in the brick fields and you realize that this is what he is replicating here in his home. And occasionally, he moves around to palm one, fondle another, even now after all these years mesmerized by the texture and design, the poetics of the thing in his hand.

Those who didn't know better considered Bishop a New Haven institution. He looked the part and certainly acted it, his death the final coda ramming home the point that the younger generation never gets around to rapping with the older generation in time. No one knew how old he was. Had he remained in Timmonsville, South Carolina, where he is purported to have been born, the information could have been easy enough to find and maintain, a digital footprint impossible to erase, but the red dust and the massive migrations it preceded were in the business of erasing such footprints, so that there was nothing but desert afterward. Red-bloods like Bishop arrive in a place like New Haven with only what they've stored in their unaugmented heads. But he was old enough to have witnessed the building of the first Colony.

A quirk and feature and sadness of the Exodust is the penchant that the first and second generations have for referring to where they

came from as the Old Country. For one the Old Country is Lara-
mie. Another, when asked, spits out Galveston like an epithet. For
another, Indianapolis is the land they left. Sometimes, Newark is the
city they are trying to forget.

He was a young man just as the pandemic was loosening its grip
on the country. The internet was ubiquitous, but what he talks about,
when he brings himself back to that time of relative optimism, is the
sound of it all. He does it now. Sometimes, when no one else is home,
the TV will be left on while he vacuums or washes dishes or sweeps
staircases. Sometimes, leaving perhaps to run an errand in the evening or to attend a meeting, the lights will be left on and they will
buzz and hum. The white noise of the Internet was the equivalent
for children born a decade into this past century. It is the drone and
bang of a washing machine at work, when everyone else is gone. Now,
without that constant connection, cut off by the Dome, then by the
radiation, he has only a thing like a TV to fill a room. The Medusa
stare changes forms, but the youthful eye drawn to it is ever overstim-
ulated and jaundiced.

The Internet, despite its vastness and its penchant for self-
replication and its bots, the Internet in all its capriciousness and
obscenity and power, the very muscularity of the thing, is simply us.
And the way Bishop tells it, it has transmogrified our personal experience of silence so that his generation now found their hellos and their
goodbyes and their please stay with me's and their chuckles and their
sobs in a series of keystrokes. The emoticon and the animated gif.
Noiseless. The music of human communication had become percussion. Complex percussion, laden with implication and innuendo and
nuance, but percussion nonetheless. A naked rhythm, rather than a
cadence or tempo wearing the sundress of consonance. There is no
longer a whine and a series of scratches signaling entry and exit from
that world. The gate has been so oiled as to open and close smoothly,
so smoothly that one thinks it has remained open all this time.

The TV, the humming of the lights left on, the washing machine.
It was all a curative. As was the Internet's percussion. It was all a
curative for the amorphous, unnamable malaise that I realize had

gripped me when I found myself in an air-conditioned bus roaming the urban desert, without the calm and safety of a lie. It is prayer. The gift afforded to those who never cyberized. Who had refused or perhaps had missed the opportunity to have the Internet injected into them. Who bled red instead of black.

Bishop was, by nearly all estimates, handsome. He was young once, too. You often arrive at your destination without any baggage, any totems of your past, digital or analog, but there is always the occasional photo or the corroborated recollection. And sometimes, there is reputation. On occasion, you would hear, at or around a site, whisper of someone who struck you as unbearably kind and trusting to a fault and you would see them suddenly as a chilling wraith hunched over their skid, each motion of their swing the turning gears of an exceptionally cruel machine. You would chastise yourself for rushing to judgment, then you would see the thing acted out, the suspicion confirmed, the mystery of a person partially solved. He grew up knowing to equate Black and beautiful, but to have never seen him around white crowds or in contact with non-Blacks is finally to notice the cracks spiderwebbing that fresco. The Exodusters are nearly uniform in their tales of humiliation and suffering, brought about because the radiation poisoning that moved in clouds over the country was attached, by scientific reconnaissance, by prejudice, to their Blackness. He was always kind to the stackers, was always kind whenever I saw him, grandfatherly, but he had suffered ruin in multitudes and when he looked up from his skid he saw a field full of children and grandchildren, Black and menaced like him.

I will never know him beyond what I saw, see, heard, hear, am told, am shown. It is impertinent for me to assume these things and perhaps there is no small amount of racism in it, but perhaps this is the price to be paid for attempting to understand a man like Bishop, what brought him and others like him here and whether or not the streets on which this caravan travels played victim to the same bomb that had exploded the old man's heart.

With Bishop's death, the first generation of New Haven residents has had sustained contact with returnees from the Colonies. Roles are slipped into seamlessly enough, but the bitter warnings Bishop may have whispered in secret found ears upon which to fall. Bishop had seen this happen before. Though he was, on this point, frustratingly vague, his travels took him throughout the Midwest, then back to the South before he made his way up the Eastern Seaboard. Over a decade spent crisscrossing the country as municipalities declared bankruptcy, people began living in space, cerulean domes appeared over cities that could afford protection from the poison, and much of the country devolved, became the image captured in the nineteenth-century daguerreotype. Linc and Kendrick are at the front of the caravan, stone-faced, and you look at them and realize that what's in their mind, what was in Bishop's mind, is not in yours. What killed Bishop will likely kill them. What killed Bishop will likely not kill you.

It is little surprise that Bishop was a long time ill before he was finally taken. By his count, he had suffered two heart attacks, and the story has it that it was his second stroke that finally killed him. On the worksite or elsewhere, his trademark loquaciousness was punctuated by prolonged silence, the mark of a man in close communion with the Divine. Another act of ethnography has me positing that those moments that saw him in that posture, angled toward the transmundane, were moments that saw him caged in his horrors. To spend all of one's life searching for a place to breathe and not be punished for it, and just as they go and fix the air, it's too late.

On the first Sunday of March, 20—, the United States Restoration Congress convened in New Haven, and for a week, on the tail end of that winter, more than twenty thousand streamed into the city from ports around the world. Each Colony sent their own delegation. An already-patchworked Dome was put into overdrive, augments hired in droves to speed up repairs to the air-filtration systems. Just as it became safe to walk around without an air mask, tents were erected, and delegates, visitors, those who took any reason whatsoever to come on the heels of this gathering, filed out into the city, attending classes, hosting panel discussions, scorching a debauched trail through parts of downtown while some of the local activists looked on, many of them having just reemerged from hibernation to continue working on their homes. The ironies running rampant throughout the episode were lost on many of the returnees, themselves only a few years removed from life on the Colony.

Professional protest coordinators had come from Seattle with the purpose of expanding the Green Wave, a tide meant to lift all boats, but that, to enlist their tortured metaphor, had only dashed already-leaky fishing skiffs into the hulls of corpulent, inebriate yachts. Eco-equity was the charge where eco-apartheid was the reality, with Fairfield awash in solar this and bio that and just two stops over on Metro-North gives you asthma, pollution, and a roof-shattering cancer rate. Their speaker, who carried so many of their contradictions, was an Asian American woman in a blazer, black T-shirt, and jeans, her bees an ever-present cloud haloing the black bob that bounced on her shoulders. Train prisoners to build a solar-powered, energy-efficient community: that was reentry. Construction of clean commerce: the green-collar worker. Green jobs, not jails.

New Haven was known as a market for bootleg augments, often refurbished or remodeled in backyard shacks or Body Shops. A protest march was scheduled to head down College Street through downtown, then fan out to locations indicated in the maps that came up on the leaders' displays. Red dots on blue mapping marked the locations of suspected Body Shops. Not only was the process of mechanization ruinous to the environment, but the mechanizing of labor took jobs away from those indigents who needed them most. It was understood that this meant ex-cons or high school dropouts, invariably Black or brown.

One branch of marchers found the Body Shop of a Puerto Rican man named Michael, who doubled as a Wrecker for the municipality. They had only found the Body Shop by accident. Residual radiation had worn at their flimsy equipment such that their maps had fallen apart. Michael's sign out front listed the price rates he charged for repairs.

A smaller event held within the auspices of the congress was a

Public Education Forum. There was less talk of revitalizing a system on life support and more talk of building said system from scratch. Though the panelists almost all sported beards, not one of them looked over thirty-five, though one would be forgiven for forgetting that they were all augments. The forum had been put together to build a future that left behind the destructive forces of privatization, school closings, and high-stakes testing. An audience member, who later identified himself as David (himself a Colonist having arrived the previous December), raised a hand and asked the panel for a definition of "grassroots." In parentheses was the observation that the community about which the panelists were speaking was 87 percent people of color from the last census. Yet onstage were thirty-two flavors, all of them vanilla.

"I didn't know it was a racial thing," replied a panelist, a mixed-race community organizer named Eamonn.

Before the first wave of returnees, the average response time of police to gunshots or a call was an hour. By spring of the following year, the police became ubiquitous. On corners, outside the entryways to apartment complexes, sauntering up and down sidewalks, battling boredom in unmarked cars. Few to whom I spoke seemed to know where they came from or what they were here for, except that, very soon after, the air was fixed. Celebration attended the event, but in many other parts of the city lay, flooding through the streets, a directionless malaise, a coin with helplessness on one side, waiting to be flipped over to reveal relief.

There was no hospital stay for Bishop.

He recalled one of those legendary figures of Black mythology, hardened by slave labor, then, having gained the wiles to survive Redemption, agile enough in body and mind to make it through Jim Crow in one piece. An easy, too-pat image is that of John Henry, the steel-driving mammoth, who raced a steam-powered hammer and won, only to have the effort itself collapse his heart. A symbol of physical strength, emotional fortitude, but also of exploited labor. A

child of the Internet made to fight for his dignity against the degra-
dations of the machine age. By the time his strokes had caught up to
him, augments had taken over the brickfields.

More people than expected filled the chapel where his funeral
service was held. Despite impediments to cross-country communication, word got out that Bishop had died. Many had come because
the stirring that precedes a riot had drawn them, just as it had drawn
them to Detroit and Chicago and Philadelphia and Memphis and
Cleveland earlier. One could only guess at the relationships all these
people had with Bishop, whose life crossed so many paths, who was
defined, like so many of his generation, by the very act of wandering.
There was no physical demarcation to mark the spiritual progression
of the journey. No South from which to flee. The entire country had
been cursed, and there was only the running of the rat in the maze.
Few of the mourners looked as old as Bishop was when he passed, but
for many of them, his terminus would be theirs. He had found peace,
then it had left him. But despite the presence of many, including, one
supposes, some acquaintance or two from a past Bishop had tried
with vigor to erase, grief did not spasm through the crowd or latch
on to one mourner in particular, seize that person with anguish, specific or generalized. This becomes all the more remarkable given that
many of the mourners have tracked soot into the church and blood
and bits of broken glass stuck to their boots. Some of them bear recently dressed wounds. Others enter only with the help of a friend or
some family. But these pews inflict numbness. In here, the destruc-
tion of out-there is remote; guilt can't follow them past those doors.
The mood was dark and thoughtful.

You search your mind, in your recollection of those interviews, for
vocal tics, aural indications of regret. You search for any cue, which
you can take for him trying to hide himself or reacting to him trying
to hide himself. Because you want to take that bit of evidence and
measure it with the recognition or lack of recognition you see in those
faces that look up toward Bishop's face in that casket. Did they know
the man the way he's being eulogized now? Or is this simply what
each of them hopes will happen to them when it's their turn? When

the course of one's life, with all of its lapses and angers and trans-
gressions and animosities, has been ironed into a narrative, has been
rendered coherent and clear, has been turned into the Hero's Journey,
what is there to see in that story except the reflection of one's self? At
the bottom of Bishop's story is that he suffered and now he is dead,
and you realize that this is going to happen to you too.

He's infected you with his God-talk, and you find yourself sub-
scribing to it because it fills in gaps. It's helpful that way. Like when
you're trying to figure out why it matters so much to you to get Bishop's
story, this story, down right, like he's your editor, and you get to that
realization that both you and he suffer and that you, like him, will
one day be dead. And the incompleteness of that hurts, because you
want the explanation of this connection to be more than that. So your
mouth forms around the word "God," and it flows like sand into the
spaces between the stones. When precious things were abandoned,
God heard the heart's wailing. God heard the quiet sobbing by the
campfire. When one of His children, Black and menaced, was faced
with the prospect of raising sons who would also be Black and menaced, and enacted on them violence so that they could avoid it elsewhere, it was upon God's ears that the anguish boomeranged when
the tuning fork of the heart sent it flying.

The Lord tasted the heart's poison, knew its general ingredients to
recognize it in others, but could also tell, connoisseur that He is, the
uniqueness of each person's envenomed character.

And just as the Lord testified to Bishop's travails and his triumphs,
so does He to yours.

When Bishop is given to humming "Blessed Assurance" and closes
his eyes, you don't need to try to follow him to wherever he's going.
You know, even in your attempt to write about the impossibility of
following him there, that you are trying. You can guess, certainly.
You can guess that maybe he is remembering pleasant conversations
or painful ones or maybe silence. But perhaps it is most respectful
just to watch. To listen.

Just as I reach that thought, deacons begin leading the mourners
up the aisle to gaze one last time upon the face of the deceased.

I am trying to assume him back to life. The deeper I try to reach into his mind, the deeper I reach, I realize, into my own perception of him. Thinking there's truth somewhere at the bottom of that, some potent, earth-shattering truth about him and about race and about writing about both, I meet only this: he is an old man dead.

The food cans, rolls of toilet paper, beer cartons, all hanging out of broken windows, the bedding and the clothes strewn throughout the streets, the dirty gang rags, the charred crescent moons of tires, the bloodstained barriers, the rubble that used to be barriers, all of it had arranged itself out so as to spell, when seen from above, the word *complicity*.

An image has appeared on newsfeeds, pinging back and forth between the Colonies and cities around the world: a row of stackers, their hammers arrayed before them, while they kneel with their hands behind their heads before a row of riot police, helmets poking above plastic shields, a regiment of Spartans. Bent stalks of smoke flank them. Another has an otherwise tall and muscled stacker with his hammer back, whole body poised to swing, against an Aries mech that stands a foot taller than him. The caption reads: DAVID VERSUS GOLIATH.

The two returnees whose phone call led to the police-involved shooting of the kid I got to know as Bugs claimed that between six and eight Blacks had accosted them. That there was one leader, and that he had threatened them quite explicitly. In the belly of a surveillance drone somewhere is that moment, frozen, perhaps itself deserving of the caption: David versus Goliath.

You leave the city limits and you remember that, before people came here, it was all irradiated jungle. The caravan has passed through the Dome on the way to the potter's field where Bishop is to be buried. They can't stay here anymore, so they will scatter. 1 Samuel, chapter 17, verse 51, comes to mind: "Therefore David ran, and stood upon the Philistine, and took his sword, and drew it out of the sheath thereof, and slew him, and cut off his head therewith. And when the Philistines saw their champion was dead, they fled."

[May 18th, 20—, 3:57 a.m.]

I'd never get the chance to ask him what he meant about Sodom and Gomorrah, whether or not he was talkin' about us. I came back to New Haven looking for him, heard he was here. Maybe you seen him around. I heard he was calling himself Bishop. Or others were callin' him that. But they musta moved on. I thought . . . I thought maybe if he'd found a place to settle, you know, to call home, maybe I could call it that too, you know?

I think he's still around here somewhere. People clear out, move on, it's a big country. But I'ma find him. He's been through a lot, Bishop. And no one lasts forever. But I gotta tell him thank you. That night at Gladden. Don't know how he did it, but he made me feel it, you know? Like I was safe. World was gettin' ready to end, and he made me feel safe. And I gotta tell him thank you for that. I think I'll do it after work tomorrow. Show him my new horse too. I think he'd dig that. Yeah, after I finish stacking, I'm gonna keep askin' after him. I'ma get to the worksite, I'm gonna find him, and I'm gonna tell him thank you. Tomorrow.

PART IV

SPRING

The morning of the fire at the Assawoman Bay refugee camp, Linc stood on a ladder scrubbing the stained-glass windows of the Church of the Nativity. Most mornings, he would be up before the other kids of the camp and would make his circuit through the chilled back alleys and down the cracked streets where Relief Agency trucks sat parked. Caws and birds going kyurr-kyurr trailed him all the way to the stone threshold, built small so that every visitor had to humble themselves whenever they came in or left. All the janitors knew about the back entrance, though, where you could come and go straight-backed where no one could see. Additionally, going through the back got you easier access to the cleaning supplies than any other point of ingress or egress. Linc didn't know why he always insisted on that front threshold, though. Maybe it had something to do with the fact that his father, once he started preaching here, had gifted him a set of keys that made him feel special, made the place feel like theirs, his. Maybe it was because of the first time his father brought him here and how he'd paused for a long time outside that entrance and something had washed over his face, the kind of soft slackness Linc hadn't seen in him since Vegas, before he stooped low, so low it hurt, and walked in. Every other church they'd stopped at on their travels had regular doors, some of them wood and some of them wood reinforced with steel, but they were regular doors you pulled a handle or pressed a button to open. And they didn't demand of his father's back what this one did. But the old man seemed to like it, so Linc did it, hoping that whenever he did, he would see what his father saw.

There was always sweeping and mopping to be done. In the early

mornings, the floor glowed with irradiated bootprints, the dirt illumi-
nating what other trash had been left behind either by churchgoers or
someone looking for a roof when the acid rain fell.

Even though Linc hadn't needed it, his father, soon after their arrival here, had quoted verses from First Corinthians Chapter 3 at
him: "Now he that planteth and he that watereth are one: and every
man shall receive his own reward according to his own labour. For
we are labourers together with God: ye are God's husbandry, ye are
God's building." It was the man's favorite chapter. Every place they
went to was a chance to see the Word played out, people pitching
tents or teaching schoolchildren or setting up domes or midwifing or
guarding the entrance to a settlement. And when the place would fall
apart and Linc would despair for their being made homeless again,
his father's voice would not falter: "Every man's work shall be made
manifest: for the day shall declare it, because it shall be revealed by
fire; and the fire shall try every man's work of what sort it is. If any
man's work abide which he hath built thereupon, he shall receive a
reward." Which was perhaps all just the old man's way of coaxing
Linc into his chores.

He always did the windows early because he had to open them to
let them dry and when he did, the patterning caught the sunrise to
spray green and red and orange and blue on the sidestreets flanking
the place. A kid wearing an oversized helmet with the RA's logo stenciled in white on it had been caught one day scampering through and
had landed on the rainbow rhomboids and had stopped in her path
and giggled, hopscotching from one shape to another. The next day,
other kids came to do the same. It grew into a ritual, Linc timing the
window-drying with the sunrise so that the kids could start the day
with their little dance routine then head off to wherever it was they
were going.

He opened the window and heard, in a high-pitched timbre,
"C'mon, Vonnie. Bang on the camera! Bang on the camera!" And saw
outside one kid, surrounded by his confederates, aiming a scuffed-up
recorder at a girl in a denim jacket and a ruffled skirt. "Bang on the
camera one time!"

"I'm not bangin' on camera," the girl said, annoyed.

One of the kids behind the camera boy popped out and curled his fingers into a sequence of gang signs while the others whooped and laughed and shouted, "Ooooh you killin' it, cuz!"

And somebody else said "c'mon crip walk" and another high-pitched disembodied voice replied, "I ain't never crip walk a day in my life, I'm a shooter." And in between bursts of giggling from the others, "I transformed into that. I was tryna skateboard at first but niggas kept tryin' me because I guess I look try-able, so we gon' see who ready to go to hell." "Mi run tings, tings nah run me!" The rest, drowned out by fading peals of laughter.

Next came the skylight, which was trickier to get to and required setting up the harness and pulling himself up to the ceiling. It was while he was horizontal to the ground that shuffling footsteps echoed in the sanctuary. He couldn't get too good a look at who had entered, but it sounded like two people. The rhythm of their walking told him that they'd turned at the entrance, which meant they were proba-bly heading to the dish that held some of the church's candles, their bottoms stuck firm in sand. You were supposed to put in a donation in exchange for a candle, and Linc wanted to tell the early comers as much but then one of them started speaking softly in Arabic and he realized it must be one of the camp's Palestinians, that wave of refugees who migrated with much of South New Jersey when the tides swallowed up the peninsula. It was often the Arab teens Linc's age who tagged the walls of the camp with their art—a pole vaulter in mid-spring over the thing or verses from the Bible—and who had smells from the food they made in Little Ramallah wafting over the whole sector. Linc generally left them alone to do their thing, as they had the look of folks who had been wandering much longer than Linc and his father had, the type who settled too easily into camps like these and hated having the skill. Hated having needed it.

The two Arabs moved from fresco to fresco and the one voice seemed to be explaining them to whoever the other person was. Long as they weren't making any mess, Linc felt content returning to his washing. He expected them to make the whole circuit, go through all the landmarks, see where this saint was buried, kiss the star-marked spot where this other saint had been born, cross themselves at the altar. They were smart to do it before the early-afternoon rush. While Linc might've preferred to do his work in silence, he didn't begrudge the duo's desire for the same. There was always so much noise in the camp. And not everybody was as good as Linc's father at pulling God and contemplation thereof out of the air.

"It is difficult," Linc's father had told a small congregation in a boat at the docks one night as they swayed on the moon-dappled water, "to look at these things, the Wall and the rebellion painted on it and not see a religion flavored by last things, by apocalypse. Revelation." He'd picked up this new way of talking somewhere in Colorado and it had gotten thicker the farther east they traveled. His sentences became longer, grew swirling, cirrus clauses. Felt less like they came out of the earth they stood on and more like he was pulling them out of the sky. More often than not, it was gibberish to Linc, who was content only to no longer have for a companion someone catatonic with mourning. Still, he'd stopped sounding like the man who'd bounced him on a knee in Vegas or who worried over him in Long Beach. Around Iowa, he'd begun to sound like a stranger.

"But New Testament liberation flowers out of Old Testament roots," he said of the camp. "That's what hope is. It's the unseen. We mustn't be trapped. Trapped in that Old Testament dogmatism that believes only in things seen, then clings to them at the expense of everything else, every other word in that message of which the burning bush, the ram in the briar patch, the parting of the Red Sea, is only a small part."

The morning of the fire that gobbled up the camp's school buildings and swallowed the bread distribution site whole, the fire that would have bodies crowded in the rubble afterward, climbing over fallen stone walls and trying to salvage the "Sawmill Site" sign that kids had taken to doodling on, the fire that chased camp dwellers to the dock that would collapse under their weight and leave them to drown, Linc figured his father was talking about himself. About their journey. Reasoning with God, who knew better than them the why of it all. The morning of the fire that would see the old man trapped in the very church Linc was now cleaning, Linc figured the man was simply puzzling in his own way over the mysteries of his life. It wouldn't occur to him until he was pulling the man's body from the charred rubble and saw the look on his face—that soft slackness—that he'd wonder if maybe the man had been talking about his son's mother instead.

The morning of the fire at the Assawoman Bay refugee camp, Linc had not thought about that woman in eight years.

No one but the stackers saw to the horses during winter, but as soon as the first drifts of snow began to melt, small crowds formed at the wood fence that had been erected around the barn. At first, just a few kids who, playing nearby, saw the new thing and were drawn, and they saw Bugs, who looked only a little bit older than them doing what looked like important work, brushing down horses and stacking bales of hay and feeding the horses and leading them by the reins in small circuits throughout the field. And the kids would watch in grinning silence. Then others would come and they'd catch sight of Bishop or Linc on a roof swiping snow or red dust to a place where it could be collected and taken care of later.

Those kids musta gone and told their mothers because then their mothers and fathers came and the kids asked their guardians what those things were and what they ate and how they moved and Linc or Mercedes or Sydney or Jayceon or Bugs would tell them and even let them pet the horses. Then the parents would thank the stackers and take the kids, on fire with questions, back home.

Whalley Avenue awoke to the clopping of hooves.

A distant, regular sound that was first heard around Edgewood Park and could be heard by the dragonchasers hidden within the Westville Cemetery, then continued past the Beechwood Gardens Housing Complex, and that was when the first residents peeked their heads out their windows to see what the noise was. The clip-clop grew clearer, sharper around the Food Market, and Destiny froze in the act of opening her hair salon when she turned and saw what was happening. She wiped at her mask to clear whatever smudge must have caused her vision, but when the sight was still there, she took the mask off completely and followed the horse as it cantered by shuttered take-out stores and banks that had been converted into county stockpiles for radiation-wear. Past the juvenile court, within view of the pranksters on the roofs of the St. Martins Townhouses, then past the liquor store and the auto repair shop run by the Dominican Miguel, not the Puerto Rican one.

The first white residents to see the source of the sound were the ones who lived in the loft apartments that had gone up in the late fall where Whalley became Broadway, far enough within the Dome that the air no longer rasped the lungs. So the rider slipped off his mask and hooked it by the pommel of his saddle as he rode down past the open-air market on that stretch of Broadway between Whalley and Elm that was just waking up.

Horse and rider ambled to the New Haven Green with its broken obelisk and crossed to Chapel Street so that it stood in the shadow of the apartment complex just as Mercedes, at the window, nursed a mug of coffee spiked with pitorro. The rider raised an arm, hailing her, knowing she was watching, and she smirked.

Then horse and rider made their way up to Wooster Square, passing the abandoned library and the city hall building on the way, and
when he arrived to find the group of stackers that spring morning on
the side of the street, he sat straighter in his saddle.

They had their hammers in front of them and had pulled their
masks and bandannas down around their necks while they drank
melted iced coffee or Malta Goya. They all had to look up to the
rider, some of them shading their hands against the sun, and a few
of them grumbled about not being able to enjoy this too-brief spring,
knowing summer with its weight and wetness was waiting just over
the horizon.

But Bishop stood to his full height and adjusted his chewing stick,
then he said, "So, Bugs, you finally decided to show up for work."

Bugs awoke from the dream smiling.

Bishop found him in the truck bed under a ratty blanket and jos-
tled his ankle. "Ready to head out?"

Bugs fumbled for his hammer, then sat up and wiped the dream
from his eyes. Then he nodded and made himself comfortable against
the wall of the truck bed. Bishop turned on the rattling truck, it rose
a little off the ground, then they were gone.

"Don't forget your mask!" Bishop hollered from the driver's seat,
but Bugs didn't hear him.

David and Jonathan passed beneath the Wooster Street archway, wirework that had at its center a wrought-iron elm tree, the city's symbol. The only bits of winter David bore were the stories Jonathan had told him, and, looking at him now, walking next to David with one hand snug in one of David's back pockets, the boy's muscles had filled out. He had developed sinew, had turned into the most delicious thing David had ever seen. Buds had only just now begun to sprout on the trees that lined the street, distinguishing them from the telephone poles that towered over the rusted, chopped-up husks of maglev cars. Nineteenth-century architecture tracked their progress up and down and along the avenues and roads. Greek style, Revival, Second Empire, Italianate. And with each house that returned David's gaze, he saw not the stripped, peeling façade of a gutted home but the colorful, robust, ancient monument it had once been. One of the first things he'd made Jonathan bring him to was the fabled sycamore tree on the west side of Wooster Street Park that was said to resemble Jesus Christ. Their tour of the neighborhood took them to the famous pizzerias to which people from everywhere had flocked and through streets with names like Chapel and Chestnut and Water.

Saint Michael Church drew them to Wooster Place. Even as a pericarp, it held that gravity David had felt in the abandoned opera houses and warehouse factories, buildings made sacred by the memory of the life that had thrummed in them. No more colored glass in the windows meant that the tall arched frames permitted an unobstructed view of the shit-colored interior. There were no wooden pews, off of which the echoes of their footsteps could bounce, nor golden organ pipes, nor statues of St. Mary Maddalena, nor frescoes of haloed New

Testament titans. Only the pebbles and litter and the innards of what remained of the walls, all of which could be seen from above through holes in what had once been the golden dome you could see from just about anywhere else in the city.

Jonathan had his eyes on the street. His vigilance unnerved David and he brought himself closer to the man to whom his soul was knit.

"They used to have a cherry blossom festival here," David said into Jonathan's ear. "Started out with a local band and a handful of neighbors under some lighted trees. Then it turned into this huge event with singers and speeches from politicians and gospel music and a band playing on a stage right there"—he pointed to some imaginary spot at a far corner of Wooster Place—"salsa music, jazz"—he chuckled—"prog rock." Jonathan's body hummed against his. "Shadow puppets. And the New Haven Clock Company would have an exhibit. All 'cause a bunch of folks decided it'd be pretty to plant some Yoshino Japanese cherry blossom trees in their corner of New England."

Jonathan leaned into him, eyes closed with the idea of it all.

"All we need here are some neighbors and some tree lights."

A motorbike engine ripped through the quiet, followed by another, until a whole chorus of them grumbled around a street corner. Jonathan pushed David behind him. The street bikes growled as a group of Black kids made their zigzag parade past them. Some of them doubled back, balanced on their front wheel, another popped a wheelie and sped forward, the plastic frames bending, nearly breaking, beneath the weight of their bravado.

"I bet he asthmatic!" shrieked one of them over tire-squeal. "And he got a ass-bag. His feet come up and his ass-bag come out!"

One of them pulled a hard turn that should have thrown him off his bike and wheeled past the two white boys on the steps of the Catholic chapel. "He slip and fall and his ass-bag come out."

A third: "Or he get knocked out, and his ass-bag come out."

The first stood up so that the wind whipped his shirt against his long torso and put some bass in his voice: "Good thing my ass-bag come out." He screeched to a stop in front of the church, his back to David and Jonathan, and addressed his coterie, who had by now stopped their bikes, the massive mosquito-buzz drone replaced by the hungry grumbling of street bikes in repose. "Now, all you niggas that's knockout-prone, be sure to cop the all-new ass-bag."

"Nine ninety-nine!" another shouted through dust-covered hands cupped around his mouth. "We got them shits for sale."

"You heard it here first, we got ass-bags for all the niggas that's knockout-prone. For when you get knocked on your motherfuckin' ass, you better hope the ass-bag come out." Their giggles had turned into thunderclaps. One of them clutched his stomach and doubled over on his handlebars. "We have the additional chitti-chest bag too, in case you get snuffed from the back." A pause. "For fifty-nine ninety-nine!" He held a hand up to stop the laughter that had by now rippled over the entire block. "We do take personal checks and all that. EBT, food stamps, whatever—"

"And we do test drives!"

"That's right. We could take you down the hall, down the street, and test out your all-new ass-bag."

"For ninety-nine ninety-five! Your all-new ass-bag."

A little kid whose shoes could only touch the asphalt by their tips revved his throttle. "Don't forget the diaper chinstrap that'll hold your chin while you fallin'." He collapsed in a fit of laughter.

"One size don't fit all! We gotta measure your chin and your ass."

They took several more seconds to get the most crippling of their howls out before their leader revved his throttle and prepared to go. The others followed suit. Before he peeled off, he looked over his shoulder at David and Jonathan and winked. They rushed by like a flock of birds, the last one, the little one, looking over his shoulder, slowing as he passed, and shouting, "Don't be afraid of us!" before the horizon swallowed his mirth.

Jayceon took a pull from his Olde English. Everyone in the semicircle around him had either a Swisher Sweet clenched between their teeth, a box of chicken in their lap, or nothing but a lollipop in their gloved fingers, leaning, as they were, against their bike frames. Some still sat astride the plastic reptiles, but the breeze was cool around them, wet with spring, and there was no storm in sight, thus, no impetus to protect their bikes. Plaster from the day's work still clung to most of them.

"I got my eyeballs raped with that one time," Jayceon said after a gulp. "Big homie was like 'You wanna see what that bitch did?' Pulled out a picture, nigga had his legs up like he was getting missionary'd."

"Nah, come on, dawg," Bugs said, tiny body, overcompensating voice. "Chill."

Jayceon had already started laughing, nearly choked on a throatful of beer. "Bitch was down there lickin' his ass." His laugh did that thing where it turned into straight percussion, a series of scrapes, his head buried in his chest, his shoulders shaking, voice tight from lack of air. "I said, 'Don't you ever show me that shit again!'"

Kendrick tried to look disgusted. "Nah," he said between stifled chuckles, "he ain't show you no shit like that."

"I swear to God, the nigga name is—" A single gunshot rang in the distance, cut off the rest of the sentence.

Sydney spoke, husky and virile, around a mouthful of dry biscuit. "My little sister took me to a gun range for Father's Day once." Sydney caught Linc's glance, knew this was the first time she'd ever mentioned her family, knew that whenever she would, it would be in the past tense. "They gave me the twelve-gauge." She swallowed, loudly sipped her orange soda through a straw. Her legs were crossed

over the sidewalk curb. "They throwin' the clay ones up. 'Pull!' BOW!
I'm shootin' everything. POW! POW! She like, 'Syd, you really know
how to shoot,' I'm like, 'yeah, I do.'" She smirked, looking up from
her lap, all matter-of-fact false modesty. Her greasy fingers rummaged
in her box for her second biscuit. She looked to her right, addressed an
invisible little sister, "That homeboy can try to run for the car, get in
his Datsun, his Hyundai, whatever the fuck he drive, I'ma peel that
dude." Belly laughs thundered up and down the block. "Looked at lil'
sis like, I'ma knock your boyfriend's waves right off his fuckin' head."

Bugs's story, told in a smaller voice at the circle's periphery, had
grown louder to fill the silence. "Nigga, I'm tellin' you I had robbed a
pawn shop. We stole a pickup truck—"

"How your feet touch the pedals, though?" Kendrick shouted from
next to Sydney.

"We ran the truck into the front window, nigga, just PSSSHHH."
Linc smirked, and Jayceon leaned over. "Nigga's sound effects."

"And then after we did that shit, we was just goin' in. Anything in
that motherfucker, gimme them necklaces, gimme that—"

Voices had grown louder around him, other stories, other jokes,
little islands of frolic apart from his own.

Bugs arched himself toward Linc who sat directly across from him,
like Linc was his only audience. "Nigga!" He guzzled some Olde
English. "I was like Mr. T when I was walking through the 'hood,
nigga. I had so many cotdamn chains on me from that fuckin' pawn
shop robbery I was Mr. T on them niggas." He had enlisted his hands,
his arms, the whole rest of his body in the telling of the story. "Yo,
my shit was draped." Some of the others quieted, others laughed with
him. "I was like DOW." He mimed drawing a sash from shoulder to
opposite waist. "Pa-da-da-dow."

Kendrick: "Ha-da-da-dow."

Bugs collapsed against his bike. Their convulsions echoed over the
block.

More than the chuckles, so powerful they hurt your stomach and
ripped up your chest, more than the Swisher smoke, more than the
forty-ounces, it was the weather that reminded Linc of Jake, of being

a younger brother, of being little and ignorant and part of a kinder life, one that didn't rasp against your throat or cancer your insides.

"Niggas don't know how fucked up my life really is," he said to no one and to everyone. "We used to live out in Long Beach when we was young, 'cause my mom and dad used to move around a lot." He made a tornado with his hands, one rotating on top, the other on the bottom. "Everywhere. And when we lived out there, my brother, Jake, my older brother, he had a five-man crew." Why did everyone wanna talk about families all of a sudden? "And they all worked at Carl's Jr.'s."

"Oh, they worked there?" someone Linc didn't see.

"Yeah. So I used to wonder"—a sly smile split his face—"why niggas was spending twenty dollars . . . for a ninety-nine-cent sandwich. Them niggas was puttin' the twenty-piece crack rock *in* the motherfuckin' hamburger." A bunch of them could no longer hold it in, struggled to stifle their chest-ripping chuckles. "Them niggas was sellin' crack from Carl's Jr., nigga." The memory of the place had crystallized, the old neighborhood, the sprawl of it, the project towers, the drive-through fast-food joints, the identical one-story houses whose only distinguishing feature was how much care had been given to the front garden, the white tank tops, black jeans, and the bandanna, red, blue, purple, black, green, yellow, the uniform. "Yo, dawg, real talk. Real motherfuckin' talk. I was so un-hip to the shit, 'cause I was young, I went inside the Carl's Jr. one time and I went up to the counter where my brother was and was like 'dat hamburger don't cost no twenty dollars!'" He struggled through sobs that came out as laughter. "Big bro was at the register like 'if you don't shut your little ass up!'" He fell over and the others were too busy closing their eyes against the pain of their revelry to notice that Linc's bottom lip trembled in between snickers, mouth fighting to grin and not to frown. He missed his mother.

He sighed the rest of it out just in time to hear the whoop-whoop of a cop car as it wound a corner several blocks down. Linc looked at the sky, squinted against the sun and saw a twinkle that signaled the Predator drone watching them from above. Kendrick sucked his teeth, and the others lumbered onto their bikes and pulled their bandannas and masks over their mouths and noses. The bikes did their little lion roars, and they circled, preparing to peel out. Bugs kicked down on his and it choked. He kicked again, each time with more fury, then with something approaching desperation.

"Nigga!" Jayceon shouted.

Bugs stomped and stomped.

Linc rolled his up. "Yo, Bugs, take mine." Before he could finish, his bike shook beneath him. "Fuck!" He trembled atop the thing as it inched backward. "Go! Go! Go!" The others made it out, splitting up and vanishing around abandoned houses and street corners, and just as Linc leapt off his bike, his and Bugs's flew out from under them, spinning upward toward the magnet attached to the drone's undercarriage. From their view on the concrete, it looked as though the bikes simply vanished into the sky.

For the first time that afternoon, Bugs couldn't control his breathing. "We didn't even do anything to those white boys." He looked to Linc, who stood firm as the cop car inched toward them. "We didn't do nothin'. They don't even live there."

"That cop don't need an excuse." He tensed, saw that there was only one cop in the car, noted the toaster's features, badge placement, the netting that separated the front of the car's interior from the back seats. "Just walk. Let's just walk away. He asks? None of that shit on the ground is ours." A few steps. "We didn't hear no shots, either."

"Linc, we didn't do anything."

"We scared white people. Come on, let's go."

Mercedes had the cigarette to her mouth before she remembered Sydney. They both sat on rumpled blankets by the window that looked out onto the glowing blue barrier that marked the edge of the Ribicoff Cottages project. Sydney absently waved away her worry, everything about the gesture a lesson in dejection. Mercedes lit up, all the while watching the girl, waiting for her to reveal what it was that Mercedes was here to do.

"I'm . . ." Sydney rasped, put her hand to her chest and tried to clear her throat. "I'm burnt." She pointed to her throat when she said it.

Mercedes knew from the first time that girl had shown up at a site and had Linc making eyes at her, the first time she'd opened her mouth, beckoned him because she didn't dare speak above a whisper, that the girl was on her way out. It still hurt to hear. "You gonna tell him?"

She looked away from Mercedes, back out the window.

When Mercedes had shown up, Sydney still had on her wristband from the hospital. Syd moved around some cushions so that Cedes had something soft to sit on and smiled an apology for how messy Linc had left his room.

Mercedes stared at her.

"You know my husband was a Congregationalist," Mercedes said to the spring afternoon outside the window. "He took me to his church. Old brick place, maybe a couple cities over. I wasn't a good Catholic after my mother died, but I did love him. Oh, how I loved him. And every Christmas Eve, they would do this cantata, the choir with their long, flowing robes, the lightbulbs switched out for actual candles, the whole thing. But the thing everyone came for was this rendition of 'O Holy Night' that one of the baritones did. He stood in front of the altar where the pastor was gonna preach after. Ooh, mija, as soon as you saw him step up there, you could feel it. The whole place is so silent you could hold it in your hands, you know? Everybody's hold-ing their breath. People are whispering to the person they brought with them. Like *this* is what they were talking about. ¡Dios mío, and then he starts singing." Mercedes closed her eyes to the memory. "And I swear, his voice singing that song is what mercy sounds like." She opened her eyes and saw that Sydney was staring straight at her, cheeks shiny with tearstain. "You know, that . . ." Mercedes searched for the word, the phrase, the thing she'd felt whenever she'd set foot in that sanctuary. "That 'and yet . . . ,' you know? Like there's more going on than what you deserve or I deserve or don't deserve. There's this thing too."

They stared at each other for a long, silent moment before Mer-cedes sniffed loudly, wiped her eyes with her sleeve, and saw that her cigarette was down to the filter. She stubbed it out against the windowsill, tossed it, and pulled out her pack to light up another. She looked up, saw Sydney's face, then put the pack away.

THE afternoon saw Sydney on the porch of their trailer wearing at the skin on her knuckles when she saw one of the Chihuahuan smug-glers haul a large board of wood from out the back of his truck. He tossed it down onto the scrubland, and it raised a puff of blooddirt with a slap. Bambi had her fists on her hips—she was getting bigger too fast—and Sydney paused at itching the skin of her knuckles to see what was gonna happen.

One of the Chihuahuans, belly spilling over his horned belt buckle, tightened his bootlaces, even though he made a show of grimacing when he handled the left boot. When he stood, it was with new deter-mination. These were special boots. Dance boots, and his compadres leaned on the truck or sat on a stool with a bottle of Sotol and two glasses between them or lay back on the flatbed of the vehicle and slept with their hats covering their faces. The big-belly Chihuahuan straightened, walked up to the board and tapped it with the toe of one boot, then stepped on it with both feet and, as Sydney watched, his feet disappeared in a blur of clip-clop-clippety-clippety-clip-clop-clop-clip-clop before stilling and Bambi fell in the dust laughing, then jumped up, excited for her turn.

The boots were too big for her. She insisted on wearing them anyway, and when she finally got them both on, she duck-walked to Sydney for help while everyone shot good-natured laughter into the air.

"Careful, Bambi," Sydney whispered as her sister fell into her arms. "We gotta stuff your dance boots." So she went inside and, under the sink, found some of the insulation that went into the boxes of cacti she delivered to the smugglers every two weeks, and she came back out and made Bambi stand still while she filled in the space around her little sister's toes and heels with the pink stuff.

Then, with a pat on the butt, she sent Bambi to the board.

Bambi spent a long time staring at it, then tried her first tentative steps, almost falling over her own legs. But the big-bellied Chihuahuan laughed and righted her, then, next to her, danced a quick clippety-clip-clop once, then twice, then this time with Bambi.

Bambi tried it again with the Chihuahuan, clippety-clip-clop, then again as the Chihuahuan let go of her and moved away and each successful sequence bred more speed, more confidence until Bambi's own feet were blurring against the wooden board in smooth and staccato rhythms. Clippety-clippety-clip-clip-clop-clop-clippety-clop-clop-clippety-clop-clop-clippety-clippety-clip.

"She's fast," the Chihuahuan said, fanning himself with his hat and grinning a gold-toothed grin at Sydney, who shaded her eyes with a hand and just squinted.

"Syd!" Bambi shouted as she switched her rhythm and banged anew with her heels and toes on that poor wooden board. "Syd, dance with me!"

Syd coughed and spat red into the dirt. "I ain't up for that shit, Bambi."

The little girl stopped and put her fists on her hips and faced her like a general, at which point the Chihuahuans barked and wheezed their laughter at the cloudless blue-red sky.

"Como el jefa," said one of the Chihuahuans on a stool and the others laughed. "¡Qué rabia!" laughed another one. But Bambi held the pose.

"C'mon, Bambi, I'll be sleepin' on the floor for a month 'fore you're done with me. You know I got a bad back."

"I'll give you my blankets!"

And that was when Sydney knew any further argument was futile. So she raised herself from the porch and took herself to the board, then stretched her muscles in exaggerated movements, at which Bambi frowned but at which some of the Chihuahuans whistled. Sydney bent double, grasped her calves, straightened, touched her toes, then swiveled her torso. To the left, to the right. Then, for good measure, she hopped up and down a few times.

"You want my boots?" Bambi asked, quietly, like she was trying to give Sydney a secret advantage in a game they were playing against the others.

"You sure you want this?" Syd asked her, challenge thick on her tongue.

"Dance!" Bambi screamed back, joyful, challenge accepted.

So Sydney shook her head wryly and settled her hat onto her head, then stepped on with both feet. And she danced a jig she remembered from before Bambi was born and she'd watched this whole big family that musta been hers all crowded around a table and laughing and eating and there was a Christmas wreath hung on the door and lights strung up along the walls, little stars fixed in place by magnetic charge, changing colors and, when the main lights got turned off, swimming into the constellations Dad used to point out to her, a jig from before when Dad's beard was closer to his cheeks and he was wearing the same sort of shirt and tie as the other men around the table and the women wore sparkly dresses and Sydney would sometimes climb up to the rafters over the dance hall's glass-covered swimming pool and watch the couples all dance and shake and some of the women with big skirts would take the skirts in their hands and ruffle them and shake them back and forth and the men would shake their heads, crazy with what she didn't know to call desire and there was hopping and shuffling and legs hooking around waists and bodies pressed against bodies and then someone in the shadows pushing a button so that slowly the dancers started levitating off the ground and Sydney in the rafters had to hold on as her feet went up in the air behind her and some of the dancers started to go horizontal and fear flashed over some of their faces but not Dad's and not the woman's across from him and their feet moved but to stay close, they hooked arms together, then with their free arms, they threaded their fingers around the other's and drew even closer as they twirled and spun through the air, a beautiful tangle of limbs as more and more bodies floated in the zero gravity to make constellations like the stars over the dinner table and Sydney had the biggest smile on her face watching her neighbors and her family and seeing Dad with his family, his brothers and sisters and cousins and lover and her family, a jig before they all went to space and Dad didn't, and that thought threw Sydney back into the present so that her toe missed a beat and the whole rhythm of it all unraveled. Spent, she bent over, chest heaving, sweat dripping down the back of her neck, soaking the collar of her shirt. Her hat had fallen off.

Bambi and the Chihuahuans didn't say anything. Not even the insects spoke. The only sound was Sydney's heavy breathing before Bambi squealed with delight and ran to her older sister and Sydney, after a beat to regain her strength, caught her up in her arms and didn't care that it hurt her back to do so.

And as she held her close, she noticed the beginnings of gray at the roots where her hair sprang from her scalp and her heart hurt. She turned a grin the way of her audience, but it slipped off her face when they all heard hooves clopping against the desert floor.

It wasn't the thunder announcing a posse, no dust cloud either. But the Chihuahuans all reached for the guns at their hips, and the guy who'd been sleeping in the truckbed pulled a pump-action shotgun to his side and hopped down.

Sydney bounced Bambi in her arms as the little girl, sensing the change in the air, grew quiet and buried her face in the sweat-stinky crook of Sydney's neck.

"If it's the law," Sydney said to the big-belly Chihuahuan, "you should prolly head home. They can't catch you 'cross the border."

The man put a hand to Sydney's shoulder. "Now, how do I look leavin' mi muñecas lindas like this?"

Sydney smirked at the man. "You got a quarter million dollars' worth of cactuses in your truck right now. Shipment gets stopped, we're all in trouble." After a beat, "We'll be fine."

He squeezed her shoulder, then whistled, and everyone hopped in their trucks and were off.

Sydney was still holding Bambi when the lawman came to a stop before her. If Sydney were younger, the lawman atop his horse woulda looked like a giant, one of them irradiated monsters that haunted the desert. But she'd seen enough to know that it was just a human on a horse. No matter how impressive they looked, one arm skinless and steel, hat castin' cooling shadow over their faces, atop a steed whose silver head and body made it glow in the sun.

"You metálico."

"And you the girl whose daddy blew hisself up a few months ago."

"We ain't got nothin' illegal here. Just me and my sister."

The man with the white face and the metal arm was silent for a long time on his horse.

"You gon' arrest us or what?"

The man took his hat off his head and held it at his side. Probably to tell Sydney that with his hands full he had no intention of drawing down on her. "I ain't lookin' to arrest you. I'm on loan from a couple counties over." A laminated sheet of paper ejected itself from a slot in the horse's flank. The lawman took it and handed it to Sydney, who took it with her free hand. "We're lettin' everyone who live here know the water's all tapped out. Last purification plant's gone down. Relocated or shut down or whatever, ain't my business to parse the language. Anyway, the aquifers are out. 'Sides, slavers are runnin' loose pickin' up every little thing. So if you're mindin' the little one there, you need to get." Sydney didn't move. After a beat, the man turned to leave.

"Why don't you do somethin' 'bout the slavers, then?"

"Little girl, I can't change the weather."

"These walking papers?" she asked, lazily flapping the already melting laminated notice.

The lawman turned back around. The sun glinted off his arm. "Chance it across the border with yer friends." He softened. "Caravan's gathering at Marfa to head east. You make it there, they'll get you fitted with a relocation packet. Send you somewhere with good water. You get to Ohio, head to Lorain County. Ask for a woman called Cayenne."

"Cain? Like from the Bible?"

"Cai-ANNE." The horse twisted under him, antsy. "She's a friend from work." Then he waved his hat by way of salutation, put it back on his head, and left.

Sydney's knuckles itched, watching him go. "Ain't never heard of a white woman named Cayenne," she said under her breath. She bounced Bambi in her arms, trying to forget the new gray in the little girl's hair and what it meant. "Bad man's gone now." She looked down and let out a mock gasp. "You ain't give back them dance boots!" The notice fell from her hands and curled in the Texas heat.

THEY'D fallen asleep on the blankets, Mercedes with her arms wrapped around Sydney, when the door banged open. Mercedes turned over. Sydney stirred against her and wiped sleep from her eyes.

Linc stood in the doorway, hunched over, held up by the doorframe, covered in blood and vomit, gasping for air, shoulders heaving, whole body held together by sheer force of will.

Sydney rushed past Mercedes, peeled back some of Linc's clothes, searched him for answers. "What? What on earth?"

"They killed him."

"What?" Sydney's eyes widened with horror. She could still hear the pawnshop robbery story as clear as if Bugs were telling her now. "Where are you hurt? Whose blood is this?"

Linc was weeping. "Those bitch-ass toasters killed Bugs."

Short Cuts: Born to Run

For me, it started with the bloody fingertips. You see a kid who got booked come out, and he's got bloody fingertips, or maybe they're already wrapped in bandages from a brief pit stop home or at some neighbor's house or the basement of some churchgoer's place to get patched up before the kid's back with the crew. Their hands are gentle around a hammer handle for a while, and they spend some time on the sidelines, trying not to look too dependent on the kindness of others. But it's more a system of exchange than anything else. Looking at them, Kendrick, Jayceon, Linc, Wyatt, even some of the younger stackers, they've all been in, and they all have to have been taken care of when they got back out.

The settlers have brought with them an increased police presence. Their return from the Colony happening under the auspices of urban development. Cyberized workers win jobs working on air-filtration centers, mech cops (affectionately dubbed "toasters") find work patrolling desolate, potholed streets on which now live white Colonists. Now that the air is cleaner here, it must be protected.

And so I watch as these denizens relearn how to avoid the police.

When running fails and they get booked, they sometimes put their fingers to the electric force field shielding the control box to which the cops put their ID badges. Their fingertips come back charred and smoking and missing the first few layers of skin, so that when it's time for their fingerprints to be taken, they are ghosts, non-people, just as they were before the police showed up. It only takes a few trips to the pen to learn this.

If you sit with them long enough, you watch them develop their heightened awareness like a superpower—what the police look like, how the different models of their mechanized bodies move, the cut of their hair, the rust patterns on their undercover cars, their routes and how they time them. Then you see them: sitting in plain clothes on a park bench with their children, in the rearview on the freeway ten cars behind. Sometimes, the body reacts first, launching a sheen of sweat, quickening the pulse, before the mind registers coordinates and escape routes.

"You don't think what they might want from me," Wyatt told me one afternoon near the end of a workday. His overalls were nearly white from overwash. "Whoever they're looking for, even if it's not you, they'll book you anyway." Timeica sat at his knee rolling a stylus around her fingers.

They practice running from each other. Maybe a Flex gets stolen or someone's old lady is trying to track them down because their daughter needs them more than the bar does. Maybe someone flicks someone behind the ear when they weren't expecting it, and the lesson begins, learning alleyways, how to leap over cars, how to watch out for rusted edges and not cut yourself on fences, weaving in and out of traffic, how to note who you went to church with and whose house was safe to hide in when the five-oh rolled past or a low-grade mech ran its scanner over license plates and addresses, instantly checking them against warrants.

With each passing week, as the celebration and industry of the new arrivals spreads and spreads, the number of police pursuits increases. The growth is exponential at this point. Some are foot chases, some are car chases, some a combination of the two. If your motorbike has gas, that's ideal, as a red-blooded stacker stands almost no chance running on his or her own from a half-mech trained officer.

And if there's ever trouble on the block or an injured stacker needs help, no one thinks to call the police. Between active hostility, then malicious neglect, followed by weary reappraisal, they've been known to do more harm than good.

Jayceon, in the middle of an afternoon, had grabbed an older stacker, a parolee, yanked him to the side and spat in his ear about why he shouldn't have called the police when he saw an old friend of his steal the stereo out of his mother's place. "You done got home like a day ago!" Jayceon hissed. "Why the fuck you callin' the law for? They coulda grabbed both of you."

Rodney had joined them and put a hand to the parolee's shoulder. "They didn't grab you. You didn't have any outstanding warrants. That buddy of yours didn't snitch on you for nothin'. But you filed a statement, brother. You gave them your government name. And now they got your girl's address as your last known. Next time they come looking for you, guess where they'll show up."

Three days later, the mech at his halfway house had been doing drug scans on all the residents. You didn't need cyberized parts to know what bloodshot eyes meant, and he booked it. He'd been planning a life on the move, following the migrant train somewhere else, a next-generation Exoduster, but just as he was preparing to leave, they found him at his girlfriend's place.

You catch how quickly they start coming back with bloody fingertips, and you remember that their reality is not yours; they stayed, were forced to, had come from other places to get here. Their parents, the Exodusters, their grandparents, they too had bloody fingertips, so that if they all put their hands to the wall of this country's history, one would find a single, uninterrupted bloodsmear, inclined inexorably toward oblivion.

inc lay on the hood of a stripped car set up on cement blocks. Kendrick's legs dangled over a pile of metal crates to the beat of the reggaeton coming from Michael's speakers. Everyone else sat or stood or lay, angled in repose, against a block of wood or metal or plastic, searching for shadows, smelling of sweat and menthol. Michael worked inside the bunker, its massive doors wide open, smudged plastic windows, rusted hinges, his truck a dusky mammoth behind him. Linc knew, without looking away from the sky, that Sydney wasn't with them. The last time they'd seen each other, he'd had Bugs's blood on his shirt and the few words she had spoken had taken knives to her throat. He wasn't ready to see her again.

"All your favorite rappers eat booty," she had told him one time. They were sitting on the stoop of an abandoned house, and they had blankets wrapped around them and beanies tugged tight over their ears. She looked like an insect curled in on itself, tufts of hair poking out like fat, ghostly red fingers on her forehead. "You say you don't, it's 'cause you're a kid. Just wait. Day's gonna come when eatin' the booty is like eatin' the box."

"You're gross," he had told her.

"You'll walk up to a girl and tell her you're down to suck a fart out her butt."

He sputtered, chuckling and protesting at the same time.

"Like when dudes used to walk up, all cool and shit, and tell a woman 'you're so fine, I'd drink your bathwater.'" She looked at him, eyebrow arched all the way into her beanie. "*That* shit is gross. To drink a motherfucker's bathwater? Now, that shit is disgusting."

"More disgusting than a fart?" She had turned into a sibling, a piece of family, because who else could you talk to about farts.

"Yes, man. The fart? It's like a bong hit. You suck a fart out your woman's butt, it'll change your whole relationship."

He shook his head, put on the frowniest frown he could manage. "Nah, I'm good."

"Used to be trendy. It'll start trending again. But if you start now, you'll be the hipster of eatin' ass."

"The original ass-eater." A bark of a laugh. "That should be a T-shirt. O.G.A.E. Original gangsta ass-eater."

Suddenly, he stood over a pile of bricks, fishing through the bats for some gold with Bugs working not too far off. "Yeah, man," Linc is telling Bugs from behind his bandanna. "Eat the ass and it'll change your whole relationship." Bugs tried to maintain his rhythm, but his hammer strokes hiccupped. "I mean, how old are you, Bugs? Really."

"—teen."

"Exactly." Clink. Scrape. Scrape. Clink. "I remember, I was in the car." He huffed while he spoke, words like train cars between hammer swings. "I was seven, eight. I'm riding a burgundy Mercury Tracer. And it's my brother, Jake, and a friend of his." Clink. Scrape. Pause. Scrape. "And a homeboy from back then, Juicy. And they was talking about eatin' pussy. And I was like 'euck, that's *gross*; that's *disgusting*; that's *nasty*; ugh, who eats pussy?'" A forearm across the forehead, dirty sweat like a menace on his eyelids. "Turns around, 'man, how old are you?' 'Ten.' My lyin' ass. 'Man, please, shut the fuck up. When you get to our age'—they were twenty-five, twenty-six—'when you get to our age, you'll be eatin' ass.'" Bugs is trying not to chuckle. "EATIN' ASS?! I'm screaming in the car 'EATIN' ASS? WHAT?! Y'ALL EAT PUSSY AND ASS?! Oh, let me out." He put his hand to his stomach and swayed back and forth over his hammer. "I'm never drinkin' after y'all again. Don't pass me a blunt no more. This and that, this and that." He propped his hammer beneath him. Leaned on it. "Nigga. They was right."

Silence sizzled in the heat between them, then their shoulders shook with laughter. As they got back to work, Linc said over his shoulder, thinking of Sydney, "You should try it, change your whole relationship; ten years from now, girl gets up, you'll be sniffin' her chair,"

knowing that this was what older brothers said to their younger sib-
lings, the joke, the tease, the lesson, hoping somewhere in it Bugs
would notice that he'd begun to matter to Linc, that he'd begun to
matter to everyone making music on that site that afternoon. Even
Bishop had been shaking his head, chest a-rumble with quiet mirth.
Didn't matter that the whole story was a lie. Jake had not been alive
to tell him all of that.

He snapped awake to the smell of burning, and snatched his elbow
from the bit of plastic the rot had gotten to. But the odor drifted to
him from inside the bunker, and Linc shifted, squinted, and saw that
the piece of metal on which Michael worked now had flesh attached
to it. A light-skinned man sat in his barbershop chair with his arm
out on a slab of metal while Michael turned it over and put his tools
to it. Sparks sprayed in an arc, Michael having turned from barber to
tattooist to mechanic. The man in the chair was saying something, a
smile playing on his lips, and Michael looked as though he were smiling too, but everyone saw them, even as they pretended not to. The
augment in the chair didn't seem to notice how some of the stackers
eyed the man's hammer or the way they glanced at each other, information passing with each brief flit of the eye until diagrams had been
drawn and coordinates mapped, a cartography written out with the
blood of their friend whose death hung like a spiderweb among them,
eager to stuff their throats if they moved.

"I mean, there's no union or anything yet, it's all just comin' together," the augment told Michael. "We find work where we can get
it. Stacking's good stuff and we can go on all day, but enough guys
get to a site, and it's gone in an hour, you know? Some of us found
work repairing the air-filtration center, you know the one going up
in Newhallville? They're tryna dome up West Rock, get it connected
with Westville, then patch up the Ivy Quarter. I mean, with all these
kids coming in, they can't get it done fast enough. And you got all
this wildlife to clear out, and then the municipality with the zoning
and all that, can you imagine what it was like before? Just empty
houses and trees everywhere? That's maybe what I should do next. Is
maybe find some work clearing forest."

Linc sat up on the car, one knee up, intently watching everything but the augment.

The sizzling stopped, and Michael lifted his mask.

"How much I owe you?" the augment asked, flexing his repaired wrist, turning his forearm over and back once Michael had scrubbed away the char.

"Uh, just the wrist? Sixty."

He raised his finger, waiting for Michael to bring his machine.

Michael shrugged an apology. "We only take cash here. Don't get a lot of augments really." At all.

"Dang." The guy reached into his back pocket, unfolded some bills, reached into the others. "This is all I got. How do we work out the rest?"

"Don't worry about it. Just, you know, bring cash next time."

A nervous smile that Michael did not return, could not because he was already walking away. The augment turned to grab his hammer and found that it was gone. Scraping filled the air, and he saw one of the stackers drag it away around the corner of another building. "Hey!" He darted down the street, heard the roar of a motorbike grow more and more distant, and by the time he finished running, he realized how silent it had become. The empty houses lining Ella T Grasso Boulevard stared down on him from atop their hills. Small drifts of snow dotted footpaths. Wooden fences, white paint chipped, hung open at the gate. Water gurgled neatly along the gutter. Farther down, project towers sprung up, and he wandered, peeking around building corners for any trace of the kids who'd been hanging around the Body Shop. A barrier blocked the end of the boulevard where it connected to Whalley Avenue.

The place held the silence of the post-apocalypse.

He flexed his wrist and forearm, newly repaired, then something swift and small like a brick thundered into the small of his back, pitching him forward. He writhed on the ground, gritting his teeth against the pain, turned when he heard footsteps tap against puddles of melted snow. Two bodies, slim, filled the mouth of the alley, the sunlight turning them to wraiths. A hammer scraped along the ground, and he squirmed around to see someone walking toward him from the alley's other end.

"Guys, guys." Before he could offer them any of what lay stuffed inside his pockets, the first hammerhead swung down, smashing his wrist. Before the scream had run out of air, another blow, this one to his ribs, and so they came down until every limb was broken, and his face had been caved in completely.

Linc had the brush in his hand and was a long time staring at the horse's flank before he remembered where he was and that he was supposed to be doing something with that brush. It was the draft that woke him out of his day-sleep. Someone had slid a door open nearby or the wind had bust open a window or maybe some piece of wood somewhere had gotten loose. He knew better than to look for Bugs or even to suspect the kid's ghost leaving footsteps in the small snowdrifts outside. But he knew that another flesh-and-blood person had entered the stables, raised the temperature of the place.

When Linc turned and saw the reporter, she had a pitying look on her face, like she wanted to help. But Linc turned his back to her and resumed scrubbing his dun-colored horse. And she knew then that shutting the fuck up was exactly what Linc wanted her to do.

So she watched him while he worked his way up and down the stalls, feeding the horses, brushing them down. The others liked to talk to the horses, even Bugs. And Linc had watched it change them. Mercedes started out speaking conspiracy with her horse, furtive Puerto Rican Spanish while she cut her eyes at whoever she was gossiping about. But other times, Linc would catch her just making conversation with the beast like she was telling it a story about what what was like when or who did what in front of whom and how things weren't set right until X did Y with Z. Whether or not there was violence in the stories or danger, there was always comedy. Maybe Mercedes had the horse convinced she was some master storyteller, best out of them if they all started from the same place, language-wise. Timeica talked to her horses like they were infant sisters. She babied them and met them at their impulses, found them carrots or, if she were riding, leaned down to murmur in the horse's ear instead of speaking through the reins. The Atlanta in Kendrick showed up more in his voice when he talked to his horse, and Jayceon, maybe thinking this made him cool or mysterious, effected a drawl that migrated from Appalachia to West Texas and all points in-between. Sydney rarely spoke to the horses she cared for when it was her turn to do the caring. She just hummed. It was a Morse Code sort of humming, short sounds and long, stretched-out ones. Musical notes. But the horses seemed to understand them well enough, because they did whatever she wanted.

But Linc hadn't seen Sydney since the night Bugs got killed. Maybe she was avoiding Linc. Maybe he made it too easy.

It came time to shovel the shit and bring it to the compost, and that was when he realized he needed to be two people. He couldn't haul the horseshit and walk the horses at the same time, so when he had put away his brush and washcloth and had rolled up some of his hose, he pushed a wheelbarrow into the main pathway, leaned on it, and inclined his head toward the stalls.

"You wanna take 'em for a walk while I clean the shit out?"

She seemed so grateful to be included it almost made Linc rescind the offer. It would take too much effort to tell her that she wasn't participating in his grief, that there wasn't any grief to begin with, not more than what there was before Bugs, before even arriving in New Haven, that when it came to grief sometimes you ran up the bill and after a while the number just got meaningless. No, she was just taking the horses for a walk. That's all.

The "vacuum," as some of the stackers liked to call it, was out by the back of the barn, away from the fence so that the people who came to watch could avoid the worst of the smell. But that meant having an unabated view of the reporter as she brought the horses out for their early-spring circuits. Her breath clouded before her face. He turned away before he had time to think her pretty. He'd never forgive himself if he got to that place. So he wheeled the barrow over to where a large box-like device rose from the ground, coming up to his torso. He unhooked and unfurled an accordion duct hose from the green box's side, positioned its end just over the lip of the shit cart, and flicked a switch up on the box's console. Bugs had made the mistake of flicking it down one time, and the storm had been quick but ruthless, and he'd run into the crowd of them in the barn screaming, almost weeping, covered in shit that the composter had decided to spray over him rather than inhale for its own digestion.

He shook Bugs out of his head while the hose worked to clean the cart.

His rhythms meant that they were always crossing paths at different points, him reentering the barn just as she was coming out with a horse, him leaving while she was finishing up a circuit, their arrivals and departures staggered so that Linc wouldn't have to talk to her. And maybe a part of her clocked this, because she fell in line with it and kept the peace. Until Linc had gotten the last of the horseshit into the composter and she'd come back out, even though she didn't have a horse to walk. She halfway blocked his path and had her arms folded across her chest, her chin sunk into her neck for warmth.

"We missed you," she said.

"We."

She flinched.

Linc let the silence hang between them, but she didn't give way.

"You should've been there."

He stopped trying to get past her and rose from the cart. "What are you doing?"

"What?"

"This." He spread his arms to indicate the entirety of his world. "What are you doing here?"

"I . . . I'm trying to get it right." Linc knew that wasn't enough, and he knew that she knew it wasn't enough, so he waited for more. "I mean, you look at how fast these stables went up. It took us two weeks. If that. And the work you do, stacking. It takes thirty seconds to demolish a home. Half a day to clear away the rubble. If I write about the people who are here already, then maybe . . . I don't know. Sometimes, people get to a place and assume nobody's been here before. And I don't want that to happen here. That's why I'm writing about you all and about the horses and the home you've made for yourselves."

Linc just looked at her. He said nothing and he didn't let his face show her any kind of feeling as she withered under his gaze.

"It's not my fault, okay?" Something had snapped in her, like a curtain rod. "I can't get rid of being white. And my guilt is useless if I can't do something with it. So I write. I educate. I'm able to go into spaces others can't, and I can walk in and walk back out with these stories that I can show to other people. And they can read these stories and know that these people who look nothing like them are just as human. I have that power. I can do that. I can be of service. How does me doing that get Bugs killed?"

Linc made to run her over and she glided out of the way to let him pass through the open doors. He settled the wheelbarrow in a corner, then found an upended bucket to sit on.

"When you write down what we say, how do you spell it?"

"Spell it?"

"Nigga. How do you write it?"

Twin roses burst to life on her cheeks.

"Do you write it with a 'u'? Or, like, a 'u-h'?"

"I . . . um—"

"I saw sometimes when white writers write Black people they use the hard R. Make it sound like we call each other niggers all the time. Like we say it the same way white people do." He paused. "I saw this one time, someone wrote nigga with a 'a' then a 'h.' What the fuck? I couldn't stop laughing. Please tell me that's not how you spell it."

She took up her position opposite him, her back against the closed stall door, and he grew quiet. A horse's head swayed over her shoulder. Its coat had whitened with the drop in temperature. It was almost the same color as her, which turned the whole sight of them into something ominous.

"Bugs didn't go anywhere. It's too easy. Heaven, Hell, whatever, none of that exists. Do you want to know why? Dying is too easy. Nigga spent the last minute of his life coughing blood onto my sneakers, and niggas is gonna cry and be upset for a week, then we're all gonna move on. That's just how it go. But you wanna fuck it all up by making his life look bigger than it was. You couldn't just leave us alone. You told them about us." He put his chin on his fists, then shook his head from side to side. "But this is what yah do." Then he was up on his feet. He had the bucket in his hand, not sure what to do with it, but knowing he needed something for his fingers to do. "Yah find people who aren't you, livin' they lives, and you gotta come and fuck it all up."

She pushed off the stall door to go after him, but he was already through the front threshold and away from the space heaters, hemispheres that lined the floor at regular intervals.

You told them about us thundered accusation in her head, and she wanted to rebut him, to catch him from behind and stop him in his tracks and convince him of her goodness, her native-ness, but she saw where he was heading. She saw the crew of young white settlers with blankets or thick woolen sweaters draped over their shoulders, leaning on the fence like they were getting ready to climb over. And she saw Linc waving them away like a man several decades older and shouting that the stables were closed for the season, even though the mayor had been talking about a series of spring events and excited murmurs had galloped through the city about this new thing blooming in the park. She saw Linc waving that bucket at those white kids, barking at them, maybe seeing among them the two white boys who got Bugs killed, and she knew then that there was nothing she could say to Linc to convince him she was on their side.

"It's not my fault," she said in a white cloud of breath.

You told them about us.

Crashes filled the reporter's home, banging, hammering, the tearing-apart of things. He left her office and walked into an apartment unit that had played host to a hurricane. He felt no joy in this. He couldn't speak for Jayceon or the younger kids—younger than Bugs would've been—who'd heard about this trip and figured it for the easy score it pretty much was. He didn't tell the others anything, just stepped over the broken glass and shattered furniture and obliterated keepsakes, and walked out the door.

SOMETIMES, Linc forgot the hammer in his hands and the radioactive dust coating his lungs and the cold that cut through the holes and the loose sole of his left boot, and he would let himself get encased in the sunlight that shot through church windows and cast the pews and the aisles in trapezoids of gilt. So many of those gilt-framed memories were like that, like his whole childhood was caught in the frozen, time-stamped impact of a bomb's explosion, and hands, older hands lined with wisdom, would hold his and pass him forward, helping him walk. And the voices of his mother and her friends would wash over his passage, and they would giggle, and Linc knew words back then but couldn't say them. So he would shuffle forward and babble and they would coo and he would shriek with joy at being loved.

When the world returned to him, when the memory ended and he stood again amid the pile of broken bricks, the sky, red with poison, was always a darker thing. The burn pinned in the tendons between his deltoid and bicep was sharpened. The numbing ache in his fingers whose tips had long since worked their way through worn gloves, that ache throbbed with greater viciousness. And he resumed his posture in the world with a cough, that signal that he had passed from the past into the present where the aureate carried poison and where people laughed or giggled instead at someone's infirmity, at someone's impairment, at a junkie's stutter or an epithet bellowed in a howl upon the errant striking of a thumb with one's hammer.

Linc delivered that day's skids to the local transporter and found himself on Ella T Grasso Boulevard where it hit Whalley Avenue. Barriers had been put up and though a straight path was cut to the Ivy Quarter from the working grounds, Ella T was now off-limits. It was a long time in Linc's mind since white folk or anyone carrying their sensibilities would have wanted to live there, constantly having to change bedding if one didn't have the right plastic because the radiation would copper-dot all your white mattresses within a week. Or checking to see if the piping had been re-coated by the last tenant and, if not, then having to deal with water that sometimes carried iridescent flakes; or having to depend on the checks for your local food runs where the price of bottled water and proper milk and cereal had risen higher and higher.

Stackers and their families or their running buddies or the people they were willing to tolerate had camped out there, though. Made it a home or something like it. But now even that had been taken. Slowly, they were being pushed out and Linc knew it wasn't for their own safety. Because if the folks who decided whether or not to kick a man and his family out on the street cared for that man's safety, he wouldn't'a had to live on that block to begin with.

What was happening in Westville, in West Rock, in Beaver Hills, was also going to happen here. If Linc blinked, it'd all be over.

Linc was a long time staring at that duplex before he turned around and walked back the other way down the boulevard, hammerhead dragging a sighed screech behind him. His path circled back so that he passed by the ruins of the old medical school. Dilapidation had swallowed that too, but the forbidden majesty of the place, or at least some remnant of it, still towered over him. It was the sense that Linc would have never been allowed in a building like that, even if he were sick and needed treatment. And there stood a barrier, not one he could see or vault over, one higher than that, invisible, that would rise to block him no matter how high he jumped and would plow into the earth to cut him off no matter how deep he dug, that kept him out.

He wanted to spit, but the air had dried his mouth.

Linc thought he imagined the thudding when he found himself on a street corner half an hour's slow walk down from Whalley. A big block of a building, short and stocky, stared at him from the opposite corner. Gold lettering had peeled away, revealing the faded black silhouettes of "R_ng On_". The percussion reminded him of the djent music Jake always tried to get Linc to listen to when Linc was little, guys who played guitar like it was a drum, polyrhythmic drummers that made you work to find the logic in a song. The door creaked when Linc nudged it in with his hammer. Slowly, so that the rusted hinges didn't give out completely.

Flakes and dust glowed in the still air. Linc walked through the soft clouds of fluorescent detritus to find, in a shadowed portion of a second space, a guy with sweat drenching his sleeveless. Giving a shine to muscles that rippled with each impact. Makeshift gloves with duct tape on 'em, pounding against what Linc discovered was a heavy bag. The chain from which the bag hung groaned every time the thing swung, and the roof moaned in tandem. Wyatt, dancing around the bag, didn't seem to hear it. Or didn't seem to care.

Wyatt hadn't heard the door open either because when Linc stood on the threshold between the first room that held the sagging canvas of the boxing ring and the ropes that hung in tatters along its side and the dumbbell weights rusted to dust and the elliptical that hadn't been touched in decades and the second room where Wyatt boxed in front of a corroded mirror, Wyatt didn't look up.

Linc leaned on his hammer, chin on his hands, back unhealthily but comfortably bent, ass out, and watched.

Wyatt's face staticked between a smile and a frown, twitching one way, then the other, so that Linc could not tell whether the fellow stacker was trying to grin or trying not to. He bounced more than he slid. He tucked his chin into his chest. His hammer lay propped against a far wall, most of the handle obscured by shadow, the head glowing red in the light that shone through the broken rafters. The rhythm thwarted Linc's attempts to follow it, but he noticed that when Wyatt's left foot slid back after a straight right, there would be a left uppercut. More often than not, the bag would cave from the right hook that followed. Jabs concussed the duct-taped leather before Wyatt would slide in and riddle the thing with a flurry of uppercuts. When he did pause, he wiped his forearm across his forehead. Sometimes he pressed his forehead to the bag and whispered a benediction. Sometimes he wandered in a loose amoebic meridian, blinking long, restorative blinks against the sweat that must have burned his eyes.

Disappointment pinched Linc's chest when he saw Wyatt take off his gloves and pick up a jump rope, though, in the movement, he became a gleaming, mythical thing, Linc paying witness to some divine manifestation. When Wyatt finished, he dropped the rope and moved over to the mirror-wall and sat down before it, chest heaving, staring directly at Linc.

"Used to take me forever to figure out how to do that."

"Jump rope?" Linc asked.

"Not surprised though, 'cause it was always Timeica and the little girls on the block doin' the Double Dutch. I dunno. You gotta swing your own rope, that's different."

"Not workin' today?"

"Don't have to," Wyatt said and grinned.

"Don't have to?"

"Who'm I tryna spend money on?"

Linc chuckled. He pushed off his hammer and dragged it over to where Wyatt sat, sat down beside him.

"Your shit's gonna fall off, you don't take care of it."

"That what you doin' here?"

"Hah-hah. See what you did there, clever motherfucker." Wyatt looked at his hands when he said this, flexed them and unflexed them, turned them over in the light.

Linc waited in the quiet, reverent and sacrosanct. "Looked like you were stacking."

Wyatt nodded softly to that. Moved his jaw like he was trying to crack something.

"You not like it when people watch you box?"

Wyatt turned his head. "Why you say that?" His knuckles glinted, the grooves in his skin ablaze.

"I dunno. Looked like you didn't wanna be disturbed is all."

"Then why you disturbin' me?" Wyatt smirked, but Linc heard the bite in it.

Linc looked at the rotting carpet they sat on, its patchwork stretching to the corridor, so as to not look at Wyatt. He wondered if Wyatt's hitting that bag was the uncurling of some Big Bad Thing or merely what hard niggas did when they flexed around the neighborhood, hiding themselves. Maybe Wyatt talked too much at the dig site to convince Linc that he could ever treat a person's head the way he treated those busted bricks. Those bats.

Wyatt nodded toward the still-swaying bag. "You wanna try it?"

"I might hurt the bag."

They both chuckled, and Wyatt came to his feet and Linc saw in the moment that he straightened a passing whisper of grief, a brief moment when, head down, he seemed to be waiting for someone to hit him, as though talking with Linc had brought him to the precipice of articulating a bit of suffering he did not know how to express, reinforcing his own inarticulateness. It was only a moment, but Linc saw that Wyatt believed he would never be able to tell someone just how much he had suffered. It wasn't the long trek he and Timeica had made from Chicago through desiccated post-apocalypse in search of clean air. And it wasn't having to swing a hammer for a living, because he seemed to enjoy that well enough. Sunlight glinted off his eyes in Morse Code. A lonely signal, answered rarely. Then, it was gone. And so was Wyatt and so was his hammer.

Linc waited for silence to settle, then turned and hit the bag with his bare fist. His knuckles sang with pain and he waved off the grief before clenching his hand into a fist and denting the bag again. Duct tape and leather bit him with each blow, but numbness began to set in and Linc forgot to move and the bag began to vanish until he returned to the world with its poisonous aureate and the way it burned the lungs, and he found that the pain pinned between his deltoid and bicep had followed him here. Had sharpened. When he stopped, he found he was huffing. The world faded back into focus. He had never seen red before, been so blinded by it. He wanted to cry. He gritted his teeth instead, fought it down, then found his own hammer. Its head had loosened, but he dragged it anyway.

On his way out, he passed through the shadows cast by a sun slanted toward the horizon. Dust clung to him, and he glowed with fury.

They didn't talk about Bugs.

They didn't have to.

When it got like this, he stopped being a person. Linc had seen it, gone through it, enough times to know that this was just how it went. Wanting things, wanting to deserve them, thinking and feeling in two different directions, all of that evaporated when it got like this and everything became inevitable. Every community disintegrated eventually. Every place was broken and whatever wasn't lost forever in the breaking crawled out through the fault lines. He stopped being a person and became, instead, an instrument. A symbol. A shell to put things into or maybe a glove for someone else's hand.

That's what he told himself up on that hill with the light of the fire warming his face. It wasn't him. It was fate or prophecy or whatever else it's called when you remember that losing what you love is part of the game too. That's what Linc told himself as he'd gone through that barn earlier and ripped open the floor heaters and set some of them on the hay for feeding the horses and set others up against the wood, exposed wiring dug into the frames, and it's what he told himself when the first columns of smoke swam through the stalls.

It's supposed to go like this.

That was the deal at the reporter's place. That was the deal with Bugs. That was the deal with this too.

And whatever was gonna come after, whatever thing he was gonna do next, after he'd erased this place they'd built from the earth, that was part of the deal too.

It was supposed to go like this.

Linc wanted to tell the horses they were screaming at the wrong person.

A few blocks down from Saint Michael Church, where the cherry blossoms had begun to bloom and the last mounds of snow peed clear into the gutters and the wind's crispness was blunted with the promise of summer, residents had turned the street into a makeshift memorial. On the spot where Bugs had lain, people had planted a pyramid of stuffed animals: silver sharks, striped tigers whose white underbellies had not yet been pimpled with bloodpennies from radiation, cards pinned in the crook of an elephant's tusk, roses sprouting from every crevice in the small mountain. Blue and yellow ribbons whipped in the breeze. Orange traffic cones set off the memorial, and posted to a telephone pole was a sign that said "SLOW DOWN" in block letters. Radiation tag ran like tattoos on the concrete: R.I.P. BUGS; Angels Never Die; Stay Golden; Black Lives Matter, all in neon calligraphy. Someone had strapped teddy bears to another telephone pole, but with plastic hand-ties so that it looked like some of them were being cuffed.

Linc doubled back and stood before Saint Michael Church, stood there so long he had watched the shadows turn with the sun. He remembered the soot-sheathed, bloodstained hammer in his hand and marched forward. The windows were already gone, but if he could take the walls from the inside, maybe he could bring the whole thing down. He hoped those white boys who'd called the cops on him and Bugs would walk by. He hoped a whole gang of them would walk by. He hoped every white person who had descended from the Colony would walk by. They wouldn't make it to the memorial.

Purpose drove him up the steps, and he hefted his hammer, prepared to swing at the nearest bench, when he noticed a familiar lump toward the front of the sanctuary. A hammer lay propped up against a pew by the altar. When Linc drew closer, he saw Bishop, utterly still, then, after a moment, turn and notice Linc. Even his wrinkles had wrinkles. The left corner of his mouth hung awkwardly.

And suddenly, everything hurt. He almost dropped his hammer, almost buried his soot-covered face into the dirty rug that ran from door to altar. But the hammer was driftwood for him to cling to. Still, everything hurt so much. Like he had just come up for air, not realizing he'd been in the process of drowning. And he tried to take a step forward, toward Bishop, but couldn't.

The old man saw him and stared for a long time at his face covered in soot before struggling to his feet and limping heavily to him. The scuff and thump of a stiff leg sweeping and a stiff foot hitting wood was the only sound inside the church. It was the only sound in Linc's ears. And Linc thought of what was gonna come after and he even thought he could hear Bishop tell him to take Sydney with him, because he knew that there was something between the two of them, and they would need each other. Linc thought he could hear Bishop say all that, even though Bishop hadn't opened his mouth. He thought he could hear himself telling Bishop that she couldn't make whatever journey was ahead of them, that she was burnt. Coughing blood into his hair, him pretending not to notice.

But Bishop got to Linc and just put his arms around Linc's, and to be touched by another human being like this, to be held with tenderness and love and care and fierceness, it made Linc drop his hammer and lean too heavily on the other man so that Bishop had to slowly lower them both to the ground.

"I miss my mom," was all Linc could bring himself to say.

"I miss my mom" was the last sentence Bishop would ever hear.

The mulberry tree was still there. And the forest growth framed the man's tiny estate the same way it did when Timeica and Sydney first came down this stretch of highway and saw him. The man with the jug of lemonade under the mulberry tree. The highway, the greenery that flanked it, the erupted pavement where broken maglev lines poked through, all of it looked just like when she'd last seen it a lifetime ago, so maybe it was routine that had her taking the pistol out of the glove box, turning it over in her hand, then putting it on the empty, ratty passenger's seat.

The man saw her coming, saw her tug her jacket tighter over her shoulders, saw the look on her face, and knew not to ask after her "lil' friend." Still, he got to his feet and gestured to the seat on the other side of his table.

"You said," Timeica managed. "You said if I came back in the springtime and helped you with the burning, I could get a discount. On the blueberries." She didn't know how else to ask for what she wanted. But, after a beat of peering into her eyes, the man loosened and said, "Follow me," and took the jug and his plastic cup indoors with him.

The humidity was below fifty percent, and there was barely any wind, which, the man said, was what today needed to be for them to do it all right. Also, it was late enough in the day that all the morning dew was gone. So the acres were bone-dry. There were suits and thick gloves waiting for them in a shed attached as an extension to the man's house, along with masks. The man put a cowboy hat on his head for reasons Timeica couldn't begin to guess at. She pulled a bandanna off the wall and used it to pull her hair back. Then they both put on masks.

The blueberry farmer strapped a five-gallon water sack onto Timeica's back, then did his own. Armed with drip-torches, they worked in tandem, the farmer lighting the straw that winter had pressed into the ground and Timeica doing her best to then follow his lead and shepherd the flames inward a little over twenty feet to create a charred strip of circle around the fields. It took several hours for them to create the firebreak. Smoke rose from the rich, thick black duff layer of decomposed leaves and other organic matter once the straw was gone. Stone poked through, steaming as well. Soon, the smoke was high enough to dim the sun, so that the angry red of the sky was a little bit less mean.

When the farmer said, "All right," they were both standing near the center of the circle. "I'ma set this for a more powerful burn." He lifted his drip-torch. "I'ma light this area here, and soon as the flame gets high enough, we're gonna make a break for that firebreak there, all right? It'll keep the burn controlled. Keep the rest of this place from burning down. Get this place ready for some blueberries." He was grinning. "Now, wait till I say 'go' before you start running, okay?"

She nodded. But something in her face musta told the farmer she was nervous, because he took her arm and gently pulled her close and brought his face near to hers.

"You're gonna be all right," he told her.

She believed him.

"*Go.*"

ACKNOWLEDGMENTS

Ultimately, whether or not a writer has been successful in achieving their aims is quite literally in the hands of the reader. Where I've come short, I have tried to, in the words of Elizabeth Bear, "fail brilliantly." But I owe much of what may be judged the book's successes to my editor, Ruoxi Chen, who has remained superhumanly clear-eyed through each of this book's many incarnations. Additionally, this was the book that helped seal the bond, personal as well as professional, between me and my agent, Noah Ballard, whom I must also thank. It would take more than four hundred pages to properly express my gratitude to them both.

My thanks, as well, to Jamie Stafford-Hill, who designed the cover that, the moment I first saw it, struck me so powerfully with its rightness. The production staff at Tordotcom Publishing are tireless and heroic, as are the copyeditors who deftly navigated every brambled path and thorn'd trail I threw before them.

Though the events of the book are undated, they directly reference our present and recent past. In that respect, I drew heavily for the prison section in "Winter" from Heather Ann Thompson's *Blood in the Water: The Attica Prison Uprising of 1971 and Its Legacy* as well as the Attica Central School District's detailed online account of the uprising at the archived Attica Correctional Facility website. Dr. Thompson's book pointed me in the direction of numerous other primary and secondary sources about the event. "The Attica Liberation Faction Manifesto of Demands" is available in Vol. 53, Issue 2 of *Race & Class,* published September 2011, and a portion of Bishop's speech during the uprising is adapted from the recorded words of one Elliott James "L. D." Barkley, a prisoner twenty-one years of age at the time of the uprising who was killed during the prison's retaking.

My first contact with the Attica uprising came during a screening in a law school clinic of a portion of a film depicting the uprising's aftermath. Meeting Dr. Thompson at a book event three or so years later and hearing her describe the uprising as a civil rights moment seared that episode of American history into both my mind and my heart.

Also inspiring the monologue in "Winter" was *The Guardian*'s Cancer Town series of reported articles on environmental pollution in Reserve, Louisiana.

Tori Marlan's January 1999 *Chicago Reader* piece titled "Brickyard Blues" provided the initial seeds for the short story that eventually grew to become this novel, and perceptive readers might be able to trace the genealogy of a few of the characters in *Goliath* to the Chicago residents about whom Marlan wrote so compassionately. To my knowledge, brick stacking has not been one of New Haven's major industries, but much of the relationship between manual labor and race and class, the depiction of which resonated so loudly with me in that feature, seems, to me at least, to transcend geographic and temporal borders.

Virginia Eubanks and her work has informed much of how I've tried to imagine the digitization and mechanization of oppression in this story set mere decades from now. I cannot recommend highly enough her book, *Automating Inequality: How High-Tech Tools Profile, Police, and Punish the Poor*.

The Church of the Nativity described in the scene at the Assawoman Bay refugee camp is modeled in part on the Church of the Nativity in Bethlehem in the West Bank. Parts of the Assawoman Bay refugee camp bear intentional resemblance to the Aida refugee camp, also in Bethlehem. Both are places within which I was fortunate to have stood in person.

For a greater general understanding of urban planning, I consulted, among others, figures with diametrically opposed visions of cities, their function, and their futures. Robert Moses, as chronicled in Robert Caro's *The Power Broker,* quite literally shaped New York City to fit his whims, treating neighborhoods and the urban projects that would destroy them less as something meant to serve the city's residents and more as a sandbox for monuments to his supposed greatness. On the other end of the spectrum stands Jane Jacobs, urbanist and critical thinker behind *The Death and Life of Great American Cities* and whose smaller works, collected in *Vital Little Plans,* did more than anything else to reshape how I think about the metropole and all the different ways a city can be occupied. The work of Ruth Wilson Gilmore also pushed me to better see the ways in which environmental racism and the racialized carceral complex in the United States are braided together and how justice movements in both arenas are and should be intertwined. For a deeper awareness of the history of housing segregation in the United States, I would be remiss not to recommend Richard Rothstein's *The Color of Law: A Forgotten History of How Our Government Segregated America.* I owe much of my education in housing insecurity, its myriad causes, and legion consequences to Matthew Desmond's *Evicted: Poverty and Profit in the American City.*

The two lines of song Michael and Linc speak to each other in "Summer" come from the ScHoolboy Q song featuring A$AP Rocky, "Hands on the Wheel," a song I fully expect to last through any impending climate-induced apocalypse.

My sincerest thanks to Jeannie Chan, Leigh Bardugo, and V. E. Schwab. Knowing you sustains me.

A hundred other thinkers and storytellers—among them, Arundhati Roy, Malcolm Lowry, Leslie Jamison, Jesmyn Ward, Mohsin Hamid, Roberto Bolaño, and Gene Wolfe—influenced the crafting of this book, and to them, I am indebted. As well as to you, Zack Fox.

ABOUT THE AUTHOR

Christina Orlando

TOCHI ONYEBUCHI is the author of the young adult novel *Beasts Made of Night,* which won the Ilube Nommo Award for Best Speculative Fiction Novel by an African; its sequel, *Crown of Thunder;* and *War Girls.* His novella *Riot Baby,* a finalist for the Hugo, Nebula, Locus, Ignyte, and NAACP Image Awards, won the New England Book Award for Fiction and an Alex Award. He holds a B.A. from Yale, an M.F.A. in screenwriting from the Tisch School of the Arts, a master's degree in economic law from Sciences Po, and a J.D. from Columbia Law School. His fiction has appeared in *Panverse Three, Asimov's Science Fiction, Obsidian, Omenana, Uncanny,* and *Lightspeed.* His nonfiction has appeared on *Tor.com* and in *Nowhere,* the Oxford University Press blog, and the *Harvard Journal of African American Public Policy,* among other places.

tochionyebuchi.com
Twitter: @TochiTrueStory